THE *GHOST*

GEORGE CHANCE • ARCHIVES 1

THE THRILLING LIBRARY:

THE GHOST

GEORGE CHANCE • ARCHIVES 1

VOLUME 1

BY

G.T. FLEMING-ROBERTS

THRILLING PUBLICATIONS

2017

TABLE OF

CONTENTS

CALLING
THE GHOST

CHAPTER I

THE LISPER

IT WASN'T a nice night that served as a prologue to the first act of a series of baffling mysteries revolving about the man who lisped. A clammy mist of the sort called Scotch mantled Manhattan's towers and stooped to drape my brownstone house on East Fifty-Fourth Street.

I find, looking back, that not the least amazing feature about the thing was that I was in on a multiple murder case literally before I knew it—a feature which the gods of coincidence will have to explain, for I cannot. Incidentally, what promises to be rather amusing to the reader of this memoir is the chance to cotton to certain clues before I did. For, you see, I didn't know they were clues when I first saw them, and I'm wondering if the reader will have any better success.

I was in my second floor study. Joe Harper was with me. Joe Harper, I might add, is always with me and has been ever since that night some years ago when he appropriated my guest room as a good place to have a hangover. I If you've spent much time on Broadway, you'll remember Joe—checkered suit, piped vest, snap-brim hat which is always offensively green regardless of what fashion prescribes. Joe, lean and wolfish, with black-beetle eyes connected with an agile brain, thin lips and thin nose, the sort of chin that would break a fist.

If you were a hick on Broadway, maybe the pitchman who tried to sell you a lifetime fountain pen for two bits was Joe Harper. Or if you liked the ponies, maybe Joe was the bookmaker you wanted to shoot after the race. Or if you were a glamour girl in your home town, trying to crash Broadway, you might have met Joe sitting behind the desk in a booking agency. Anyway, it's certain that Joe knew you before you knew Joe. He'd make your business his, and he'd have done pretty well for himself at the same time.

As I said, Joe Harper was in the study with me. His lean legs bridged the gap between a leather lounge chair and the top of my desk. His green hat rested on a plane determined by the tips of his close-set ears and the bridge of his nose. Except for the hat I might have thought him asleep. He almost never goes to bed with his hat on.

I was working, getting down on paper the complicated moves of a trick with giant cards which had brought me considerable fame when I was traveling with vaudeville circuits. It was an invention of my own, and if I could put it down on paper comprehensively I intended to pass it on to my students at the School of Magic. Since the working of it was considerably easier than the explanation of the method, I had got no farther than the title: "The George Chance Card Monte," when Joe Harper spoke to me, his parted lips scarcely moving.

"It was a swell day for a funeral."

I GAVE him an amused glance and caught the glint of his beady eyes watching me like little black beetles from the shadowy nook formed by the brim of his hat. Experience told me I was about to be touched. I have met some artistic chiselers in my life, but Joe Harper is the only one who has a thousand different approaches to asking for a loan.

"Oh, you went to a funeral today," I said, being conversational. "An old friend?"

"Max Gerrich," he said. "Just a ham actor. I didn't know him very well. He tried everything from male juveniles to heavies. Ended up doing walking parts with a split-week company. His funeral was the only thing he ever had the lead in. Incidentally, he bumped himself off."

Joe's voice was crisp and a little nasal, not an unpleasant sound against the mushy stirring of cars and pedestrians in the damp street outside.

"What for?" I asked.

It has been said that the reasons for suicide can all be included under two heads, money and love, but there are many variations, and I was interested in the subject.

Joe shrugged. "Dunno, but his interment marked the first time you could have stuck up an S.R.O. sign in the same block with Max. Funny, too, because he must have had a little money once. And now what? Scattered flowers and sand in his face—?"

"And," I cut in, knowing where the touch was coming, "he couldn't take his money with him, could he?"

"That's it." Joe took his feet off my desk, pushing up his hat, regarded me unblinkingly for a moment. "George, you and I got the same philosophy about money. Enjoy it, is my motto."

"Enjoy somebody else's is your motto," I corrected. "How much?"

Joe looked offended, but not much. "This isn't a touch. This is a chance to make some money, George. After funerals, I always get hunches. I think I could take a hundred bucks and run it up to a grand tonight at Snooky's. We can split the take."

I took my wallet from a drawer in the desk and counted out five twenties. "Aha!" said Joe Harper. And raked the bills into his palm, rolled them, stuck them into the tight slit of his trouser pocket.

It was then that the glass insert on the top of my desk glowed and I knew I was about to have a visitor.

Through the medium of mirrors arranged for a periscopic effect, I am able to see, from my desk on the second floor, whoever approaches the front door. On this glass screen, which is an integral part of my desk top, I could see a man of medium height, dressed in a pearl gray top coat, gray gloves, a black derby hat. A system of electric eyes on either side of the door turns on the light illuminating the periscope.

Joe Harper placed a forefinger bluntly on the reflection of the visitor's thick shoulder.

"Who's the guy in the iron hat?" he asked. "All he needs is a bunch of orchids to look like a stage door godfather."

"The guy," I said, "is Taylor Owens, active in several civic organizations and at the present time chairman of a benefit party entertainment program. He wants me to put on an act for the show. Let him in as you go out."

Joe said okay and hurried off. How long he would be out depended entirely upon how long it took Snooky to relieve him of my hundred dollars.

THIS WAS the second visit from Taylor Owens in the past week. He had a nearly round head with a few black hairs brushed tightly across from ear to ear. His nose was a sore-looking shade of rose and potato-shaped. He had a square pair of jaws and he used them for clamping the bit of a short pot-bowled pipe. I let him in and he sat down in the chair Joe Harper had been warming, his knees close together and his derby in his lap.

"Well, well, well," my visitor said in a descending scale.

He looked pleased to find an ash tray handy, gently tapped fluffy gray ash from his pipe, began reloading the hot briar immediately from a striped silk roll pouch.

"The party," he declared, "is all arranged for tomorrow night. Can we definitely count on you to perform?"

I nodded and watched Taylor Owens grope for a match. He stopped groping for a match and groped for a pencil which he found. On a white card he wrote: "The World's Best Magic by Mr. George Chance." And so I was included on the benefit party program.

"You slice your baloney thick enough," I told him.

Taylor Owens smiled all over his face.

"Not at all," he said. "The magician who has baffled our best psychologists and entertained the crowned heads of Europe has to be the world's greatest."

He returned pencil and card to pocket, remembered he was looking for a match.

"But," he warned, holding up a forefinger shaped like a wiener sausage, "you'll not fool me, Mr. Chance."

I sighed. "Of course not," and I lighted a match and extended it toward his pipe.

"Thanks," Taylor Owens said, bending forward.

When his pipe was near the flame, I thumb-palmed the match. The disappearance of the match pushed Taylor Owens' blue eyes a little farther out from their sockets. He stood up and said he'd be damned and tried to see on all sides of me at once. When I apparently reproduced the match fully lighted from my vest pocket, he laughed, cautiously took the match from my fingers.

"Elastic," he said between puffs, and sat down again.

"Think so? By the way, you neglected to tell me who's backing this benefit."

"Union of Civic Clubs," he said. "Know the president, Leonard Van Sickle? He's probably been bothering you about the details of your part in the performance. He's a glutton for details. Nothing ever escapes him. If he ever committed murder, he'd never be caught because he'd never leave a clue."

I remembered seeing Leonard Van Sickle's name and picture in the papers. He was a manufacturer who had recently been forced into retirement by some sort of a merger which had been brought about by financial difficulties in his own company.

I told Taylor Owens I had heard the name.

"A good egg in small doses," Owens said.

He took a chubby grip on the brim of his hat and stood up. I saw him downstairs to the door where the cloud of his pipe smoke mingled with the cold, clinging mist. I closed the door. Three steps up the stair, and the phone rang. I decided to take it on the living room extension.

"Mither George Chanth?" An unfamiliar lisping voice asked.

CHAPTER II

THE MAN DIED LAUGHING

// THITH ITH Leonard Van Thickle," said the voice, pleasant in spite of the lisp. I was surprised. I couldn't quite associate the robust man I had seen in the news photos with the lisping voice.

Van Sickle had appeared tall, well-made, young-looking for his middle age. So this was Leonard Van Sickle, I thought—the man Taylor Owens had humorously said would never be caught if he committed a crime. The voice went on.

"I underthtand from Mither Owenth that you will perform for the benefit party tomorrow night. I wanted to athk a thpecial favor."

"No harm asking. Go ahead." I smiled. This Van Sickle's chuckle was catching.

"Could you play a trick on me? I have a childith ambition to get up on the thtage with you and have you pull thomething out of my pocket."

I couldn't help laughing. Of course I agreed—it would be very convincing to pull a serving of hot mush out of Van Sickle's mouth.

Still chuckling, the man thanked me profusely and hung up.

I returned to my work in the study. A little later, Joe Harper returned. He didn't stop at the study to say goodnight, so I said a mental good-bye to my hundred dollars. Had he won, Joe would have come in with champagne under his arm.

Soon his snores sounded from what I had once called a guest room. I went to my own bed. If Joe's Broadway conscience was clear enough for sleep, so was mine.

I had been asleep for about an hour and a half when the extension phone on my night stand burred softly. I reached for it without opening my eyes and got the right end of the phone to my ear.

"George Chance speaking," I said.

The gruff voice of Police Commissioner Edward Standish came from the receiver.

"Calling the Ghost," Standish said in a low voice. "You alone, George?"

George Chance

I told Standish I was.

"I'm speaking from the private wire in my apartment. I've got something you might be interested in."

I swung my legs over the edge of the bed and sat up.

"Shoot, Ned," I told him.

"Maybe you've heard of Leonard Van Sickle—"

I was startled. Who wouldn't be?

"Yes," I said. "What about him?"

"The guy killed himself about forty minutes ago! Opened a window in the Cronner Hotel and went for a walk—twenty stories straight down. Underneath him was a lot of hard ground."

Standish cleared his throat, something which usually indicated he was about to hang up.

"Wait, Ned!" I cried.

I got my mind back over the unbelievable short interval which had passed between the present moment and my talk with the chuckling Van Sickle on the phone.

"Ned, I don't get this," I said. "I was talking with him only a little while ago—he was in the best of spirits—"

"He's *with* the best of spirits now, I hope," Standish remarked dryly.

"You're sure—"

THE COMMISSIONER grunted. "Twenty-five years with the police department I've been, George Chance. And by now if I don't know a dead man when I see one, it's me who should pull a grave over my head and find out what it's like. And there's a payoff to this, George. We can't find the man's false teeth. They weren't in his mouth, they weren't on the sidewalk where he landed, they weren't in his clothes, and they're not in his apartment." And with that, Standish hung up.

I slowly replaced the phone. Standish, whom I knew well enough to call by his nickname "Ned" couldn't be mistaken about a corpse when he saw one. If Standish said you were dead, you could go right ahead and order the flowers. The point I didn't get was the suicide verdict. Nobody in a suicide mood calls up a magician and laughingly tells him to play a trick on him.

"Matter, George?"

I looked up quickly, shuddered at the sight of Joe Harper in a purple bathrobe.

"Leonard Van Sickle knocked himself off," I said.

Joe yawned. "Guys do that. Ain't I just semi-fresh from the funeral of a 'sooey?'"

"They don't laugh an hour or so before they do it," I said, taking off my pajamas and reaching for my clothes. "Or at least I don't remember your mentioning it in the case of Max Gerrich."

"I knew something was wrong," Joe said. "I got the jumps like a bowlegged lady before a burleycue try-out. Was that Standish?"

I nodded. "Standish is worried. A set of missing false teeth bother him. Standish thinks he might fumble something big."

"And the Ghost never fumbles," Joe said. "Not yet." He went over to look for cigarettes in my pants. "The Ghost taking a hand, George?"

"That's why Standish called," I told him. "Let's have the pants."

Joe tossed me the pants only after he had helped himself to cigarettes. There was a dour smile on his thin lips.

"You need them, George. You'll also need a bullet proof vest and an armored bath tub when some of the tough boys I know discover that the Ghost and George Chance are the same guy."

"That's impossible," I said.

The shoulders under the purple bathrobe rose and fell.

"Things get discovered. Look at America."

THE GHOST *is George Chance.* It looks odd on paper. It's a secret I have never before disclosed. Sometimes I've chuckled inwardly about it, and then again my double identity has been like a two-ton safe suspended by a thread over my head. There is reason for the latter. The Ghost's enemies in the underworld are too numerous for comfort. But it is my own doing. You can't create a wraith-like manhunter, materializing out of the darkness to become a tangible foe, laughing ghoulishly at frantic efforts of discovered criminals to escape, and expect the underworld to take kindly to him.

All things considered, it's only natural that the Ghost should have become the focal point for so much sincere hatred on the part of the criminal gentry. My only consolation is that George Chance, so far as he knows, has no enemies at all.

Now then, to understand fully how the Ghost has managed to spank public enemies who would have welcomed a clash with the police, you should know a little more about George Chance.

I was born in the show business. My father was an animal trainer and my mother a trapeze performer in a circus. Both my parents were generous to a fault, so that when I found myself an orphan at an early age, it was entirely dependent upon my own ability whether or not I was to eat regularly in the days to come.

Thanks to early circus training, I am a fair tumbler and contortionist. I learned much of the secrets of makeup from a clown named Ricki. To the grave-eyed man with the long black burnsides who traveled with the show under the name of Don Avigne, I am indebted for knowledge that has made the knife one of the deadliest of weapons in my hands.

Then there was Professor Gabby, who taught me principles of ventriloquism which are today responsible for the hundreds of voices of the Ghost.

But most important of all, while I was hanging around the circus, I won the confidence of Marko, the Magician. His sideshow sorcery caught and held my fascination. Marko was a German. Incidentally, I got the sorrowful word recently that he died in a German concentration camp.

I will never forget the day he called me into his dressing tent and gave me a half-size set of multiplying billiard balls.

"You haff goot hands for tricks unt gimmicks, George, mine poy," he told me. "Learn to use these unt some day you vill know magic. Unt der vorld vill know you."

I still have the billiard balls Marko gave me, and the supple fingers they developed. To me, they're the foundation of my reputation as a magician which has spread around the world. Magic was the ladder that helped me climb from the circus to vaudeville and from there to my own revues. Magic made me a fortune so that I finally retired from the stage to establish the New York School of Magic where amateurs, bitten by the unending craze to create illusions, are taught.

I first met Commissioner Standish in person when I was performing magic at a policeman's benefit party. I could tell him truthfully that I had always followed his work with more than average interest, since criminology and magic have one thing in common—both depend on keen judgment of human nature and more than rudimentary knowledge of psychology.

STANDISH AND I took to each other at once, and my comments on criminology aroused his interest sufficiently for him to invite me to take a hand in a murder investigation. When I exposed the real criminal by means of a spirit-slate trick that has been known to conjurers for years, he said: "I'll take a second helping."

"What do you mean?" I asked.

"I mean that when I need you again, I'll certainly call on you," he answered soberly.

We looked at each other. I think the idea was born simultaneously in our brains.

"I'll study up on it," I said.

In the days and weeks that followed, I found one concept more and more dominating my thoughts—Magic and Crime-Detection, how to merge the two and make them one. And so, not all at once, but gradually, slowly—but surely—the idea of the Ghost took form.

Not until then did I take Standish into my confidence.

"Ned, do you know that the late Robert-Houdin, the father of modern magic from whom the great magician, Harry Houdini, took his name, was sent by the French government to Algeria to put down the *marabouts?* Do you know that Robert-Houdin filled the natives with so much terror that they decided not to rise against the French?"

"I've heard something like that," Standish replied. "But why burden my policeman's mind with such queer data? Give me something that will work on some of our modern troublemakers right here in New York, and I'll say you're talking."

"That's what I'm doing," I said.

"What do you mean?"

I told him.

Standish couldn't quite grasp it at first.

"It won't work," he objected. "You'll be getting yourself knocked off. You're a great magician and you've acquired a pretty thorough theoretical knowledge of criminology. But that's not the same as being a

Glenn Saunders

cop, with a cop's training. You're a pretty rotten shot with a pistol. And what do you know of police procedure?"

"Almost nothing," I admitted, "yet to my mind the very fact that I would be unhampered by orthodox police methods might be an asset. All I'd ask of you and the Department is a fair amount of co-operation."

For a moment, enthusiasm for the idea flamed in the commissioner's eyes and then gradually died.

"Suppose it works," he said. "Suppose you catch one member of a criminal gang. Don't you suppose the members who go free are going to put the finger on you? It'll be an added expense on my budget, ordering flowers for your funeral."

I shook my head.

"I've thought all that out," I said. "Suppose, Ned, I had the perfect alibi?" I grasped his arm. "Suppose it was possible for me to do what all criminals dream of doing! Suppose George Chance were to be apparently minding his own affairs and at the same time be out chasing gunmen!"

STANDISH THREW back his head and laughed.

"I've seen you do impossible things, George, but nothing like that. Nobody—positively nobody—can be in two places at the same time."

It was my turn to laugh but I only chuckled.

"I can," I said. "Ned, if you saw my last stage revue, you've seen me in two places at once."

"What are you trying to tell me?" he demanded.

"Remember the climaxing illusion? I am handcuffed in a mail sack. At the crack of a gun, the mail sack falls limp and empty to the stage. And at the same time I appear, running out of the lobby of the theater and into the audience?"

"Yes, I've seen that one," Standish said.

"Well, Ned, there's only one way that trick could be accomplished."

Comprehension dawned on Standish's face. He leaned forward in his chair, his mouth slightly agape.

"You've got a double?" he almost whispered.

I nodded. "An identical double. Now then, suppose my double were to live the life of George Chance while the real George Chance, suitably disguised, is out playing cops and robbers, annoying criminals with his magic, possibly handing over a few murderers to the police!"

Standish's eyes held a gleam now; he rubbed his hands.

"A Dr. Jekyll and a Mr. Hyde, eh?"

"Never cared much for Hyde," I said. "Make it George Chance and his ghost, if you've got to be dramatic about it."

So much for the history of George Chance and the origin of the Ghost. Now to get on with the case of the lisping man.

As soon as I had dressed, after hearing the commissioner's news about Van Sickle's suicide, I went down into the basement of my house. I have a workshop down there where many new tricks and magical devices are developed. Glenn Saunders was there, working on a piece of apparatus for use in that clever trick which consists of dropping a ball-bearing through a plate of glass without breaking the glass.

Glenn Saunders usually works at night, entering my house under the cover of darkness. You would understand why if you saw him. For, by a curious quirk of nature helped a little by plastic surgery, Glenn Saunders is the identical double of George Chance.

His height measures up to my own six feet-one inch. He has the same broad shoulders and lean waist. His face reflects my own—blue eyes, ruddy gold hair waving back from a fairly broad forehead, thin nose and mouth, prominent cheek bones. He apes every move I make, and does it so well that sometimes when I look at him I could almost be in doubt as to who is who. Ever since the birth of the Ghost, he has acted as my double in exchange for all that I can teach him about magic as an art and a business. It is a considerable sacrifice for a man to shuck his own identity, but Saunders thinks it is worth it.

FOR ME it is an immeasurable advantage. I can withdraw from my usual haunts, adopt a new identity for the purpose of stepping into the underworld, while Glenn Saunders literally wears the shoes of George Chance. Glenn Saunders is to the Ghost what every criminal dreams about—a perfect alibi.

When I went into the shop, Glenn Saunders laid aside his tools, picked up a cold briar pipe and lighted the remaining heel of tobacco in it.

"Nice night," he remarked, his voice a natural echo of my own.

"Nice for murder," I said. "Glenn, you're performing for a benefit party tomorrow evening. The Ghost is going for a walk."

Glenn smiled one-sidedly.

"What's up this time?"

"A suicide," I explained. "A suicide that couldn't have happened."

I walked over to the bench and took the pipe out of Saunders' mouth.

"From now on until further instructions, Glenn, you're George Chance. And I don't smoke a pipe."

"No pipe," Glenn said. "Only your cigars and cigarettes."

"My pajamas you'll find thrown over my bed. Get in them and get some shut-eye. Tell Joe Harper I'll probably need him."

Glenn nodded.

"Right, chief."

And my double and I parted.

CHAPTER III

THE GHOST WALKS

I N A small basement room brilliantly lighted, I began altering my features. I always use as few makeup materials as possible, for I have found that a simple makeup is less likely to be detected and is nearly always just as effective as a complicated one.

To create the character of the Ghost, I take small wire ovals and put them into my nose, tilting the tip and elongating the nostrils. For the somewhat ghastly effect proper to a ghost-character, I darken the inside of each nostril. Simple, eh—yet one must know how.

Brown eyeshadow goes on to darken my eye pits. Pallor comes out of a powder box. I highlight my naturally prominent cheek bones. Over my own teeth I place shells the color of old ivory.

After that, I have only to affect a fixed vacuity of expression and my face becomes something very much like a skull.

Yet—and this is important because it gives me freedom to get around without attracting undue attention—if I allow my eyes their usual animation and keep my lips closed over the yellow teeth, the Ghost is serviceably hidden beneath the exterior of an ordinary man who is merely a little less attractive than the average.

This done, I returned my makeup materials to a case the size of a tobacco tin. From a closet I removed a black suit—black because the color apparently reduces the width of my shoulders and decreases my height. The suit has other virtues in the way of secret pockets and clever holders of magical gimmicks I find useful—even more useful than the small flat automatic I carry or the nasty little throwing knife.

Before I went out, I put on a black felt crusher hat and took a look at myself in the mirror. The possibility of recognition as George Chance no longer existed. I looked like the ghost I had chosen to be—a rather husky, happy ghost, however—for the time being.

As soon as I got outside my door I "turned off the Ghost." I took a walk to Fifth Avenue, where I signaled a cab. The driver took no interest in me except as a potential fare, nor did I expect him to. The cab let me out in front of the Cronner Hotel where it towers above Central Park, and in one of the apartments of which Leonard Van Sickle had once lived and breathed—and lisped to me over the telephone.

The efficiency of the New York police system was pretty well evidenced. The only things outside the hotel to indicate that this was the site of a recent tragedy was a hotel employee diligently engaged in mopping at an ugly stain on the sidewalk, and a uniformed cop talking about the weather to the doorman.

I walked into the lobby. Nobody noticed me. There's a lot of obscurity in a black suit.

SINCE QUITE a while had passed since I had talked with Standish, I wasn't surprised to find that all the bustle attending sudden death was over. Evidently the homicide boys and my friend Robert Demarest from the medical examiner's office had concluded their job. It may seem that there was no particular point in my visiting the scene of the crime before seeing Standish. But I always prefer, when possible, to start at the beginning of a mystery maze instead of plunging into the middle of it.

Almost at once I ran into something queer. When I reached the door of the Van Sickle suite, there was no police guard in the hall. The point is this: Standish, even though he had not said so, suspected murder.

Otherwise he wouldn't have asked me to take a hand in the game. Well, where there had been murder, there should have been a policeman.

I tried the door, found that it was unlocked, pushed it open part way.

Something was wrong. I could not push the door all the way open. And the reason for that was pretty much of a shock—the body of a man blocked it.

I stepped over it, into darkness that was total, and closed the door behind me. My idea of getting in on the beginning of this thing was already pretty well shot. Here I was, already in the middle of it.

I knelt beside the man on the floor, using my fingers for eyes.

My hands traveled lightly over the body on the floor—the body of a man wearing close-woven suiting, a man with a sizeable paunch. My fingers met a bullet-studded belt and an empty holster, passed upward over a rising and falling chest to touch the cold, smooth surface of a shield.

I understood now why the door was unguarded. This man was a policeman and he had been slugged.

I stood up, looked through darkness. Coming from what must have been another room was a faint twinkle of light—the guarded rays of a flashlight. No sound came, however—footsteps were muffled by a rug.

I moved closer. It was a man's hand that held the light. A shadowy figure was kneeling in front of a desk. False drawers of the desk were open, revealing the door of a steel safety deposit box. The man was just closing the door. The light went out. I heard furtive movements.

I was invisible in the darkness because of my black outfit. I flattened myself against the wall, lowered my head to the lapel of my open coat. My left hand whisked upward from a vest pocket, fingers closed over a small rubber balloon. As the man moved cautiously about the extensive suite, I put the nipple to my mouth and quickly inflated the balloon under the cover of my coat. A twist of the valve and the balloon held its air.

THE PROWLER entered the room in which I was waiting for him. I could hear his quiet breathing. Then his needle of light jumped about the room, paused on the prostrate form of the cop. I saw the prowler's hand in reflected rays from the light. There was a peculiar bluish tattoo mark encircling his wrist like the coils of a small snake.

The light began moving in my direction, as though some sixth sense told the man hidden eyes were watching.

I pulled the balloon from under my coat.

If you have seen spiritual materializations as accomplished by magicians on a black stage, my balloon stunt may be disillusioning. The balloon I had inflated had a ghastly skull face painted on it with luminous paint.

The prowler saw the glow skull face, uttered a gasp, dropped his light. In utter darkness I could hear his shallow, frightened breathing as I advanced slowly toward him, keeping the balloon at arm's length to the right. I dislike being shot at.

"S-stop," the man's whisper ordered. "Stay where you are. I've got a gun. Stop, I tell you!"

His whisper mounted to something close to a hysterical cry. I judged it time to give the balloon a flick that carried it through the air toward him. At the same time, I called up my powers of ventriloquism and gave the prowler the benefit of a derisive, ghoulish laugh.

His reaction was the expected one—he fired.

It was a good shot. The balloon burst, the sound of its bursting lost in the roar of gunfire so that the glowing head must have seemed to have vanished in mid-air. But the man's gunfire had pinned a ruddy sign of his exact location and I made for it, slipped in behind him, clicked my knife from my sleeve.

The knife is good steel and I let him have the tip of it in the quivering muscles of his back. At the same time I uttered the rollicking, macabre chuckle which generally heralds the entrance of the Ghost. It is a rather horrible sound, and I never blame any of its victims for being frightened by it.

"Drop your gun."

My voice was flat, dead, unemotional.

The plunk of the weapon to the carpet sounded.

"Over to the door," I ordered. "You'll turn on the lights and then turn around slowly. No tricks. The knife is a key for unlocking hell for you if you try anything."

The man obeyed, moving slowly, avoiding the unconscious cop. I heard the whisper of his fingers along the wall as they sought the light switch. Then there was light and I backed a step so that the man could turn around. By this time the muscles of my face had once again frozen into that death's-head expression which makes those who see it think they are smelling their own graves in advance.

The man's piggy eyes were some time taking me in. Then his dry, pallid lips whispered.

"*What* are you?"

He asked "what," not "who." They usually do at first.

Then his wits returned to him; the play of his thoughts showed in his face; memory of gossip in the underworld made him guess at the truth—

"My God," he muttered, "you're—"

"Yes," I said softly—

"The Ghost…" he whispered, and I could hardly hear him.

CHAPTER IV

CRIME STRIKES TWICE

O **F MEDIUM** height, the man wore gray. His face was as ordinary and uninteresting as a bowl of cold porridge. In a crowd of six men you'd have lost him. He wasn't dark and yet not blond. His small, furtive eyes varied between green and brown. He was just a guy with a serpent tattooed on his wrist.

I flipped my knife from the right hand to the left—an easy gesture for a magician—and stepped in close to him. I set the point of the knife at his throat, and his prominent Adam's apple went up and then down in his attempt to swallow his terror.

"Wh-what are you going to do?"

I let him wonder about the answer to that one and how close he was to becoming a ghost himself. My right hand went through his pockets. Except for a few bills held together with a dollar sign money clip, there was nothing in his trouser pockets. But the inner pocket of his coat yielded the loot from the dead man's safe—a sheaf of bond certificates which I took no time to examine, and a chamois skin bag containing what might have been unset gems.

I pocketed these. Ned Standish would eventually get them.

I nodded toward a comfortable-looking chair with a chrome-trimmed smoking stand beside it.

"Sit down," I ordered.

Watching me with his piggish eyes, the man backed to the chair. He sat down as though he had a couple of overripe eggs in his hip pockets. Nervously, he fumbled with an ornament topping the smoking stand.

And his fingering called my attention to something that lay on the smoking stand.

From where I stood, it looked like a dime that was a little the worse for wear. I went over to the stand, my knife still jutting threateningly in my left hand. I picked up the round disk and flipped it from fingertips to palm. It was a spiral of inflexible wire, like a coiled watch spring except inflexible, as I said, and the wire was round and the color of gun metal.

"What's this?" I showed the man the coil.

"You got me." His voice was husky, maybe naturally that way, maybe because he was scared half-witted.

"I know I got you," I said, "but—"

The door of the room opened. I sprang backwards, twisted around, trying to see the intruder and the man with the tattooed wrist at the same time. I got only a glimpse of the person at the door, a woman, when the man with the tattooed wrist decided he could beat me to his gun which still lay on the floor where he had dropped it. I could see by the direction of his glance and the way he was gripping the arms of the chair exactly what was in his mind.

I warned him, but he was already in motion. As he stooped for the gun, my fingers slid down the length of my knife to the tip. I threw the knife, pinned his arm to the floor, the knife passing through the cuff of his gray coat as he reached for the gun.

NO BLOODSHED, no noise. Fear and the knife held the man in a crouching position on the floor. My right hand brushed the bottom of my coat, came up with my automatic delivered from a smooth acting gimmick-clip which had originally been designed to hold a magician's handkerchief-dying tube.

I bowed slightly to the woman in the doorway.

"Won't you come in? And close the door, please."

She was calm enough, but that was because I had "turned off the Ghost." She was an attractive, rounded woman, red-haired, with soft brown eyes. My first glance said she was thirty, my second that she was forty. But attractive and less flustered, I believe, than anyone else could have possibly been under similar circumstances.

She looked at the man with the tattooed wrist.

"Hugo!" she said.

"I see you know each other," I said. "You'll have to pardon Hugo's rather odd position on the floor."

I went over to him, retrieved my knife, retained it in my left hand while my right put my gun in my pocket. Hugo straightened and backed shakily to his chair.

The woman in the doorway was looking in wide-eyed wonder at the cop groaning on the floor in front of the door. And then her brown-eyed gaze moved to me.

"Who are you?" she asked.

"On the contrary," I said, "who are *you?*"

"I happen to be a friend of Mr. Van Sickle."

"Who is dead," I said; "who jumped out of his window. And there seems to be some slight reason to believe that he was urged."

The announcement made no visible impression upon the woman. Her rounded face was an admirable picture of studied calm.

"And after suicide or murder," I went on, with a glance at Hugo, "a little robbery—"

"Mrs. Kurtzner," said the man with the tattooed wrist, "this guy just cracked Van Sickle's safe. I don't know what he got. I had an appointment with Van Sickle and when I came in—"

"You socked the cop," I concluded for him. "Tell me, when you go to a business appointment, do you generally club the first person who opens the door?"

"*He* socked the copper," said the man, meaning me. "I didn't even know there was a cop here nor what he was here for."

MRS. KURTZNER took a decisive step to the telephone which rested on a small table at the left of the door. The woman apparently had courage and understood the advantage of a receiver off the hook when there was a man with a gun in the room. Her soft brown eyes were fixed on my face as though she wanted to remember me.

"Send the police up to Mr. Van Sickle's suite," she said. "Burglars."

"The police, madam," I said, indicating the cop on the floor "are at your feet."

I went to the door.

"He's trying to escape," Mrs. Kurtzner said calmly into the phone. "He's wearing a black suit and a black hat. His face is dead white and queer-looking."

For Mrs. Kurtzner's entertainment, and also to return my knife to its place in my sleeve, I turned my head slightly and "swallowed" the knife. I was applauded with a faint gasp from the lady. She dropped the phone in place, turned a little pale under her rouge. I saw her lips frame the words: "The Ghost," although no sound came from them.

"Yes," I admitted. "Good night to you."

I stepped out into the hall.

I passed the elevator shaft and glanced at the indicator. A car was on the way up. It was not in my plans to meet the police as yet. I walked to the end of the hall to the red-lighted doorway opening on the fireproof inner stairway. I went up the steps instead of down.

The Sky Room on top of the hotel is a cafe. It was a swank place George Chance had visited often enough. I found the cafe crowded, which was only to be expected at midnight. I kept my hat and slid into a table not far from the lavatory door. It had been my intention to go to the lavatory at once so as to switch disguises in private, but the plan had to be revised upon my seeing a fat man in evening clothes reel into the lavatory. So I took the table and waited.

One of the waiters approached, asked if he couldn't take my hat. I said he couldn't, and told him to bring some beer.

"We have some imported Braumier Pilsner special for this evening only," he said. "We are getting some very nice compliments on it."

I told him to bring whatever could be brought the quickest. He eyed me strangely. I watched the lavatory door, lighted a cigarette. It was only a short time before the alarm would spread throughout the hotel.

My friendship with the commissioner makes everything okay in case the cops pick me up, but an arrest, even though temporary, would mean questions embarrassing to both Standish and me. Also, the pinch would be bound to make the papers, and the Ghost's prestige in the underworld would be damaged. A good deal of the Ghost's terror-inspiring reputation in the underworld springs not alone from the fact that its members do not know who he actually is but because they believe the police do not know either.

MY BEER came. I left it untouched. The band was breaking into one of Raymond Scott's hectic bits, and while the bodies of the dancers on the floor were getting keyed up to the torrid tempo, my own pulse was beginning to get a bit jumpy—not from the music but because the fat man still occupied the wash room.

I got up and went to the lavatory door, opened it.

The fat man was bending over a wash basin, tie and collar off. He was scrubbing his moon-like face, his pointed ears which reminded me of Mercury's wings, and even splattering cold water on the top of his nearly bald head.

I was amused, but not at that. Once again fate was reaching out for me and taking me by the hand. Certainly in no previous case had cir-

Merry White

cumstances combined so often to save me time and trouble in gathering in the threads. But I am jumping ahead too fast.

"You're supposed to take your bath before you come to a joint like this, mister," I said.

He looked around at me, gripping the edge of the wash basin with soapy hands. I had thought that possibly I might have been mistaken, but he was the man I had taken him for at first sight—Theo Quinn, president of the concern which had absorbed Van Sickle's manufacturing plant after fortune had taken a slap at Van Sickle.

Looking at me, he got soap in his eye, which was my fault, according to the reasoning process of his drink-numbed brain.

"To hell wishu!" he said.

I backed out and left the door open. Quinn continued his washing.

Then, in the foyer outside the plate glass and chrome doors of the Sky Room, I saw a police detective—a man named Hullick. He was just coming out of the elevator.

I turned my back on the door through which Detective Hullick had to pass, and headed for the stairway.

CHAPTER V

BLOCKED

IN ANOTHER minute I knew exactly how a baseball player feels when he's caught between bases. I hadn't gone down more than a flight of stairs when I heard someone coming up toward me.

"It was the Ghost," a woman's voice was saying. "No doubt of it!"

"Then you were a sap to inform the police, Lulu. We've got to block him off before the cops do."

"The call was already in before I knew it," the woman justified herself querulously. The voice was that of Mrs. Kurtzner. I didn't recognize the voice of the man who was with her. It wasn't Hugo.

They were hunting the hotel for me, for some reason then obscure, and it looked as though Fate had pointed out a short cut toward the achievement of their purpose.

There was only one thing to do. I bounded back up three steps to the landing I had just left, pushed open a door, went into the hotel corridor. No safety zone there. The cool-nerved Lulu Kurtzner and her scratchy-voiced pal would certainly look in on every floor on the way down. I headed for the door of the first room on my right, knocked on the panel as though the hotel was on fire.

"Telegram for Mr. Reed!" I called out, and pounded the door again.

If the door didn't open in another instant, I knew that Mrs. Kurtzner would spot me.

The door opened. A seedy, inoffensive-looking man who might have been a birdseed salesman from St. Louis or a cartoonist's conception of tax-burdened John Public, blinked out at me with sleepy eyes.

"You've made a mistake," he said.

I shoved the door open and showed him my gun.

"Don't rub it in," I said. "I acknowledge the fact I have made a mistake. Sorry about this, old man."

I slammed the door behind me just as Mrs. Kurtzner and her fellow searcher came into the corridor.

Wide-eyed with astonishment, his trembling body setting up waves in the pink stripes of his pajamas, my Mr. Public stared into the muzzle of my gun.

The smartest thing for me to do at the moment would have been to tap the little man on the head with the gun barrel, but I couldn't do it.

When coincidence is unkind enough to throw some innocent bystander into the game of cops and criminals, I think the bystander ought to be spared a lump on the head. So I planted my left hand on Mr. Public's meager chest, shoved him into the bathroom and shut the door. I was counting on the impression my gun had made to last long enough to keep him there while I switched disguises.

I removed the wire ovals that distorted the shape of my nose and the yellow shells of my teeth. A piece of cloth quickly took care of the makeup material on my face. I got a pair of metal "plumpers" from my makeup kit and put them into my cheeks. This added apparent pounds to my thin face. A few touches with a lining pencil at the outer ends of my eyelids created crow-foot wrinkles.

THAT BLACK suit of mine is a work of ingenious tailoring. All I had to do was remove it, snap out the silken lining with its pockets and holders for magical apparatus, turn the suit inside out, replace the lining, and dress again. I was then wearing a suit of gray herringbone.

The Ghost's black crusher hat stands any amount of abuse. I rolled it up and stuck it into a secret pouch at the tail of my coat. Shoulders hunched a little, some white powder worked in my hair at the temples, added ten years to my age.

This took a little time, but the meek little man in the bathroom had offered no word of protest. I opened the door of his room and stepped into the hall. Between me and the stairway stood Mrs. Lulu Kurtzner.

With her was a tall man in evening clothes. His face was one nobody could forget in a hurry—deeply tanned skin, a thin hooked nose, a knife scar on his chin, rivet-clinching lips, cruel slots of eyes. He and the Kurtzner woman were talking in low tones.

I don't think a faint heart ever deceives a fair lady, so instead of showing only my back to Mrs. Kurtzner by going to the elevator, I walked straight toward her, headed for the stairway. The plan would have worked without a hitch, but I had reckoned without my Mr. Public.

As I reached the steps, a door in the corridor behind me was wrenched open violently. I ducked down the stairs. I couldn't see what happened but I could form a mental picture of it—the meek Mr. Public's trembling in the corridor of the hotel, catching sight of the couple near the stairway, running to them, telling them about the invader of his privacy.

Mrs. Kurtzner and her boy friend would need nothing more, in spite of my disguise. They would put two and two together and cotton to the fact that it must have been the Ghost who had passed them. I ran down the stairs.

I never saw the man whose room I had appropriated again, but I will always remember him for having prepared what promised to be a hot fire for me to land in as soon as I had jumped out of the frying pan.

Whether I got out of the hotel without any further difficulty depended a whole lot on how fast I could descend the stairs and how lucky Mrs. Kurtzner's friend in evening clothes was in catching an elevator.

It turned out that I didn't get any sort of a break. When I reached the lobby, the man with the scarred chin and hooked nose was waiting for me.

He had taken the elevator which must have descended without a stop. He was watching me even before I spotted him standing between two elevator shafts.

The lobby was quite crowded. At the three visible exits, police lounged near the doors, evidently on the lookout for the man Mrs. Kurtzner had described over the phone.

BUT THERE was a bright spot among all these spots of unpleasant promise. Leaning against one of the marble pillars that supported the lobby ceiling was the familiar figure of Joe Harper, green hat far down over his dark eyes, one of my cigarettes dangling from his lips.

I gave him a sign perceptible to him alone—the letter "G" formed by the fingers of my left hand in the symbol employed by deaf mutes. Nothing escapes those black beetle eyes of his. He tilted his cigarette in token that he had caught it, otherwise betraying no recognition.

Extremely important, this care we always exercised in concealing any connection. For, if the friends of George Chance were proved to be the friends of the Ghost also, it is obvious how easy it would be for the Ghost's underworld enemies to deduce the connection between the Ghost and George Chance.

Joe Harper had tailed me. I had half expected that. I never know when, as the Ghost, I am going to need the man. And his shrewd eyes and his brain that bulges with facts about Manhattan and Manhattan's crooks, are valued accessories.

True, at the present time I couldn't see exactly how he was going to be useful. I couldn't see how the man with the scarred chin could start anything with the police around. Yet there was a certain tenseness in the air. I knew Joe Harper sensed it. Back turned toward me, he headed for the nearest exit. I knew he intended I should follow him.

I started for the same door and the man with the scarred chin moved toward me. He wasn't looking at me, but that very fact, coupled with the fact of his simultaneous movement with me, assured me that he was trying to head me off.

CHAPTER VI

DEATH AT MY ELBOW

BREATH BATED, out of the corner of my eye, I saw the man with the scarred chin cut around in front of a semi-circular lounge backed up against the same post against which Joe Harper had been leaning. But I also noticed something else. I had been mistaken about there being only one bright spot; there were two.

A girl was sitting on the lounge—a girl masked from the waist to the crown of her head by a wide open newspaper—and something about that girl was delightfully familiar.

The man with the scarred chin passed her. She lowered the paper half a foot. I recognized her black hat and her curiously beautiful green eyes. The girl was Merry White, the feminine attraction in my magical shows and in the private life of George Chance.

If you have seen any of the George Chance magical acts at any of the benefit parties in and around New York, you will remember Merry White—tiny, black-haired, green-eyed, with a roguish smile that wins the heart of even the coolest audience. She has a ten thousand watt personality plus the sweetest face and the most graceful figure. But perhaps I am a bit prejudiced. After all, someday she is to be Mrs. George Chance.

Obviously she had come to the hotel with Harper. She is continually mixing with the affairs of the Ghost, frequently throwing him helpful hints with only a vague idea of their full significance. She has been both a big help and a big worry. Having little conception of the meaning of fear, she's a dark-haired angel stepping in where a fool would fear to tread, her abrupt, impulsive actions utterly unpredictable.

It's a very difficult thing for even a perfect stranger to pass Merry White without giving her a couple of second glances, but that's what I did. The man with the scarred chin kept to his course and I kept to mine.

And at the cigar stand he deliberately bumped into me. He was lean and light-looking, but height added weight to his body. I was thrown off balance.

"I beg your pardon!" he said, catching at me with his left hand. "How perfectly careless of me. Wasn't watching where I was going."

"That's all right," I told him.

I noticed he was standing considerably closer to me than was necessary and that his right hand was in the pocket of his jacket.

His left hand began dusting mythical lint from the shoulder of my coat. Whether it was intentional or a mere coincidence, I noticed that the two of us were pretty well surrounded at the moment by a group of Broadway night hawks who had dropped in for a time at one of the several supper clubs in the hotel.

The man with the scar crowded closer and I felt the nudge of the gun in his pocket.

He spoke in low but distinct tones:

"Silencer on this baby. Knock you off pretty damned quick. The grill and make it snappy—*Ghost!*"

AT THE moment I was more chagrined that alarmed. It was the first time the Ghost had ever been spotted unless he had wanted to be spotted. My eyes flicked across the lobby. Toward the north side a neon arrow pointed to the entrance of the grill and tap room. I looked into the man's hard inscrutable face. His hawk's nose was close to my face. His pincer lips formed a tight straight line. The scar on his chin was like a second mouth.

I had an uncomfortable moment of wondering whether or not he would shoot. The pop of a silenced gun attracts more attention than the average man supposes. And within twenty feet of us were police on the lookout for me.

For all of that, if I ever saw the will to kill in a man's eyes, I saw it now. I silently debated whether I should reach for my knife and let him have the length of it in his abdomen—I could have done that quickly enough—but I decided that it was what Joe Harper would have called bad percentage. The thrust of the knife would have caused a reflex-pull of his trigger-finger.

If the situation seemed tight, it was a lot tighter exactly two seconds later. I heard the crisp click of high heels on the marble flooring. Merry White, the short skirt of her black suit switching, her green eyes snapping with something that bordered between genuine fury and pure devilment, came toward us. She is unpredictable!

She sleaked her way between two top-hatters who were arguing about the virtues of a recent Broadway comedy. She gave friend Scar-Chin an elbow jab in the ribs and let loose a stinging left-handed slap to the side of my jaw.

At the same time, she cried:

"Here he is, officer! Help! This way!"

Two cops came from the doorway, saw Merry White hanging onto my arm as though afraid I would make a break for it. One of the cops wedged in between Scar-Chin and myself, and that was a great comfort.

"What's the matter, lady?" the cop wanted to know. "This man bothering you?"

Merry looked at me, stamped her foot. Her eyes blazed.

"He's a masher. Just an old hotel lobby masher! Didn't you see him trying to make a date with me? And when he pinched me—"

The hand of the law seized me roughly. The voice of the law was heavy with outrage.

"Annoyin' this lady, was you?"

I was hauled roughly to the door.

Merry's heels clattered after us. She grasped the cop's coat tail just as we reached the street. He turned, still holding onto me.

"Ooh!" Merry uttered a prolonged, hurt cry—it was a masterpiece of sincerity.

Her small gloved hand went up to her mouth. Her head downcast, her eyes rolling upward, I could feel my cop becoming slightly less useful.

"I've made a dreadful mistake!"

She looked at me as though she was seeing me for the first time.

"That isn't the man at all. He was a little like him, but not much. He was wearing black, I remember. A black hat and suit—"

The cop let go of me.

"Where, lady?" he demanded testily. "When was all this?"

"Why not ten minutes ago. Right here in the lobby!"

She turned her eyes on me, gave me that sweetest smile.

"Please forgive me. I wouldn't have caused you all this trouble for anything."

"Mistakes happen in the best of families," I said with a smile, and sauntered toward the curb.

"Dames," the cop said in disgust.

Joe Harper had just called a cab. When he saw me coming, he started to get into the cab and was slow about it, giving me a chance to catch up with him. But such is the peculiar relationship between the Ghost and the friends of George Chance that Joe and I had to put on a little act.

I tapped Joe on the shoulder as he was about to get into the taxi. "Beg your pardon," I said gravely, "but this is my cab."

Joe faced me, that smoldering cigarette still dangling from his lips.

"Like hell it is," he said. "Where do you get that stuff?"

The doorman from the hotel came toward us, evidently to act as intermediator in what appeared to be an incipient brawl. I gave Joe a push in the chest and sent him back three paces. He took one step forward, swung wildly at my head, missing by a foot. I ducked into the taxi and shoved a five dollar bill under the driver's nose.

"Get going," I ordered.

CHAPTER VII

IN SECRET COUNCIL

EAST FIFTY-FIFTH STREET, not far from my house on Fifty-Fourth, has an old church with two lean spires that sway when a high wind sweeps across the city. In its shadow is a square brick house formerly used as a rectory. The brick house is always vacant, always displays a For Rent sign on the front door. The rental, in fact, is kept prohibitively high. And the owner of the rectory is George Chance.

The place has a bad reputation with small boys in the neighborhood. Its windows are always shuttered and it is somehow squat and evil-locking in the shadows of the steeples that might be the home of Poe's ghouls. The place is said to be haunted, and I would never be the one to deny it. You see, I haunt it. It is the headquarters of the Ghost.

I left the taxi a block away and walked to the Ghost's haunted rectory. It was about three o'clock in the morning. Darkness lay heavy upon the street. There was silence, too, except for the swift swish of tires on the wet pavement of Madison Avenue not far away.

I turned into the narrow way between the walls of the church and the walls of the rectory. The walk led to a small court at the rear of my hideout. I mounted three steps to the back door, unlocked it, stepped into darkness, closed the door behind me. I went down basement steps, unlocked another door and closed it before turning on a light.

This basement is no spider's lair. No bones are lying in the corners and there are no chains for ghostly clanking. The basement of the house contains several liveable rooms and it is home to the Ghost when he is working at his unique job of haunting criminals into the electric chair.

I went into a living room furnished with modern simplicity. At a small bar, I mixed a quart shaker of pink ladies, drank one, stretched my spine on the studio couch, loosened tie and collar. Facial muscles relaxed, I suppose I looked a little more like George Chance—a fat-cheeked George Chance. I took from my pocket the oddest assortment of clues I think I have ever run across.

There was first of all the sheaf of bond certificates the man Mrs. Kurtzner had called Hugo had swiped from Van Sickle's small safe. These were bonds on the Deistel International Corporation, a concern I had never heard of.

Opening the certificates, I found that each bore the registered name of the owner—Fabian Deeming, a man as unknown to me as the company itself. There were ten such bonds of two thousand dollars' each.

I TOSSED them onto the cocktail table beside the couch and took out the chamois skin bag which I supposed contained jewels.

When I opened the bag I got the surprise of my life. It contained twenty-eight human teeth.

Bonds and teeth—a queer combination.

Then there was that curious spiral of inflexible steel wire, a little more puzzling than the teeth themselves. I turned it over in my hand and made nothing of it. It was about the most purposeless thing I had ever seen. Sort of a springless spring.

The spiral, the teeth, or the bonds—one or perhaps all of these had been of vital importance to the man with the scarred chin. Otherwise, there would have been no reason for him to try that stick-up in the hotel lobby. I could take that one of these three things was what criminologists call "the essential clue." I put the spiral on the table with the teeth and bonds.

That was the entire lot of crazy pieces that might, when properly fitted together, give a complete picture. Or they might each represent a piece from a separate puzzle. I'd seen crimes without clues. This one had too many.

Thus far three of my friends were already involved in the Van Sickle affair. I now reached for the phone and called up Tim Terry.

Tim is my oldest friend and certainly the smallest. Nearing middle age, he still isn't tall enough to see over the average table. The midget, for such he is, had been my friend in the old circus days, and now that he had retired we kept in constant touch with each other. He is one of the six persons who know that George Chance and the Ghost are one. And Tiny Tim of the circus is one of the cleverest of the Ghost's agents.

I told Tim where I was and asked him to come over in spite of the hour. Merry White and Joe Harper would probably drop in, and the four of us would go over the details of what had happened. I hadn't any of the police angles on the Van Sickle case, but those could wait until tomorrow. I wanted Robert Demarest to have completed his medical examination of the corpse before I got any of the police opinions.

Shortly after I had talked to Tim Terry, I heard the opening of the back door of the old house. Only the six who share the Ghost's secret with me have keys to the house, and a moment later I heard Merry White's light step on the stair. She came in, wearing the same smart black suit she had worn when I had last seen her in the lobby of the hotel.

SHE STOOD in the door, a queer little smile on her lips.

"Wasn't I good tonight, darlin'?" she asked.

"You were perfect," I said.

I got over to the door fast, took her in my arms, and kissed her. One arm around her, I led her back to the bar and poured her a cocktail. We went over to the studio couch and sat down.

"Whose idea was it?" I asked her. "You and Joe looked as though you were about two jumps ahead of me."

She shook her head, sipped her drink.

"About two blocks behind. Joe knew where you were going and took one of your cars. He picked me up and we went over to the Cronner together. Joe said: 'George will sure as taxes get himself in a jam. I got that kind of a hunch.' And then when he saw the man with the scarred chin in the lobby, he thought his hunch was a sure bet."

"I see. Who was the man?"

"Scar-puss?" Merry put down her drink. The boxey shoulders of her jacket shrugged. "I don't know. But I could see he was out to do you no good. So I did what I did. Just an impulse. He was gunning you, wasn't he? I could see the lump in his pocket. I thought I was pretty good."

"You were perfect," I said again. "Like always."

I indicated the pile of stuff on the cocktail table.

"Make anything out of that stuff?"

I explained where I had obtained each of the objects. It was a waste of time, because when Joe Harper and Tim Terry came in a bit later I had to give them the whole story as well.

"What's the curley-cue?" Merry asked, looking at the wire spiral.

"I don't know. I don't think we can tie up any of that stuff yet. What I do know is that we're in for some trouble and maybe some brain exercise."

Merry stared at the objects on the table. Her slim, fragile-looking fingers toyed with the curl of dark hair above her forehead.

"It could be like this," she said. "The villain is a dentist. He pulls out people's teeth. And when people find what a sissy lisp they have after the operation they go and jump out of hotel windows. Check."

She leaned back, cuddled into my arms.

"How do you know Van Sickle lisped?" I asked curiously.

"He would if he didn't have any teeth, wouldn't he?"

"And those are his teeth, aren't they?" She added as an afterthought.

"Maybe," I said. "According to Ned Standish, Van Sickle had false teeth and they're missing. At least no teeth were found in his mouth, so the assumption is he had false ones."

We remained silent for a time enjoying just being together.

JOE HARPER and Tim Terry came in finally. Tim, immaculately clad in one of his tiny double-breasted suits, the largest of cigars grotesquely clenched in his babyish mouth, came gravely to me and shook hands. Joe Harper didn't say anything, but dumped his loose-jointed body into a chair which he hitched far enough forward so that he could get his feet on the cocktail table.

I poured cocktails around, all the time giving out the details of my actions since the moment that I had concluded my telephone conversation with Standish.

When I had finished, Tim Terry—bent double from the chair he was curled up in, put his glass on the floor.

"Well," his child's voice piped, "whatever the answer is, I know my job. I'm to have another kiddy role. I get pushed around in a baby carriage in Central Park. Merry pretends to be my nurse. Cops chuck me under the chin—and the next cop who does that, damn it, will get his finger bit off, so help me."

Merry dimpled at the midget. "Tim, if you knew how adorable you are in a little lacy bonnet."

"Quiet, frail!" Tim shrilled.

Merry laughed. Joe Harper grunted. He was staring at the heap of incomprehensible clues on the table. I asked him if he could make anything out of them.

"It's by me," he said. "All I know is you can thank Merry for putting over a fast one on a dangerous guy tonight. You'd have decorated the floor of the Cronner lobby if she hadn't done what she did. You know who that guy was?"

"Who?" I asked.

"Part of a business firm that went unnamed, but quite a few guys in Chicago knew the telephone number of some years ago. I got that tonight at Snooky's, so I guess you got value received for the money you gave me tonight, huh? The guy was at Snooky's. Snooky pointed him out to me."

"Who is he?" I asked. "What does he do?"

Joe Harper's lip-dangled cigarette spilled ashes on his vest. He flicked at the ash with his fingers. A tight scowl you can always take as a sign of nervous apprehension formed between his brows.

"His name is Elmer Tanko," Joe said. "His business is murder."

CHAPTER VIII

WERE THESE MEN DEAD?

MERRY WHITE puckered her pretty mouth and uttered a prolonged whistle.

"Such a nice man. George, why didn't I sock him one, too, when I was slapping faces?"

"Don't interrupt, babe," Joe Harper said. "You see, it was this way. Up to the time of the St. Valentine's massacre, the tough boys did their own gun-slaying. Then up Chicago way, along came a couple of mugs named Tanko and Henning. Gus Henning was the other guy. They hung out their shingle, though not in public, and made themselves a nice piece of change murdering for money. You could get a D.A. knocked off for a grand. That was about top price. Smaller fry came cheaper. Henning kicked off with a bursted appendix and Tanko was probably too touched by his pal's death to carry on."

Merry looked at me, eyes wide open. "Darling, I believe I'm good for something after all. But what have you got, besides me, that Tanko might want?"

I nodded at the clues on the table. "Take your choice," I said.

"One thing," Tim put in, his baby face screwed into a puzzled knot, "there's a hook-up between the Kurtzner woman and Tanko and the man with the tattooed wrist. Tanko knew that something had been left in the Van Sickle suite that shouldn't have been. Mrs. Kurtzner didn't know that, otherwise she wouldn't have called the cops. Tanko did know it, and he was in favor of getting to the Ghost before the cops did. That's why he was hunting the Ghost. You've got something, George, that Tanko wants."

"I know it," I said drily. "My life. And—one or all of these clues."

I watched the little man a moment as he sucked great lungfuls of smoke from his fat cigar. He had summed things up very well and I said as much. Tim reddened with pleasure. Merry clapped her hands. Joe snorted.

"Unless you just want to be melodram about this," Joe said, "the tattooed guy is Hugo Wayne. I know him, and he's dirty and cheap. He's a one-night-stand investment broker. Let me handle him, will you?"

I put my finger on the stack of bonds. "Then these are probably what Hugo Wayne was after. Bonds belonging to Fabian Deeming. Ever hear of Deeming?"

"Complete stranger to me," said Joe. "Wonder what Van Sickle was doing with bonds belonging to another guy."

NOBODY HAD an answer to that. Nobody had any more answers to anything. There was an interval of silence in which Merry White bent over the human teeth on the table, a distasteful expression on her face.

"They look good as new," she said, "except that one has been filled. I say they're Van Sickle's."

"Hunch, Merry?"

"Hunch."

"All I know," I said, "is that when Van Sickle talked to me shortly before he jumped out of the window, he lisped."

"And all I know," said Joe Harper, "is that he doesn't. Or didn't. I saw him at the Erlanger not long ago. I saw his teeth and heard him talking to the good-looking red-haired lady he was with."

"Good-looking and red-haired fits Mrs. Kurtzner," I said.

Joe reached for another cigarette, put it in his mouth, didn't light it for a moment. Behind his keen, dark eyes, his shrewd brain was grasping at something.

"What's the matter, Joe?" I asked. He took out the un-lighted cigarette, twisted it in his fingers.

"I was just remembering—I went to a funeral today. A friend of mine, Max Gerrich. Max Gerrich killed himself. He was a financial flop and a ham actor. He killed himself by jumping in front of a midnight suburban train. He left a suicide note under a brick beside the track."

"Did he lisp?" Merry White interrupted.

Joe gave her a look.

"Did he lisp! Well, you take all the people from the Battery up to the Bronx, and you'd only find one person who'd ask a question like that. What's lisping got to do with it? Will you let me speak my piece? I was saying, at the funeral they didn't open the casket because old Max wasn't fit to be seen because of what this train did to him, and you have the nerve to ask if he lisped."

Joe snorted again and continued more rapidly.

"Max Gerrich couldn't have played a first class bloodhound to the best Lisa that ever trouped, but his diction was strictly Barrymore. His big trouble was that he always wanted to re-write his parts. He thought an English-speaking audience should never be bothered with words of French or Latin derivation. He hated anything in the world that wasn't Anglo-Saxon."

You may wonder why I didn't get impatient at this seemingly irrelevant matter Joe was spouting. That's because you don't know either Joe or my other aides well enough yet. When they talk, I listen.

"What I started to say before I got side-tracked," Joe went on, "was that when I got a little low on funds a while ago, I went to see Max Gerrich." Joe sent me a sidelong glance and lighted his cigarette.

"Max owed me something, I guess. I put him in more bits than anybody else. When I was a percenter I used to put the sting on a lot of producers to give him a walking part in this or that show. Even after everybody knew he was finished, I stuck up for him."

It was the others who were growing impatient, so I prodded Joe.

"What are you getting at?" I demanded.

"Yeah," Tim piped. "You were touching Max, so what?"

"WELL," JOE went on, "he said the damnedest thing, when I asked him for money. He said he didn't have any. He made the excuse that he was keeping up a big insurance policy that was keeping him strapped. I asked him what for, since he didn't have any immediate family. I said: 'Max, you can't take it with you, can you?' And he said: 'Only if you're smart.' "

"I still say, so what?" Tim said, impatiently.

Joe Harper shoved fingers up under his hat and scratched his head.

"Well, Boss," he said, "are you wondering the same thing I'm wondering."

"Yes," I said softly. "Body and face turned into mincemeat by a train… 'only if you're smart'…."

"What in blazes are you two talking about?" Tiny Tim shrilled.

"George and I are just wondering if Max Gerrich is dead, that's all," said Joe casually.

I looked at Merry White.

"Just why did you ask if Max Gerrich lisped?"

She shrugged. "I just thought the question sounded profound and intelligent."

"Maybe it is," I said, "maybe it is…. I'm just beginning to ask myself another question: is Leonard Van Sickle dead…?"

CHAPTER IX

DETAILS OF THE CRIME

N **EXT MORNING** early, a cab dropped me off in Broome Street at the side of Police Headquarters Building. I was not myself. I had borrowed a look of wisdom by means of a pair of impressive Oxford glasses, and an appearance of sober dignity by virtue of a moustache. These items, plus a few added touches, sufficed to establish my identity as Dr. Stacey, a role I frequently assumed, since it gave me access to the Police Department without embarrassing Standish.

It was early for Standish to be in his office, so I killed some time by walking around to the Centre Street entrance. I hesitated an instant when, going in the front door ahead of me, I spotted my caller of the evening before, Taylor Owens. His black derby sat straight on his head and his purplish potato nose looked irritated by the fog of smoke from the stump pot-bowl pipe in his mouth. And of course he didn't know me from the King of Siam. I wondered what had brought him to Police Headquarters.

Owens wandered about the corridor and I passed him to go directly to Standish's office, where his secretary immediately admitted me.

Edward Standish is not an imposing-looking man. You don't realize the full weight of his driving personality until you've known him for a while. Medium height, with a taste for subdued clothes, heavy from the belt upwards, his is a typical cop's figure—hard, muscular, but spindle-shanked. He has pronounced chops, a black square of mustache, close-set hard gray eyes. In his early forties, he has nevertheless grown gray in the service of the police department.

Standish got out of his swivel chair to greet me with a crushing hand clasp.

Sitting beside his desk, slumped down, heavy eyelids drooping over protruding eyeballs, was my friend, Robert Demarest, medical examiner, as gloomy and saturnine an individual as ever came out of a morgue alive.

"Did you find Van Sickle's teeth lodged in his liver or something, Bob?" I asked.

Demarest gave me a glum look.

"Don't be funny," he mumbled. "It ill becomes a ghost. The man didn't have any teeth, false or otherwise. And how he expected to maintain *vite* by gumming his food I don't know. Investigation proved his teeth had been extracted. We've checked with his dentist and the dentist doesn't know why it was done."

"Then I take it that Van Sickle's dentist didn't do the extracting," I said.

"What's more," said Demarest, "the condition of the gums of the cadaver indicate that he had never worn plates. His gums hadn't yet been conditioned for plates."

I took out the chamois bag of teeth and passed them over to the medical examiner.

"What's this?" he asked. "The family jewels?"

"That," I said, "is probably what a lad named Hugo Wayne thought. He took them out of Van Sickle's safe last night together with a pack of bonds. He slugged one of your cops on the head, Ned."

Standish nodded. "We're looking for Wayne this morning. And not finding him."

Demarest opened the bag of teeth and looked at them. He cursed.

"Another anatomical clue, huh? One of Ned's bright boys brought me a pickled appendix he had found in Van Sickle's suite. Wondered what it was. This Van Sickle must have had a horror of letting his accessory parts go out of his possession."

"Ned," I said, "is the body definitely Van Sickle's? Could it be somebody else's?"

"George," Standish said, "that sounds like a crazy question. I'm forced to admit, however, that after a man falls as far as Van Sickle fell, the corpse is apt to have a kind of anonymous look about it. The face was beyond recognition."

"It was Van Sickle," Demarest said testily, sifting the teeth back into the bag. "I examined the contents of his stomach, I checked with what Van Sickle had eaten at the hotel. They agreed. Also, the body had on Van Sickle's clothes and the man jumped out of Van Sickle's window. If you think that adds up to somebody other than Van Sickle, then I suggest that it must have been two other fellows."

"Ignore him," Standish said to me with a grin. "What did you do last night?"

I gave him the whole story. I showed him the bonds Hugo Wayne had removed from Van Sickle's safe, asked him if he knew the owner, Fabian Deeming. Standish didn't, but he put a man out to find Deeming at once. I turned the bonds over to the police.

The inflexible spiral of wire brought no enlightening comment from either of the men. Demarest said it looked like "something out of or off something" and I returned the clue to my pocket.

Standish showed me the suicide note which had checked with other samples of Van Sickle's handwriting. It read:

Dear Lucretia: This is good-bye to you and the world. I am the complete failure. What was once my business is now the sole property of Mr. Theo Quinn. My personal property, I hope, will settle my hotel bill.

   I have provided that a portion of my life insurance shall be paid you in memory of our friendship, which is the only thing I leave regretfully.
Leonard Van Sickle

"I presume Lucretia is Lulu Kurtzner," I said immediately.

"We've already talked with her," Standish said. "She seems on the up-and-up. Damned attractive woman. I'm inclined to think that her association with Elmer Tanko is nothing more than an innocent hotel acquaintanceship. She made an extremely favorable impression on me. I'm glad that Leonard Van Sickle took care of that detail."

"HE THOUGHT of *every* detail," Demarest growled. "He was a plain crank. Inside the breast pocket of his coat, he had a special pocket tailored in there, just the right size to hold kitchen matches. Apparently didn't care for book-matches."

"Just a minute," I objected sharply. "If Van Sickle just did the Dutch and provided for Mrs. Kurtzner, then everything is rosy. But somehow I got the impression that this was murder. You helped to give me that impression, Ned. So suppose you tell me what first gave you the impression that it wasn't suicide."

"It *was* suicide," Demarest snapped. "Maybe Van Sickle was pushed out of the window, but you can't *call* it anything but suicide. There's no proof of anything else. This note was written by Van Sickle and nobody else. The body is Van Sickle's and nobody else's. Those teeth George has appropriated were probably Van Sickle's—"

Standish interrupted. "Answering George's question, it's this business of teeth that gave the suicide a shady touch—missing teeth. At first we thought Van Sickle had false teeth. If so, why remove them to jump out of a window unless he was crazy enough to think he'd have use for them again. If he removed them, where did he hide them? And now that we know his teeth had been extracted recently by a dentist who remains a mystery, why such concern about his health if he was going to kill himself?"

"Correct," I said. "It was not suicide, in spite of the suicide note and the fact that Van Sickle wrote it. Ned, I want to test the craziest piece of coincidence that was ever left like a foundling on a detective's very doorstep. Do something for me."

"What is it?"

"An old actor named Max Gerrich jumped in front of a suburban train a day or two ago. He left a suicide note. I want that note."

Standish belled his secretary and sent him to the files for the note. Demarest eyed me sleepily.

"George, you're crazy," he told me. "Do you know how many people voluntarily shuffle off the old mortal coil in this little town of Gotham every week? Now if you try and connect all those suicides, make murders out of them, you're just crazy. But if you want to know about Gerrich, I'll tell you as much as I could gather from an M.E.'s viewpoint. The chances are remote that he ever knew Van Sickle existed. He was so heavily in debt that the only thing that would get him out and clear his name was suicide. He had life insurance. So did Van Sickle. But so do a lot of other men who commit suicide. His body was an unrecognizable mess. So was Van Sickle's. But so are the bodies of many other suicides.

What do you want to do—establish the fact that nobody commits suicide in this town anymore, that they're all murdered instead?"

HADLEY, THE commissioner's secretary, came in with the Gerrich suicide note at that moment and saved me the job of answering Demarest's tirade. I did not know it yet, but I held part of the answer in my hand.

I compared the Gerrich suicide note with the one Van Sickle had written. It took only a glance to show that there was no similarity whatever. I coupled this with what Standish had told me—that the writing was similar to other samples of Gerrich's script.

So far, nothing.

But I re-read the note and something caught me.

> Life for me is a ghastly travesty. Why continue it? But a few minutes from now, I, Max Gerrich, answer my last exit cue.

"Anything there, George?" Standish asked.

"Nothing," said Demarest.

He has a habit of answering questions that are not addressed to him. He was about to say more but something in my face must have stopped him.

"Yes," I said slowly, "there is something there. I believe if that body was Max Gerrich's body, Max Gerrich was murdered...."

Standish and Demarest stared at me, wordless. At last Standish said:

"Are you intimating that Gerrich didn't write that note—that his handwriting was imitated?"

"No," I said. "Gerrich wrote the note all right—I'm willing to take the word of the experts on that. It's the *wording* of the note that has suddenly struck me as significant. Max Gerrich, I happen to know, had a peculiar dislike for words originating in the Latin languages. That dislike was intense, probably springing from certain Teutonic prejudices ingrained in Gerrich.

"Now, I maintain, such being the case, that Gerrich, if he had been contemplating suicide, would never have used the word 'travesty' in his suicide note. The word is French. He would have used in preference to it the word 'farce.' Maybe not even 'farce,' since that word, too, is of French origin, although he may not have known that.

"Secondly, he would not have used the word 'continue.' He would most likely have said 'go on.' I say Max Gerrich would not have used those two words—"

"But the handwriting, man—the handwriting!" Standish cried. "You yourself admit that Max Gerrich wrote that note—"

"Wrote it, yes," I said, "but it was dictated."

There was a second of silence. Then Standish sat way back in his chair and emitted a long whistle....

CHAPTER X

THE SHAMUS FROM BOSTON

SHAKING HANDS, I got up to go.

"This case has got more angles than a cubist drawing," Standish said. "We'll get hold of Hugo Wayne and this Fabian Deeming. We'll try to find out who pulled Van Sickle's teeth. We'll nail this hot rod, Elmer Tanko. And we'll see how far that gets us. So long, George."

But I was not destined to take my leave yet. Hadley entered and announced that a Mr. Taylor Owens and a Mr. Ken Vickers were waiting to see the commissioner in regard to the Van Sickle business. Standish looked at me and I nodded, resuming my seat.

Standish, apparently, had been expecting the callers. Vickers, he quickly told me, was a private sleuth who worked out of the home office of the Boston life insurance firm of which Taylor Owens was the local representative. Owens had called Standish on the phone, asking permission to bring Vickers over and introduce him. When I had seen Owens loitering in the hall, he had evidently been waiting for this Boston gum shoe.

Hadley showed the two men in. Vickers was one of these personalities who is hell-bent on being dynamic. He pumped my hand and Standish's, regarded Demarest a little as though he was just being introduced to a corpse. He told us who he was in the explosive manner of a young man who is working his way through college selling magazines. In the end, it was Vickers who introduced Mr. Taylor Owens, instead of the other way around.

Owens was his cordial self. While Vickers was making his speech, Owens sat next to me, his gray suede shoes close together, his derby resting on his knees.

"Associated with the police, Dr. Stacey?" he asked me. I replied that I was connected with the medical examiner's office in an advisory capacity, but I don't think he paid any attention to what I was saying, for at the moment he was attending to the business of scraping soggy, sizzling dottle from the bowl of his stubby pipe.

Vickers explained that the insurance company had sent him to look into the Van Sickle suicide, because Van Sickle's death was costing the company half a million dollars.

"Whether it figures suicide or murder, your company still has to pay up, doesn't it?" Demarest dourly remarked.

Vickers nodded energetically. "Absolutely. Pay without question. But not go on paying any more such claims without question. You grasp the fine distinction. We don't want it to become a habit. And this is the second large suicide claim we've had to pay in the past week."

I looked at Demarest and smiled.

"You're referring to the claim covering the death of Max Gerrich, aren't you?" I asked.

"Yes, that's right—" Vickers let his sentence hang and twisted around in his chair to eye me shrewdly.

"On the police force, Dr. Stacey?" he asked.

He clipped his words much closer than any Bostonian I had ever met before.

"DR. STACEY is one of my and Dr. Demarest's most valued advisors, though in no way connected officially with the force. If there's anything smelly about this suicide business, Vickers, I can assure you of his full and complete cooperation."

"Fine," Vickers said. "That's fine. Commissioner, could you have dinner with me at Charles' Restaurant at seven sharp? Some important matters I'd like to go over with you in regard to Van Sickle's financial set-up. We could go into the matter here, but the man who knows the most about the subject is not available until evening. Dr. Demarest, will you join us?"

"Too many people die, I don't have time to eat," the saturnine M.E. said.

Vickers looked at me. "Medical opinions are always valued. How about you, Doctor?"

I told Vickers I would be there.

A little later, from a drugstore pay station, I telephoned Joe Harper. He was just getting out of bed. I told him to get on the tail of Hugo Wayne to see if he could find out anything about the bonds taken from

Van Sickle's safe and also something about the identity of the mysterious Mr. Fabian Deeming. And then I called Tim Terry, asked him if he wouldn't put on knee pants, get over to the Cronner Hotel with Merry White and keep an eye on Mrs. Kurtzner.

Somehow, I couldn't feature Lucretia Kurtzner as a lily white lady. I've always been prejudiced against Lucretias. One of the poisoning Borgias had that name.

In my identity of Dr. Stacey, I visited a rental agency and rented, sight unseen, a small apartment on Amsterdam Avenue, made note of the address, went from there straight to the office of the *Herald,* and inserted an ad.

The ad announced that Dr. Stacey, at his Amsterdam address, would pay one hundred dollars to the dentist who had extracted the teeth of Mr. Leonard Van Sickle if the dentist would call in person after making an appointment on the phone. I gave a telephone number which is not listed in the directory but which rings the phone in the Ghost's own haunted rectory.

By that time it was afternoon. I got a bite of lunch at a drugstore soda fountain, a setting which didn't exactly suit the dignity of Dr. Stacey's Oxford glasses but filled a vacancy in George Chance.

After that, I took a taxi up Fifth Avenue to Thirty-Fourth, got out, walked half a block to the entrance of the Starret Building. Taylor Owens had his office there, and I wanted to see him about certain details in Van Sickle's life insurance policy.

Owens' office was on the fourth floor, not a large place, but attractive because of an ornamental blonde who sat behind a desk and was, at the moment, occupied with filing her nails. I learned that Owens wasn't in, but was expected any moment. I sat down to wait. The phone rang, and the blonde answered. No, Mr. Owens wasn't in. She asked who was calling.

A SHRILL, excited but masculine voice announced:

"This is Jonathan Marvin." Marvin's voice was so loud that I could hear every word he uttered though I was ten feet from the girl.

"Miss Rice," Marvin said, "I must get hold of Owens at once. It's a matter of the gravest importance, even of life and death."

Miss Rice jotted Marvin's telephone number down on a pad, promised to get Mr. Owens as soon as she could. She hung up, looked at me, smiled slightly.

"That man sounded as though he was dying at the very least."

I returned her smile, with considerably more warmth than I felt. The lady looked impressionable, and I now had a reason to impress her. Mr. Marvin had sounded like a living case of jitters to me.

"I couldn't help overhearing, Miss Rice," I said. "If it's really important, I don't mind telling you that when I came up here I was perfectly aware that Mr. Owens wasn't here. In fact, he was talking to a gentleman in the cigar store on the corner."

Miss Rice looked slightly dazed.

"But I can't see why you came here then," she said.

Her cheeks flushed a little, because it was evident that she understood, or thought she did.

I laughed slightly. "Did you ever look in a mirror, Miss Rice?"

I stood up and stepped to her desk. The Oxford glasses robbed my eyes of the ardor they were faking and frightened the little blonde. She laughed uneasily, stood up, slipped around to the other side of the desk.

"Really," she said, "I must go find Mr. Owens. This is really important."

Miss Rice skipped to the door where she turned, gathered courage.

"You better not let my boy friend hear about this. You ought to be ashamed of yourself, at your age!"

And then she was gone and I heard the beat of her toes as she ran down the corridor toward the elevator shaft.

I picked up the phone. A reflection of Dr. Stacey's dignified countenance reproached me from the nickeled rim of the phone transmitter. I did look a little too old to be chasing blondes!

And then I called the number Miss Rice had written on the pad. Jonathan Marvin's shrill voice exploded in my ear.

"Owens? That you, Owens?"

I had heard Owens' voice exactly four times and if what I knew about voice control and ventriloquism would not enable me to impersonate it, I felt that I would not be worth my salt.

I said I was Owens and asked what was bothering Mr. Marvin.

"LISTEN," MARVIN said, "you won't believe this, but it's God's truth. It's the damnedest plot you ever heard of. And I'm in it, Owens. I'm not dishonest at heart, Owens. You know that. You know me—"

"Yes," I said in Owens' voice. "I know you. What are you getting at?"

"In a moment of weakness, I fell for the scheme. It isn't right. It isn't legal. It makes me a criminal! And I can't go to the police. You've got to advise me!"

"What, man?" The excited flow of words from Jonathan Marvin had increased my blood pressure a little, too.

"Owens, it's—" And Marvin interrupted himself with a small, startled sound. Then, as though he were speaking some distance from the phone, I heard him say:

"It—it's impossible!"

And the connection was broken.

CHAPTER XI

POISON

LOCATING THE address of Jonathan Marvin took a little time. When I had done that, I left Owens' office. The blonde Miss Rice, indignant and not looking the worse for the flush of color in her cheeks, stepped out of the elevator as I entered it. She gave me one of those looks and a toss of her curls, and clicked off up the corridor. She hadn't found Taylor Owens where I had said I had seen him, which was natural enough, seeing that I had fed her pure fiction.

I was three minutes waiting for a taxi to pick me up at the curb. Just as I got in the cab, settled back in the seat, I happened to look across the street. Coming out of the door of the building was the tall, gaunt figure of Elmer Tanko.

He stepped hurriedly to the curb, and his shrewd, dark eyes met mine through the back window of the taxicab.

It was impossible for him to recognize me as the man he had stuck up in the lobby of the Cronner Hotel on the night before. Yet that glance he threw at me, which might have been the purest coincidence, gave me an odd, uncomfortable feeling. For just a moment, I had the notion that something had gone wrong. I couldn't dismiss the premonition, because of something I had learned during my early life as a magician.

At one of my first public performances, I was pulling the old cut-and-restored rope trick, the version in which two pieces of rope are employed, the piece that is actually cut being jerked beneath the tails of the coat by an elastic pull.

At this performance, I had just offered the second piece of rope for examination as "proof" of the fact that my magic had healed the cut, when that curious, inexplicable premonition of danger came over me. And I dismissed it. That time I dismissed it, but never again.

For when I turned my back to the audience in order to take up my wand for the next trick, howls of laughter sounded in the auditorium. And I discovered that something had gone wrong with the elastic pull and several strands of cut rope dangled from the base of my spine, in full view of the audience!

If you've ever had the experience of stooping over in a crowded street and thinking that you've heard a rip, you have a conception of how I felt when I found I had bungled the rope trick. I felt about the same when Tanko's eyes spotted me through the window of the cab.

For just a moment, I had an impulse to have my driver stop, turn around, and if possible follow Tanko. But then I lost track of the gaunt killer in the crowd. Then, too, if this man Marvin was involved in some sort of a plot, it was probable that he merited attention before anything else.

The plot in which Marvin had found himself must have had something to do with insurance, otherwise why had he sought the advice of Taylor Owens? And some sort of an insurance swindle, I believed, was back of the Van Sickle "suicide" and possibly the Max Gerrich affair; though up to this point in the case I had little to go on but hunches.

JONATHAN MARVIN lived in a three story house which had been converted into small apartments. A glance at the row of mail boxes in the entry way and I knew where to look for the man. I walked up a flight and knocked on the door. The echo of my knocking whispered along the dingy corridor. I knocked again, and still no answer.

Fingers covered with a handkerchief, I tried the knob of the door, found the place unlocked, opened the door, walked in. A man was sitting in a lounge chair, his white, shaggy head just visible over the back of the chair, his right arm, dangling over the arm. On the little table beside him was a tall glass with an inch of liquor remaining in it. I closed the door quietly, not that there was any danger of waking the man in the chair, and went over to the table.

The shaggy man's heavy-set figure had that crumpled attitude of the newly dead. His face was livid, ghostly, even in the pale light that seeped through an unshaded portion of the window.

Beside the liquor glass was a small bottle plainly labeled Hydrocyanic Acid. And had the man lived over ten minutes after drinking a highball of that stuff he had an unusual constitution. The poison bottle was weighing down a piece of note paper on which was written in pen and ink:

When a man takes his own life, it is customary to leave some sort of an explanation. Here is mine.

I have recently been placed in a position of great trust as the secretary of Arnold Smock. Mr. Smock, I found, was not only a man of wealth but a man who is careless with his money.

All of his money matters were turned over to me. I took advantage of my position, embezzled certain of the funds entrusted to me, planning to make a killing on the stock market. Of course I lost.

In order to repay Mr. Smock the full amount owed, this is the only thing I can do. The entire record of my fraud will be found clipped to life insurance policies in which Mr. Smock is named beneficiary. He will be repaid.

Jonathan Marvin.

It was a puzzler. The note conformed to the conversation I had had with Marvin over the phone, except for one thing. Marvin had said that he had been involved in "the damnedest plot you ever heard of." While embezzlement might be damned, there wasn't anything novel about it. And I knew perfectly well that this man had not committed suicide but had been murdered.

But the proof? There was none. I could see what was coming. It was a set-up. Jonathan Marvin's records would show that somebody named Arnold Smock had been swindled by Jonathan Marvin. Mr. Smock would turn out to be an individual whose past record was clean. And Mr. Smock would collect on Marvin's insurance policy.

It was something you knew instinctively to be crooked, yet you felt also that its set-up was law-proof. The brain behind the scheme was a clever one. Even if Arnold Smock himself was Marvin's slayer, the chances were that he would walk off with the boodle.

I intended to prevent that, but as yet I did not know how I could.

I telephoned Police Headquarters, said I was Dr. Stacey and that I would like to speak to Commissioner Standish. I was put through to Ned's private office at once.

I gave him the story as briefly as possible.

"Get a man on the tail of this Arnold Smock," I said. "Watch Smock day and night. Don't put a restraint on the insurance company, but urge immediate payment. And when the check goes through and Smock cashes it, find out what he does with the money. I'll repeat that, *find out what he does with the money!*

"If he keeps it, there's a chance he's the ringleader of the whole business. That being the case, we'll probably find ourselves up a dead-end street unless Smock can be broken down. But if he's just a hireling for

Robert Demarest

the master brain, there's a chance that the route the money takes after it leaves Smock's hand will bring us to the man we're after."

"Hang on," Standish said, "while I issue those orders." I waited and he came back on the wire.

"We've got a trace on this bird, Fabian Deeming," he told me. "A man by that name reserved two passages for Europe on a ship leaving New York on the twentieth of this month. He paid for the tickets, had them sent to a post box at Grand Central Annex. But the pay-off is that we can't get a description of him. He managed the whole deal by mail. His letter to the travel agent was mailed at Grand Central and it was written in a penciled print-script. Cash was enclosed in the envelope. The passengers were to be booked as Mr. and Mrs. Fabian Deeming. I've got a man watching the post box mentioned as the return address. There's an envelope in the box right now for Fabian Deeming and from the travel agent. It hasn't been claimed, yet, but when it is, we'll have Deeming by the neck."

CHAPTER XII

ON TANKO'S TRAIL

GOING OUT of Jonathan Marvin's apartment, I was an entirely different person than when I had entered it. Reversing the suit I had worn in the identity of Dr. Stacey, I was now clad in sage green Shetland. My rather heavy mustache was gone and in its stead I wore a Van Dyke beard and a mouse-tailed mustache. Additional pomade gave my eyebrows an upward curl at their outer extremity. In Marvin's medicine cabinet I found cotton and adhesive tape and with this made a bulky dressing for an imaginary wound on my left cheek. Dr. Stacey's Oxford glasses I put away.

Why all this precaution? Nothing explains it except that curious premonition that something had gone haywire and that Tanko might have had the X-ray eyes to pierce my disguise.

Next, what had Elmer Tanko been doing in the building across from Owens' office? Nothing could keep me from trying to find an answer to that one, so I taxied back to Thirty-Fourth street, entered the building across from the Starret, went immediately to the building superintendent.

The superintendent was an accommodating man somewhere in his fifties. He regarded my bandaged face with only casual interest and I began at once to get what information I could out of him. I said I was looking for a friend of mine.

"A tall man," I said, "deeply tanned, with shrewd dark eyes, a knife scar on his chin. A man with a nose that is both thin and hooked."

"Mr. Avery?" the superintendent questioned. I nodded, hoping that his Mr. Avery was my Elmer Tanko.

"Mr. Avery rented an office on the fifth floor," the superintendent told me. "A queer duck. Not very talkative."

I laughed. "That's Avery, all right. Close as a clam. Mind telling me the number of his office?"

"Number five-twenty," the superintendent said.

"Avery is queer," I went on, "until you get to know him. He knows a lot of queer people, too. Tell me, have any of his friends visited him recently?"

The building superintendent said he couldn't be sure they were friends or not, but he had noted a couple of men who had visited "Mr. Avery's" office. One, he had noted particularly, had a glass eye. The other man was squat and neckless, and not the sort of man you'd like to meet up a dark alley.

I laughed again.

"Avery," I commented, "knows the worst people. He writes about them. I guess I'll run up and see him."

"Go right ahead," said the superintendent. "Do you happen to know when Mr. Avery will move in his office equipment?"

I DIDN'T know. I supposed, though, that all the office equipment Mr. Avery needed was a silenced revolver and a few rounds of ammunition.

"Probably something is holding him up," the superintendent speculated. "He's had his phone connected for two weeks. And he visits his office quite frequently. I hope you find him in."

Fervently, I echoed the superintendent's wish, but mentally added that it would be nice if I found Avery before he found me.

I took an elevator up to the fifth floor, found the door of five-twenty locked. It's a pretty lucky thing that the Ghost has enlisted on the side of law and order, however, for he knows a bit about getting into places where he is not wanted. A skeleton key, smudged with lamp black and inserted in the lock, gave me the exact position of the tumblers. Some manipulation with a piece of strong wire, and the lock was picked.

I went into a clean, barren room, where late afternoon sun streamed through a window. I went to the window and there found the only piece of "office equipment" that the place contained besides the telephone— a pair of French field glasses in a worn leather case.

The window faced the Starret building, and looking out of it I could see the gold lettering on the window of Taylor Owens' office. I borrowed the field glasses, brought them into focus. Through the window, I could clearly see that Taylor Owens was occupied. He had his right arm about the blonde Miss Rice's shoulders. And the blonde Miss Rice was crying into a handkerchief large enough to belong to Owens himself. Probably she had committed the crime of filing her nails when she should have been filing reports, bringing down the insurance man's wrath and subsequently his forgiveness.

"Reach for the ceiling, mister!"

The order in a low-pitched voice came from behind me. I turned slowly, the field glasses in my hands. Three feet this side of the door stood a man. He was squat as a toad. His head grew from hunched but powerful shoulders and the only indication of a neck that he had was a narrow collar which seemed to include his heavy chin.

His right hand dwarfed the proportions of the black automatic he held, but I couldn't say that it reduced the potential danger to me in any way.

"Friend of Mr. Avery?" I asked, as pleasantly as you could ask anybody who looked like something off a branch of the toad family tree.

"I said reach, didn't I? Put 'em way up or I'll drill you, wise guy. We don't exactly give snoops the glad hand when they come in here."

THE FIELD glasses in my right hand, my left hand started slowly upward, the left elbow out from the body. Naturally, my suit coat gaped on the left side, but something else happened, too. A black silk pouch, well known to magicians and attached to the left side of the lining of my coat and also to the top of my pants, opened, ready to receive anything I cared to vanish, from a palming coin to a small goldfish bowl.

A flick of my right wrist, and I threw the field glasses into the pouch. Hardly had I felt the jerk which signified that the glasses had disappeared, than the fingers of my right hand flicked downward to nip the knife in my right sleeve.

All this was accomplished in less time than it would take you to wink an eye, and my gaze had not left the squat man's face. To him, it must have appeared as though a pair of field glasses changed into a knife. It was disconcerting, a bit bewildering to him. He squeezed the trigger of his gun instinctively and I still think the noise of the shot startled him more than it did me.

Anyway, he was running backwards to the door when he fired. I heard the whine of the bullet, but didn't feel the impact of lead smashing bone.

I let go with the knife in that fumbling moment when the squat man was trying to get through the door. I'd have pinned his left hand to the door except for the fact that his hand and the knife moved simultaneously and not in the right directions to meet. He went through the door and I was after him. A second to jerk the knife out of the woodwork where it quivered like a living thing, a second to get out my own gun; and then I was in the hall, running after the squat man who was fronted with the hopelessness of an empty elevator shaft.

But the squat man had got out of places in a hurry before. I called on him to stop as he darted around a corner in the hall, going toward the stairway. He didn't stop, and I fired at his stumpy legs. But when Ned Standish said that George Chance wasn't the world's best marksman, he hadn't exaggerated much. My shot was a clean miss and I had to go flat against a doorway as the toad-like man tried a shot from around the corner.

Other office doors on the floor were popping open. People were coming out in the hall, complicating matters for me, but not for the squat man who threw his lead without any particular discrimination, and then plunged for the stairway. I followed. The guy was worth nailing. Any friend of Elmer Tanko was worth nailing. But I had to get him alive. Inside his fat head might not be too efficient a think tank, but it might contain the answer to half a dozen riddles that had popped up in the past couple of hours.

HOW THE man's short, thick legs ever got him down the stairs as fast as they did, I don't know. And at every turn in the landing, he would try a shot at me. Between us we made a lot of gun noise and did very little else until the squat man reached the landing between the second and third floor. Then, as he turned after trying a shot at me, he saw a cop corning up the stairs toward him, gun drawn.

He was blocked out. He tried to go over the banister for a short cut to the floor some twenty feet below. The cop had him covered, was shouting his warning. The squat man tried a shot at the cop, the cop retaliated, and when the squat man went over the banister, it was head first.

Somewhere below, a woman screamed. Men pelted along the corridor. The cop who had shot the squat man turned around, went down the steps to the hall below. When I got there, there was a knot of people standing around the spot where the squat man evidently lay. I heard somebody say the man's neck was broken. Then I slipped out the front door of the building, avoiding the crowd and the copper's questions.

More than the squat man's neck had been broken. An important link in the mystery chain had been broken as well.

CHAPTER XIII

I PLAY THE DANGER GAME

BEN VICKERS had ordered a good dinner in the little private alcove off the main dining room of Charles' Restaurant, but Dr. Stacey was not there. The premonition that the Dr. Stacey identity was unhealthy for me persisted, and I turned up as a chesty, red-haired, entirely fictitious Detective-Sergeant Hammill, who, according to Commissioner Standish, was in charge of the Van Sickle suicide mystery.

Ken Vickers, his blond skin almost transparently clean, shook hands with me, asked Ned Standish where Dr. Stacey was. Ned alibied the missing "doctor," and we were both introduced to Theo Quinn, the man who now owned all the Van Sickle manufacturing interests.

Theo Quinn, sober, was entirely the reverse of the fat, bald men whom I had seen taking an impromptu bath in the wash room of the Hotel Cronner Sky Room the night of the Van Sickle tragedy. He was grave, slow-speaking, though not entirely courteous toward Standish and me. It seemed that he had the not unusual conception that the police department is an inefficient, tax-eating octopus paralyzed in at least seven of its tentacles.

Taylor Owens was there.

"No real reason why I should be here," he said to me, plastering at the countable hairs that crossed his cranium. "All this business of crime and corruption is way over my head. But inasmuch as it's the insurance company I represent that is standing Vickers' expenses, I thought I might as well take advantage of the free meal.

"I'm sorry I won't be able to linger over the coffee. Eat and run. I'm on an entertainment committee for this Union of Civic Clubs benefit party given tonight. Got to be there. Got George Chance the magician to donate part of the show. He's clever."

Owens then told me about visiting George Chance's house, about how George Chance had vanished a match right under his nose, and then explained the trick to me, its author, as a "simple thing anybody could do with a piece of elastic."

I smiled inwardly, and had to discount my own skill by agreeing that a piece of elastic was probably back of the match-vanish illusion.

After dinner, we pushed back from the table and Ken Vickers discharged a fire-cracker volley of words at Theo Quinn.

"About Leonard Van Sickle, Mr. Quinn—you're intimately acquainted with his financial resources. How come he hit the financial skids?"

Theo Quinn pondered, savoring his cigar.

"Purely a matter of bad luck. Leonard Van Sickle was the most careful man I've ever known. Spent too much time fussing over minor details. But he was very astute in business."

TAYLOR OWENS scraped a soggy heel of tobacco from his stumpy pipe and filled the pot bowl from a striped tobacco pouch. He borrowed a match from me, and I could scarcely resist vanishing it before his pipe was going again.

"Was Van Sickle resentful of you when you took over his business?" Vickers shot at Quinn.

The fat man mused again.

"Not any more than could be expected. The merger was more in the nature of a foreclosure for debts long due." Quinn's baby-smooth forehead crinkled a little. "Is this absolutely necessary, Mr. Vickers?"

"Quite," Vickers said. He got half-way to his feet, one of those surprising moves born of unrestrainable physical energy. "And Van Sickle retained absolutely no hold on what had formerly been his property— nothing that would have made it easier for you if Van Sickle had been out of the way?"

It was a tactless question. Theo Quinn stood up. He eyed us all frigidly.

"This is something I should have expected," he snapped. "It is also something I will not tolerate—an insinuation that I might have something to do with Van Sickle's death. Gentlemen, I am afraid my time is too valuable to be spent in the character of the wicked witch in a fairy tale compounded by the police. Goodnight."

He walked out on us. Vickers saw he had pulled a boner. He tried to alter our opinion of him by ordering after dinner cordials.

"None for me, thanks," Taylor Owens said. "Maybe a bottle of beer. Braumier, if they've got it."

It was while we were drinking that I saw the man with the glass eye. He came into the restaurant, disregarded the table designated by the headwaiter, came to a small table not far from the door of our alcove.

Now there must be thousands of men in New York who wear counterfeit eyes. But this man had a certain furtive attitude that often marks the bum and the criminal alike. Also, I was conscious of the fact that he was paying us a lot of attention. I remembered what the building superintendent had told me about the glass-eyed friend of the killer, Elmer Tanko.

Was Glass-Eye looking for Dr. Stacey, whom premonition warned me had been marked by Elmer Tanko's gun-sight eyes?

"Tell me, Vickers," Ned Standish said, "just who benefitted from Van Sickle's death besides Mrs. Kurtzner to whom Van Sickle addressed his suicide note."

"A protégé of Van Sickle's—a woman named Mrs. E.L. Long." Vickers took out a notebook and revealed Mrs. Long's Hoboken address.

Standish and I made a note of it.

"I delivered the company's checks in person to both Mrs. Kurtzner and Mrs. Long. Mrs. Long ought to appreciate it. The house she lives in is a rat's nest."

"ANOTHER THING," I put in, "what about this man Jonathan Marvin, who did the Dutch today? Is he insured with your company?"

"Yes. To the tune of three hundred grand."

Standish fiddled with the thin stem of his half-filled wine glass.

"The Marvin case is damned confusing. In his suicide note, he mentioned gambling on the market. We've checked with every stock broker in town, and no one ever heard of Marvin. He was working as secretary for a Mr. Arnold Smock over in Brooklyn. Smock's an eccentric who raises pigeons. He just moved into a fancy house he's rented, seems to have had a little money. But when we told him about Marvin, showed him the suicide letter Marvin had written, Smock phoned his bank, discovered that they had never received three hundred thousand which he had sent Marvin to deposit some time before."

"You mean," Taylor Owens gasped, "this Smock person sent his secretary with three hundred thousand dollars in cash? Incredible!"

"But true," Standish insisted, "according to what Smock says. And we found Marvin's insurance policies and the beneficiary had been recently changed to Arnold Smock, in an effort on the part of Marvin to clear up his name. It's all damned mid-Victorian and unconvincing. If a man has so little conscience as to embezzle that amount of money, why commit suicide for the sole purpose of paying it back?"

"I'm going to instruct the company to withhold Smock's check until further investigation," Vickers said decisively.

Standish remembered my instructions and advised Vickers against doing that, giving my reasons. Vickers agreed that they were sound.

I was still watching the man with the glass eye. Whenever I'd glance at him, he'd be looking our way. I reached into my pocket and speculatively fingered what I had there—something I had brought especially for the purpose—the Oxford glasses that characterized Dr. Stacey.

Again that disconcerting premonition of danger came over me. Had the man with the counterfeit eye been sent there by Tanko to eliminate Dr. Stacey? If he had, I felt certain that in spite of the putty nose I was wearing, in spite of the red toupee, if I were to put Oxford glasses astride my nose, Glass-Eye's interest in me would receive a powerful boost.

And I was determined to find out. It was just a little bit like a man who suspects he is dying of an incurable disease and wants the truth from his physician. I wondered a little if I wasn't scheduled to die of an acute case of Oxford glasses.

I got up and moved to the door of the alcove. No one was in the same line with me and the glass-eyed man. My right hand was within inches of the gimmick-holder that held my automatic. If Glass-Eye thought he could get to his shoulder holster before I could get to my gun, he had the privilege of trying.

I raised my left hand to my coat pocket and took out the Oxford glasses.

CHAPTER XIV

THE TRUTH—BUT NOT ALL

ALTHOUGH IT was on my nose that I placed the Oxford glasses, I might also say that the glasses struck the furtive man at the lonely table directly between the eyes. His mouth was open, a forkful of food six inches from it, but there was a perceptible pause before he conveyed his fork the rest of the way. And immediately, he looked away from me and away from the alcove where we had eaten. Up to now, he had been watching Ken Vickers' party closely. After the appearance of the Oxford glasses he studiously avoided looking our direction.

I was a marked man, but I couldn't reproach my sixth sense for not warning me. I went over to Vickers and shook his hand, told him I'd have to be going. I said good-bye to Ned Standish and Taylor Owens.

As I left the alcove, I slipped a mirror ring over the middle finger of my left hand, turning the mirror setting inward. A mirror ring has its uses in magic and in detection. With it I can see what goes on behind me and at the same time appear to be ironing worried wrinkles out of my forehead. I knew, then, as I passed the one-eyed man's table, that he was prepared to tail me.

At Charles' Restaurant, there's a private dining room reached by a little hall to the left of the main dining room. The place is used chiefly by luncheon clubs, and is seldom occupied at night. It wasn't in use tonight. I entered it, unobserved except by Glass-Eye.

Inside, the place was dark except for what light filtered in through windows which opened on a little driveway for delivery trucks at the side of the building. In what light there was, I could make out tables draped with white cloth. Beside the door was a hat tree which I carried to the opposite side of one of the draped tables.

I stripped off my coat, used a table cloth from another table to add bulk to the shoulders, hung the coat on the clothes tree, putting my hat on top of it. Anyone entering the room would have thought there was a man standing behind that table, his legs hidden by the table itself.

From a large flat pocket in the lining of my trousers, I took out a flat pack of black silk. Folding the silk is no easy job, but unfolding it can be done with a flourish. Unfolded, it becomes a black domino suit with a maskhood which will cover me from head to ankle. In the darkness the black domino is as good as the legendary Invisible Cloak.

In my black robe, with black rubber gloves on my hands, I waited for the glass-eyed man. Fingers of my right hand were about the handle of my knife, but the blade of the knife was pointing upwards.

Evidently as soon as he found an opportunity to slip to the private room without being observed by any of the patrons or waiters, the glass-eyed man pushed open the door. I saw the glint of a gun. I saw him look right and left, as though he was prepared to find me hiding behind the door. And then he saw the impromptu dummy I had rigged up behind the table.

I got a big laugh out of watching him pussy-foot toward the dummy. And then I closed in on him quickly. My left hand slapped across his mouth to gag him with the clammy palm of my rubber-gloved hand. My right let him have the butt of the knife handle back of the ear. He went limp in my arms and I let him slide down to the floor.

I got out of the black robe and gloves, wadded them up, and, after I had put on my coat, stuffed the robe up under my coat front. This gave me a little paunch, but to fold the robe and return it to its original pocket would have taken longer than to stuff a magician's production cabinet with twenty silk handkerchiefs.

I carried Glass-Eye to the nearest window opening on the truck drive, eased the window up, lifted him over the sill. He dropped like a sack of bones on the pavement. I followed, stooped, got his left arm across my shoulder, and made for the street. Out on the street I pulled a ventriloquist act, dug a drunk song from Tin Pan Alley's junk heap of memories, made the unconscious man appear to sing. I got a cab right away.

When I got in with Glass-Eye, ventriloquism made Glass-Eye say in a mushy voice:

"Where we goin', pal?"

And I replied: "We're headed for bed, Johnny." Maybe I should have said my "dummy" Charley.

Out of the cab half a block from the Ghost's haunted rectory, I lugged Glass-Eye the rest of the way, let myself in through the back door of the rectory, went down to the basement. Joe Harper was sitting on the back of his neck, his heels cocked up on the coffee table, asleep.

I stretched Glass-Eye out on the floor and when I looked around, Joe Harper was awake and watching me, although he had not altered his position in the least.

He looked at me and shook his head.

"Haven't you got your roles a little mixed, Ghost? What's the idea of wearing Dr. Stacey's glasses?"

I indicated the glass-eyed man on the floor.

"This guy was sent to Charles' Restaurant by our pal Tanko to bump off a man who wore Oxford glasses—Dr. Stacey, specifically, but to this one-eyed gent, just a man wearing Oxford cheaters. There wasn't anybody in the party with that kind of glasses on, so I obliged."

The man on the floor groaned, moved slightly. I told Joe Harper he'd better go into the next room because the glass-eyed man was coming around. Joe helped himself to several cigarettes from my humidor and went into the adjoining room.

I knelt down and frisked my captive. He had dropped his gun when I knocked him out. There was nothing important in his pockets. I went to a small cabinet that stood at one side of the room, took from it a hypodermic syringe and a bottle of scopolamine, or truth serum. My friend Dr. Demarest would have laughed at my technique, but as soon as the glass-eyed man became conscious, I tested his heart and finding it okay gave him a shot of the drug.

THE DRUG works differently on different people, but mostly the first effect is something like a stroke of apoplexy. That's how it was with Glass Eye, and that's why it was necessary for me to test his heart first, for I didn't want to kill him.

He turned purple, had a slight convulsion, and when he had relaxed a little, his one good eye stared up at the ceiling and was almost as glassy as its counterfeit mate. I knew his conscious mind was subdued. I spoke to him in a gentle voice.

"What's your name?"

"Thomas Ivor," he answered hoarsely.

"Tonight you were sent to Charles' Restaurant. You had a gun. What were you going to do there?"

"Stick up a gent. He had on glasses with a black ribbon. Nose pinching glasses. He wasn't there at first and then he was."

"What were you supposed to do with the man?" I asked.

"Stick him up. Avery said he had a little curley-cue of wire in his pocket. I was to get it and kill the man."

I drew a long breath.

"What was the curley-cue of wire? What was it for?"

"Don't know."

"What was the man you call Avery going to do with it?"

"Don't know."

"Did the curley-cue belong to Avery?"

"Don't know. He wanted it. Avery isn't his real name. His real name is Tanko. He's some hot rod."

"You work for Tanko?"

"Yes. He's the boss."

"Who's Tanko's boss?"

There was a long pause. I repeated the question.

"A man," came the answer.

"What man?"

"Don't know."

"What does he look like?"

"Never saw him. He just telephones and Tanko talks to him."

"Do you know what kind of a game Tanko and the boss are playing?"

"They're after money. Big dough."

"Whose dough?"

"Don't know. I just do what I'm told. I'm a good guy to have. I do what I'm told."

Before the man could come out of his trance, I sealed his eyes shut with tape and taped his lips. I called Joe Harper into the room.

"As soon as this guy can navigate, get handcuffs out of my drawer and lock him to you. Get one of my cars, take him over to the other side of town, handcuff him to a police call box. Telephone Commissioner Standish and tell him where to have his cops pick the man up."

JOE NODDED. "Okay. Say, can that guy hear what we're saying now?"

"He'll forget as soon as he's out from under the scopolamine. Why?"

"Nothing much. I got a couple of phone calls here while I was waiting for you to come back. Glenn Saunders called up. He just wanted you to wish him luck with his performance at the benefit party."

"He doesn't need luck," I said. "He's using my best tricks."

Just about now, I reflected, Glenn Saunders would be performing as George Chance at the party. Taylor Owens would be informing whoever would listen that all the tricks were accomplished with elastic.

"Somebody else called up. A man. He said he wanted to speak to Dr. Stacey. He wouldn't leave his number."

I wondered if the ad I had inserted had brought results already.

"And I didn't find Hugo Wayne," Joe said.

"He may have lammed out of town."

"Not Hugo. Too smart. He knows this town as well as I do and it's the easiest place in the world to lose yourself. Look how long Lepke stayed around until he gave himself up to the G-men. I'll get Wayne yet."

"After you get through tying Glass Eye to a call box, how would you like to take a run over to Hoboken and find out what you can about a Mrs. E.L. Long. She's the lady who gets the other half of Van Sickle's half million dollar life insurance."

Joe agreed to this and I gave him the address Ken Vickers had mentioned. Our friend with the glass-eye showed signs of coming out from under the influence of the drag and Joe Harper got the handcuffs and took him out.

I was alone in the Ghost's haunted rectory. The *brrr* of the phone brought me out of my chair. I picked it up.

"Dr. Stacey?" a man's voice asked.

"Yes," I said.

"This is Dr. Chalmers, a dentist. I saw your ad in tonight's paper. I'd like that hundred dollars."

"You can give me information regarding the extraction of Van Sickle's teeth?" I asked.

"I certainly can."

"Can you identify the teeth? Can you give me a brief description of them?"

"I can. They were good teeth. There was one pretty bad hole in one of them, but it was filled."

"Which tooth was filled?"

"An eye tooth, I believe," went on the voice.

"Why did you do the extraction?"

"Van Sickle wanted his teeth out."

"All right. Meet me in an hour at my apartment on Amsterdam Avenue."

I HUNG up. I did not believe this Dr. Chalmers was a dentist. Dentists did not say "hole" when they meant "cavity." Nor did they, when talking to either a medical or a dental colleague, call a "canine" by its common name of "eye tooth."

I had a pretty good hunch that Dr. Chalmers had a thin, hawk-like nose, close-set dark eyes, tanned cheeks, a knife scar on his chin, and that his real name was Elmer Tanko.

Sometimes, when you know the location of a trap and about what to expect, you will risk walking into it. But what I expected and what I found weren't the same thing.

CHAPTER XV

DEATH ACROSS MY DOORSILL

THE LOGICAL next step was to call up Merry White at the Cronner. Or rather, I called "Miss Miesnest" which was Merry's idea of a good alias. She told me she would run down to a pay station and call me back—she didn't trust hotel switchboard operators. I smoked a cigarette half down before she called.

"How's everything?" I asked.

"Oh, swell. Tim's right here in the phone booth protecting me," Merry laughed. "He looks so cute with a lollipop in his mouth."

"Cut it out, frail!" cried Tim.

"Find anything out about Mrs. Kurtzner?" I asked.

"Oh, sure. Her husband died of something wrong with his gall bladder. She has her hair done at Maurice's. She likes children, especially little boys like Tim—"

"About the money she realized from Van Sickle's death."

"Oh, yes. I went with her down to the bank to get the insurance company check cashed," Merry said. "I make friends quick."

"Pretty crazy set-up, eh, Merry?"

"Pretty crazy insurance company."

"They're acting on our advice."

"Honey, I never saw so much money in all my life."

"So Lucretia goes to the bank with a quarter of a million dollar check," I said, "the bank cashes it, and she takes the cash—just like that. This is quite a case, Merry."

"And she goes back to her hotel carrying all that cash," Merry said.

"She had guards, all right," I said grimly, "only you didn't see them. They watched her plenty. You do the same. Lucretia is up to something. She's by no means the pure white lily she so skillfully pretends to be. She's in the mob somewhere. If so, somebody will come after that money. If anybody comes, give them a lot of room, you understand? But if possible, find out what they look like and get in touch with me or Standish immediately. Got that?"

She had it.

I called a taxi company and ordered a cab to meet me on a corner two blocks away, altered my makeup to the extent of removing the red wig and remodeling the putty on my nose, locked up the rectory and went for my cab.

I gave the driver the address of the furnished apartment I had rented but had never seen, settled back in the seat and removed from my pocket the steel wire spiral that Tanko took so much interest in. I carefully transferred it to a secret compartment in my cigarette case.

MY CIGARETTE case is a double purpose affair, for holding cigarettes and also for serving the purpose of a magician's card box. In other words, it has a false bottom, undetectable unless you know the secret. The flat spiral of wire was safe beneath the false bottom.

As I rolled along I tried to figure out by what means Tanko had discovered that the man known as Dr. Stacey had possession of the wire spiral. There was only one possible explanation—Tanko knew that Dr. Stacey and the Ghost were one.

From the window of his office he might have watched me, as Dr. Stacey, prowling around in Taylor Owens' office. But all that proved was that Dr. Stacey—well, it simply proved that Dr. Stacey was in Owens' office.

No matter where I started, it always came out at that unsatisfactory conclusion. Unless Tanko had Owens' wires tapped and had heard Dr. Stacey impersonating Owens over the telephone, while knowing that Owens was elsewhere.

And even then the tie-up with the Ghost would not have been definite.

I figured that the tapping of a single telephone leading off the trunk line that served a building the size of the Starret was impossible without the special aid of the telephone company. And that was absurd.

And then something else hit me between the eyes—the idea that the blonde Miss Rice was in league with Tanko! When I had sent her from the office on the pretext of finding Taylor Owens, she might have tiptoed back to the office door, listened to my telephone impersonation of Owens, and informed Tanko. That was the most logical explanation of all. I mentally added Miss Rice to my list of people who ought to be watched.

The apartment I had rented on Amsterdam wasn't particularly fancy, I noted, as soon as my cab pulled up. I paid the driver, and let him go. Then I walked around the four story apartment building, saw that there was a fire escape that might prove a convenient exit, returned to the front door, went in, pressed the bell button marked "Janitor."

When the janitor appeared, I told him I was the new tenant and asked him for the keys.

"Sure, sure," he said, groping in his overall pockets. "I'll show you to the place myself. Good thing you wasn't here today, Mister. They'd have pestered the daylights out of you."

"Who?" I asked.

"Oh, enterprisin' people from the neighborhood shopping district. A new family moves in, they all get out and try to get you to use this milk, an' that cleaner, or the other bakery."

"Just give me the keys," I said. "I'll find the place myself. You needn't bother."

"No bother at all," he said.

Tiny Tim

BUT I couldn't risk taking the janitor into anything that might include hot rods like Tanko and his men, so I gave the janitor a buck tip *not* to show me the apartment, went off up the stairs with him gaping behind me.

I found Apartment B6 at the end of the second floor corridor. What the janitor had said was true enough. Shopkeepers from all over the neighborhood had been here to solicit the patronage of Dr. Stacey, for I could see their advertisements and hand bills sticking under the edge of the door.

My eyes caught sight of a square of white cardboard down on the floor, something that stood apart from the other litter. On the square of cardboard was a large black skull and crossbones. Beneath this death's head were the two words:

SURE DEATH!

My gun out, I gave the door a push with my knee and dropped to a crouch to pick up the death's head card. And then hell broke loose.

CHAPTER XVI

TANGLED THREADS

A **RUDDY FLASH** like a bolt of lightning, a stunning explosion, the scream of shot, and instinctively I dropped from a crouch to a position flat on my belly. I rolled to the left. Echoes of the blast died. An interval of silence, and then the confused babble of voices of occupants of other apartments. Doors opened and closed, footsteps thudded on the floor, a door in the corridor behind me opened and a woman screamed:

"Someone's been killed!"

I sprang to my feet. The woman in the corridor behind me screamed again, ran back into her room and slammed her door. I gripped my gun and stepped across the door sill and into the dark. My hand found the light switch and flipped it. The tiny living room blazed with light.

There on a straight-backed chair a few feet from the door, I saw my would-be murderer—a shotgun, tilted so that its charge would rip into a tall man's heart and lungs. The gun was tied to the chair and a network of string leading from the trigger, through a staple, and across the door made this as simple and effective a murder machine as I had ever seen.

I turned to the door. People were standing in the hallway.

"No cause for alarm, folks," I said in a calm voice. "Accidental discharge of a shotgun. Sorry to disturb you."

The woman who had screamed put her hands on her hips and glared at me.

"Sorry to disturb, are you! Blow up half the building, scare a person out of a year's growth, and you're sorry to disturb!"

I looked down the hall and could see the damage the spreading scatter of shot had done to plastering and woodwork. But even so, the indignant woman had exaggerated a little.

"We'll not have people like you for neighbors," a pompous little man said. "No, sir. Anybody that don't know when a gun is loaded isn't safe anywhere outside of an asylum."

I stooped, picked up the death's head card, closed the door in the pompous man's face. He didn't need to worry. I wouldn't be his neighbor any longer than I had to.

In the bright light of the living room that had come so close to being a dying room, I examined the death's head card. On turning it over, I read in printed letters:

YES! SURE DEATH TO MOTHS IF YOU SEND YOUR GARMENTS TO BURTAMAN'S, THE CLEANER WITH THE REPUTATION!

And that may have something to do with the fact that George Chance, ever since then, always has his cleaning done at an establishment known as Burtaman's.

BY THIS time, I had come to the conclusion that Elmer Tanko was a thorough-going individual. The set-gun had been arranged just in case Glass-Eye failed to polish me off. When I went to settle with the janitor for the damage done, I learned that about two hours before my arrival, the janitor's wife had unlocked the apartment for a man who claimed to be Dr. Stacey but who answered the description of Elmer Tanko.

As soon as I could get away from the janitor, I went back to the Ghost's rectory.

In the basement room, I found no less a personage than Medical Examiner Robert Demarest, his sleepy, heavy-lidded eyes watching the frost form on the outside of a tall glass he held in his hand. When I went in, he lifted the glass to his lips, took a slow drink, licked his lips. I went through the business of getting putty and makeup off my face.

"How's ghosting, George?" Demarest asked.

I told him ghosting was okay and how was my liquor. My liquor, he said, tasted like embalming fluid, but maybe that was because he'd had a hard day's work in the morgue. I had a drink with the doctor, neither of us saying much. Demarest is a queer egg, but I usually enjoy his secret visits to the hideout.

I had to tell him all that had happened. His only comment was that I was a swell magician. On his way from the morgue that night, he had dropped in on the Union of Civic Clubs' benefit.

"This George Chance," he said, "is pretty good stuff."

"Thanks," I said, knowing that he referred to Glenn Saunders, my double.

"What's-his-name Owens was master of ceremonies at the party," Demarest said; "If I had a nose like his I'd never get up on a stage. I left before the party was over. I ought to go get some sleep, but this damned suicide epidemic is driving me nuts. Aren't you getting anywhere?"

I said I didn't know. I went over to a small writing table, took out a piece of paper, began doing a bit of pencil-thinking. I doodled, but all my pencil could draw was a lot of little curley-cues like that spiral of wire I thought was an essential clue to the case. Then I wrote down some names.

HUGO WAYNE, who was linked with bonds belonging to Fabian Deeming. Wayne was missing and Fabian Deeming was an unknown quantity entirely.

Then there was Taylor Owens' beautiful secretary, Miss Rice—was she hooked up with Elmer Tanko? And the red-haired Kurtzner woman—a woman who had a suitcase full of money she wouldn't have had if tragedy had not come to Leonard Van Sickle.

I added Arnold Smock to the list. He was to get a nice piece of change, apparently owed him, because of Jonathan Marvin's death. Who was Smock, anyway? An eccentric who raised pigeons. I drew a not very good sketch of a pigeon on the paper while I was thinking. I got an idea.

"Listen, Bob," I said.

Demarest's sleepy-looking eyelids flickered a little, indicating that he was all attention even if he appeared to be half man and half cadaver.

"Have you heard Standish say what kind of pigeons Arnold Smock raises?"

"I never heard of Arnold Smock."

"Well," I said, "he has a flock of pigeons, I hear. Sometime tomorrow, he's going to cash a check from Marvin's life insurance. If he's the brains of this mob, maybe he'll just keep the money. If he's just a tool, he'll try to get it to the head man, won't he? And the cops will be watching him, he'll know. Bob, that's where the pigeons fit in, if pigeons fit in at all."

"You mean carrier pigeons?"

"Yes. A flock of them could carry a lot of money in large bills."

"And should that be so?"

"It must be looked into," I said. "The Department will put an aeroplane onto that angle, Smock's pigeon roost will be watched, the watchers will be in communication with the Department, and the Department will contact the plane by shortwave."

I then added the name of Mrs. E.L. Long of Hoboken to my list. She netted a small fortune by Van Sickle's death, too, and her relationship with him was even more vague than that of Mrs. Kurtzner.

Lastly, I put down an X that stood for the dentist who had pulled Van Sickle's teeth.

Lighting a cigar, I settled back in silence to think. Demarest's heavy eyelids finally closed all the way. Like most doctors, he had learned to sleep in a chair. I hadn't. I went over to the davenport and lay down without removing my clothes. I must have made a good picture of a dead-tired man at a dead-end.

And at exactly four o'clock in the morning, I was awakened by someone coming slowly down the basement steps, dragging one foot behind the other. I sat up, half blinded by the light to see Joe Harper stagger in the room, his hair matted with blood.

"God!" he said hoarsely, "somebody get me a drink!"

Slowly his legs crumpled under him.

CHAPTER XVII

THE LISPING MAN

J OE WAS out cold. I got him across my shoulder like a sack of meal and carried him to the couch on which I had been lying.

Demarest was awake. He came over, looked at Joe, grunted. He revealed a gash in the forehead.

"Hot water," Demarest said to me. "And don't worry, he'll be okay."

I went to get a basin of water and some towels. On my way back from the Ghost's basement bathroom, I got a bottle of whiskey. I thought that would do more toward putting new blood in Joe's veins than anything else.

Demarest bathed Joe's wound. It wasn't deep. Swabbing the cut with iodine brought him around. He looked at me.

"Hi, George."

He looked at Demarest.

"Well, I always did expect to wake up in a morgue sometime. Get this vulture out of here, George."

"Hold still, parasite," Demarest said sourly. "I don't know why I bother with you."

I poured Joe a drink and he took it neat. He tried to light a cigarette, but his hands were too shaky and the cigarette wobbled in his lips. I helped him get lighted. Then he leaned back on the couch. No use trying to prod information out of him. When he was ready to speak, when he got his thoughts in order, he'd tell us what had happened, but not until then. He dragged in deep lungfuls of smoke, let ashes fall where they would. Then he told us his story....

As soon as he had left the Ghost's rectory with Glass-Eye, he drove south for a dozen blocks or so, taking a circuitous course in order to prevent the man with the glass eye from ever doubling back on the trail and finding the Ghost's hideout. At a police call-box on East Forty-First Street near Madison, he had left Glass-Eye—securely manacled to the call box. Then he had gone to a telephone and called Commissioner Standish. He failed to find Standish at Headquarters or at his home, but finally found him at Charles' Restaurant where, evidently, he was still in discussion with Ken Vickers.

That done, Joe called a taxi, drove over to Hoboken Ferry, got out, crossed the river and ran up another taxi bill finding the house of Mrs. E.L. Long.

It wasn't much of a house—one story frame with mid-Victorian filigree trim on porch and eaves. The place needed painting and repairing. Blinds were down, but through the lightning-like cracks in the green shade cloth, Joe could see streaks of light.

Joe went to the door and knocked. The door was opened immediately by a woman. She looked about forty years old and she had tried to do something about it in the way of an elaborate paint job. Her hair was straw-blonde and rolled up on patent metal curlers. She had on a man's bathrobe which didn't entirely conceal the fact that her figure was still okay.

THROUGH THE half open door, she eyed Joe Harper. Joe had his hat pulled well down over his face.

"You from the boss?" she asked in a brassy voice.

"Sure," Joe said.

She opened the door and let him in to a living room which conformed pretty well with the general scheme of things in the Long house. The furniture was gaudy and worn like Mrs. Long's face and the scroll work that decorated the outside of the house. And like Mrs. Long's bathrobe, the place was dirty. Joe found a chair that was covered with wildly colored tapestry and sat down.

"Haven't you forgot something?" Mrs. Long said as she took a cigarette for herself and passed the box to Joe.

Joe didn't know what it was he had forgot. Not the woman's face. The more he studied it, the more sure he was that he had seen it before.

"Wasn't you in the second row of the chorus in the curley-cue business once?" he asked. "Isn't your name Patsy Moore?"

"Maybe so," she said. "Haven't you forgot something?"

Joe got it then. He was supposed to have some sort of a letter or countersign to show the woman to prove he was from "the boss." He didn't have it. He didn't know what it was he was supposed to have.

The woman came up to him, stood squarely in front of him, eyed him closely. Pretty soon she said: "Sa-ay!" drawing it way out. And then she pulled a nickeled revolver from the pocket of her bathrobe and turned it on Joe.

"Push your hat up a bit, sonny boy," she said.

Joe pushed his hat on the back of his head. He knew what was coming. If this woman was Patsy Moore, he had got her a job or two back in the days when he was acting as a booking agent. She'd been quite a song and dance girl until she'd put on too much weight.

"I'll be damned!" she said. "The ten-percenter! The gyp artist! Joey Harper in person! Listen, you two bit mug, what the devil do you want?"

She moved in close with the gun. Joe Harper looked at her coolly. His right hand went up to remove the cigarette from his thin lips, then suddenly struck out at her gun. He slapped the muzzle to one side. Patsy made the gun speak, or maybe it spoke out of turn, but Joe didn't get the slug; the chair-back got it.

Joe came to his feet, got the woman's gun hand and lifted it so the gun-muzzle pointed at the ceiling. He wedged a finger in between the back of the trigger and the guard.

She squeezed the trigger, but mostly squeezed his finger. She spat in his face. He took that because this was a lady. He doubled her gun arm around her back in a hammer-lock because even that was fair in love and war and this wasn't love. She dropped the gun and cursed him. He shoved her back and picked up the gun.

"NOW," HE said, "another squawk out of you and I'll let you have it."

There was no way of telling that he wouldn't have let her have it, so she didn't squawk. She just watched him with those large, tired-looking eyes of hers.

He thrust the gun into her back. "Ladies first, always," he said.

He gun-shoved her through the house and found that all the rooms in the place were just like the living room except that they were dirtier. In the bedroom, under the unmade bed, he found a Gladstone bag which he made the woman open. She said she didn't have the key to the bag, but he told her to get it or he'd look for it. She produced the key from her bosom, and giving Joe a lot of new names, opened the Gladstone.

Commissioner Standish

It was stuffed with money—the dough she had cashed in on with the check from Van Sickle's life insurance.

Joe looked at the dough. "Listen, Patsy, there's a lot of mazuma in that bag," he said. "Maybe we could split it and go somewhere."

Patsy shook her head.

"It's mighty generous of me," Joe said. "I could take the whole works myself."

She laughed at that.

"You couldn't get a block from this house with the dough. Not half a block. And I don't cross up anybody. It ain't much of a life, but it's the only one I got."

"This boss of yours—who is he?" Joe asked.

Her rouged lips came together as though they were going to stay that way. She paled a little. Joe kicked the Gladstone closed and shoved it under the bed.

"Let's look in here and see what we find," he said, meaning the bathroom.

He shoved her ahead of him into the bathroom. On the wash basin were a lot of cosmetic jars. The porcelain was dirty and stained with rouge. Everything was there on the ledge around the basin except what Joe was looking for. But he found it in the bathroom closet—a pair of shears and a safety razor.

There was just one way to third degree a woman. If you could hurt her vanity you could get somewhere. He took Patsy back into the living room.

"Sit down," he ordered.

"Wh-what are you going to do?" she stammered.

And then she got a grip on her courage and unleashed a vocabulary that would have withered a saint but had no effect whatever on Joe Harper. When she got through, Joe came in close with the shears and razor.

"Murder me, damn you!" she said. "See where that gets you!"

Joe shook his head.

"I guess a woman can take more physical pain than a man. I'm not going to hurt you."

He lifted the shears to Patsy's straw blonde hair and snipped off a lock of it. He dangled the hair in front of her eyes.

"See?"

SHE LOOKED at the hair and her eyes widened.

"I'm going to cut it all off," he told her, "as close down as the scissors will take it. Then I'm going to shave you bald. Get a picture of what you'll look like, Patsy. You'll want to bury yourself alive. You won't want to live. You'll look terrible with a bald head."

"You—you wouldn't dare!" she defied him.

Joe shrugged, raised the shears, snipped off another piece and dropped it into her lap. Then he raised the shears a little and snipped at the air a few times. And Patsy broke. She fell down on her knees and started to cry.

Joe stood back from her, the shears in his hand. His black eyes squinted through the fog of cigarette smoke.

"Well," he said, "you going to answer a few questions?"

"Wha-what do you want to know?"

"Who's your boss," Joe asked. "That's all I want to know. It's just a personal matter. You give and I'll go away. You don't give and I'll make your head look like a cue ball."

"I don't know! Don't ask me that, Joe. Because I don't know. I've never seen him. I don't know anything about this racket. All I know is that I get a grand for collecting the money. Listen, if there was a way of blowing with the dough, wouldn't I do it? The boss would kill me. You can't get away from him. Nobody can."

Joe sighed. "This hurts me almost as bad as it does you, babe."

And he advanced with the shears.

"No!" she screamed. "Don't touch me. Don't do that."

Tears swelled into her eyes again. And maybe it was just the tears, but anyway Joe thought she was telling the truth.

"Listen," she said, "you take a thousand bucks out of that suitcase. Go get ten C notes. I was to get a thousand bucks, and I'll tell the boss I took my thousand bucks out. You get a grand. Can you use the dough?"

Joe laughed.

"Anytime, babe."

But he didn't take the money. He took the woman into the bedroom and instead of taking out the Gladstone, he went to the closet.

Her clothes were hanging there—not many clothes, but gaudy stuff. And on the same rod was a man's suit. The man's suit was good stuff— good cloth, tailor made. Joe thought he's seen the suit somewhere before. It was a little too conservative, in his mind, but it was an unusual cut. There was something about the breast pocket of the coat, something funny.

Feeling in the pocket, he found there was a shallow, narrow pocket sewed into the lining. In the pocket were half a dozen kitchen matches. He searched the side pockets of the coat. They were empty except for a business card. He took the card out, couldn't read it because of the dim light in the closet. He held the card in his left hand and scuffed a match on his heel.

Behind him, somebody lisped:

"Thtick up your handth!"

Joe dropped the match, pivoted on the balls of his feet, lashed out with his fist. The blow didn't connect. The man who had come up from behind moved fast to slice the air with his gun and bring the muzzle down on Joe's forehead.

CHAPTER XVIII

DEATH AT MY ELBOW

PIERCING THE scintillating explosion of lights in front of his eyes, Joe glimpsed the man's face. And what he saw was more of a shock than the blow on the head, though the blow brought him down to his knees. And there was another man in the room—somebody with a black cloth tied over his face. Nothing about the man's face stuck with

Joe except the eyes. The eyes were somehow relentless, stabbing, and infinitely cruel.

"Finish him off!" the masked man said.

The gun raised again above Joe's head. Joe fell backward from his kneeling position, legs doubled under him. Then he remembered that Patsy Moore's revolver was still in his possession, the pearl butt of it sticking out of the slit of his pants pocket. He pulled the gun, fired, got the man through the arm somewhere because the man dropped his gun, ducked to retrieve it with his left hand.

Joe got to his feet. Somewhere sounded the chill skirl of a police whistle. On the other side of the room, through the red haze that swirled over Joe's eyes, Joe saw the man with the mask kick out a window with the heel of his shoe. The masked man had the Gladstone in his hand. He tossed it ahead of him and was going through the window when Joe turned the revolver on him and let loose a pair of shots. He didn't know whether it was a hit or a miss. The masked man was gone.

Joe reeled across the room. The other man, who had surprised Joe in the closet, had picked up his gun and started to follow the masked man through the window. Patsy—Joe didn't know where Patsy was. He didn't care. Because coming through the door of the living room was a cop.

Joe swung to the right, blundered through the kitchen door. The cop warned and then fired high over Joe's head. Joe went through the back door, running. He didn't know exactly where he was running. He didn't know how long he could keep those leaden legs working—up and down. Somewhere in the backyard he fell over an ash can, didn't think he could get up. But he got up just the same and kept running....

"AND THAT," Joe Harper concluded, "is about all there is to it. I made a fizz out of the whole business, maybe. But here's this."

He reached into his pocket and brought out a crumpled piece of pasteboard—a calling card. He handed it to me.

Demarest and I had listened closely to Joe's narrative. When he had mentioned the match pocket in the coat of the suit he found in the closet, Demarest and I had exchanged significant glances. I looked now at the calling card. In conservative engraving was the name:

MR. LEONARD VAN SICKLE

I handed the card to the medical examiner. Demarest grunted.

"Why didn't you nail something besides a card?" he complained.

Joe flicked his cigarette into an ash tray.

Joe pivoted as he heard a voice
say—"Thtick up your handth!"

"Listen, cadaver, did you ever have a corpse coddle up to you and sock you on the head with a gun? Maybe you don't believe it, but a dead man can sure hit hard."

"You're nuts," Demarest said.

"What Joe is trying to tell you," I said quietly, "is that Leonard Van Sickle is living over in Hoboken with a Patsy Moore and is going under the name of E.L. Long."

"Nuts!" Demarest said. "Did the man you say was Van Sickle have the scar of an appendectomy on his side?"

Joe sneered.

"Sure. After he socked me, I told him to take off his pants and tell me about his operation! What do you think this was—a reception after an opening night?"

"Joe, did you see the man's face clearly?" I asked.

"George," Joe groaned, "you don't see clear with more lights dancing before your eyes than a top-billed star gets. But I saw and heard enough. Sure, those suicides are murders, but I don't think Van Sickle was the guy who was murdered. The racket's been worked before. Van Sickle collected half of his life insurance himself. He'll have to split with the mob. The other half went to the Kurtzner woman who is probably strictly legit. Right, George?"

"Can't say," I answered. "It may look that way but it doesn't necessarily have to be that way. For one thing, I can't see Leonard Van Sickle living in a rat's nest in Hoboken with an ex-follie's dame. That's a false note in this queer drama of human folly and greed. There have been other false notes. I expect that the cooing of a certain Mr. Arnold Smock's pigeons will add to the discord."

THE FOLLOWING Tuesday, Mr. Arnold Smock received his check from the Boston Insurance Company.

He was about as insignificant a person as I have ever seen. Though his chin and forehead both receded and his nose was prominent, you couldn't say there was anything sharp about his face.

My first impression was that the master brain behind the suicide epidemic did not lurk behind the dull blue eyes of Arnold Smock. He did not impress me as a man who could manage money, with or without the assistance of Jonathan Marvin, who had clarified to be Smock's secretary.

Still, first impressions are not necessarily correct.

I watched Arnold Smock cash his check. I was the whiskered ancient who stood behind him in the line at the branch bank in Brooklyn where he cashed it. But other eyes besides mine were on Arnold Smock. Ken Vickers, the insurance company detective, was there. And there was one of New York's most capable plainclothesmen on his tail.

And all that day, Arnold Smock and his house were watched by the police. In addition, up against the lowering gray ceiling of sky, a small red plane droned—a man-made bird set to watch pigeons.

It was no holiday for the cops. Hoboken police, cooperating with their New York colleagues, were on the lookout for the lisping man Joe Harper had sworn was Leonard Van Sickle, and inasmuch as Joe also claimed to have wounded the man, hopes of a speedy capture ran high. Newspapers had the story and captioned it:

LEONARD VAN SICKLE BELIEVED ALIVE

I read the story later in the Ghost's rectory. It was the usual police handout, colored by a reporter's imagination. It made good reading. Then there was something else that struck my eye in an adjoining column:

MYSTERY MAN IN VAN SICKLE CASE CAPTURED

It was about John Fabian Deeming. Not much about him. Mr. Deeming was a salesman for an Iowa farm machinery manufacturer who had registered at a New York hotel, and that was about all that

Joe Harper

there was to it except that the mystery man emphatically denied all knowledge of the affair and had threatened suit for false arrest.

I telephoned Commissioner Standish.

"What about Deeming?" I asked.

"Oh, that." Ned Standish sounded slightly annoyed. "The man's clean. He's just not the same Fabian Deeming. Got more alibis than a suburban estate has mortgages. We let him go, poured the old oil on his troubled waters. This Fabian Deeming business looks like a dead end. But we got a lead on Van Sickle."

"I thought you thought Van Sickle was dead," I said.

"Listen," Standish sighed, "I stopped thinking. There's no percentage in it. But the Hoboken police have picked up the trail of a man and a woman. The man was toothless, answered in a superficial way to Van Sickle's description. And the lady with him sounded like Patsy Moore. The man's carrying a slug in his arm. He had a run-in with a doctor last night when the doctor refused to treat his wound. The doc was lucky to get off with his life."

And that was that until at about three o'clock that afternoon, there was an "accident" at Arnold Smock's house. All of his pigeons got loose at once.

The cop in the plane saw Smock's frantic and ineffectual attempts to corral his birds. They seemed to fly everywhere at once and it was utterly impossible to follow them because of lowering clouds, a fog that rolled in from the sea, and the fact that the birds didn't make off in a body as expected.

This last fact did not contradict my theory of carrier pigeons but rather confirmed it. The answer was that some were carriers and some were not. Those who were not just flew. Those who were—if my theory was correct—flew toward a destination, bearing bills of large denominations. But the aeroplane could not determine which group to follow, and percentage dictated that it would follow the wrong one.

It had been a clever move, but we were prepared with counter-moves. Standish's detectives searched Arnold Smock's house immediately, over his strong protest, and did it legally, for they had a warrant ready. But the money he had brought to the house in cash was gone. Smock claimed he had hidden it and refused to tell where it was. He was arrested.

Two hours of questioning couldn't break him down. He contended that the money was legally his as the beneficiary of a life insurance policy, that as such he could do with it what he pleased, and furthermore did not have to account for what he did with it to anybody.

LEGALLY HE was right. By four o'clock, it looked very much as though the police and the Ghost were stalemated. I did not think so, however. There was still Joe Harper to reckon with, and he had promised me he'd catch up with Hugo Wayne. At half past four the break came. Joe Harper phoned me.

"I've got Hugo Wayne," he said. "I found him in a Tenth Avenue hideout. I softened him up with a few well-chosen punches and he came across. Who do you think Fabian Deeming is?"

"Leonard Van Sickle," I said promptly.

There was a whistle on the other end of the wire.

"George, what does a guy have to do to surprise you?" Joe said. "Listen to the payoff. A few days before Van Sickle's suicide, apparent or otherwise, Van Sickle called up Hugo Wayne. He wanted Hugo Wayne to transfer the title of the shares of stock Van Sickle held in the Deistel International Corporation, the stock you hijacked from Hugo Wayne. Van Sickle got hold of Wayne, made him swear to keep this dark. Van Sickle had Wayne register the stock in the name of Fabian Deeming.

"The stock," Joe went on, "was practically worthless at the time. But evidently Van Sickle wanted to hang on to it. He must have been riding a hunch. Hugo Wayne didn't know why, but he wormed it out of Van Sickle that Van Sickle was going to do a disappearing act. Van Sickle bought, or had Hugo buy for him, two passages to Europe, one for Van Sickle and one for Mrs. Kurtzner. The transaction was carried on through the mail and the tickets were to be sent to a post office box."

"I know all that," I said. "Why did Wayne swipe the stock?"

"Because Van Sickle's hunch came true. The stock boomed. Hugo Wayne was on his way to the Hotel Cronner to tell Van Sickle about the stock jump, when Van Sickle, apparently, jumped out of his window and killed himself. Do I have to go on, George?"

"No," I said. "Knowing that Fabian Deeming didn't really exist except in the mind of Van Sickle, who had seen the name somewhere, stored it up in his subconscious, and then resurrected it when he needed an alias, and believing that Van Sickle was dead, Hugo Wayne went to Van Sickle's suite right after the homicide boys were through. Wayne knocked out the cop who was on guard, opened Van Sickle's safe, took out the certificates. Wayne's idea was to put himself in the place of the fictitious Fabian Deeming and cash in on the stock. While he was about it, he snatched that bag which he thought contained jewelry but which, as we know so well, turned out to be a set of human teeth. So much for Deeming. What about Mrs. Kurtzner?"

"Well, what about her? I think she's legit. Wayne met her at Van Sickle's before. According to him, Van Sickle was in love with her. I think the two boat tickets to Europe prove Van Sickle's intentions. The whole thing boils down to this—Leonard Van Sickle is alive, and just to guess, I think he's the brains behind this whole damned business!"

CHAPTER XIX

THE MISSING QUARTER MILLION

V **AN SICKLE,** in Joe Harper's mind, had undergone as many transformations as a chameleon. From Leonard Van Sickle, he had changed to a man named Long who was living with Patsy Moore in Hoboken. And from Long he had changed to Fabian Deeming who would have liked to elope with Mrs. Lucretia Kurtzner. A very fickle person, according to Joe.

The door of the rectory opened and I heard the sharp clack of a woman's high heels on the steps. It couldn't have been anybody but Merry and I went to meet her.

I lifted her to lip level, and pressed her warm mouth to mine. This time her lips were less clinging. She wriggled from my grasp, darted across the room, bounced into a chair. Her breath coming in shallow gasps and color had gone from her cheeks. I crossed the room to her. "What's the matter?" I asked.

"Plenty," she panted. "Oh, I've run ten blocks if I've run one. They've got Tiny Tim. Tim and I followed them in a taxi. They stopped up the street at a liquor store. Tim got into the trunk of the car, so now they've got him. He shouldn't have done that."

Her fists clenched tightly and she bit her lower lip.

"I could spank Tim!"

She bounded out of the chair, grasped my coat lapels in her hands.

"We've got to do something. And I don't know where to start."

"At the beginning, Merry," I told her. "Up to now, you haven't told me anything. *Who's* got Tim?"

"I don't know!"

She pulled off her hat and tossed it across the room. Her hand brushed up the dark hair above her brow.

"We were watching Mrs. Kurtzner, like you said," she began. "Ever since Mrs. Kurtzner cashed that quarter of a million dollar check and carried the money away in a suitcase, we've been watching her. Tim drilled a hole through the panel of the door and one or the other of us have been watching Lulu's door, which is just across the hall, most of the time. You said somebody would come for the money. Somebody did. This evening at dinner time."

"Who?" I asked.

"Don't know." Merry shook her brown curls vigorously. "A couple of real tough-looking men. They knocked at the door and Mrs. Kurtzner let them in without a word. Tim and I watched through our hole in the door. And when Mrs. Kurtzner's door opened again, we could see Mrs. Kurtzner sitting in her living room, taped to a chair, her mouth taped shut with that sticky black tape.

"The two men came out and both of them were carrying square bundles of newspaper, tied up tight. It was the money, as sure as anything. It's going to look as though Mrs. Kurtzner had been robbed, only we know it wasn't that. It couldn't have been. She didn't look scared of the two men she let in. There wasn't any noise that you could think was caused by a struggle, because Tim slipped out of our room and went over to listen at Mrs. Kurtzner's door."

"Right," I said. "Mrs. Kurtzner will claim she was robbed. She always keeps her skirts clean. What happened after that?"

"TIM AND I followed the men from the hotel. It was exciting. Tim was good. He stopped in front of a candy store and yelled for me to buy him some candy, just like a kid. The two tough men up ahead couldn't have known what we were up to. Pretty soon, they got into a parked car. Tim and I grabbed a taxi and followed them. They took their time. About eight blocks from here—you know that liquor store with the purple and green sign that—"

"Yes," I interrupted hastily.

"Well, the two of them went in and bought a bottle of whiskey. They carried their newspaper packages with them. Tim and I were in the cab parked not far behind them. Tim got out and ran to their car. I tried to stop him and he turned on me in his excitement and called me names that didn't sound very little-boyish. The taxi driver decided that Tim wasn't a kid. He wanted to know what this was all about. He thought it was something crooked. He was sort of a cute cab driver with a cleft chin and a little black mustache, except for which he would have looked something like Richard Greene—"

"Yes. Let's have the rest."

Merry shrugged her shoulders, lifted her hands in a helpless gesture.

"That's all. Tim got into the trunk of the two tough men's car while I was arguing with the cab driver. The tough men came out of the store and drove away. The cab driver said he wouldn't have any part in the whole business. Gosh, but you'd have thought he was virtuous! He wanted to be paid off. I tried to pay him off, but when I opened my purse I was sort of reminded that I'd lost my last dime to Tim Terry in a dice game we played to kill time in the hotel. The driver said we'd call it square if I gave him a kiss."

I scowled.

"I'll let you guess whether I gave the kiss or ran straight here," Merry snapped at me. "What do we do now? Get Mrs. Kurtzner and put her on the grid?"

"Put her on what?" I asked.

"The grid. Grid, griddle, grill—what's the difference, and who cares so long as Lulu Kurtzner cares enough to come across with the truth? That redhead lady is no angel. She's mixed up in this. The robbery was faked and I don't know how we're going to prove it otherwise. But we've got to do something. Tim's smart. He can take care of himself as long as it doesn't come to a fight. But when I think what one of those tough men could do to him, I turn cold all over."

She shivered a little and I put my arm around her. The ringing of the phone startled us both and drew our nerves taut.

I reached for it, heard Tim's voice coming out of the receiver.

"It's Tim," I whispered to Merry and listened again to the midget's shrill voice.

"Listen," Tim piped, "I've got them! That is, I know where they're staying. You'd better come. I'm down on Oliver—"

AND THAT was the end of it. Just a crash in my ear and then the monotonous buzz of the disconnected phone. I dropped the instrument back on its cradle. Merry must have read anxiety in my eyes. She asked me what the matter was and I told her the line had gone dead, and started for the room in which the Ghost keeps his particular kind of wardrobe.

"Maybe he'll call back," Merry said.

Her optimism is always on hand when she thinks I need a lift. In the dressing room, I put on the outfit I had worn that morning—a dark suit that needed pressing, gray whiskers, bushy false eyebrows, a gray wig capped with a slouch hat.

I took a furled umbrella which has certain special properties not allotted to the usual run of umbrellas, and as I walked from the room my shoulders drooped with the weight of an incredible number of fictitious years.

Tim was down on Oliver—did that mean Oliver Street, not far from Chinatown?

CHAPTER XX

THE HOUSE OF DEAD BIRDS

D **ISGUISED IN** the character of the whiskered old gentleman with the umbrella, I rent a garage in the neighborhood where I keep a dilapidated-looking sedan, the dented hood of which hides an eight cylinder modern power plant. Merry White and I hurried to this garage and got into the car. The garage is back of a small knit goods store which is deserted after five o'clock, and the secluded court in which it is built makes it ideal for the secret comings and goings of the Ghost.

With Merry beside me, I drove down Madison and into Broadway, dropping as fast as traffic would permit into lower Manhattan, cut across the little Orient of Pell Street and came into Oliver Street.

I parked the car and we got out. I was an old, inoffensive man then, leaning on my umbrella and partly on the arm of a girl who might have appeared to be my granddaughter—something of a nuisance on the crowded sidewalks of the Ghetto. Any of the shops and dingy dwellings might have been a place where Tim Terry and disaster had met.

I think if it hadn't been for the dark-haired, dark-eyed kid we found playing on the curb, we wouldn't have found the place at all.

My pegging umbrella tip nearly spiked the boy's hand. He jerked it away and stood up, cuddling something up against his ragged shirt and looking at us with offended eyes.

"Watch who you're steppin' on, gran'pop!" he yelled at me.

I stopped, looked at him, asked him what he had in his hands. He said it was none of my business.

"It's a kitten," Merry said, smiling at the boy. "Isn't that what it is!"

"No. I ain't got a kitten," the boy said. "It's a bird, that's what it is."

"Hold it tight," Merry said. "It'll fly away from you."

"It won't," the child said, warming a little toward Merry. He stroked the feathered form with his fingers. "It can't fly. It's dead."

I took a step forward. "Let me see the bird," I said.

The child backed into the gutter.

"I won't. You can't have it. It's mine. I found it and it's mine."

"Would you let me see it?" Merry asked sweetly.

She put out an appealing hand. The kid lifted one hand slightly and we could see that it was the body of a dead pigeon.

"Where did you get that?" I demanded.

The kid pointed across the street.

"Over there. That pet shop. There was lots of them in the trash this afternoon."

I looked across the street, saw a gloomy doorway and unlighted windows. I gave Merry's arm a tug and we made our way across the street. The place pointed out by the boy bore a faded sign unillumi-nated except by the gray glow of the city night. The sign said Pet Shop, the words lettered on it with black paint.

MY PULSE picked up. Dead pigeons from a pet shop. Was this black little hole the destination of the carrier pigeons that Arnold Smock had released?

"Go get the car, Merry," I said to the girl. "Park across the street. Keep the motor running. This place needs a little looking into. Thanks to Tim, we've found it."

"Right!"

Her whisper was tense. Her eyes glowed excitedly. She released my arm and started back toward the place where we had left the car.

I went past the pet shop, entered the narrow walk between it and another equally dark building. If this was the destination of Arnold Smock's winged messengers, it seemed logical that the pigeons had been destroyed lest their cooing attract the attention of some cop who knew that pigeons had been the object of considerable worry from his superiors during the past few hours.

In the darkness along the side of the building, I moved faster than my apparent old age would have admitted. Windows in the wall were dark not because blinds were pulled but simply because there were no lights behind them. The uncomfortable thought struck me then that the place was as deserted as it seemed. Perhaps poor little Tim had been taken on one of those one way rides. His body would have been easy to conceal.

At the back of the house, the same darkness and silence. I approached steps leading up to the back door. Near the steps were several cages made of wood and heavy mesh wire and there were crates such as dogs and other animals might have been shipped in. My foot was on the bottom of the three steps when I heard the husky croak of rusty metal, saw the door opening slowly inward. I dropped behind the pile of crates and cages.

A man came out of the door, down the steps. Two feet from where I was hiding, he stopped, fumbled for a cigarette, put it between his lips, scuffed a match on the side of a match box. The flame, cupped between his hands, highlighted his face. He was narrow-eyed, heavy-jawed, flat-nosed. If this was one of the men Merry and Tim had seen going into Mrs. Kurtzner's suite, I didn't wonder that Merry had described him as tough.

I stood up slowly as the man turned his back toward me, let him take one step, then swung my umbrella. The innocent-looking handle of the umbrella is loaded and it would have taken more than this man's dark felt hat to resist the skull-cracking force of that blow. It was something like hammering a nail into soft mud, the way he went down.

I BENT over the man. From a concealed ball dropped on the left side of my coat lining, I brought out one of those large red billiard balls a magician delights in manipulating. My right hand coat-sleeve gave up my knife which I used to pry his clenched teeth apart. I wedged the ball between his jaws and tied it in place with a handkerchief. I used a length of strong silk cord from my pocket to bind his hands and ankles.

Then I walked up the steps and to the back door.

The man had not locked it. I stepped inside.

Beneath the balls of my feet, a floorboard gave perceptibly. I stepped forward quickly, but not quick enough to prevent the loosened board from doing its work; for somewhere in the dark shop a bell tinkled. There was no other sound.

The place smelled. The close-pressing darkness reeked with animal odors intermingled until each lost its distinction. I took out a tiny flashlight, let its beam shine through its rice-grain sized lens. I was in some sort of back store room. At my right, a basement stairway yawned. On the left, more shipping crates were piled to the ceiling, some of them bearing the labels of well-known pet foods. Ahead of me was another door.

I stepped to the door and pushed it open.

The small needle of light fell upon canary cages with their downy yellow occupants heedlessly sleeping. The beam passed on toward the dirty front windows.

A puppy barked shrilly, frightened from its nap. A green parrot pulled its head from beneath its wing and screamed at me.

I turned out my light. No other sound than that of the frightened puppy and the indignant green bird with the sharp eyes. The shop was empty; I went back the way I had come in, flashed my light into the basement stairway, started down the steps. Somewhere in the dark ahead of me, an electric signal *brrred* like a rattler's warning.

No other sound.

I kept on going down the steps and came to a door that was standing part-way open. I knew I could squeeze through without touching the panel. I stepped into the darkness, and the beast-odor of the place became almost overpowering.

I sensed movement behind me. Light blazed. I turned swiftly, glimpsed a man who was holding an electric torch. And at the same time the heavy, stagnant air above me stirred.

I ducked instinctively and something dropped over my head, shutting out the light. Someone who had waited behind me had dropped a sack over my head.

The sack had a draw string that tightened at my throat with such stricturing strength I thought I knew what it was like to be hanged.

CHAPTER XXI

THE MASTER MIND

FOR TINY TIM TERRY'S sake, it was most important that these men did not discover I was anything but what I seemed. I can say without bragging that I could have given the pair a little more trouble than I did when they tied me up. But I tried to match my struggles with my apparent age and so was comparatively submissive while they bound my hands and feet.

"Who is this old buzzard?" one of the men asked his companion in a harsh voice.

"Looks like Santa Claus to me," said the other. "Tie his umbrella up against his back. It'll stiffen him up so he can't wiggle out of the ropes. We'll save him until Tanko comes back with the boss. Some night's catch, ain't it—a midget and an old snoop like this. Don't hardly give a guy's muscles a chance to exercise."

I sighed. They were saving me for the boss. There was a pretty good chance, then, that they were also saving Tiny Tim. In complete darkness, with a cord about your throat half strangling you, any kind of wait is a long wait. I had no idea how long it took for Tanko to return with the boss. Just a lot longer than I liked.

The two men lingered in the room and I heard the clink of whiskey bottles on glass. I would have given a lot to feel a stiff slug of whiskey rasp down my throat.

Pretty soon, I heard the opening of a door. "Hi, Tanko," somebody said. "Good evening, boss."

"What have you there?" a muffled voice asked the two thugs.

"Some damned old snoop," one of the men said.

"Take the bag off," said the muffled voice.

A man bent over me and the cord about my throat was loosened. I needed a long breath and took it. The bag was pulled from my head and I blinked at the light, groaned realistically, looked around.

Elmer Tanko's gaunt figure was lounging against one wall. The two men who had welcomed me at the door were standing beside me. Neither of them were impressively large, but they looked capable of killing for a dollar's worth of postage stamps.

The man who had been greeted as the boss stood over me. He wore a long, shapeless topcoat that concealed any characteristic lines his figure might have had. A hat was pulled well down over his eyes, and the lower half of his face was hidden by a black triangle of cloth. I couldn't see his eyes, but I was aware that they were studying me closely. I put a lot of hope in my own disguise.

"PLEASE," I said in a quivering voice, "let me get out of here. This is no way to treat an old man. I just came to buy a package of bird seed for my little yellow bird. I couldn't get in the front way so I went to the back door. I thought somebody must be at home because I saw a man coming out of the back door."

"That was Wilkie," one of the men said. "He had a date with a dame, boss, so he went out just a little while ago."

I didn't think Wilkie would be entirely acceptable to his dame after he got out of a crate that had been used to ship dogs in.

The boss spoke and I had to repress a jump. "Tho you were jutht after thome bird theed, were you?" he said.

The lisping man! To all appearances here was Leonard Van Sickle, alive after Demarest, the best medical opinion in town, had pronounced him dead? Van Sickle, now called the boss! Joe Harper had heard that lisp in that house in Hoboken, and now I heard it here.

The boss thrust his gloved hands into his coat pockets and turned to the others.

"Got the money?"

"In those newspaper packages in the closet. We fixed up Lulu so it looked like robbery—"

"Thut up!" the lisping man cut in sharply.

The speaker blinked at the masked man.

"What the hell? What if the old bird does hear it? We're bumping him, ain't we?"

"No," said the boss. His lisping voice was mocking. "I do not believe in the wanton dethtruction of human life."

Elmer Tanko laughed harshly.

"You're getting chicken hearted, chief."

"Lock the old man up," the boss said. "When you get through with the midget and get him to thpeak, you can give the old man a beating to help him learn not to thnoop."

"And the midget?"

"Perhapth you'd better kill him after he talkth," the lisper said.

Then he and Tanko went out together.

One of the men, the larger of my two captors, got hold of the ropes at my ankles and dragged me across the basement floor, into what proved to be a windowless room. He left me on the floor in clammy, stinking darkness, went out, closed and locked the door.

I felt pretty certain I knew why my life was to be spared after I had been given a beating. I was sorry, but I didn't think I could stay to endure any punishment at the hands of the two toughs. My first objective was to get Tiny Tim out of the jam into which he had fallen.

THE UMBRELLA roped to my spine made escape a little more difficult than it would have been otherwise. I couldn't bend my back a whole lot. Even so, I didn't think it was going to take me long to get out of the place. I didn't dare take long because I didn't know what kind of resistance Tiny Tim could put up against this pair of crooks. And once he talked, they wouldn't take long to kill him.

I opened my mouth wide, lips drawn way back from my teeth. I drew in air through my mouth, let it dry my teeth thoroughly. When my whole mouth felt as dry as a wad of cotton, I bent my head until it seemed my neck would snap.

My early days as a contortionist had been well spent. My teeth locked on the edge of the button at the top of my coat, pulled it off. The button held in my dried teeth, I brought my tied hands up to my mouth, inserted the edge of the button between the tightly drawn pieces of cord and left it there.

I closed my mouth, allowed saliva to collect, then turned over on my belly, hands up to my mouth again. I soaked the cords and button with saliva, drew my hands down toward my chest and waited for the moisture to soak through the thin coating of carbon that covered the button.

If the criminal world knew that the top button of the Ghost's coat is always made of metallic potassium it's likely that no one would have taken the trouble to bind my hands with cord. No sooner had the moisture soaked through the coating of the button than the potassium reacted with the water in the saliva, liberating hydrogen gas so rapidly that enough heat resulted to cause the hydrogen to burst into an intense flame. It's just a bit of chemical magic which was never precisely intended for the use to which I put it—it's a little hard on your hands. You get burned a bit.

The cords burned through instantly and I dropped flat, smothering the flame with my chest. The pain of the burn was less than you'd imagine because I had smothered the flame quickly. I immediately got my knife from my sleeve and cut myself loose from the ropes, but let the ropes drape across my chest and legs so that it appeared I was still tied. I moved to one side, got the umbrella in my hands.

I've said the umbrella has peculiar properties. The silk cover, unfurled and removed, reveals a white lining which is silk and unfolds to cover the black outside. The cloth is coated with a magnesium compound such as is used in magician's "flash paper." At a touch of flame, the cloth bursts into a blaze of light and is almost instantaneously reduced to ashes.

The frame of the umbrella isn't exactly ordinary. The ribs are readily detachable and I took off all but two of them. The remaining two can be operated as usual by the sliding ring on the central rod. A length of silk thread is attached to this ring in such a manner that the ring can be slid up and down by the thread. This causes the two ribs to raise and lower.

IN ADDITION, a pencil-shaped cigarette lighter with automatic mechanism is attached to the central rod up near the tip. This is concealed, usually, by the cover. A second silk thread operates the lighter. Finger-rings tied to each of these threads enable me to operate them readily. The central rod of the frame is very ingenious, for it is made of telescoping sections of tubing painted dead black. The whole central rod can thus be expanded to the length of about twelve feet, forming what the fake spirit mediums call a "reaching rod." This is very convenient for making a ghost walk.

I draped the white silk cover, now expanded to the size of a small sheet, over the two ribs of the umbrella. A pull on one of the silk cords raises the ribs, causing the "ghost" to flap its silken wings as I've been told some ghosts are in the habit of doing. Expanding the reaching rod, I could lie flat on my back, apparently a helpless old man tied hand and foot, and make my ghost perform at a distance of twelve or more feet from me.

I lay there on the floor, listening to what went on in the next room. I could hear Tiny Tim's shrill voice above the voices of the two toughs. Tim was saying that his two captors could go to a warmer climate. He was denying emphatically that he was a police spy.

"Listen, yah little squirt," one of the men threatened, "how'd you like to have your arm twisted off, huh? When we said give, we meant give."

I thought it was time for the Ghost to intervene.

CHAPTER XXII

ESCAPE

CERTAIN MUSCLES in my throat drew tight. From my parted lips sounded the rollicking ghoulish laughter of the Ghost. At the same time I extended the umbrella-reaching-rod with the white silk cloth draped over the movable arms. Two fingers of my left hand were in the rings that controlled the silk threads that made the white silk put on its surprising performance.

In the room outside, there was an interval of silence. Then a man's hoarse voice asked:

"What was that?"

"Somebody laughing," came the answer.

"But where? The old man in there?"

"That wasn't an old man. That was—"

I didn't hear the rest because I gave out with more ghoulish laughter. In the next room, a man cursed and strode to the door of my prison. He unlocked it, swung it wide. Light falling through the open door was sufficient to barely illuminate my prone figure, but the whiteness of the "spirit" I operated stood out clearly.

I made the spirit flap. The man in the door turned, saw the white thing that danced twelve feet from me. He jerked out a gun, fired a shot. The spirit soared toward him and the Ghost's laughter screamed.

The second man pushed through the door, took one look, cried out hoarsely. He too pulled a gun, tried a shot. I jerked the second thread which fired the cigarette lighter under the magnesium treated cloth. There was a blinding flash of light. The two men ducked their heads. And as my dancing spirit vanished in the blast of flame, I swept the reaching-rod across to the door and used it to slam the door shut behind them.

In the total darkness, the ventriloquism of the Ghost is his best weapon. The laughter echoed from every corner as I got to my feet, pulled my gun from its gimmick. The laughter drew fire from one of the crooks, but his shot struck the wall yards from the source of my laughter. Gun-flame targeted the man and I fired two quick shots and moved swiftly toward the door.

It was a break that at least one of my slugs struck the man. As Ned Standish always says, I'm not the world's best shot. I heard the man strike the floor. His companion beat me to the door, yanked it open. He twisted in the doorway and tried a panicky shot back into the room. He was nearly as lucky as I, for I felt the bullet jerk at my sleeve.

I didn't retaliate. The man was on the run and I didn't think he'd stop in a hurry. What I wanted was to get to Tiny Tim and then have a little time to look around the pet shop in search of a clue.

I heard the man race up the steps, heard the door slam. And I went out into the room where Tiny Tim Terry was tied to the top of a small table. He looked at me, his baby face screwed up into a knot.

"It's about time, Ghost. About time."

I took out my knife and cut him loose.

A QUICK search of the shop revealed nothing that could be construed as evidence. The man I had shot at was dead, one of my slugs through the center of his forehead. I picked Tim up under my arm and carried him up the steps and out the front door of the shop. Across the street, Merry was waiting for us with the motor of the car running. We piled into the front seat with her and got going.

Merry looked at Tim. The little man was shaking all over with excitement, groping in his pocket for one of his enormous cigars.

"I got to quit smoking," he said, as he lighted up. "It's bad for my health. In fact, it pretty near ended my career. As soon as I got out of the trunk of the car which those two mugs were riding in, I skipped across the street to call you, George. They must have glimmed me from the pet shop.

"I needed a smoke bad, so while I was calling you in the store across the street, I lighted a cigar. Pretty soon, the two mugs came in, put a gun on the proprietor, mobbed me in the phone booth. I'm sorry, George. I shouldn't have broken the rules like that."

"Sorry I haven't time to give you the bawling out you deserve for taking such chances," I said. "Let me off up here at the corner, Merry. I want to call the cops."

"You should have captured some of the men and put them on the grid. Or griddle or grill," Merry said to me.

I shook my head.

"They don't know who their chief is. He wouldn't wear a mask around them if they did. Besides, there's one of the gang tied up in a crate at the back of the house. I'll have the police pick him up and let them do the grilling," I smiled down at Merry. "Or maybe it's griddle or grid."

It was a funny thing, but Merry's "grid, griddle, grill," kept running through my head like the strain of a popular song.

I got out near a shabby lower east side hotel and Merry and Tim went on with the car. From a booth in the hotel, I contacted Ned Standish and told him about the business at the Oliver Street pet shop.

"You'd better send some men to clean up and stop up the hole so the rats can't get back. Not that the brain behind this mob would ever think of using the same place again."

"I wish you'd come around where I could talk to you, Ghost," Standish said. "You see, we've picked up the lisping man. We got him on ice—in the morgue."

WHEN I stepped through the door of that gloomy building on the north side of Bellevue Hospital grounds, close to midnight, I was in my plainclothes sergeant's guise. I went directly to the room in the morgue which Medical Examiner Robert Demarest calls his own. Demarest himself admitted me, and I knew by his greeting that he was either alone or that only Standish was with him.

"How's ghosting?" he asked.

I stepped into the room and went over to shake hands with Standish. The commissioner looked a little grizzled about the chops. His hard gray eyes seemed to have sunk farther back in his head. His black mustache looked a little ragged.

"Don't think you've got the brains of this outfit in your morgue, even if he does lisp," I said at once.

"Who said he lisped—the brains, I mean?" Standish asked.

"I said so," I informed him. "He was talking with me a couple of hours ago."

Standish plumped out his cheeks and let the air explode out of them.

"Then why in hell didn't you—" he stopped.

"Sorry, George," he said. "This thing is getting the old man down. I suppose if you could have brought Mr. Brains in with you, you would have."

I nodded. "I was hampered by a few yards of clothesline and too many people looking on. Too many guns, too."

I told them of what Merry and Tim had discovered about Mrs. Kurtzner and about the adventure at the pet shop.

"Get Mrs. Kurtzner and put her on the fire," Demarest suggested.

"You mean the grid, griddle, or grill," I said.

Demarest looked at me as though he thought I was crazy. I didn't bother to deny it.

"Mrs. Kurtzner," I said, "is perfectly clean. She's got that appearance, anyway. You can't do much about her if she says she was robbed, and I expect the robbery has been reported at Headquarters by now. You can bet there was some pretty good evidence left behind to prove, in the eyes of the law, that she had been robbed. You couldn't get to first base with a case against her, and you know it."

"I'm not disputing that," Standish said. "Want to see our lisping man? He's the chap with whom your pal Joe Harper had a run-in over in Hoboken. His name's E.L. Long and he died resisting arrest. He left Hoboken and came over here, tried again to get medical attention and the doctor was smart enough to get word to the cops."

We went out into the refrigerator room and Demarest readily found the proper crypt and opened the door. He hauled the dead man out on the roller slab and I looked down into the face of the corpse. And I could see where Joe Harper, his head reeling from the gun barrel blow he had received, might have thought this man was Leonard Van Sickle, especially just after discovering one of Van Sickle's suits in the closet of the Long house in Hoboken.

"It's too bad Long died," the commissioner said. "We might have got something out of him about the identity of the man behind these suicides."

DEMAREST SHOVED the body back into its crypt and closed the door.

"I wonder if Long knew who his boss was?" he mused.

I shook my head. "Perhaps Tanko knows, because Tanko is the brain's strong-arm man. But so far as Long or Patsy Moore or Arnold Smock or any of the rest go, you'll find they don't know who their chief is."

We walked back to Demarest's office, and there pulled up chairs around the desk, had a drink, and lighted cigars. We did some summing-up.

"We're stalled," Ned Standish said tiredly. "We can't even establish murder."

"We can," Demarest disagreed. "We've got circumstantial evidence to prove that Van Sickle didn't intend to commit suicide. The stuff that the Ghost and Joe Harper have dug up would indicate that Van Sickle, under the name of Fabian Deeming, was going to cash in on some stock and run off to Europe with the Kurtzner woman. On the Max Gerrich case, I'll admit we're stuck. There's nothing but that business of Latin-deviation words in his suicide note to indicate that he might have written it at someone's dictation. And the murder of Jonathan Marvin—" Demarest shrugged.

"I suggest concentration on the death of the lisping man," I said. "And I mean Leonard Van Sickle. We can prove *that* was murder."

Ned Standish wriggled in his chair, looked from Demarest to me. He was frowning.

"This may be an idiotic question, but have we decided that Van Sickle is dead?"

"Beyond a shadow of a doubt!" Demarest snapped. "The man scraped up off the sidewalk in front of the Cronner was Van Sickle. If George says the master mind lisps, why then there just has to be a third lisping man somewhere."

"That'th tho," I said, lisping, and Ned Standish darted a glance at me and opened his mouth slowly.

"I get it," he said.

"Anybody can lisp," I said. "The only really dumb play the chief criminal has made, he made tonight. He didn't investigate the old man with the umbrella thoroughly enough. I mean yours truly, of course. If he had killed me, I'd have gone into the big black elsewhere thinking that the murderer was pretty smart. There's only one reason he put on that lisping act tonight. He read in the papers that Van Sickle was believed to be alive. He thought that if he lisped in my presence and then didn't kill me, I'd go out of the pet shop and tell the cops that the brains of the business was Leonard Van Sickle. Van Sickle is dead and I know who killed him."

DEMAREST RAISED one of his sleepy eyelids and glared at me.

"Would you mind being more specific?"

"Gladly. I've now got three points to go on. First of all, the murderer had to be a man who was in the Cronner Hotel the night Van Sickle was pushed out of the window. Our murderer was in the hotel that night.

"Second, the murderer left behind him a material clue of such importance that he sent Tanko back to the Van Sickle suite to get it."

"You mean that crazy little spiral of wire?" the commissioner asked.

"Yes. I think I know what that clue is and who it belongs to. The third point is in the nature of a question. Tanko knew me as the Ghost when I was wearing the disguise of Dr. Stacey. How did he know? Answer that one and you've got the whole thing in a nutshell."

"It's in your nutshell, maybe," Standish said, "but I'm damned if it's in mine."

The man jerked a
gun and fired—

"I say I know who the guilty party is," I went on, "but I'm not announcing him because I haven't as yet got enough proof to stand up in court. And that's what you want."

"You might give us the killer's name anyway, just so we can write it in our diaries," Demarest said drily.

"Your list of suspects is as long as mine," I said. "Arnold Smock, Theo Quinn, Elmer Tanko, Lucretia Kurtzner, a blonde named Miss Rice, a private-detective named Ken Vickers, Taylor Owens, Hugo Wayne, Patsy Moore—"

"Oh, let it go," Demarest said.

"One of them fits the picture," I said. "And the killer's scheme is so perfect that if you pinched him he'd have an even chance of breaking Standish for false arrest. Worse, if you pinched him, there would be no guarantee that his murder-machine couldn't go right on functioning."

The phone on Demarest's desk rang. The medical examiner reached for it lazily and then passed the instrument to Standish. Apparently, it was Standish's secretary Hadley on the wire. We heard Standish say: "Okay, Hadley, you have him call me here at once. If he's not one of those cranks, I'll talk with him."

Standish hung up. A man by the name of Hurst had been trying to get hold of him. Hurst claimed to have an entirely new angle on the Van Sickle affair, according to Hadley. Hadley had checked on Hurst, found that he was David John Hurst, who had once held a responsible position in Wall Street and was a man of considerable weight even today.

WE HADN'T long to wait before the phone rang again. Standish answered, smothered the transmitter against his chest and whispered to us:

"It's Hurst."

The commissioner listened for a moment and then said that he would be right over. He hung up and turned to me.

"This Hurst chap says he's got the McCoy. He says he knows what kind of a scheme Van Sickle and Marvin were trapped in, because he's in the same sort of a trap himself. He says he can see through the scheme and will tell the whole business, point his fingers and name names. He's got a place out on West End Avenue, wants me to come out right away. I think this man is sincere. He sounds it. Will you come along, George?"

"Of course," I said.

Demarest got up and reached for his hat.

"I might as well go too," he said gloomily. "If Hurst doesn't need the medical examiner now, he'll need one by the time we get there."

Demarest was a little bit wrong, but not much.

CHAPTER XXIII

MASKED DEATH

HURST HAD a place in the eighties—a small but comfortable-looking brick house. We parked out in front, went to the door. A tall, distinguished-looking man with piercing blue eyes opened the door for us.

"Mr. Hurst?" Standish inquired pleasantly.

The man nodded. "Come in, Commissioner." We went into a nicely appointed living room and Standish introduced Demarest and me. I thought that Hurst turned a shade paler when he discovered that Demarest was the medical examiner. It must have been a little bit like having an undertaker offer you his business card.

We made ourselves comfortable in chairs. Hurst, sitting very straight upon a stool, lighted his cigarette and held it awkwardly between his fingers.

"How much life insurance do you carry, Mr. Hurst?" I asked abruptly.

He looked at me, startled.

"Why—why, that's exactly what I called you here to talk about. I carry two hundred thousand dollars' worth. If I were to die tomorrow, the proceeds would be divided equally between my daughter and a charity organization—"

"Have you a daughter?" I cut in.

"I have. She lives in Chicago—"

"All right," I said. "I believe you have something extremely important to tell us. I perceive, however, that you are under the strain of a considerable fear, and so may tend more or less unconsciously to hold back certain things. Suppose, therefore, you let me give you my conception of the matter—in other words let me tell you what I imagine you were about to tell me, checking me where you find me wrong in any particular. That will make it easier for you. Agreed?"

"Agreed," said Hurst, and he relaxed a little. "What is your conception of the matter?"

"It's an insurance swindle," I answered promptly. "You know it to be such, and so does your daughter who is to be part-beneficiary. The charity you speak of is simply a myth and you also know it to be such. It is simply the collector for the criminal who is behind the whole scheme. The idea is that the criminal who plans the hoax should collect half of the total insurance, and that you should collect the rest of it through your daughter who has agreed to the plan. Right so far?"

"Right," said Hurst, wetting his lips. "Go on."

"According to the criminals, your death is to be faked. That is what they have told you. Your daughter will collect one hundred thousand dollars and pass it over to you. The criminals, through this fake charity, will collect the balance as payment for originating, devising and carrying through the scheme. Right so far?"

"Right," said Hurst.

AN EXCLAMATION broke from Standish. He was staring at Hurst curiously.

"I wouldn't think that anybody, much less a man of your obvious intelligence, would fall for a scheme like that," he said.

"You're wrong," Hurst said. "A lot of men would. A lot of men have stinted themselves all their lives, paying money into life insurance companies, and all the time wishing that they could enjoy the full face amount of their policies while still alive. That's why they'd fall for it, that's why the plan's a natural. Only"—he paused—"I didn't fall for it. I didn't because I saw through it, saw what was beneath it, hidden from the sight of those whom the criminal devisors of the scheme approached as prospects."

"What did you see?" I asked.

Hurst smiled a little sadly.

"I think you already know what I saw and don't need me to tell you. You seem to know so much, perhaps more than I do. But since you ask, I'll tell you:

"The idea was brought to me not by the criminals themselves but by a friend of mine, Stephen Perkins. *He* was completely sold on it and had readily agreed to fall in with the criminal scheme.

"I listened to Perkins. I was tempted. Then, all at once, I saw something in it that frightened me."

"You saw murder," I prompted.

"Yes," he said, almost in a whisper. His voice rose. "But I didn't think that what I saw was possible. Then came Leonard Van Sickle's death. The thought came back to me, and I felt certain that Van Sickle had been sucked into a scheme from which he himself would never benefit."

"You thought in other words that Van Sickle was really and truly dead," I said.

"Yes," he answered.

At this point I asked Standish if this Stephen Perkins had turned up on the "suicide" list yet. He said "no."

"Why did you agree to the idea?" Demarest snapped at Hurst. "You say you're caught in the same trap, yet you suspected almost from the very beginning that the criminals were not going to be on the level with their 'clients.'"

"Van Sickle was a friend of mine," Hurst said. "So I told Perkins that I'd be glad to listen to the particulars of the proposition. A man by the name of Tanko came to me and we had a talk. I seemed to agree. Actually, I was just doing a bit of amateur detective work. I hope you believe me when I say that."

"Naturally, we do," I said. "We certainly don't think that a man in his right mind would enter a scheme like that just for the sake of making himself a candidate for murder. But I don't think you were very sensible—"

I BROKE off. Hurst had gotten to his feet. He had been sitting facing the door. The commissioner, Demarest and I were in chairs facing Hurst. Hurst's eyes stared glassily at the door. His mouth worked wordlessly. I got out of my chair, at the same time drawing my gun. I turned.

A masked man stood in the door, an automatic in his hand. Beside him was a masked hood of similar build to the one who had escaped me at the pet shop, and this one was nursing a tommy-gun.

Demarest on my left and the commissioner on my right, both stood up and raised their hands. The masked man said harshly: "Drop it," meaning my gun.

But I didn't. He thought I did, but I didn't. A snap of my right wrist and I vanished my gun into the pouch attached to the left side lining of my coat.

"All right," the masked man said. And that was a signal to the man with the machine gun. As Tanko advanced toward me, the deadly chatter of the tommy-gun cut through the taut silence within the room. I saw Hurst curl up like the leaves of a sensitive plant, spin half around on his heels, hit the floor. I released my right-pocket gun down onto the floor over to my left and to Demarest's feet. My knife appeared in my right hand as I rushed the masked man. The masked man's gun blazed, but my left hand had already jammed it upward. I felt the hot flame from the muzzle across my face, drove my right hand forward to sink the knife blade into the masked man.

I never quite knew where my blade got him, because at that moment somebody shot out the light. It was Standish who did for the light

I caught the masked man's wrist.

thereby preventing a slaughter. Anyway I left my best knife in the masked man. And when the black-out came, the masked man eeled out of my grasp and opened up with his gun again.

He was going into retreat, marked by a blaze of gunfire to the door. I knew my shooting wouldn't stop him unless I was lucky. As for Demarest, I think he was somewhere behind a chair, popping shots at the man with the tommy-gun.

No sooner was the knife I had used on the masked man out of the grasp of my right hand, than I retrieved the gun I had vanished with my left. I think the hood with the machine gun had a grudge against Ned Standish because his tommy-gun was riddling every piece of furniture behind which a man could have hidden.

Then I saw Standish come out from behind a Japanese screen. He moved across a window and was dimly illuminated by the night glow for just a moment, his heavy jaw jutting as fiercely as the Police Positive his right hand carried. He tried for the masked man as that individual went through the door, drew machine gun fire, and flattened to crawl

behind a davenport. And then I lost track of the commissioner and Demarest.

I went through the door after the masked killer. I saw him legging across the lawn toward a parked car. He tried a shot over his shoulder that came close, but I kept going.

THE KILLER had a man at the wheel of his car and the motor was going. Almost as soon as he struck the running board, the car rocketed from the curb. I sprang into the police car and kicked at the starter. The starter-motor whined. I leaned forward, watching through the windshield as the car which carried the killer turned west at the corner. The starter-motor of the police car still whined. And I knew that was that. They had pulled a portion of the ignition cable before entering the Hurst house.

I had a pretty clear idea of the "what" and "why" of the tragedy so recently enacted. Hurst had been slated to die. It was that which had drawn Tanko—for I was sure it had been Tanko—to the Hurst home. Not our presence, for he had had no way of knowing that we would be there.

But, reaching the house, he had seen the police car. He had leaped to the quick and correct conclusion that Hurst was spilling the beans. He had seen only one course open to him—to kill! To kill quickly and thoroughly and unanimously, all of us!

Well, he had failed, except for poor Hurst who had been the victim of his own desire to play detective.

I went back to the house. There was no sound of gunfire—only the chatter of neighbors knocked from their sleep by the thunder of our warfare. Lights came on in the Hurst living room. I went through the open door.

The man with the machine gun still had his weapon. His arms were folded around it and his legs were drawn up under him. His head was twisted around so that I could see one side of it, and two fatal wounds showed.

Ned Standish was standing over the man, his smoking revolver in his hand. With all due apologies to his successors, I don't suppose New York ever had a police commissioner who was as thoroughly a cop as Ned Standish. The man could stand up under gunplay or physical punishment, always the same iron man, hitting hard, shooting with the same accuracy that had won him a medal when he had gone through his first police training.

Demarest was sitting on the arm of a chair, his chin in one hand.

"Some men," he said, "are born crazy. Others get that way, meaning you, Ghost. You left a nice, gentlemanly profession like magic to play in a slaughter house."

I didn't say anything. All this reminded me of a game of chess. We were taking the criminals piece by piece, but the checkmate was still a good distance away.

CHAPTER XXIV

MAN ABOUT TO DIE

"WHAT NOW?" asked Standish.

We were both wondering if the criminals would have the colossal nerve to try to collect the insurance money made available to them after the wanton murder of David Hurst. I didn't think they would. Standish did.

"They'd have the nerve, only the insurance company won't pay," he said. "Yet they'd have a legal case if we couldn't establish a connection between them and Hurst's murders."

"True," I said. "It is an established judicial principle that no man may be permitted to profit by his own wrong. So we've got to pin the wrong where it belongs. The charity beneficiary is a fraud, of course, but the named beneficiary is probably the secretary of some charitable institution."

"Well, you can lay a bet," Standish said grimly, "that if the money is paid out, we'll grab the collector of it."

"Who won't know the name of the brains behind this business," I said.

I went to the rectory and there I found Joe Harper asleep on the couch. He woke up when I came in to tell me that a dentist by the name of MacKay had been calling for Dr. Stacey most of the evening. Joe had taken the telephone number. Could it be that the advertisement I had inserted, in an effort to find the dentist who had pulled Van Sickle's teeth, was going to bring me something besides trouble? I telephoned MacKay at once.

The dentist explained that the reason he had not answered my ad earlier was that he hadn't seen it. He had been called out of town to attend a funeral. Looking over an accumulation of newspapers on his return, he had found the ad. Could he still earn the hundred dollars?

I told him that there would be a check for him in the mail tomorrow if he would answer my questions over the phone. Needless to say it would be a cashiers check to protect my anonymity. I did not need the information anymore but I had inserted the ad, so it was a kind of promise I felt obligated to keep.

MacKay told me what I had already inferred—that Van Sickle had come to him voluntarily and had asked him to extract all his teeth. MacKay had argued against it, because the teeth were good, but he had needed the money and Van Sickle had been insistent.

Anyway, I now had enough material to reconstruct the crime of the murder of the lisping Leonard Van Sickle. I thought, I could do fairly well with reconstruction of the other murders as well, though I would have to play on my imagination a little.

MY NEXT job was to visit Mr. Stephen Perkins, the man named by David Hurst as another prospective victim of the criminal's suicide-murder scheme.

At three o'clock in the morning, I found Stephen Perkins in the lower half of a Bronx two-family house, sleeping the sleep of the just. I was still wearing the disguise that identified me as Sergeant Hammill and the official shield that went with it, so that when Perkins staggered to the door in his pajamas, his eyes puffy from sleep, there was really nothing he could do but let me in to see him.

"The police," he said. "Yes, the police. J-just wait until I put on my robe."

I followed him into his bedroom where he put on a bathrobe, then I told him to sit down on the bed. He was a tall man, with blonde hair that was becoming a bit sandy now that he had reached middle age. There were many wrinkles about his eyelids and his prominent nose. His mouth was lax-lipped. I felt that I could do a pretty good job of impersonating him.

Perkins sat down gingerly on the edge of the bed and I stood in front of him.

"You got yourself into what appears to be an insurance swindle, didn't you?" I said without further preliminaries.

"Wh-what do you mean?" he asked, fingering the bed clothes.

"You're a damned poor liar," I told him. "Hurst told us what you were up to before he died."

"Hurst? David Hurst—dead?"

I gave him the details of Hurst's death and smeared it on pretty thick. He needed something to wake him up.

"And," I added, "among other bright men who thought they were going to have a good time on their own life insurance, are Jonathan Marvin and Leonard Van Sickle. Perhaps you've been reading about *their* 'suicides.'"

"B-but they're not really dead," Perkins objected. I could see more clearly than ever before, how anyone who would permit himself to be victimized by the same plot would have to believe that.

Perkins bit his lip. "You shouldn't have made me say that," he said in a frightened voice. "They said they'd kill me if I breathed a word—"

"I know," I interrupted. "But what *you* don't know is that they'd kill you anyway. Would you care to avoid filling a grave for a while, Mr. Perkins? If so, you'd better tell me exactly what the plan was."

"Well," Perkins began slowly, "a man came to me and wondered if he couldn't sell me more insurance. He was a tall man with a scar on his chin."

My friend Tanko again.

"I OBJECTED on the grounds that I was having trouble keeping up the insurance I had, and that, having been left pretty much alone in life, I could see no reason why I should provide insurance that would enable my spendthrift nephews to have a good time after I was dead. Besides, I wanted to have a little fun myself."

"There was a woman, eh?" I asked suggestively.

"Yes," he said. "But she isn't mixed up in this. She couldn't be. She's too good and beautiful. Just a harmless widow.

"The proposition made me by this man was extremely attractive. I have about a hundred and fifty thousand dollars in life insurance. It was suggested that I change the beneficiaries on my policies. Seventy-five thousand was to go to this widow lady who would hold it for me until we could skip the country together. The rest of the insurance money was to go to the son of a man I had never heard of. This man, I was told, would commit suicide in my place and in such a manner that his features would be completely obliterated. In other words, the body of this man would be identified as Stephen Perkins."

"And," I interrupted, you were supposed to collect through the widow, while the criminals collected through the son of the man who killed himself in your place. And you really thought that somebody would be willing to commit suicide to accommodate you?"

Perkins nodded.

"Certainly. The man was in poor health and was going to die in a few weeks anyway. He had no way of supporting his son."

"Didn't you ask the man with the scarred chin to show you this suicide proxy?" I asked.

Perkins shook his head. "I didn't bother. I went confidentially to my friend Hurst and talked the matter over with him. Hurst said he'd like to get in on the scheme, so I thought it was all right."

"Now Hurst is dead," I said. "Hurst saw there was something crooked somewhere and wanted to play amateur detective. But Mr. Leonard Van Sickle, with his love of details, although he fell for the scheme too, demanded to see the man who was to be proxy for him in death."

And that, I knew, and the reader has perhaps guessed, was the reason Van Sickle had had his teeth removed. Demanding to see this man who was going to commit suicide for him, the criminals had brought out Mr. Long, Joe Harper's lisping assailant from Hoboken. Van Sickle saw that there was a superficial resemblance, but also noted that Long didn't have any teeth. So that was the reason Van Sickle had had his teeth removed.

Van Sickle had carried the teeth away from the dentist's with him, hiding them in his safe, keeping them just as he had kept his removed appendix, as though he could not bear to part with anything that had once belonged to him.

I looked squarely at Perkins.

"Didn't it ever occur to you that after you had changed your insurance policies to the two new beneficiaries, that all the criminals had to do to collect was to murder you?"

PERKINS BLINKED his wrinkled eyelids.

"I—I never thought. I— Good Lord!"

"They had to write a suicide note, I suppose?" I said. "Get it for me." Perkins went to his desk, took out the note. He brought it back to me in trembling hands.

"You—you don't suppose that my friend, that sweet lady—"

"The widow, you mean? Van Sickle was going to run off with a widow too. Be that as it may, the gang still stood to collect seventy-five grand and not by any proxy-suicide arrangement either. To make sure that the body was identified as yours, *you,* and you alone, would be the one to die."

"You—you mean they would murder me?" he gasped.

"Of course. They'd do it subtly so it would look like suicide, plant this note beside your body, and leave you alone. Very much alone in a lot of blackness."

Perkins shuddered. Then he stood up and grasped the lapels of my coat.

"What can I do to avoid this? You've got to tell me! You've got to help me!"

"That's what I'm here for," I said. "I'm taking you out of this house at once and secretly. This time, there'll be a proxy for the suicide act."

I didn't tell him so, but I was going to be that proxy.

CHAPTER XXV

I DIG MY GRAVE

E **ARLY, BEFORE** dawn in fact, Perkins was out of the house and off to spend some time in Tim Terry's apartment. And before dawn I took Glenn Saunders, my double and assistant, into the Perkins house in the Bronx and explained some changes I wanted made in the place.

That was high-handed of me, but Perkins owned the place so I didn't care much. After all, it was a small price to pay for saving his life.

Glenn Saunders, skilled artisan that he is, was to install a trap door in the floor of the living room and make certain changes in the lighting of the place. And in spite of his likeness to George Chance, no one would have mistaken him for me. In carpenters' overalls and dark glasses, his face smudged with dirt, he was pretty well disguised.

It was now time to double-check my deductions by having a talk with the manager of the Hotel Cronner and also the proprietor of a little shop on East Forty-Fifth Street.

As soon as I was through with this double-checking, which I am keeping under my hat for the present, I visited Police Headquarters and talked with Ned Standish. I told him exactly what I planned to do, and what cooperation I expected from him.

I then spent some time with Stephen Perkins in Tim Terry's apartment, carefully watching the man, memorizing his characteristic movements, every line of his face and figure, paying particular attention to the way he talked. I took a few snapshots of Perkins, had them developed at the police laboratory. After that I was ready to step out of the shoes of Sergeant Hammill.

THAT NIGHT, the combing of my hair changed, its color changed, too, with powder that made it appear sandy, I moved into the duplex of Stephen Perkins. With putty and plumpers, I had built the contours of my face to match those of Perkins. I had matched the color of his complexion, added penciled wrinkles about my eyes. Alone in Perkins' house, I talked to myself, but in Perkins' voice, until to speak as Perkins spoke was second nature.

And I was perfectly willing to meet any sort of "suicide" that Tanko and the master mind of the criminal gang had planned. If death was to come with bullets, I was prepared with a bullet proof vest. If I was to drink poison, I had the proper magical cup to drink it from, for it was made after the manner of a magician's Foo-can for vanishing liquids. I even had a knife with a telescoping blade which I thought might come in handy.

Finally, beneath my arms, close inside the armpits and held there with pieces of adhesive tape, were small wooden balls, one ball in each armpit. These balls had a most important place in my scheme of things.

I inspected the workmanship of Glenn Saunders. It was, as usual, perfect. No magician's stage ever was rigged up better, with concealed traps, mirrors, and ultra-violet lighting. On the bed, in the bedroom was a special sheet, a double affair with flexible ribs of metal concealed inside.

Robert Demarest was taken into the secret of the sheet and he knew exactly how it was to be used.

In a rented room across the street from the Perkins place, Merry White waited for a signal from me. Joe Harper was not far distant, either. And in a closet in the hall between living room and kitchen in the Perkins house, were black robes and carefully constructed death masks. There was a death mask made with a photograph of the late Max Gerrich as a model, another made in the image of Leonard Van Sickle, a third modeled after Jonathan Marvin, a fourth made up to resemble the face of E.L. Long of Hoboken. A fifth mask was made from the dead face of David John Hurst. And a sixth mask had been modeled after the living face of *Stephen Perkins,* whom I was impersonating!

And with all these preparations, nothing happened the first night that I was alone in the Perkins house.

The next day came and went, and the night followed. Nothing happened. And the next day Commissioner Standish sent me a letter, for we didn't think it was smart to communicate by phone from the Perkins house.

"Of all the brass-lined guts!" Standish's note read. "They're going to try and collect on the Hurst killing. Half of Hurst's policies are payable to a man named Paget who is secretary of a beneficent society for the protection of oppressed children in the Far East. Paget, who looks pious as a monk, has put through his claim. What's to be done?"

NOW THAT I was established in the identity of Perkins, living in Perkins' house, it would have been extremely risky for me to leave the house in any other identity. For all I knew, the criminals might be watching me twenty-four hours a day. So I left the house, walking as Stephen Perkins would have walked, looking like Stephen Perkins, my lips drooping dumbly as his drooped. I went to a nearby drugstore and into the phone booth at the back. I gave Ned Standish a ring and got him on the second trial.

"Listen, Ned," I told him, "this is going to be okay. You just keep the chief suspects on tap where you can get them quickly. About this chap Paget, just keep an eye on him. Have Vickers let his check come through. And when Paget cashes, grab him. Hustle him and the money down to Police Headquarters. Just tell him you're checking on him to see that his charity is legitimate. But you don't check on him. What you do is get the money away from him, see?"

"No," Standish objected.

"You will when I get through. Do you know what *naphthionate* is?"

"No," Standish said, "unless it's something to clean clothes with."

"It isn't. You talk to Demarest about it. It's a powder. All you have to do is get Demarest alone with that money for a little while. Have him dust every bill lightly with naphthionate. When he gets that done, you pack up the money and return it to Paget with profuse apologies. Add Paget to your list of suspects, but don't watch him so close that he won't have a chance to pay the money over to his big boss. The naphthionate won't come off. Once it gets on the hands, it's scarcely visible and mighty hard to wash off. Now do what I say and stop worrying."

That done, I bought a cigar and went back to the Perkins house. The rest of the day I waited. All this watchful waiting was driving me batty, but there wasn't anything I could do about it. The move I had told Standish to make would convince the criminals that their plan was fool proof. They would certainly make an attempt to kill the man they thought was Perkins.

Night came. At eight o'clock, the Perkins phone rang. I picked it up and answered in Perkins' voice. Elmer Tanko's voice came out of the receiver.

"Mr. Perkins, if you've got some time tonight, I'd like to talk over our little plan with you. A few matters to settle. When will it be convenient?"

"About ten o'clock," I said. "I'll be expecting you."

He didn't know how much I'd be expecting him!

I hung up and went at once to the front of the house where I stood in the window and lighted a cigarette. In the house across the street, where Merry White waited, a second story window shade went down. Everything was okay. Merry had my signal. I had dug my grave, but anybody who thought I was going to stay in it was wide off the mark.

BY THE time Tanko arrived at the Perkins house, the police had moved—not with the screaming of sirens and the thump of heavy feet, but with all the subtlety and silence of approaching shadows.

It's a popular conception that the police of New York are dumb. They aren't. I've worked with them and I know. I know of no more efficient group of men in the country than the New York police.

Tanko came in smiling. He shook hands with me, and there wasn't a shadow of a doubt but that he thought I was Perkins. I took him into the living room and pointed out a chair for him near the only lamp in the room that was lighted. I took my place in a chair opposite him.

In the floor at my feet was the cleverly concealed trap door which Glenn Saunders had arranged at my instruction. At my side was a table and on it the magician's Foo cup from which I intended to "drink" poison, if that was the design that had been arranged for my death.

In the dim light, Tanko's face was as evil as Satan's. That scar on his skin stood out lividly like a second mouth on some sort of a pagan idol. His close-set dark eyes glowed like polished lumps of jet.

"All set, Perkins, for the cleverest swindle of the age?" he said.

"I—I'd rather you wouldn't refer to it as a swindle," I said in Perkins' timid voice. "It makes me feel like a criminal."

Tanko laughed. "You're nothing of the sort. It's about time these insurance companies got some sort of a trimming. They've fattened enough. Tomorrow you'll be seventy-five thousand dollars richer. You have your suicide note all ready?"

I nodded. Tanko told me to get it for him. I went to Perkins' desk and got out the suicide note I had seen before. When I turned around, Tanko had an automatic in his hand. At least, it appeared to be an automatic. He was holding it with the muzzle against his right eye and was pulling the trigger with his thumb. The gun emitted a buzzing sound. I hadn't looked for anything like this. I asked him what he was doing.

"The damnedest thing I've ever seen," Tanko said, laughing. "I got it in a novelty shop; this afternoon." He dropped the gun into his pocket. "You look into the barrel and pull the trigger. There's a battery in the handle which illuminates the picture of a bubble dancer. And does she dance!"

Tanko gave me a significant wink.

My heart beat a little faster. If I asked to see the gun, he would switch the toy in his pocket for a real gun. I would put it to my eye, pull the trigger, and then what? If I didn't ask to see it, or express some curiosity, Tanko's suspicions would be aroused. So I said:

"Let's see the gun. Some of these novelties are pretty clever."

TANKO SMILED, put his hand into his pocket. My left hand went to my own coat pocket and palmed a hollow rubber ball. Tanko passed me the gun.

"Just put the muzzle to your eye," he said, "pull the trigger and keep your eye open. Boy, oh boy, what a kick you'll get!"

I took the gun in my right hand, muzzle toward me. My thumb slipped into the trigger guard.

"It has the feel of a real gun, doesn't it?" I said.

Tanko admitted that it did. And I knew damned well it was a real gun. I was supposed to put it to my eye and pull the trigger. I stood up. Holding the gun with muzzle toward me, I raised it slowly....

CHAPTER XXVI

DEATH OF A GHOST

UP TO my heart the gun was when I "accidentally" pulled the trigger. The crash of the shot, the stab of gun flame, and I am certain that a look of surprise and pain passed over my features.

The look wasn't counterfeited. Up to that time, I had the impression that getting shot by a .32 caliber bullet while wearing a bullet proof vest would be something like getting hit with a paper wad. It was more like taking the kick of a mule. For just an instant, I thought I was knocked out. And I didn't dare go unconscious, because this show had to go on.

I twisted sideways. My right hand still clutched the gun. My left came up to my chest, squeezing on the hollow rubber ball. The rubber ball was filled with red stain closely resembling blood, and as I pressed it close to the hole the bullet had made in my coat, "blood" squeezed out between my fingers, I fell to the floor, writhed over onto my back, getting rid of the rubber ball in the upper breast pocket of my coat.

I let my eyelids sag a little, rolled up my eyeballs. Tanko dropped to his knee beside me.

"That wasn't the way it was supposed to go," he whispered. "But just so's you're dead... just so's I don't have to put another bullet in you." He laughed. "You damned dumb cluck!"

Tanko got the Perkins suicide note out of my coat pocket after he had pulled a silk glove over his hand. He put the note on the table beside the chair. Then he took my left wrist in his hand.

A smile of satisfaction spread slowly across his face. He could actually feel my pulse ebbing away into something imperceptible. It was one of the oldest tricks of the Hindu *fakirs*, who claim to be able to control the beat of their heart. Remember that under each armpit I had attached a small, hard ball. All I had to do to stop off the flow of blood through the artery that leads down through the arm, was to press the upper arm against my side so that the ball in the armpit cut off the flow of blood in that artery.

Tanko stood up. He was satisfied I was dead. He quietly left the house. Though he didn't know it at the time, he was quietly walking into the arms of the waiting police.

Tanko's career as a criminal was just about over.

I suppose I didn't alter my position for twenty minutes. Someone from the family in the upper part of the duplex summoned up enough courage after hearing the shot, came down, discovered my "corpse," took one look, called the police.

A group of homicide men came in answer to the man's call, and with them Robert Demarest to officially pronounce me dead. Demarest was nervous about the job. Maybe I looked too realistically dead with my eyes rolled back, fake blood all over the front of me, my jaw hanging open.

Demarest stood up after a bit of poking at me. And then the front door of the house opened and Commissioner Standish came in. He wasn't alone. Quietly, he had gone about rounding up our suspects and they filed in behind Standish, escorted by a uniformed cop.

HUGO WAYNE, the shady investment broker, was directly behind Standish. Following Wayne came Lucretia Kurtzner, as lovely and as perfectly possessed as ever. Behind Mrs. Kurtzner was Ken Vickers, a somewhat puzzled frown on his ordinarily smooth forehead. Taylor Owens, his face white, his potato-shaped nose purple, followed Vickers, his stubby pipe cold but gripped tightly between his teeth, his derby hat in his hand. Theo Quinn, fat, bald, pompous, followed Owens, and Quinn was mightily indignant about the whole thing.

"Nothing but a farce!" Quinn exclaimed. "A damned farce, Commissioner. I'll break you for this!"

And then he saw me, the corpse, and decided that it wasn't such a farce.

Behind Quinn was the blonde and beautiful Miss Rice, Taylor Owens' secretary. Arnold Smock, the insignificant-looking man who raised pigeons, followed. And Elmer Tanko, handcuffs on his wrists, brought up the rear somewhat involuntarily.

Standish and his men placed chairs for the suspects at one end of the room, facing the door of the hall that connected the living room and kitchen. The blonde Miss Rice sobbed into her handkerchief. Taylor Owens wriggled into his chair and groped in his pocket for matches which he didn't find. He sucked his cold pipe and it bubbled noisily.

"What's the meaning of all this?" Quinn demanded.

"This," Standish said, "is murder. One of you killed Stephen Perkins. Elmer Tanko may have been the instrument of murder, but another person planned it—the same person who plotted the deaths of Max Gerrich, Leonard Van Sickle, Jonathan Marvin, David Hurst. We're here to find out the truth."

"Commissioner," Hugo Wayne ventured, "you got me all wrong. I didn't have anything to do with this."

"Do—do we have to sit here and—look at that—that on the floor?" sobbed the blonde Miss Rice.

Taylor Owens reached over and patted her head in a fatherly manner.

"Demarest, you might cover the corpse with a sheet," Standish said.

Demarest went into the bedroom, came out with the gimmicked sheet. He spread it out over me, pressed it over my body from head to heels. I had chosen my place to "die" carefully. Because of the concealed ribs in the sheet, now bent to conform with my body, I could drop out from beneath the sheet and still it would appear that a human body was beneath the white cover.

Under the sheet, I tapped gently on the floor. It was a signal to Joe Harper, who had entered the basement of the house at the same time the police and the suspects had come in the front door. The trap beneath me opened swiftly and silently. I fell through to a soft mattress on the basement floor. I sat up, looked up through the trap. The mound of white sheet was undisturbed. In the dark basement, Joe Harper helped me to my feet.

"All set upstairs?" I whispered.

"All set," Joe answered. He, too, felt the tensity of the situation. He clipped words short in his nasal voice.

"Glenn and Merry are up there waiting for us. We're timed like a radio show. Let's get moving."

WE WENT quickly and quietly up the steps leading from the basement. Joe Harper was wearing a black robe that reached to his ankles. Merry and Glenn would be dressed the same way. There was a similar robe waiting for me on the kitchen table. While I was getting into it, no easy job in the darkness even with the help of Merry and Joe, I could hear Commissioner Standish talking to the suspects in the living room.

"You who are innocent," Standish was saying, "may wonder how these murders were accomplished. For they were murders, even though there has been every appearance of suicide. The whole idea behind the plot was to convince the victims that they would benefit by an insurance swindle, that a fake suicide would be arranged. In other words, the victims were convinced that their suicide would be accomplished by proxy so that they might collect on their own insurance and go on living under assumed names in some other part of the world.

"But this was no hoax on the insurance company. The joke was on those foolish men who sought to profit by agreeing to assist the criminals in the scheme. For at some convenient time after the victims had written their suicide notes, which they believed would fool the insurance company and the police into believing that they had killed themselves, the victims were either murdered by the criminals, or baited into unknowingly killing themselves.

"The beneficiary clause in their life insurance policies had been changed so that the criminals could collect after the victim's death. Not changed by any criminal means, understand, but the changes were made voluntarily by the victims themselves, who were led to believe that at least half of the entire amount paid on the policies would be returned into their hands after the faked death.

"Sometimes," Standish went on, "the criminals employed an attractive woman to lure the victims into making such an agreement—an agreement which amounted to a death warrant. We know that Mrs. Kurtzner worked such a scheme on Leonard Van Sickle."

"That's not true," Mrs. Kurtzner's voice said.

But you could tell she was much less calm than before.

Standish went on talking, and I stepped across the kitchen, opened a cupboard. In it Glenn Saunders had installed a small switchboard and a microphone. The switchboard operated lights in the living room. The microphone was connected with a loudspeaker concealed beneath the davenport in the living room.

This cupboard was not far from the hall which led from the kitchen to the living room. In this hall, Glenn had installed a full length mirror, so placed that anyone standing in the hall and in front of the mirror, would appear to be standing directly in the door connecting living room and hall.

IN THE closet in the hall, not far from where the mirror was, the death masks of the murder victims were waiting, so placed that they could be readily found in the dark. The masks had been treated with ultra-violet paint so that in darkness they would not be visible. This same ultra-violet paint, when subjected to ultra-violet light, is clearly visible. Needless to say, ultra-violet lamps had been installed in the little hall and also in the living room and could be controlled from the cupboard switchboard.

Merry, Glenn, and Joe, dressed in their dark robes, had crowded into the hall closet. Each waited his cue. And I was at the microphone, one hand on the switchboard.

In the middle of a sentence uttered by Commissioner Standish, I turned out every light in the house. Mrs. Kurtzner and Miss Rice screamed. Men cursed.

A copper warned: "Don't move, anybody. Every exit is covered. Try to get out and you'll be shot. Something must have gone wrong with the lights."

"That's true police reasoning for you," Theo Quinn said gruffly. "Something has gone wrong with the lights!"

Muscles in my throat tightened. I raised the microphone, uttered the ghoulish laugh that the criminal world has learned to recognize as that of the Ghost.

"My God!" Hugo Wayne said hoarsely. "The Ghost!"

And "My God!" Ken Vickers echoed in an awed whisper.

CHAPTER XXVII

DEAD MEN'S TALES

YAWPING INTO the microphone, my voice was charged with mockery.

"Don't bother to look behind you, Mr. Vickers. You couldn't see me. You don't *want* to see me, do you?" I laughed again. "Hello, Tanko. How do you and your boss like to be alone in the dark—with the Ghost? And alone with the spirits of the men you have murdered? They are here.

"Remember Max Gerrich, the old actor? He was too old to earn a living, but not too old to enjoy living. Not too old to be enticed into your insurance swindle with the hope of finishing his life in a bed of roses which you promised him. Bed of roses? That's a laugh. Bed of cold, clinging clay, shared with the worms. Take a look at him *now!*"

And that was Joe Harper's signal. Wearing the death mask of Max Gerrich, he stepped from the closet. As he did so, I pressed the switch that turned on the ultra-violet light in the hall. Black light, it is sometimes called, because ordinary objects cannot be seen in it. But the ghastly mask that Joe wore could be seen, because it had been treated with ultra-violet paint, used in many magical effects.

To those in the living room, it must have appeared that the dead Gerrich's face was floating in the air between the doorposts of the living room door, thanks to the angle at which Glenn Saunders had placed the mirror. Actually, Joe was in the hall, safely beyond the reach of bullets.

The object of all this was to strain the killer's nerves to the breaking point. Quickly, I changed my voice to something which I hoped would resemble the voice of Max Gerrich. I had never heard Gerrich speak, but I thought that in the voice of a "spirit" this wouldn't make much difference.

"I was Max Gerrich," I said. "You, *murderer*, came to me with a plan by which I could appear to die and yet go on living to enjoy at least half of the life insurance money which would be paid at my death. The other half was to go to you by an indirect route, in payment for inventing the plan. I was a little terrified at the whole idea of becoming involved in a crooked scheme. You asked me to write a note explaining my suicide, and I was so nervous I didn't know what to say. But you dictated what I was to write, and I wrote words which I ordinarily would not have used. Had it not been for those words, my murder would have gone undiscovered.

"For you murdered me. You took me by force to the railroad, threw my body in front of a midnight train. *You* are the man who plotted my death."

I switched off the ultra-violet light and this gave Joe a chance to vanish. Merry White stepped from the closet and she was wearing the death mask which had been molded from the face of E.L. Long. I turned on the ultra-violet and gave the Ghost's laugh into the microphone.

"REMEMBER THIS** man, Tanko? He landed in the morgue. He died resisting arrest because you involved him in your murder scheme.

"Long was the man presented to Van Sickle as a supposed proxy for Van Sickle's suicide. Van Sickle was cranky about details. When you told him you had found a man who would kill himself in Van Sickle's place, whose body could easily be mistaken for Van Sickle's, so that Van Sickle might collect on his own insurance, Van Sickle insisted upon seeing that proxy. Since the proxy was merely a fiction in the mind of your boss, you, Tanko, had to find some criminal friend of yours who resembled Van Sickle in some way. So you brought Long to Van Sickle and told Van Sickle that this man was the proxy.

"Van Sickle insisted upon Long wearing one of his suits—a suit later found in Long's house in Hoboken. Van Sickle also noted that Long didn't have any teeth. So in order that there would be no hitches in identifying Long's body as that of Van Sickle, Van Sickle had his own teeth pulled.

"Poor Van Sickle! All that unnecessary preparation, when all you really intended to do was to murder him as soon as he had written his suicide note and transferred his insurance so that two agents of the murder machine could collect. Those agents were Patsy Moore and Mrs. Kurtzner!"

I switched off the ultra-violet light, and Merry, with her death mask, disappeared. Out of the closet came Glenn Saunders, and he was wearing a mask which closely resembled the face of Van Sickle as it had been in life. When I turned on the ultra-violet this time, Theo Quinn uttered a harsh cry.

"This has gone far enough!" he shouted. "I—I'm not going to stand for any more of it."

"You'll stand for it, Quinn," I whispered into the mike in the Ghost's voice. "You'll listen to the story of Leonard Van Sickle. Because it's the Van Sickle case that upsets the criminal apple cart. Van Sickle believed what the criminals told him so completely that he prepared every detail for his future life after death—or after the death of his proxy. He and Mrs. Kurtzner were going to Europe, Van Sickle thought. He even bought the steamship tickets—bought them in the name of Fabian Deeming. And so sure was he of the sincerity of the plan you murderers put before him, that he had certain stocks of his, which he thought were due to boom, transferred to the name of Fabian Deeming. Hugo Wayne knows all about that, isn't that so, Wayne?"

"I—I tell you—you got me all wrong," Wayne gasped. "I'll come clean. Sure, I took the stocks out of Van Sickle's safe after I heard that he had died. Since there wasn't any real Fabian Deeming so far as I know, I thought I could cash in on the stocks. But I didn't have anything to do with Van Sickle's suicide—or murder, whichever it was."

"Shut up, Wayne," I went on. "Listen to what the spirit of Van Sickle has to say. He will tell you all the truth. He will tell you how he was murdered, after he had been led to believe that someone was to take his place in death."

I PAUSED briefly, changed my voice, impersonating that of Van Sickle as closely as possible.

"They came to me that night, thoth killerth, to talk over the complete plan, tho they thaid. They thought up an excuth to get me to the window, when they knew that I had tranthferred the inthurance polithies so that they could collect. I had written the thuithide note at their requetht. Onth near the window, they threw me out. It wath murder."

I switched lights, vanishing Van Sickle. Again I spoke in the voice of the Ghost.

"The master criminal helped with the murder of Van Sickle. He was in the Cronner Hotel that night. And he was also in Van Sickle's suite. I know that because he left behind him a little spiral of wire which served to identify him. I picked this piece of wire out of the ash tray and carried it away. When the master mind found that the spiral was gone, he sent Tanko to look for it. But I had taken the spiral from Van Sickle's room. Tanko followed me down into the lobby of the hotel. He cornered me with his gun. Tanko said: 'The grill, Ghost,' and I naturally thought he wanted me to go to the grill room of the hotel. But Tanko was talking about the spiral of wire. That spiral of wire is a *grid* which might be called a grill, I suppose.

"But," I went on, "it was something that occurred just before the murder of Jonathan Marvin that gave me my final clue."

Again I switched on the ultra-violet light, and Joe Harper, wearing the mask of Jonathan Marvin was standing in front of the mirror so that the reflection of the ghastly mask could be seen in the living room.

I spoke into the mike in the voice of Jonathan Marvin as I had heard it over the phone in Taylor Owens' office:

"I fell for the criminal plot, too. I didn't know I was to be murdered. I simply thought that I was to be involved in a swindle. That bothered my conscience, for I was an honest man. As the time for what I supposed to be my faked death approached, I became more worried until finally I decided to call my friend Taylor Owens and tell him the entire truth. I called Owens at his office. That is, I *thought* I was talking to Owens. But it was the Ghost, impersonating Owens. I knew—"

In the living room, a shot crashed out. The mirror that reflected my "spirits" was shattered, for the man with the gun was simply firing at a reflection. I jammed the third switch on my switch board. This turned on the ultra-violet lamps in the living room, and, I hoped, marked the murderer. I sprang into the living room, dark, of course, because the ultra-violet lamps shed only black light. But in that black light, I hoped something would be illuminated.

As I sprang into the room filled with confused and frightened people, I saw the hands of the murderer, glowing in the darkness! The trap had worked! Here was complete proof of guilt, for, acting on my instructions, Standish had treated the money the criminals had collected from the Hurst murder with naphthionate powder. Naphthionate glows in ultra-violet light just as ultra-violet paint does. The glowing hands proved that here was a man who had handled the money!

BECAUSE OF the glowing hands, I marked the master criminal easily in the darkness, and in another moment I had him by the throat with one hand while the other hand twisted the gun from his grasp. The man was broken. He had tried to kill Jonathan Marvin's "spirit" with a gun!

"Lights!" I shouted.

Back in the kitchen, Glenn Saunders heard the cry, turned on the switch that brought on the regular living room lights. The murderer was struggling in my hands, trying to break that hold on his throat, gurgling out his denials. But when he saw my face close to his in the light, saw that it was the face of the very man he supposed he had had Tanko kill that night, fear made him submissively limp.

Still holding on to Taylor Owens' neck, I thrust him into the hands of the police. "Take your killer," I said, "with the compliments of the Ghost."

All eyes in the room were upon me. For here I must have appeared as Stephen Perkins, and they had just seen me, a little while before, to all appearances, dead. Theo Quinn, pompous in spite of his fright, shouted:

"I won't stand for it! You're dead! I'll sue you. My health will never be the same. You ought to be under that sheet!"

I backed toward the door.

"What sheet?" I asked.

For in all the confusion, it had been very easy for Glenn Saunders to go down the basement, pull the gimmicked sheet through the trap in the floor, close the trap. There wasn't even so much as an "X" on the spot where the "body" had been. I laughed at the gasps of astonishment, and as I went through the door, I said:

"You see, there's a trick to it!"

I ran across the front lawn, the black garb I wore fluttering out behind. In the car parked at the curb, Merry White, Joe Harper, and my double, Glenn Saunders, waited for me.

CHAPTER XXVIII

THREE QUESTIONS

QUIET REIGNED. Merry White and I were alone in the Ghost's rectory. The clock was well around toward one in the morning. We were just enjoying being together, Merry cuddled up in my arms when the back door opened and Ned Standish came down the basement steps. He looked haggard and older than his years, but the bright light of triumph glowed in his eyes. Merry got out of my arms to go and fix him a drink. Standish sat down slowly.

"My congratulations," he said. "And you'll be glad to know that Taylor Owens confessed. We haven't calculated the exact amount the criminals collected through their several agents, but Owens says his lion's share is well over a million. He seemed to want to drag all the others in after him, too."

"How were my reconstructions of the crimes?" I asked.

"Perfect. You'd have probably got the Marvin killing all right, too, if Owens hadn't broken and spoiled your show. Owens simply walked in on Marvin, offered him a friendly drink which Owens poured out of his own flask. The drink contained poison. Marvin died almost at once. He had already written his suicide note, and Owens placed it beside the body together with a bottle of the poison which had been in the drink. But what I want to know—"

Merry skipped across the room and tickled Standish under the chin.

"You want to know how my sweet man figured it all out."

Standish stroked his black square of mustache and blinked.

"That's it, I guess. He said that he based his case on three points. The first was the question: what was that wire spiral found in the ash tray at Van Sickle's?"

"It was," I said, "just about what Tanko called it when he tried to get it from me in the lobby of the Cronner. Tanko was asking me for the grill, not telling me to go to the hotel grill. He really meant the grid. I got the idea from Merry, though I don't suppose she knows it. I had heard of a pipe grid, and had Tanko asked for the grid instead of the grill, I might have recognized the wire spiral as a pipe grid. This particular one was a kind I had never seen before, hence I didn't identify it for what it was when I first saw it. Owens probably brought it back from his last trip to Europe."

"What's a pipe grid?" Merry asked, sitting on the arm of Standish's chair.

"It's a wire screen or grid made to fit into the bottom of a tobacco pipe. I double-checked with my tobacconist over on East Forty-Fifth. With a pipe grid in your pipe, your tobacco smokes dry right down to the bottom, leaving a dry gray ash. Without a grid, you have something pipe smokers don't like—a wet, soggy heel."

"But," Standish objected, "some other smoker might have had one."

"True," I said. "But I *knew* Owens had one. When he visited me the night of the Van Sickle job, the ashes he knocked into my ash tray were gray and dry. At the time, that fact meant nothing. But it was to mean something later, looking back.

"Every time I saw him *after* the Van Sickle job, he was digging soggy, wet tobacco from the bottom of his pipe. So it looked as though he might have lost it at the scene of the murder. Which he did. Knocking out his pipe into Van Sickle's ash tray, he lost the grid."

"The second point," Standish said, "was that you knew the murderer was in the Cronner hotel that night. How did you know that Owens was in the hotel?"

"Because at the dinner Ken Vickers gave at Charles' Restaurant the following night, Owens asked for Braumier Pilsner beer, an imported brand which made its debut in this country for the first time at the Sky Room of the Cronner the night that Van Sickle was killed!

"I checked on that, too, and learned that the Cronner had a sample shipment, just large enough to try one night at the Sky Room. Evidently Owens was there, drank some of the beer, and liked it enough to ask for it at a place where he couldn't get it the next night. But that second point only became significant in the light of the first—the grid."

MERRY GIGGLED. "Isn't my man bright? Question three coming up."

"Yes," Standish said. "How did Tanko know that Dr. Stacey and the Ghost were one and the same person?"

"Nobody but Owens could have told him," I said. "That's why Owens went haywire at that spot in our show tonight. You see, I was in Owens' office disguised as Dr. Stacey when Marvin called to spill the whole plot to Owens. I got Miss Rice, Owens' secretary, out of the office, called Marvin back, impersonating Owens' voice. I was trying to get some information out of Marvin. Marvin was talking to me, addressing me as Owens, and suddenly he stopped. He said: 'This is impossible' and hung up. Why? Simply because the real Taylor Owens called at Marvin's at that time, probably to arrange for Marvin's death! There Marvin was, thinking he was talking to Owens, and suddenly he sees Owens!

"Marvin saw something was wrong, but he still thought Owens was his friend. He didn't know Owens was mixed up in the insurance swindle at all. Owens, having heard Marvin address someone on the phone as Owens, asked questions. Marvin told him that he was calling Owens' office. Therefore someone was impersonating Owens from the other end of the line.

"Owens simply called Tanko, who was hiding out in the building across from his murder partner, Owens. Tanko used field glasses, looked into Owens' office, saw me, as Dr. Stacey. Since Dr. Stacey was doing the impersonating, Dr. Stacey was probably the Ghost. And the Ghost had to die because he had the wire spiral which could incriminate Owens."

"And then," Ned concluded, "after he had put Tanko on your trail, Owens knew he had to kill Marvin at once. He offered him a friendly drink of poison."

"Nice man," Merry said.

"And goodnight," I said.

Standish looked puzzled. "Good night, who?"

"You," I said.

Standish looked at Merry. He grinned and took the hint.

"I'm so glad you're George Chance again," Merry said when Standish had gone.

"I'm glad too," I said. "Even a ghost gets tired."

"And yet," Merry murmured, her lips close to mine, "if Ned Standish were to call you up ten minutes from now with another case for the Ghost, you would go."

"Wouldn't you want me to?"

Merry sighed, then laughed.

"I'd go with you," she said.

"We'll worry about the next time if the next time comes," I said.

"It will," Merry said. "It will."

And I knew it would....

II

THE GHOST
STRIKES BACK

CHAPTER I

MURDER IS NO LAUGHING MATTER

THE MAN in the rain was the most unprepossessing individual I had ever seen. He wasn't just thin, he was gaunt—almost starved-looking. He was all but chinless. His eyes were protruding and glittering. He was rigged out in a seedy-looking cutaway coat and baggy striped trousers. An almost colorless fuzz adorned one-third of his peaked cranium, noticeable only when he removed his black fedora hat.

He stepped out of the shadows of the dark areaway at the stage door entrance as Merry White and I approached. In the drizzle of that rainy spring evening he was like a materialized spook, a stooped figure of a man, the yellow light over the door giving his cadaverous face the appearance of a parchment mask.

Merry, my fiancée and valued assistant, drew closer to me and shivered.

"He looks like he has a moldy mind," she whispered. "Who is he!"

"Doctor Seer," I murmured. But even if I had not known, the untidily elegant scarecrow would not have left us long in doubt. He bowed ironically and shoved one crocked hand against my spotless shirt front where it showed above the vee of my partially opened topcoat.

"You are George Chance, the magician," he stated rather than asked.

"Right," I said, studying him keenly as I gently but firmly removed his claw-like paw. This particular "thin man" had no reason to bear me any good will.

"I am Dr. Seer, the great psychic," he informed us with an almost fanatical air. "If you persist in this mockery of this evening, this obvious intention of casting reflection upon the living truth of spiritualism, you will regret it."

"I doubt it," I replied, coldly polite. "Besides, how does this concern you, Dr. Seer? I understand you're a crystal gazer, not a spirit medium."

"I, sir," he said, drawing himself up and placing his tented right hand on his hollow chest with all the dignity of a ham actor, "am a disciple of truth—a prophet of the future. Cancel this blasphemous performance while there is yet time. If you persist in your vile efforts to discredit the eternal truth, doom will be called down upon your head. Beware the death and destruction! Beware the doom to come!"

With that parting admonition Dr. Seer took himself off, his thin body seeming to melt away in the blackness of the rainy night.

"Here!" I called after him. "Would you like a pass to see the performance!"

But he was gone, and Merry was trembling. I bent my head to her lips in a reassuring kiss. A long moment later Merry's slender fingers took hold of my chin and gently pushed our faces apart. Her beautiful green eyes looked deeply into mine, and there was trouble in their depths.

"George," she whispered, "I'm having a hunch."

Merry frequently had those flashes of intuition. Her hunches, I might add, have frequently helped me out of tight spots on those occasions when I have played a somewhat different role than that of George Chance, the magician.

"It's a bad one this time," she went on, her voice still a whisper. "It isn't just because of what that old fake said, either, but I feel that—that something terrible is going to happen tonight."

"You're silly," I said, and laughed. "Come, let's go in before we get all wet out here."

That was my last laugh for the evening. Murder isn't a laughing matter.

PERHAPS I'D better explain at this point just what led up to that rather spooky meeting with Dr. Seer outside the theater. I'll begin with the visit of David Palmer to me a week before. Innocently he brought one end of a murder chain to thrust into my hand, and I had no idea how far out I was sticking my neck when I accepted it. The gift of prophecy might have belonged to Dr. Seer, but it was not included in the regulation bag of tricks of even a master magician.

I received the young financier cordially. He had been previously introduced to me by Merry, and that made him okay with me.

"Mr. Chance," he said as we shook hands, "I have come to ask a favor."

"Consider it granted if it's within my power," I assured him.

"Have you ever heard of a medium and crystal gazer who calls himself Dr. Seer?" he asked.

I nodded. It is not strange that magicians and mediums, being professional enemies more or less, should know about each other.

"He is a fake and a charlatan," said Palmer with sudden heat.

"There are many fakes," I agreed. "You seem upset. Why?"

"I have a sister," explained Palmer. "She has become involved in this spiritualistic stuff. Up to now, I have never interfered with Margaret's foibles, but she is going mad over this stuff, and is being played for a fine sucker. I'm growing weary of seeing my money disappear through such outrageous frauds. Dr. Seer is her present guiding star.

"In short, I want to expose him, and you're the man to do it. I want you to put on a spiritualistic performance to prove that all this mumbo-jumbo that is unbalancing my sister's mind is nothing more nor less than sheer nonsense. I want you to do a regular mediumistic show and then reveal that you have done it all by your stage magic. It isn't the money that's important but the state of my sister's sanity.

"I'm turning to you, the greatest living magician, for help. I remember that the great Kalaban, before his death, had a standing offer of ten thousand dollars for any medium who could materialize any spook or perform any miracle that he couldn't duplicate by admitted magic. Since his death, I understand that a great many fake mediums have tried to win the two-hundred-thousand-dollar trust fund he left for the person who could contact his astral body and give to his widow the exact message they had previously agreed upon as an authentic communication between them. So far no one has succeeded."

I nodded. I was well acquainted with Irene Kalaban and had been a friend of her husband's.

"What has the Kalaban offer to do with your problem?" I asked.

"Kalaban was a foe of fakery. So are you. I know I'm asking a great deal of you, but I will foot all expenses gladly. Will you do it?"

I REPRESSED a chuckle. Of course I would do it, but what made me chuckle inwardly was that Palmer would not know I was doing it in two capacities—not only as George Chance, the Magician, but as George Chance, the Ghost. David Palmer had brought a *personal* problem to George Chance, but at the same time, without knowing it, he had brought a *criminal* problem to that other side of George Chance which was the Ghost.

I had no quarrel with honest spirit mediums who worked without reward and honestly sought the truth. But I was doubly glad to aid Palmer because at the same time I would be striking a blow at a racket that annually mulched a hundred million dollars out of several million dupes. The Ghost was willing to walk at any time when such an issue was involved.

A word about how George Chance came to be the Ghost.

I was born in the show business. My father was an animal trainer and my mother a trapeze performer. Most of what I am today I owe to them and to my early life with the circus. I'm a fair tumbler and contortionist. I learned makeup from a clown named Ricki. Don Avigne taught me how to throw a knife. Professor Gabby patiently trained me in ventriloquism.

None of this, of course, made me a magician. It was to Marko that I owed that. I have never forgotten the day he called me into his dressing tent and gave me a half-size set of multiplying billiard balls.

"You haff goot hands for tricks unt gimmicks, Ghorge, my boy," he told me. "Learn to use these unt some day you vill know magic. Unt der world vill know you."

I still have the billiard balls Marko gave me, and the supple fingers they developed. They were the first rung on the ladder that helped me climb from the circus to vaudeville and from there to my own revues. Magic made me a fortune so that I finally retired from the stage to establish the New York School of Magic where amateurs, bitten by the unending craze to create illusions, are taught.

I first met Police Commissioner Edward Standish when I was performing at a policemen's benefit. We took to each other at once. I expressed an interest in police work. He invited me to take a hand in a murder investigation. When I exposed the real criminal by means of a spirit-slate trick, Standish showed what I thought was exaggerated enthusiasm.

"I'll take a second helping," he said.

"What do you mean?" I asked

"I intend to call on you again."

We looked at each other. I think the idea was born simultaneously in our brains.

"I'll study up on it," I said.

In the days and weeks that followed I found one concept more and more dominating my thoughts—Magic and Crime Detection, how to merge the two and make them one. And so, not all at once, but gradually, slowly—but surely—the idea of the Ghost took form.

DAVID PALMER was waiting for my answer.

"Okay," I said. "I'll put on the show."

He grasped my hand, shook it gratefully. He was still thanking me when I ushered him out.

I announced in the papers my intention of producing better spirit manifestations than any medium in the city and to do it without laying the slightest claim to supernatural powers. Further, I offered to take anyone from the audience who would volunteer, place him or her in a spirit cabinet, and let him act as my medium, guaranteeing a perfect job. This, I argued, would prove definitely that the professional spirit mediums were frauds.

The following day David Palmer announced through the papers that he thought my idea a splendid one and that he would act as my medium.

So here we were, Merry White and I, and Dr. Seer himself had just de-materialized like one of his pet spooks.

CHAPTER II

I CALL UP
THE DEAD

I WANTED TO strike a note of informality in my performance tonight, making a friendly meeting of it rather than a show. So, when I had escorted Merry to her dressing room, I went around to the foyer of the theater and entered with the crowd.

There were several people whom I knew in the group. As I passed up the aisle I paused to speak with Irene Kalaban, widow of the Master-mentalist to whom Palmer had referred.

Irene Kalaban maintained an open mind on the subject of spiritual-ism. Her famous husband had done the same, as attested by the proviso of his will which set up the two hundred thousand dollar reward. Kalaban, being a magician and therefore knowing the tricks, had precluded any possibility of fraud by arranging a secret code message with his wife.

As a spirit Kalaban would try to communicate with his wife through a spirit medium, revealing this code message to her, through the medium, as proof that it was really his spirit speaking. This would prove spiritu-alism a fact rather than a theory, inasmuch as only Mrs. Kalaban and the trusted executor of Kalaban's will knew the message.

Naturally hopeful of hearing this message which would prove her husband's immortality, Irene gladly went to any and every spirit medium in the city who volunteered to give a séance for purposes of calling up Kalaban's spirit.

I always admired Mrs. Kalaban. She was a pale, blond woman who possessed a particular type of fragile beauty. Tonight she gave me her thin hand and a wan smile as she introduced me to her escort, Robert Martin.

This Martin was virile, square-shouldered. He had an aggressive jaw. His eyebrows were like wads of dental cotton. He tried to cripple me with his handshake.

"Y'know, Mr. Chance," he said, "you're dabbling in dynamite tonight."

I smiled at the dogged, rock-hard face that did not invite smiles and asked Robert Martin if he was a disciple of Dr. Seer.

"Dr. Seer," Martin said, "is the most remarkable medium I have ever encountered. A true medium. His powers are supernatural. He will some day give Mrs. Kalaban that long awaited message from her departed husband."

I was a little surprised to find that Martin was a spiritualist. He didn't look the type. Not at all the type to sit in a dark room waiting for a medium to crack the knuckles of her big toe and announce that was the spirit of dead cousin Elmer rapping.

Irene Kalaban laughed a bit uneasily and gave me a pointed look.

"Mr. Martin," she said, "is as determined a believer as you are an unbeliever."

I understood. Martin was a man whose faith could not be shaken. If I produced any unusual manifestations tonight by confessed material means, Martin would declare that I was a true spirit medium and didn't know it.

"Your privilege to believe or not, Chance," Martin rapped. "But y'know, I wouldn't be in your boots tonight for anything."

MY MEDIUM of the evening, David Palmer, was in the front row with his sister. She was a dark-haired, neurotic-looking person. I went up to the front of the theater and Palmer introduced me to her. Margaret Palmer gave me a look. Meeting her was a little like stepping into a refrigerator.

As I got up on the stage, I saw that Dr. Seer was also occupying a seat in the front row. A very nicely mixed audience of skeptics, believers, and fence-straddlers, I had that night.

I gave a little preliminary talk, at the same time going through a bewildering cigarette routine in which the fags floated, vanished, and were reproduced. The cigarettes showed up well against the black curtain.

I announced that the cigarette tricks were no less miraculous than the feats of the mediums, for whether a cigarette was produced or a spook, skill, showmanship, and material apparatus were used.

This produced a snort of reproach from Robert Martin in the audience. And on the front row I could see Dr. Seer twisting around in his seat, as though trying to find a comfortable hollow for his angular hip bones.

The black curtains behind me were pulled aside by Merry White in the wings. My setting was simple. There was a black drape background, and in the center of the stage a spirit cabinet, which was simply a framework of steel tubing on which black curtains were hung reaching to within eight inches of the floor. There was a table of light construction in front of the cabinet and on the table was a tambourine.

"Remember," I said to the crowd, "the only difference between George Chance and a spirit medium is that I warn you ahead of time that you will be fooled. The spirit medium voices no such warning. He *knows* you will be fooled."

While I was talking, Merry White was arranging folding chairs in a semicircle about the spirit cabinet. She was my best misdirection. All eyes must have been on her. She was dressed in a flaring white satin skirt that failed to reach her knees by eight inches. Her red satin blouse fitted like a coat of paint. That ten-thousand-watt personality of hers was evidenced in every movement of her graceful body and in every arch glance of her green eyes.

I called upon the audience for a volunteer committee of six to come up on the stage and examine the spirit cabinet. I believe Robert Martin was first on his feet. He strode up the aisle, arms bowed, fists clenched. He stood on the stage, fiercely challenging the audience with his belligerent glance. At my request he announced his name.

I DIRECTED Robert Martin to enter the spirit cabinet and examine it carefully while other volunteers joined me on the stage.

The next man up the aisle also cut an imposing figure. His skin was deeply tanned and as smooth as satin. Though closely shaved, you could see the coarse blackness of his beard beneath his skin. Something about his bearing or the cut of his clothes gave out the impression that he might be a romantic figure out of a bit of colorful light opera—a Cossack soldier, perhaps.

As he stepped upon the stage, the audience whispered. Here was a man the women would call handsome. Men would look up to him as small boys look up to some storybook pirate.

The man's self-confident smile showed a gleam of polished teeth against the duskiness of his complexion. He shook hands with me, announced that he was Carl Van Borg.

This was a break for me. Van Borg was a well-known author. There was no chance of anyone supposing that Carl Van Borg was my confederate.

"I sifted up here not out of curiosity, Mr. Chance," his deep baritone voice spoke loud enough for everyone in the audience to hear. "I want to help. I've watched fakers the world over, and they're an ugly lot. I'm bound to congratulate you, Mr. Chance, for the work you're doing."

"Thank you," I said. "Glad you don't mind helping."

Van Borg gave me his smile; it was like heat lightning behind thunder clouds. "It's an anticipated pleasure. A privilege, really."

And then when Robert Martin had come from the spirit cabinet, Van Borg went in to give it the once over while I called upon other members of the audience until I had a committee of six.

I asked for someone in the audience to come upon the stage to play the part of spirit medium, and as was expected, David Palmer got to his feet. At the same time he did so, his sister seized his arm. Her strident, hysterical voice could be heard clearly throughout the room:

"David, for the love of heaven, don't go up there. *Don't do it!*"

Gently, David Palmer broke the hold his sister had upon his arm. He walked up on the stage. I shook hands with him, turned to address the audience:

"Many of you know David Palmer. You know him to be a man of integrity. He denies all knowledge of trickery and has also stated that he does not believe in the supernatural powers of the spirit medium."

I stepped to the spirit cabinet which had been examined by each of the committeemen in turn and revealed the inside of the cubical to the audience. The cabinet was equipped with a blue shaded light mounted at the bottom of it which would illuminate the medium's feet beneath the lower edge of the curtains, proving that the medium was securely tied during the performance.

Palmer took his place in a chair inside the cabinet and was securely bound, the knots sealed with wax.

THE LIGHTS were dimmed to deep purple. At one side of the stage, I took my place in a chair and clapped my hands.

"I call up the spirits of the dead," I said distinctly.

And my spook show began. I duplicated every stunt that I had ever seen a medium pull. A tambourine rattled, a small table tipped, ghostly hands floated out from the cabinet, and finally I produced some ectoplasm, that stuff of which spirits are supposed to be made. Into the ectoplasm, which was a simple bit of chemical magic producing a vapor, I caused a "ghost" picture to be projected.

The audience was considerably impressed. There was some commotion in the front row and I heard Dr. Seer's high-pitched musical voice:

"Mr. Palmer is a true medium, though he may not know it."

"That's true!" Robert Martin's voice sang out.

This was nothing more than I had anticipated. I called for lights, promising that I would repeat the performance with anyone in the audience taking the place of David Palmer.

I went to the spirit cabinet, parted the curtains.

The committee crowded around me. Palmer's face was somewhat ghastly in the pale blue light that pushed up from the lamp at his feet.

"That's all, Mr. Palmer," I said.

Palmer didn't reply. Robert Martin shoved in front of me and looked hard at Palmer.

"Mr. Palmer is a medium!" Martin sang out. "He's still in a trance!"

The impressive figure of Carl Van Borg shouldered Martin out of the way. His rich, deep voice broke a taut, ill-omened silence:

"Damn it, Chance, look here a minute! Is there a doctor in the room? Mr. Palmer isn't well!"

And as I cut away the cords that bound Palmer to the chair I knew that medical aid would be futile.

David Palmer was dead.

CHAPTER III

THE BOX OF THORNS

THE DOCTOR got to the stage by a succession of apologies and elbow jabs. The audience was in an uproar. I knew that no one should be allowed to leave until the cause of death had been established.

A faded, near-sighted individual, dressed in tails and carrying a topper with which he might well have covered his totally bald head, popped up on the stage. He pushed a pointed, inquiring nose up into my face.

"Say, Mr. Chance, everybody ought to be made to stay here until the police arrive. Somebody just went out through that exit opening from the right box."

"Glad you mentioned that," I said to the bald man.

I reached over and yanked Van Borg's sleeve.

"Will you see what you can do to keep the people from leaving? Block off the entrance and see if you can get word to the police."

Van Borg nodded. "I'll see what I can do." He sprang from the stage.

My eyes traveled across the audience. Dr. Seer's gaunt form stood out clearly as the medium fought his way toward the front exit of the building. But he couldn't get out, because Van Borg was way ahead of him, blocking the doors.

I saw that Irene Kalaban had got up near the stage and was comforting the dead man's sister. Always thoughtful, Irene Kalaban.

Back of me on the stage, the doctor straightened.

"This man is beyond help, Mr. Chance," he announced.

"What killed him?" I asked, turning around.

The doctor frowned. "It might be heart failure, of course," he said. "Palmer was obviously excited by the role he was playing tonight."

"Heart failure!" Robert Martin snorted, his nostrils spread like those of a war horse going to battle. "All death is heart failure, y'know. But that's not saying what killed Mr. Palmer. And you won't say, either. But y'know, don't you? Any man who persists in deliberately mocking the spirits of the departed—"

"Bosh!" said the doctor.

Martin squared off in front of the doctor and would have used his fists had I not wedged in between the men.

"He'll not bosh me!" Martin insisted. "Y'know, I'm not to be trifled with."

"I was about to say," the doctor continued mildly, "that it is possible that Mr. Palmer may have been poisoned."

"Poison!"

Though the word had been spoken for my ears alone, others had overheard. And the word spread like fire across a field of ripe wheat. Poison and its ugly brother, murder! And immediately a score or so of people remembered that they had to get home at once.

At the entrance Van Borg had his hands full. Smiling broadly, he blocked the door, shook his head when somebody requested to be allowed to go. One man insisted upon going so vehemently that Van Borg let go with his fist and the man went back violently, making a hole in the crowd that was in front of the door.

IT WAS a relief when a pair of uniformed police put in their appearance. The cops took one look at Palmer and phoned the homicide bureau.

One of the officers asked who was in charge of this meeting. Somebody pointed to me. The cop was a fat, red-faced person who didn't look too good-natured. He asked me what the purpose of the meeting had been.

"Spook crooks, isn't it?" he said when I had told him. "Well, listen, everybody." He faced the audience. "I want yuz all to take the same positions you was in when the body was discovered. Those that was on stage, up on stage now. The rest of yuz should be in your seats."

The doctor who had pronounced Palmer dead asked permission to take Palmer's sister out of the crowd. The cop said he might take Miss Palmer to the lounge but that they were not to leave the building.

Ten minutes later there was no chance of anybody leaving the building; the most efficient body of sleuths in the world, the New York Homicide Bureau was in control. And after a look at the body, Inspector John Magnus quietly announced that everyone on the stage would have to be searched. Though Medical Examiner Robert Demarest had not yet arrived, John Magnus seemed to need no medical attention to determine that David Palmer had been murdered.

The curtain was dropped over the stage to insure privacy. Detective-sergeant Hullick was to search the members of the committee which had assisted me in the fateful experiment. The search was to be an unpleasant ordeal to which, Carl Van Borg announced, "We might just as well submit without blowing off any steam."

Robert Martin blew off steam, however. In fact, he virtually exploded, which resulted in his being searched first. Hullick went through Martin's pockets swiftly and brought out a small, mean-looking automatic.

"Carrying a permit for this, Mr. Martin?" Hullick asked, eyeing the man coldly.

Martin snorted and produced the permit. Hullick examined it carefully, handed it back, and then turned to me.

"If you are going to search me," I said, "I request that you do it in private. As a magician, I carry certain articles necessary to tricks and which I would not care to have revealed to the public eye."

Hullick nodded. "I'll take charge of you in the men's dressing room, Mr. Chance. You're a friend of Police Commissioner Standish, aren't you?"

I said I was but that I didn't expect any special privileges on that account. We went into the men's dressing room. Hullick's usually hard mouth twisted into a friendly smile as he closed the door behind us. He massaged his jaw with the palm of his hand.

"I don't suppose this is really necessary in your case, Mr. Chance, but I'd better give you the once over. I'll try not to ask too many pointed questions about any magical stuff you've got on your person."

HE WAS as good as his word until he removed from my right sleeve a black metal tube about a foot long. Almost at once his attitude toward me changed. His mouth was once again hard, his eyelids clamped to slits.

"What's this?" he asked.

"A cigarette dropper," I told him. "I pulled a few cigarette tricks tonight. That tube holds cigarettes until I'm ready for them."

Hullick looked into the tube, found it empty, which was natural since I had used all the cigarettes in my act. He put the tube aside from the other objects taken from my person. I noted that he paid much closer attention to what he was doing after that.

In the right hand pocket of my coat he found a safety match box. This surprised me, because I'm not in the habit of carrying matches in that pocket. However, Hullick didn't seem to attach any particular importance to the match box.

"If you don't mind, I'll keep this stuff and look it over more carefully, Mr. Chance," he said. "Now tell me, was anybody assisting you tonight?"

"Miss Merry White. She always assists me."

"Go back stage and get her, will you?" Hullick began stuffing my magical gimmicks into his pocket. And as he did so, he dropped the match box. The box came open and several little brown sticks that looked like burned matches scattered out on the floor.

Hullick knelt, picked up one of the little brown sticks, uttered a prolonged whistle.

"What have you here, Mr. Chance?" He looked up at me, his slits of eyes glittering shrewdly.

"I don't know, I'm sure," I said.

"Why not? They came out of your pocket, didn't they? Don't you know what they are?"

I shook my head.

"They're thorns, Mr. Chance."

CHAPTER IV

BLOOD AND ROUGE

I DON'T KNOW what significance Hullick attached to the box of thorns. All I knew was that they weren't mine and I told him so.

"We'll see, Mr. Chance," Hullick simply said. "If you'll just have Miss White step in here a moment. I want to talk to her. I want to get this thing straight and you and she are the ones to help me."

So I left Hullick to ponder over the match box full of thorns and went backstage to get Merry.

She wasn't there. I went into the wings and looked on stage. She wasn't there either. I went backstage again and to the stage door where a uniformed cop was on guard.

"Have you seen a young woman around here anywhere?" I asked the cop.

He wanted to know what sort of a young woman. I guess my description was enthusiastic. No, he hadn't seen such a little lady, but he would like to—especially in that costume that she wore.

I looked beyond the cop and into the alley outside. Perhaps the cop divined my thoughts for he took up a position completely blocking the doorway.

Merry White is the most unpredictable person I have ever known, but somehow I couldn't figure her leaving the theater here without me before the show was over.

I recalled the near-sighted bald man who had popped up on the stage directly after the discovery of the body to tell me that someone had gone out of one of the exit doors connecting the auditorium with the rooms back stage. A moment later a repetition of that thought gave me the "cauld grue" as I stooped over something clearly marked on the floor not far from the stage door.

"What have you got there?" the cop asked, altering his position and squinting in my direction.

"Blood," I said. "Three drops of fresh blood here on the floor."

Three drops of blood, Merry White unaccountably gone, the opening and closing of a door leading back stage—three ingredients of a nice dish of worry for me.

I straightened and looked at the cop who had come over to see the three sinister dots on the floor. The cop was a formidable person, but then George Chance is no pigmy either. I knew suddenly I was going to walk out that stage door. And I meant walk, not run.

"You got a four-bit piece?" I asked.

He looked at me and fished down into his pocket, his mouth screwed into a knot.

"Maybe I have, Mister. This ain't a touch, is it?"

I told him it wasn't. I just wanted to show him something. I took his fifty cent piece and held it at my fingertips.

"Watch it," I said. "Watch it closely. Because now you see it and now you don't."

THIS TIME he didn't. I back-palmed the coin, and when he wanted to see the back of my hand I changed over quick to a front palm while I turned my hands over to display the back of it. And then I apparently picked the coin out of the air and told him to watch again. I pulled the same stunt, except that this time I purposely fumbled, dropped the coin. He stooped to recover it, and when he straightened he looked into the muzzle of his own revolver which I had pulled from his holster.

The cop brought his whistle up to his lips. His cheeks bloomed angrily. But before he could get a tweet out of his whistle, I slapped the side of his head with the barrel of his gun. He fell forward to the floor, face down.

"I'm sorry about this," I said, but I don't think he heard me. I left his gun beside him and walked out of the door.

There were a couple of cops in front of the theater, keeping the curious crowd moving along the sidewalk. They didn't pay any attention to me. I was just part of the crowd. I didn't see Merry anywhere, but then I hardly expected to. If you're not too optimistic you're less apt to be disappointed. Certainly I didn't have anything to be optimistic about.

There was a taxi stand a few steps from the front of the theater and a cab had just pulled up. I walked toward it. I didn't know where I was going. Perhaps to Merry's apartment or to my own house—any place where there would be a chance of getting some word from Merry. Those three drops of blood on the floor back in the theater weren't much.

Perhaps it wasn't even Merry's blood. It was her unaccountable disappearance that was giving me the creeps.

"Taxi, Mister?"

I didn't answer just then. Against the curbstone, painted to indicate that the space was for cab parking only, I saw red marking. Something red as blood, but something that wasn't blood.

I bent over the curbing, looked at the mark. Large sized numbers were marked in red on the curb—703. I scraped a little of the red stuff onto my finger nail. It was lip rouge, the same scented brand that Merry used, I was certain.

This mark was intended for my eyes, put there by Merry. She knew I would have to come to this stand for a taxi. 703—the numbers meant less than nothing to me. It was certainly not a telephone number. It might be part of an address.

"Mister, do you want a cab?" the driver said, leaning out of his window.

I looked up. The cab was painted white with red numerals on its door.

"Is there a cab in your crew numbered seven-ought-three?" I asked.

The driver nodded. "Jimmie Caldwell drives it. Why, Mister? Jimmie will be checking in at the office by now. That's why I'm here, Mister. I'm as good a driver as Jimmie, but if you'd rather risk your neck on your feet—"

I pulled open the door of the cab.

"Get moving. Take me to your office. I've got to see your pal, Jimmie."

It was just a shot in the dark but it might hit a bulls-eye.

I SETTLED myself back in the cab, forced myself to relax. It was the first moment I had had, since the finding of David Palmer's body, in which to do anything like connected thinking. And all that I could do was to try to get the facts in chronological order.

First, David Palmer had taken his place in the cabinet. He had been tied by the volunteer committee. I had lighted the electric light inside the spirit cabinet and pulled the drapes. Palmer had been alive then—alive and confident that what he was doing would have considerable influence on his sister who was rapidly falling into the web of Dr. Seer.

Then what? Well, then I had found Palmer dead. That interval between the closing of the curtains and the parting of them, that interval was the chasm of uncertainty over which there was no bridge of fact.

Had Palmer been murdered? I didn't know. The doctor had suspected poison. Supposing there had been poison, how had it been introduced? Palmer had eaten nothing, had taken no drink. Bound inside that cabinet, what chance would he have had to take poison? But poison can readily be introduced through the skin and into the blood stream. A poisoned dart, perhaps—

And my thoughts bounced back to the finding of the match box full of darts in my pocket. That was a point I had overlooked in my anxiety about Merry.

Poison darts, of course. It all seemed very fantastic. Zulus killed with poison darts, but I hadn't seen any such savages running around New York. No, the more you thought about it the crazier the poison dart business sounded. How could a dart have been shot through the heavy velvet drapes of the spirit cabinet? It was impossible.

But it all came back to the one unalterable fact—David Palmer was dead. There's nothing more unalterable than death. How he had died, why he had died, might have a dozen answers. The fact remained that he was dead, and if poison darts had done the job, I might be in a bad spot.

It looked like the Ghost was going to have to take over the investigation. The Ghost had made all of New York's underworld his happy haunting ground. And if it takes a crook to catch a crook, why not a Ghost to catch a spook crook. But there was a joker in the deck, and had Merry White been with me we might have enjoyed the irony of it together.

Here's the joker: If George Chance and the Ghost were the same person and the half of the dual identity named George Chance got pinched for the murder of Palmer, how in the devil was the Ghost to solve the crime and bring the real criminal to book?

That, I decided, was almost as impossible as the idea that somebody had fired a poisoned dart into David Palmer through the walls of the spirit cabinet. Not quite as impossible, as I will explain a bit later.

CHAPTER V

THE MAN WITH CLAWS

MY CAB came to the office of the taxi company. I paid the driver and promised him a tip if he would locate Jimmie Caldwell who drove cab number 703.

The tip was easily earned. We met Caldwell just as he was coming from the door of the office. He was a dumpy little man with a head too big for his visored cap.

"This gentleman is looking for you, Jimmie," my cabby announced.

Jimmie took a cigarette out of his mouth.

"It don't cost nothing to look," he informed me.

"Did you pick up a fare near the entrance of the Thespian Club Theater—a small, dark-haired girl who was wearing an abbreviated costume—"

Jimmie was already nodding.

"You bet I did. She came running out of the alley alongside of the theater. A Yellow cab was just slowing down to pick up a man who run out ahead of this girl, see. The girl lunged at me where I was waiting for a fare. She told me to keep an eye on the Yellow. And then she outs her lipstick and marks something on the curb."

Jimmie pushed back his cap and scratched among the half dozen hairs that topped his head.

"I thought the girl was screwy, but maybe it was some new kind of a treasure hunt. I remember once—"

"The girl," I said. "What did she do?"

"Oh, the girl got into my cab after she had written on the curb stone. She said I was to follow the Yellow cab, which was what I did."

"Okay," I said. "You're taking me to the same place you took the girl. Only by the shortest route, and I'll be responsible for any traffic rules you violate."

What, I argued, was a mere traffic offense to a man who was apt to be pinched for murder?

On Ludlow Street not far from Essex Market, Jimmie Caldwell braked his cab.

"This is the dump," he announced, waving at a blackened brick building front crowded close to the sidewalk. "It was sure none of my business, but I thought what a place for a lady."

"You're right," I said, "it was none of your business." I got out and told Caldwell to wait.

Six narrow stone steps between two gas pipe hand rails led me to the door where a sign advertising rooms for rent was hung. I didn't look for a bell push but shoved against the weathered wood panel and stepped through into a dingy lower hall. Two sliding doors flanked the hall and ahead of me a stairway led to the second floor.

The place was dead quiet—that sort of quiet you don't like to break. I walked on tip-toe along the side of the stairway and to the end of the hall. There was a door leading out into a rear court. At the back of the hall there were doors on either side of me, tightly closed. Behind one of them I could hear somebody snoring. I tried the knob, found the door locked.

I went back to the stairway and quietly up the worn treads. The upper floor was darker than the lower. It was a good place to fall down stairs and break your neck.

A SMALL, faint sound came to my ears. I stopped, listened for a repetition of the sound. It came again and I recognized it as a moan. It came from behind a door on my right. I went to the door, pressed my ear to the panel. The sound was not repeated. I tried the knob of the door, met with better luck this time, stepped into a totally dark room, closed the door after me.

I listened again. Somebody in the room was breathing steadily. I groped around the edge of the door with my hands, trying to find a light switch. There was none. I might have guessed that such a house would have pullcords operating from central lighting fixtures of the type designed for both gas and electricity.

I moved forward, sliding my feet cautiously. A string brushed my face about midway across the room. I pulled it and brought a saffron-colored light globe into life. Immediately I looked down at the floor. Not eight inches from the toe of my right shoe was Merry White, huddled on the floor. Except for the bluish bruise on her pale forehead, she might have simply curled up for a nap.

I dropped beside her, gathered her into my arms. Her eyelids quivered and then squeezed tight shut against the pain of a headache. Her hands clung to my arms tightly. She sighed and relaxed.

For a moment, I couldn't drag my eyes from her sweet face. Her regular breathing, the steady drumming of her heart, relieved my fears. It was just the thought of what might have happened to her that paralyzed me.

Finally, I got my eyes from her face and let them wander about the room. A closet door was open and I could see that it was empty. A scarred, gray-enameled bureau had every drawer open. The bed was unmade.

I looked down at Merry in time to see her closing one eye. A faint smile lingered around the corners of her sweet mouth. I whispered her name.

"Don't bother me," she said. "I like it here."

"Well," I said, "I can run along then—"

Her hands gripped me hard. "I mean in your arms. And I'm sleepy. Aren't I the lucky girl to get rescued by tall, blond, handsome you?"

"Merry, what happened to you? Why did you leave the theater?"

"Don't bother me," she said. "I like it here."

I picked her up and carried her downstairs and to the taxi. Jimmie Caldwell got out when he saw me coming and started to straighten his tie. I told him he needn't bother because the lady was asleep.

"The lady," Merry said, "is not asleep. But when she opens her eyes things go 'round."

I lifted her into the rear seat of the cab, held her close while the cab got underway. I told Caldwell to take us to my house on East Fifty-Fourth.

MERRY CUDDLED into a more comfortable position in my arms.

"Darlin', I hope you're not jealous. I left you at the theater to follow a man. If you could see the man, you wouldn't be jealous, would you?"

I didn't say anything.

"It was a strange man," she went on. A shiver coursed over her body. "The most hideous man I've ever seen."

"What was he like?" I asked.

"Like a mummy, darlin'. I was sure a brave girl to follow him. Right after you found Mr. Palmer dead, this man came through the exit door that led back stage. I said: 'Where do you think you're going?' He didn't say anything. I tried to get in his way. He ducked aside and fell into the wall. There was a nail sticking out of the wall and he gashed his cheek on it. Funny thing was, he didn't seem to know he'd hurt himself."

That explained the blood on the floor, thank heavens!

"I thought he was the murderer, if Mr. Palmer was murdered. So I followed him and lettered the number of my cab in lipstick where I thought you'd find it."

"You followed him to that house?" I asked.

"Uh huh. And he hit me on the head with his suitcase when I went into his room. He was packing in a big hurry when I caught up with him. He was awful. He didn't have any hands."

"No hands?" I echoed.

"No hands, just claws. Yellow claws like a chicken. What do you make of it, darlin'?"

"Claws," I murmured. "A cut cheek and no pain. Honey," I ended softly, "unless I'm mistaken, there's a leper loose in New York."

CHAPTER VI

ON THE BIG
BLACK DOT

BY **THE** time we had reached my brownstone, Merry thought she could walk, but declared she wasn't going to try.

"You've got to carry me across your threshold one time or another," she said, "so tonight you can practice."

Joe Harper opened the door when I kicked on the panel with the toe of my shoe. My home doesn't belong to Joe Harper, but he doesn't know that. He found my guest room a good place for a hangover one night years ago and he became a permanent fixture. The man's intestines are made of brass tubing. Incidentally, he's one of my staff whom the Ghost couldn't well do without.

Joe Harper had his green hat on, but he wasn't going any place. A cigarette dangled from his thin lips and he had a highball in one hand. From the shadowy nook beneath the brim of his hat his sharp, black eyes looked at Merry and me.

"She must have got her spirits out of a bottle, George," he said.

I placed Merry on the divan, and she promptly asked for a glass of sherry.

Joe Harper got the wine for her. Then, hands stuck in the tight slots of his trouser pockets, he asked what was what.

There's no getting around Joe Harper. Those eyes of his are like the probes of my friend Robert Demarest, the medical examiner. Joe Harper's career is as checkered as the suits he wears. He has been race-track bookmaker, theatrical booking agent, pitchman, gambler. He knows Broadway from the crust on down—all the way down. He is an invaluable agent for the Ghost. Beneath his calloused, sophisticated veneer he carries a very genuine and loyal friendship for me. He is one of the six persons who knows that George Chance and the Ghost are one and the same person.

Lounging on the back of his neck, cigarette ashes raining down on his gaudy, piped vest, Joe Harper listened to the events of the evening. When I had concluded, he said:

"No wonder Police Commissioner Standish has been calling here trying to get you, George. It looks to me like you were in the middle of a black dot. When Merry pulled her exit right after Palmer couldn't take his curtain call, you shouldn't have piled into that cop the way you did. Assaulting an officer"—Joe shook his head—"bad stuff, George. I should have been there. I have hit cops and got away with it."

"Maybe you'd better call Mr. Standish and fix yourself up," Merry said. "It will be all right when he finds out you had to play hero for me."

I went over to the phone.

"By the way, Joe, this man with the claws—you ever see anybody like that running around?"

Joe nodded. "But I wasn't sober then. When I saw him he not only had claws but he also had a tail like a peacock."

I RANG the apartment of Police Commissioner Standish. He wasn't at home, so I tried his office at Headquarters. Hadley, his secretary, put me through at once.

"Ned," I said, "I guess you want to talk to me."

"George," he said, "I guess I do. By all that's holy, what the hell was the idea of running out on a murder investigation and slashing one of my cops with his own gun?"

I explained about Merry's disappearance, knowing that Standish could fix me up all right on that score.

"But you're suspect number one for the murder of David Palmer," Standish said. "Oh, I know you didn't do it, but Palmer was a well-known figure. There's going to be all kinds of a smell raised about this."

"Tell me about the murder," I insisted. "What did Demarest find?"

"A thorn sticking in the back of Palmer's neck. The thorn was covered with a gummy substance which Demarest thinks is curare. And Hullick found poisoned thorns in a match box in your pocket. Also a blow gun—"

"Listen," I cut in. "That blow gun was nothing but a cigarette dropper. You can't call it anything else. I can show you the thing in the suitcase of any magician who is going to pull a cigarette routine."

"Now, *you* listen, George," Standish said, his voice soft and I thought a little worried. "When you find poison thorns on somebody and you find any kind of a hollow tube through which the thorns could be propelled, that tube becomes a blow gun even if it's a soda straw."

"So I did it," I said. "I unpinned the cigarette dropper from my sleeve. I have X-ray eyes that could see Palmer's neck through the back of the curtains of the cabinet. The curtains offered no resistance to the thorn.

The thorn, shot from one side of the stage, curved, went through the back of the cabinet. It's as logical as snow in August. Hullick and Magnus have a motive all doped out, have they? What was I after? Palmer's money. You know I don't need money."

"You never have so much of the stuff you don't want more, they say. And George, you once told me that a spirit medium puts atropine in his eyes so he can see his way around in a dark room. You could have pulled the same trick, walking to the back of the cabinet, parting the curtains, shooting the dart into Palmer."

"Am I pinched?" I demanded.

"Don't get me wrong," Standish said. "This is a difficult situation. Palmer, a prominent man and well-liked—"

"And I don't see how I can be cut to fit into the picture at all," I interrupted.

AT THE other end of the line there was an interval of silence. Finally the commissioner said:

"Magnus is building up a swell case against you, George. You've got to realize Magnus' position. There has to be an arrest or there will be the devil to pay. And damned if you don't look like the murderer. What you ought to do is go to bed and get some sleep. Don't worry. *There's a way out for you, you know.*"

And Standish hung up!

I turned slowly from the phone. I knew the way out he mentioned. Standish was one of the six persons who knew that I was the Ghost. And Standish knew that the Ghost could be two places at once—in Tombs prison awaiting trial for murder, and at the same time at large trying to clear himself. Standish knew the secret of this seemingly impossible thing.

So that was what Standish had been hinting at. That was the thing he expected me to do. Seriously, he didn't suppose I had killed Palmer. But if other members of the police force thought that I was a murderer, there was nothing Standish could do about it.

You see, the only other official on the police force or connected with it in any way who knew that George Chance was the Ghost was Dr. Robert Demarest, the medical examiner.

"Well?" Joe Harper asked, examining me critically with his dark eyes.

I worked up a smile which I let Merry and Joe share.

"Standish says I'm to go to bed and not worry. I think I'll drive Merry back to her apartment and then turn in. Tomorrow, I think the Ghost will have to take a hand in the murder case of David Palmer."

And I knew that maybe my noteworthy story went over the head of Merry, but I hadn't deceived Joe Harper. Joe knew that Standish had said I was wanted for murder.

CHAPTER VII

MURDER MOTIVE

GO TO bed, get some sleep, don't worry—that was the commissioner's prescription. I filled it by dozing off about dawn and pounding the pillow for maybe three hours. The soft buzz of the front door signal virtually pitched me out of bed. I staggered into the second floor study which is adjacent to my bedroom.

In the top of my study desk is an illuminated glass screen. A periscope arrangement is employed to "pipe" a view of the front-entryway up to this screen, so that I can see who is demanding admission into my house.

Pictured in the screen was not the burly figure of Inspector Magnus, as I had half expected. Instead, I looked down upon the lean, cadaverous image of Dr. Robert Demarest, Chief Medical Examiner of New York City.

Unless you know the man you are apt to consider Demarest the most gloomy and saturnine individual alive. He looks unhappy, what with his peculiar protruding eyes with their heavy, sleepy-looking eyelids. His job is certainly the most cheerless one in the city. And, as though he realizes that his position is not one for making friends, he has carefully cultivated an attitude which seems to alienate people. For all that, his sleepy eyes front for the keenest brain in the field of pathology. His slow, tired movements are but a counterbalance for the nervous energy within him.

I went into the bedroom long enough to slide into slippers and pull a bathrobe about my shoulders. Then I hurried down the steps in order to let Demarest in.

Half-way down the steps, I heard someone open the front door, and Demarest's voice intoned:

"George, you couldn't be in a worse mess, aside from turning up as the prone and silent partner at an autopsy."

"I'm afraid you're mixed up again, Doctor," said the voice of the man who had let Demarest in. "George is still in bed."

That voice—the voice that answered Demarest—is an auditory miracle. Hearing it unexpectedly like that always gives me the uncomfortable feeling that I have somehow escaped from my body. The voice was like a perfect recording of my own natural voice in pitch, accent and inflection.

"Damn this seeing double!" Demarest said. "Why don't you keep a pipe in your mouth, Saunders, so I can tell you from Chance?"

And by that time I was far enough down the steps to see Demarest talking to Glenn Saunders, my assistant.

Little wonder that Demarest sometimes got Glenn and me confused. To see us together is enough to make a chronic alcoholic hit the water wagon. For by some quirk of nature augmented by a little plastic surgery, Glenn Saunders is my identical double.

THERE IS a Chinese proverb which states that there is always a twin. And in Glenn Saunders I had found my twin. His height measures up to my own six feet, one inch. He is broad at the shoulders and lean at the waist as I am. His face is like a reflection of my own—blue eyes, ruddy gold hair that waves back from a fairly broad forehead, thin nose and mouth, prominent cheek bones.

I encourage Saunders to ape my every movement, to develop a perfect imitation of my natural speaking voice. For Glenn is the reason why the Ghost has a perfect alibi. When the Ghost is on the haunt, stalking some criminal in any one of his many disguises, Glenn Saunders fills the shoes of George Chance, proving to my enemies that though the Ghost may employ magic in his investigations, he simply can't be George Chance!

Saunders leaves and returns to the house under cover of darkness, usually. When he is not playing the part of George Chance while I am ghosting he is busy in his basement shop, working on some new piece of magical apparatus. For magic is a mania with him. In exchange for all that I can teach him about the art, he has deliberately shucked his own identity.

So the Ghost's secret remains a secret. And when the Ghost seeks sanctuary from his enemies in the identity of George Chance, his real identity, his enemies never manage to pick up his trail.

So careful is Saunders to efface himself unless he is called upon literally to wear the shoes of George Chance, that he would never have presumed to open the door that morning were it not for the fact that Robert Demarest is one of our intimates.

Seeing me now on the stairway, the medical examiner looked from me to my double, a dour expression on his face.

"I am charitable only to myself when I say I hope neither of you ever turns up at the morgue," he said. "I would never know who was who."

As though to make sure that Demarest didn't become confused again, Glenn Saunders stuck his briar pipe between his teeth. It's his mark of distinction, since I smoke cigars or cigarettes.

I motioned toward the door of the living room, but Demarest shook his head.

"No time to sit down, George. So many people die I'm getting so my knees don't hinge because I'm standing over the autopsy table so much. I just thought I'd stop by and tell you the worst."

"Let's have it," I invited, smiling a little.

"Why, this murder business—you killing David Palmer," Demarest said. He pointed a bony finger at me. "Listen, Inspector Magnus is going to nail you to the wall on this job. Opportunity, murder weapon, everything points to you clearly as though the trail was marked in neon lighting."

DEMAREST WAS not a man to exaggerate. I considered what he had just said.

"Except motive," I said. "Palmer's money doesn't mean anything to me."

"Money," Demarest said, "isn't the root of this particular evil. It's the other thing. I mean women."

"What woman?" It was my turn to frown.

"Why, Merry White, of course. Hasn't Magnus found an autographed photograph of Merry White in Palmer's place?"

"Has he?" I asked Demarest.

"He certainly has. David Palmer was mad about Merry. And when you're arraigned before twelve men who have been pretty thoroughly educated by the tabloids of this city, it pans out that you killed David Palmer because of jealousy."

Knowing Merry White as I knew her, I laughed a little. But not much. Because a smart prosecutor could paint the same picture Demarest had done with much more glowing colors. Merry had introduced me to Palmer. Merry had very probably carried on a harmless flirtation with the wealthy bachelor. It would be like her. It is as natural for her to flirt as it is for her to breath. With a personality like hers, nobody could be a wall flower.

But the idea of jealousy—it was absurd. Merry's loyalty to me had been tested too many times.

"George, that doesn't sound good," Glenn Saunders said.

"It sounds rotten," Demarest said. He took the brim of his hat in both hands and pulled it well down on his head. "And if I can make it sound rotten, wait until the D.A. gives his version. Under the circumstances, if I were a magician, I'd vanish myself."

Demarest turned, reached for the doorknob. I told him to wait a minute. He shook his head.

"Magnus is probably on his way here now. I can't be found here by the inspector."

Demarest hurried out.

"You're not going to go down to Headquarters with Magnus, are you?" Glenn said.

I asked him why not.

"Because you're in a tight squeeze," Glenn insisted. "Demarest wouldn't have come here—"

"Demarest is a calamity-howler," I said, going into the bedroom for my clothes.

Demarest wasn't anything like a calamity-howler. I wasn't kidding myself at all. I was in a jam. But it was a jam I was going to have to wriggle out of myself.

While I was dressing, I could hear that Joe Harper had joined Glenn Saunders in my study. The two were talking in low tones.

I joined them a moment later. Joe wasn't dressed. He was draped in that atrocious purple bathrobe of his which must once have belonged to a prize fighter.

HIS CRISP, nasal voice attacked me the moment I entered the room.

"Listen, George, if you think this self-sacrifice act you're trying to pull is going to reap a hand from me, you're screwy. Glenn told me what Magnus has dug up. You're a smart guy, George, but you don't know what Broadway uses for a brain as well as I do. When the papers get hold of this, make a gooey scandal-murder out of it, the people will lap it up. You can't ad lib your way out of a mess like this."

"I was thinking the same thing," Glenn put in. "So suppose you let me face Magnus when he comes. Let him take me down to Headquarters. They'll go easy on me, thinking that I'm George Chance who is a friend of the commissioner. Maybe I'll be indicted, but you know how a trial drags along. You'll have plenty of time to find the man who did the killing."

I put a hand on Glenn's shoulder.

"That's nice of you," I said, "but I can't take the chance."

"Where's the chance?" Joe said. "The Ghost has tackled harder jobs than this. A lot harder. But if you're in the Tombs, you can't ghost yourself out of this mess."

"Nothing doing," I said.

Yet there was logic in what Joe preached. As Commissioner Standish had pointed out, Inspector Magnus had a job to keep, and if he couldn't produce the murderer of as prominent a man as David Palmer, things wouldn't look so good for him. Not that Magnus was deliberately framing me—*somebody had already done that*—but if he didn't arrest so palpable a suspect as I was, there'd be a holy howl from the press.

The why or wherefore of Palmer's murder hadn't occurred to me yet. That the fanatical Dr. Seer had somehow managed to cause it merely to keep me from convincing Margaret Palmer that professional spirit mediums were fakes was too far-fetched, although I did not rule it out as a possibility. There was an underlying motive beneath the whole thing that smelled like something the Ghost should be investigating, but I felt I must draw the line at the point where I would risk sending my double to the electric chair in my stead.

So I turned my back on the idea and went downstairs to await the call of the capable and thorough-going Inspector Magnus.

CHAPTER VIII

MAGNUS MAKES HIS PINCH

INSPECTOR MAGNUS put in his appearance promptly. He was accompanied by a plainclothesman. He came to his point with admirable brevity.

"I'm sorry, Mr. Chance, but you're under arrest for the murder of David Palmer. Those poison thorns, you know, and your magic blow gun. Motive, jealousy."

"The motive is haywire, Inspector," I said. "I grant that Miss White may have had some sort of a harmless flirtation with Palmer. Maybe Palmer, who didn't strike me as being particularly smart about women, took her seriously. But suppose a man named John Doe is murdered and an autographed picture of some Hollywood movie queen is found in his bedroom—you wouldn't think anything about it, would you?"

"That's different," Magnus said. "That's a whole lot different. The fact remains that you had every opportunity to kill Palmer. You had the weapon used in your possession after the crime. Palmer was in love with the girl you intended to marry. It don't make a lot of difference whether Miss White was serious or not. Palmer was plenty serious. It was Merry White or nobody as far as he was concerned."

Magnus jingled handcuffs.

"We better go down to Headquarters, Mr. Chance. I want to make everything as easy for you as I can, so if you'll agree to come quietly—"

I smiled a little. "I don't think your handcuffs would mean much to a magician, Inspector, so let's just dismiss that little formality. I'll get my hat."

In my house there is a large closet just off the hall. I went out into the hall to go to this closet. Magnus and his man followed me. I opened the door of the closet and stepped inside, groping for my hat in what light there was that came into the closet from the hall.

And then suddenly there wasn't any light at all. The closet door closed. I heard a quiet, furtive movement at my elbow. I had scarcely time to realize that I was not alone in the closet before something crashed on the top of my skull. In the darkness there was suddenly light, but no light you could see by. The brilliant, flashing array originated inside my own brain, and when the lights went out, so did everything else, including my ability to reason that somebody had laid a sap on top of my head.

WHEN I came to, it was a gradual process in which headache and nausea were my first sensations. I was propped up by pillows and lying on the floor of my own basement, a mattress under me. Joe Harper was sprawled out in a deck chair not far from my furnace. He was fully dressed, which included his hat, and beneath the light of a single globe he was reading the latest issue of a Broadway magazine.

I tried to say something to him and couldn't. I couldn't move my jaws. I lifted my hand to my face and then to the top of my head. Somebody had tied an ice bag on the top of my head.

Sensing that I was conscious, Joe put down his magazine, came over and unbound the ice bag from my head.

"We had to get tough, George," he said. "When a man won't read his lines as they are written, you got to get tough. Glenn was in that closet, waiting for you to get your hat. He had to sap you and give you a goose egg for your head instead. You'll feel all right by nightfall."

I knew how it was. That closet into which I had stepped has a trap door in the floor. My house is filled with similar tricks which I have used to baffle guests. Glenn Saunders had waited in the closet, sapped me, dropped me through the trap, came out of the closet with my hat on.

In other words, Glenn Saunders had been arrested as George Chance—arrested for the murder of David Palmer, though I don't suppose that Glenn had ever seen Palmer in all his life.

"Now you can go to work on the case, Ghost," Joe Harper said. "If you fail, you can spill the whole fraud to the cops and have Glenn released from the death house in time. Only," he added as I began to protest, "it isn't going to get as far as that. The Ghost has cracked tougher cases than this."

"Okay," I said, shrugging. "I go ghosting after the killer of David Palmer. Meanwhile get the best lawyer available to defend Glenn."

"Of course," agreed Joe imperturbably.

"And thank Glenn for knocking some sense into my head when you go down to see him," I went on. "I was acting like a sap."

"So we thought," replied Joe. "That's why Greek met Greek."

"Eh?" I said, frowning.

"Sap met sap," said Joe in a tired voice.

"A pun is the lowest form of halfwit," I retorted. "I was thinking, Joe—clearing George Chance of the murder charge is really only the preliminary to a nasty job. The question is, who actually did kill Palmer, and why."

"Yeah," Joe grunted. "You find that out."

"I will," I promised grimly.

I went down to that secret room just off the workshop in which Glenn Saunders and I have created some of those illusory miracles which have astonished and entertained the play-going world. This secret chamber was brilliantly lighted and contained, among other things, the paraphernalia of the Ghost. There was a large wardrobe and a tall three-panel mirror. In front of this mirror I began the process which brought that wraith-like hunter of men, the Ghost, to life.

I USED as few makeup materials as possible. Small wire ovals go into my nose, tilting its tip and elongating the nostrils. I darken the inside of each nostril with brown pigment. Brown eyeshadow goes on to darken the eye pits. I get an effect of pallor out of a powder box. Next I highlight my cheek bones which are naturally prominent. And over my own teeth I place celluloid shells the color of old ivory.

That done, I no longer look like George Chance. Dressed in a specially made suit and crusher hat, my appearance does not attract any particular attention. I am just another man, not very attractive, yet not particularly hideous.

But that's about half of it. I have only to part my lips in a skull-like grin, affect a fixed vacuity of expression with deeply sunken eyes staring glassily, and my face becomes something ghastly, like that of a skull. It is an instantaneous change which is the result of long practice in front of the mirror, this "turning on the Ghost" as I call it. I have seen many a hardened criminal quail before it.

The suit I had put on is always prepared. It includes secret pockets for bits of magical apparatus which I carry around and which have many times proved their value. A magical gimmick originally designed for quite another purpose holds my flat automatic.

Commissioner Standish has more than once told me I am a rotten pistol shot. I admit it. But sheathed in my right sleeve I constantly carry a weapon in which Don Avigne long ago taught me to have great confidence—my nasty throwing knife which has a double edge and a needle point. Coupled with trapeze-strengthened muscles, the Ghost has little trouble fighting his way into and out of corners.

So as dusk dropped on Manhattan I left my house by a special back exit which permitted me to drift onto the block without seeming to have come from the home of George Chance. Leaving there was like divorcing myself from my own identity. I was the Ghost in grim earnest this time and would be compelled to live the life of the Ghost until the real murderer of David Palmer was brought to justice.

My first move was to step into a telephone pay station near Columbus Circle and call Commissioner Standish.

"This is the Ghost, Ned," I said when I heard his gruff salutation. "How are tricks?"

NEEDLESS TO say, he was startled. After all, he was under the impression that Magnus had put the Ghost in the Tombs along with George Chance when the inspector had arrested Glenn Saunders.

"Thank heaven you had the sense to see this thing right," he growled back at me, recovering.

"I didn't have the sense," I replied. "Glenn had a blackjack."

"Good!" The commissioner chuckled. "Somebody else was fooled, too. Merry White is in my office right now using her considerable charm trying to get you clemency by denying that there was ever anything between her and Palmer and that Palmer knew it and you knew it. In short, she's generally making a nuisance of herself."

"Give her my love," I said, "and tell her she doesn't have to prove anything. Just how serious, however, is this case against George Chance?"

"Well," he answered gravely, "it's circumstantial, of course, but I've known men to burn on flimsier evidence. Damn it, just where did those thorns come from?"

"They were planted on me. Don't ask me who did the planting. At the time I discovered Palmer dead there were a number of people on the stage, any one of whom might have slipped that box into my pocket. One of them did, and that makes a horse of George Chance, a magician who was out-magicked."

"I'd call it a strike," came back Standish dryly, "and I don't mean because it was a match box, either. But why were you singled out for the goat? Why was David Palmer killed, anyway? The only person to benefit is his sister, and she didn't need anything. It seems pointless."

"It does, but I'm afraid it has a point that is quite deadly. I'll keep in touch with you."

"Good luck... Ghost...." Standish whispered.

CHAPTER IX

A BRACE OF THUGS

L EAVING THE telephone booth, I hailed a cruising taxi at the next corner and gave the driver the address of the Palmer home in Washington Heights. I had nothing definite to connect Dr. Seer with the murder save that he could have been the person to plant the poison thorns on me.

The Palmer place occupied a large part of one of the blocks south of Fort Tryon Park. I was not surprised to see several luxurious-looking cars parked in the drive. Sympathetic friends of the family were paying duty calls.

Dismissing my cab a block farther on, I walked back and cut across the lawn in the dark. I came out of deep shadows and surveyed the house. The place was well lighted. Several windows were open, but the screens had not yet been put up—a nice advantage for anyone who might wish to enter without arousing the occupants. I took advantage of the opportunity, and entered from the rear.

Several callers were gathered in the drawing-room with Margaret Palmer who was simply dressed in a black gown which heightened her pallor. I recognized only one of them—the bald-headed and near-sighted man with the inquisitively pointed nose. He was the party who had called my attention to the fact that somebody had left the theater through one of the box exits.

I was intent at the moment on searching David Palmer's study, but I didn't get the chance as the guests were leaving. I had to retreat down the hall in a hurry to get out of sight. I opened the first door I came to and slipped into the room. Through the crack of the door I watched Margaret Palmer tell her well wishers good-bye. Then, to my great consternation, she came swiftly along the hall and entered the room in which I was. As I quickly closed the door behind her I saw that it was a downstairs sitting-room, obviously for private comfort.

"Don't cry out, Miss Palmer," I warned. "I want to help you find your brother's killer."

I didn't "turn on the Ghost," you can be sure of that. Thanks to what I had learned of ventriloquism and voice impersonation, I didn't sound like George Chance. In fact, I put all I knew of hypnotic appeal into that word of warning to Margaret Palmer. And she didn't cry out.

Hands at her throat, she stood straight and tall and somewhat pathetic, looking at what she could see of me in the shadows.

"You—you are from the police?" she asked. "Please go away. I've begged you not to question me now. I'm tired—so very tired."

I KNEW she was all of that. When a woman of Margaret Palmer's neurotic temperament holds herself together at a time like this it amounts to nothing short of heroism.

"No, I'm not a policeman," I said quietly. "I am simply a friend of your brother. I want to be a friend to you. I want to find out who killed David."

"David wasn't killed. It was simply his time to die," she said. "I knew it all along."

"You knew it? Why in the world did you permit him to go to George Chance's spirit show last night?"

"It would have made no difference where he was. It was his time to die."

"And yet you worried when he went into the spirit cabinet."

"Yes, something within me cried out against the inevitable. Doctor Seer predicted my brother's death at one of his séances. Naturally I believed him."

I repressed a start. So Dr. Seer had predicted Palmer's death!

I pretended to take this important piece of information casually. "That's rather interesting," I said. "Do you regard this doctor as infallible in his predictions?"

"Yes," she said flatly. "He prophesied the death of another man correctly—a man named Michael Holland."

It was another shock. I remembered having seen the name of Michael Holland, scientific worker, in the newspaper. He had died in some kind of accident while working in his laboratory.

"Have you spoken of these two prophecies to anyone else?" I asked.

"The followers of Doctor Seer knew about them. Tomorrow the world will know when it reads the newspapers."

"I see. Who was that bald man with the sharp nose in your drawing-room with your other guests?"

"His name is Harkness. I didn't know him, but he is associated with some bank where David had connections. He said he was a friend of David's. Mrs. Kalaban introduced him to me."

Margaret Palmer began twisting her handkerchief. I could see by her thin fingers that she was nearing the breaking point.

"Thank you very much, Miss Palmer," I said gently. "You've been a great help. I won't trouble you with any more questions, but there is one thing further. There must have been a reason for your brother's death— even admitting Dr. Seer's gift of prophecy. I would like your permission to look over his private papers or things of that nature which he kept here at home."

"Please, no."

"Why not?" I asked a little sharply.

"Our lawyer instructed me to keep everything locked up in David's safe and not let anybody go over his papers until—"

THE FAINT sound of a crash in the next room—as though somebody had knocked over a pedestal on a heavy rug—came to us. I glanced at the closed door and then shot a quick look at the bereaved woman. She seemed as startled as I.

"Where is your brother's study?" I demanded in a low, terse voice.

"There," she whispered, indicating the room from whence had come the sound.

With one leap I was at the door. It was locked. Margaret Palmer opened her mouth to scream.

"Don't!" I snapped at her so sharply that she stared at me in open-mouthed but silent amazement.

Twisting the knob and exerting pressure in a manner taught me by my old circus friend, Hercules, I lunged all my weight against the door. The latch snapped out of the keeper, and the barrier shuddered open. I sprang on into the room at a crouch. Margaret Palmer followed me across the threshold.

The room was a mess. And the cause of the mess was still present in the guise of as villainous a pair of thugs as I had ever encountered. One of them must have been an ex-pugilist, for he had a beautiful pair of cauliflower ears. The other had a face like a shark and eyes just as mean. Sort of a soup and fish pair, if you get what I intend.

Like the bull in the china shop, they had been giving David Palmer's study the works. Desk drawers were open, book cases had been emptied, litter was everywhere. But I didn't have time for a detailed survey. At my feet was a pedestal ash-stand with a leaded bottom. That was the object one of the china shop bulls had overturned.

The thug with the garden variety of ears let out a hiss like a punctured locomotive and charged at me. I grabbed up the ash-stand and twirled it like a drum major's staff. It cracked him squarely across the shins and he fell on his face like a ton of second-hand bricks.

Shark-face used more discretion. He went the other way—toward the draped windows—but he drew a vicious-looking automatic that seemed as big as a cannon. Perhaps that was because of the silencer he had on the end of it. Anyway, it was a one-shot weapon because of the silencer, but he must have had plenty of confidence in his ability to use it.

"Lay still, Bull!" he grated. "I've got 'im." And he leveled down on me with an expert motion.

It was touch and go. There wasn't any help for it. So I stayed in my crouch and twitched my right hand against my left coat-sleeve. Before Shark-face had time to slip his safety catch and squeeze his trigger my right hand flipped forward in the manner of a snake's darting tongue.

There was a silvery flash and then a faint thud just as he pulled his trigger. But that shot was really reflex action and the slug buried itself in the wall above the door. The shaft of my throwing knife was sticking out of Shark-face's upper arm muscle.

He let out a scream a calliope would have been proud of, whirled, and dived head first through the draperies behind him. Bull scrambled to his feet, took one glance, and followed through before I could snag him. Margaret Palmer cut loose now with her hysterics.

BY THE time I got to the drapes I saw the window had been left open by the two prowl artists and that they'd got away—fast. The butler was banging on the door which opened into the hall by now, a door which Bull and Shark-face had also locked against intrusion.

"Wait!" I snapped at Margaret Palmer. "Before you let anybody in—is your brother's safe in this room?"

That question shut her up as though I'd drawn a knife across her thin throat. She darted startled eyes toward a small tapestry of a dancing girl in a Turkish coffee house. Without waiting for her words, I sprang over there and swung the tapestry aside. Behind it was revealed the closed door and shiny knob of a wall safe. Using my handkerchief to avoid leaving prints of my own, I tried the door.

The safe was locked, intact, and the combination was not set.

"So they didn't get into it—yet," I said sharply. "Call the police at once. Get Commissioner Standish to come here in person and impound everything in this safe. Thanks for everything, and good-bye."

I took a header through the window after the pair of routed prowlers.

CHAPTER X

WARNING ON THE WALL

REACHING THE street, I saw neither hide nor hair of the two fugitives. Getting my breath, I slowed to a circumspect walk and hailed the first cab I saw. I had plenty to think about, and I knew I would get the dope from Ned Standish if there was anything of importance in David Palmer's wall safe.

So I headed straight for Irene Kalaban's home, intending to hunt out Shark-face and his playmate Bull a little later. I employed my time by fitting the bald-headed Harkness into my pigeonhole of suspects along with Dr. Seer and all the others I could identify who had been on the stage with me at the time of Palmer's death.

As George Chance I had frequently visited the Kalaban home on the upper Riverside Drive, so I knew the place well. To my faint surprise I found one of the luxurious cars which had been at Palmer's home now parked in front of the apartment building. I dismissed my cab and walked boldly up to the chauffeur of the limousine.

"Who owns this car?" I demanded, just as though I had the authority to do so.

"Mr. Harold Harkness," the chauffeur said. "Who wants to know?"

"You'd be surprised," I said and walked away toward the front entrance of the house.

A maid opened the door in answer to my ring. She informed me that Mrs. Kalaban was busy at the present time. I told her that I must see Mrs. Kalaban immediately and that she might announce to her mistress that my visit concerned George Chance.

I stood around in the vestibule, waiting for the maid to make her announcement. Through the door of the living room, I could hear the voices of two men. One was clearly Robert Martin and I presumed the other to be this Harold Harkness.

The maid reappeared and told me that Mrs. Kalaban would receive me in the library, which was a small room opening off the right of the vestibule.

I opened the door of the library and stepped in quietly. Mrs. Kalaban was facing a spinet desk, her back toward me. At the moment I entered the room, I heard her give a small, frightened cry. Her hand went out to something on the wall—a slip of paper held there with a pin or tack. And then she knew that I was in the room with her and turned around.

Irene Kalaban was always pale so that the color of her skin was scarcely an indication of the emotions that went on within her. But she was taking in short, choppy breaths and her fragile-looking fingers crushed that slip of paper into a ball as she greeted me.

"Mrs. Kalaban," I said, naturally keeping the ghost well turned off, "I am a private investigator. I'm interested in the case of Mr. George Chance. As you doubtless knew, Mr. Chance was arrested this morning on the charge of murdering David Palmer."

"I know," she said. Her hands went behind her and fingered with something on the desk. "I was deeply shocked. George Chance wouldn't murder anyone. I have known him for a long time."

"You were at this spook show that Mr. Chance put on?" I asked.

I KNEW what her answer would be, of course, but I was trying to lead up logically to a question concerning Mr. Harkness who was even now talking with Robert Martin in the living room. When Mrs. Kalaban nodded, I immediately put my next question:

"Immediately following the discovery of the body, a man by the name of Harold Harkness approached Mr. Chance while the latter was standing on the stage. Mr. Harkness informed Chance that some member of

I seized the wrist of one and jerked his arm upward.

the audience had passed out of the room through a rear exit. I want to check on the integrity of Mr. Harkness. I believe you are acquainted with him, as was the dead man, Mr. Palmer."

"Mr. Harkness is entirely reliable," Mrs. Kalaban said at once. She moved away from the desk and I saw that her hands were entirely empty.

My glance darted to the surface of the desk and the only receptacle on its surface into which she could have dropped that piece of paper she had taken from the wall was a hammered copper inkwell. If it was like most inkwells in these days of fountain pens, it was for ornamental purposes only.

"What experience have you had with Mr. Harkness?" I asked. I fumbled in my pocket, searching for a pencil which I purposely did not find. I took a step to the desk. As I did so, I brought my left hand out from behind my back, bringing with it a rubber plug, shaped very much like a sugar pear, and attached to a length of strong black elastic. I palmed the pear-shaped thing with what you might call the stem-end outermost.

"You have a pencil over here? I seem to have left mine somewhere."

Without waiting for her consent, I fumbled in a tray of pencils with my right hand while my left simple wedged the rubber "pear" into the glass lining of the inkwell. A quick glance had shown me the wad of paper in the bottom of the dry well.

As I picked up the pencil with my right hand, I raised my left hand, released the pear, turned quickly toward Mrs. Kalaban at the same time. The rubber plug and the elastic carried the lining of the inkwell together with that wad of paper under the back of my coat. My left hand lied about what it had been doing by bringing a notebook from my pocket.

"Mr. Harkness," Mrs. Kalaban was saying, "was named executor of my late husband's will. Also, he is trustee of the two hundred thousand dollar reward my husband posted to be paid to anyone who successfully communicates with the spirit of my dead husband."

I pretended to note all this down.

"By the way," I asked, "if Mr. Harkness is trustee of that reward, I presume that he knows the secret code by means of which your husband's spirit will get in touch with you."

"That is true," Irene Kalaban said. "He knows and I know. No one else knows. Perhaps no one else will ever know."

BUT I wasn't thinking about that abstract matter at the moment. I was suddenly wondering if I would get out of this room alive, if my little disappearing act had gone undetected by other eyes than Irene Kalaban's. In short, I was wondering if I knew the owner of the pair of feet behind the Chinese lacquered screen in the corner.

How the devil my usually keen eyes had come to miss that pair of brogans I don't know, but there they were, and somebody was in them. Still pretending to be deeply interested in what Mrs. Kalaban was saying, and praying that she didn't say anything either of us would not want an eavesdropper to hear, I carelessly drew a little rod from my breast pocket and tapped my lips meditatively.

Suddenly I placed it between my teeth and blew sharply through it. At once I returned it to my pocket, but a fine cloud of dust puffed out like a lance toward the Chinese screen and then billowed in a faint cloud that settled over and enveloped the Oriental piece of furniture.

There was an instant of silence. Then gagging and gurgling sounds from the corner. And finally a terrific ker-chou! Two of them! Half a dozen!

Sneeze powder, of course. It came in handy sometimes.

But the big surprise was on me. The screen toppled outward and fell flat, exposing not one, but two eavesdroppers. As ugly a pair of mugs as I had encountered at the Palmer home—but a different pair.

"I thought things came in threes," I murmured as Irene Kalaban uttered a tiny scream. "Somebody must have had the numbers wrong. They come in pairs."

That was my last quip for the evening. The two thugs, still sneezing and wriggling their noses, charged for me in a first-class line-buck that would have given Army and Navy a few pointers. I was caught flat-footed, without gun or knife.

I swept Irene Kalaban out of the way with a straight-arm gesture and set myself to meet the stampede. But it is harder to fight two men who are trying to flee than it is to defend yourself from attack. That precious pair swerved to each side and went around me like a freight train passing up a tramp. They hit me from each side and as I clutched them they ripped free from my grip, one of them leaving an entire coat-sleeve with me, and fairly tore through the door.

I felt as if I had been squeezed between a pair of twenty-ton tracks, but I recovered my balance and took after them. It was a photo finish to the front door, and the pair of thugs won by a nose—my own. The slamming door nearly took it off me.

Then I made a mistake. I allowed my impetuosity to overcome my caution. I flung open the door and dashed out.

The thugs had anticipated just that, and that was why, instead of continuing their flight, they stood waiting, automatics handy. But even they were unprepared by the violence of my exit. My slam-bang eruption from the house, while placing me in danger, also worked to save me. I catapulted into them, and all three of us went flying off the porch.

THE REST happened very fast. I reacted instinctively. I seized the wrist of one of them and jerked his arm upward. The other was behind me. I knew he had an automatic too, and I kicked back, connected. But the next instant I knew I had not disabled him. There seemed no help for it—I would have to take his bullet and the most I could hope for was that it would wound but not kill.

Then I got the break—and it came oddly enough, from the one I was struggling with.

"Don't shoot!" he rasped hoarsely. "There's a beat-cop close. Sap him!"

And the other sapped me. I went down, stunned, but dimly grateful for the sudden change in my antagonists' plans. Their caution had made up for my lack of it. They got away, of course. It was a minute before I could stand on my feet.

Of course, that pair of housebreakers must have left the note that Irene Kalaban had found pinned to the wall. And I thought that I had recognized them, too. They looked strangely like a pair of hoods who belonged to a gang of crooks operating under one McTeeg. But McTeeg was a racketeer. He didn't go in for spirits unless they came out of a bottle.

What was he doing mixed up in this affair?

I thought of the note I had filched. In the taxicab I hailed I removed the glass liner of the inkwell I had stolen from its copper receptacle and shook the wad of paper out into my hand. Opening the wad, I found these words scrawled in pencil:

> We weren't kidding you at all, were we? We're watching you all the time. Get wise and come through.

CHAPTER XI

THE AVENGER

THE FOLLOWING day, a familiar figure entered the Centre Street entrance of Police Headquarters Building. Gray templed, his grave eyes encircled by gold Oxford glasses, his brow scored with many tiny wrinkles, the man known as Dr. Stacey went at once to the office of Police Commissioner Standish.

Hadley, the commissioner's secretary, greeted the doctor warmly. He hadn't seen Dr. Stacey for some time, he said, which was understandable considering the fact that the Ghost hadn't been haunting Headquarters for some time. For Dr. Stacey is simply the Ghost in one of his various roles.

When I entered Standish's office, I found the commissioner entertaining Carl Van Borg, of all people!

Standish shook my hand, turned to Van Borg, managed an introduction.

"Doctor Stacey is an intimate friend of mine," Standish explained, "and also an unofficial advisor."

"Unofficial meddler, the better term," I said in the voice I always employed while carrying the identity of Stacey. And then I had to return that powerhouse grip of Carl Van Borg.

We were seated finally. Van Borg slumped in his chair, but his powerfully built body was nonetheless impressive for all his slovenly attitude.

"I suppose, then," Van Borg said, his teeth flashing brilliantly against his dark skin, "I can speak in perfect freedom before Dr. Stacey, Commissioner?"

Standish stroked his dark square of moustache and nodded.

"I dare say it's nothing to become alarmed about," Van Borg began, "but I sifted down here with the idea of shedding a wee bit of light on something that happened some days ago. Perhaps you remember a man named Michael Holland. Bit of an inventor, something of a genius—Mike Holland."

"Yes," Standish said. "He met with an unfortunate accident."

"Maybe not," I said. "It's a curious coincidence but I too came to talk about Michael Holland. Do you happen to know that this spiritualist, Dr. Seer, predicted Holland's death?"

"The hell he did!" Van Borg frowned, leaned farther back in his chair, stuffed his hands into his pockets. His tanned forehead was rippled by a frown. "Oh, well, that might have been as coincidental as our meeting with the commissioner this morning to discuss the same subject. Was Holland a friend of yours, Doctor Stacey?"

I told him that I hadn't heard of the man until a little while ago.

"Nothing we can really do about Holland," Van Borg said. "The man's dead and I understand that his death was accidental. But the fact remains that if a certain person had had his way, Holland would have been *murdered.*"

IT WAS a startling pronouncement.

"Explain, please," Standish said rather brusquely. Standish hated hints and preferred directness.

"I wouldn't have brought the matter up at all," Carl Van Borg said, "if it weren't for the fact that—well, this man Chance—"

"What about Chance?" Standish cut in. "Suppose you begin at the beginning."

Needless to say, I too was rather interested in hearing the answer to that question.

"I attended that spook show Chance put on the other night," Van Borg said. "I was followed there by what I believe the police call a suspicious-looking character. At first glance you'd have thought some bum had sifted into the theater. At second glance—well, you wouldn't take a second glance if you could help it, he was that ugly."

Inwardly I tensed. That reference to ugliness had suddenly recalled to me Merry's man—the man with claws!

"I am not certain, understand," Van Borg went on, "but I believe that man who followed me would very much enjoy seeing me cooling my spine in the morgue. If this man is who I think he is, he would have also enjoyed seeing Michael Holland in the same position. And there are one or two others who might make pretty good targets for his vengeance."

Van Borg spoke slowly. An author, he was building up suspense. I concealed my impatience.

"His name you've probably all forgotten. At one time he was an outstanding explorer. His name is Eric Emboyd and he hasn't been in New York for years. In fact he has been confined to a leper colony in the tropics. Quite naturally he hates the men who discovered his disease and sent him to the leper colony."

There was no doubt of it any longer! My assumption had to be correct! Merry's man with claws! Leprosy, in certain stages, stiffens the joints of the fingers, making hands look like claws. And there was that other matter of the man ripping his cheek open on a nail and not seeming to notice it. Leprosy also destroys the sense of pain.

"A leper here in New York?" Standish breathed.

Van Borg let out that slow, easy smile of his.

"That's not so alarming. People lock lepers up because they are superstitious of them and because they aren't nice to look at. The ailment isn't spread by mere physical contact, though it used to be thought that it was. The alarming thing is that it was Michael Holland and I who discovered that poor old Eric had the disease. We dragged him to a medical friend of ours—a man by the name of Livingston—and it was Livingston who was instrumental in having Emboyd sent away. Interesting, isn't it, Doctor Stacey?"

"Yes," I said. "I can understand how this Emboyd might not care for you and Holland."

"Exactly," Van Borg said with a smile. "In fact, he swore to settle the score, which in his imaginings might have been multiplied several times over. Emboyd was about to be married and of course the discovery spoiled that for him. Naturally, he's bitter."

"What does all this have to do with Chance?" I asked.

VAN BORG'S brow furrowed. "I don't know. Only you know how you'll meet a person and then take a fancy to him? I met Chance the other night, and damned if he looked like a murderer to me. I just thought you ought to know that Eric Emboyd may have been in that audience, and if so, probably had murderous intentions in his heart."

"Was David Palmer one of Emboyd's enemies?" Standish asked. "Or rather a man whom Emboyd might have considered as an enemy."

"I don't know that Emboyd even knew Palmer," Van Borg said. "That's a possibility, of course. But here's another one: Eric Emboyd might have been firing poison darts at me, where I sat up there on the stage. He might have missed me and hit Palmer. In other words, this might have been an accident."

I made no comment. I hated to admit it to myself, but if I couldn't have blown a poison dart into the back of Palmer's neck from my side of the stage, a man sitting out in the audience certainly couldn't have done so.

Van Borg shrugged and stood up.

"I suppose you police do get a bit fed up with us layman detectives. Well, it was just an idea. You might keep an eye on Randolph Curtis. He's some sort of a consulting engineer, runs in and out of the city a lot. But he happens to be the man who married Eric Emboyd's girl friend, just another idea. I'll sift along and get out of your hair now, Commissioner."

Van Borg shook hands with us and left the office. When he had gone I said to Standish:

"Michael Holland was murdered."

Standish was taken aback.

"What makes you say that?" he demanded.

"Doctor Seer predicted his death," I said gravely. "I'm stubborn about some things, Ned, and one of those things is that nobody here on earth can predict a healthy man's death unless he's planning that death himself or knows some person who is planning it!"

CHAPTER XII

THE ROAD GOES NOWHERE

OVER ON East Fifty-Fifth Street, not very far from the brownstone house of George Chance, there is an old church with two gimlet-like spires boring into the sky. Beside the church squats a square house of brick which was formerly used as a rectory for the church pastor.

The rectory has the reputation of being haunted, if you believe what the small boys in the neighborhood tell you. It has a shabby, somber appearance, and if it isn't haunted why is it continually unoccupied?

Well, it isn't always unoccupied, though it may have that appearance. The house belongs to George Chance who keeps the rent prohibitively high so that the place will never be tenanted.

If any of the children in the neighborhood were to smash one of the locked windows and get into the dusty interior, they probably wouldn't stay long because of certain ghostly effects which had been installed for the purpose of keeping the curious kids away.

But the haunting of the rectory is not all effect. It's haunted. I ought to know, for I am the Ghost who haunts it! The basement of the building is well furnished in the modem manner, and the entrance to the basement is kept carefully locked. Only the Ghost and his six intimate friends have keys, and they are pretty cautious about entering the place so as not to be seen.

It was this house that the Ghost called home during the troubled days that followed the arrest of George Chance—or perhaps I should say Glenn Saunders. For it was Glenn Saunders, remember, who filled my shoes, who was indicted, tried and convicted of the murder of David Palmer.

The night that Glenn Saunders was sent up to Sing Sing, there to await the deposition of his lawyer's appeal from the death sentence, I met with my aides in the basement of the Ghost's rectory. Joe Harper was there, green hat tilted over his eyes, a chair supporting a portion of his back and shoulders, his heels cocked on the glass top of a cocktail table.

Merry White was also there, looking tired and worried. She had been compelled to testify at the trial and the ordeal of the court room had been a little too much for her.

With Joe and Merry was Tiny Tim, my smallest and oldest friend. As you might guess by his name, Tiny Tim Terry was a midget I had known in circus days. He is hardly tall enough to see over a table, though well along toward middle age. As an investigator for the Ghost he is priceless. Wearing a boy's suit, he can pass for a child. Merry White has even packed him into a baby carriage at times, but he's a bit resentful at being goo-gooed by women.

However, in juvenile disguise, he can get information for me without running the risk of being suspected. His small body can slip through openings too small to admit the average adult. His is a child's body, you might say, but his brain is that of an adult.

"THERE ARE several angles to work on in this business," I said to my friends.

"One angle that seems to be played out is this man with the claws," Joe Harper said. "I went to that address where the man with the claws was hanging out, tried to trace him from there. But I think Merry must have scared him away."

"The police haven't had any better luck than you, Joe," I said.

"There's that moldy-minded Doctor Seer," Merry said. She swirled across the room in one of those unsuspected and graceful movements of hers, to land where I hoped she would—on the couch beside me.

"Yes, there's Doctor Seer," I said. "Seer, the death-prophet. If said deaths were murders, and we're sure Palmer's death was, then Seer, if not the murderer himself, is in some way connected with him."

Tiny Tim shoved an enormous cigar into his baby mouth and when he lighted it Joe Harper bummed a match off him for a cigarette.

"I want you to know I'll do anything," Tim said, getting a couple of lungfuls of smoke off his chest. "If it's another baby act with the frail playing mama, I'll even suck a pacifier if it will help."

The "frail" was Merry. Tiny Tim was very slangy.

"Another angle we've got to consider is the fact that somebody is trying to throw a scare into Irene Kalaban," I said.

"Where's the hook-up?" Joe asked, his cigarette wagging up and down in his lips as he spoke.

"Well," I explained, "when Kalaban left that two hundred thousand dollar reward to anyone who could prove communication with his spirit after death, he opened the door to a lot of crooked activity on the part of the spook crooks. Dr. Seer is the biggest spook crook in town. Suppose Seer has some way of knowing ahead of time when certain people are to be murdered. He makes his predictions based on that knowledge. Mightn't he do this for the sole purpose of throwing a scare into Irene Kalaban?"

"I don't get it," Merry said. "Clearer, please."

"Suppose," I tried again, "Seer convinces Irene Kalaban that he can predict death. Then suppose he predicts that Irene is to die. Then he goes to Irene and says that he can communicate with spirits and maybe he could prevail upon the forces of life and death to spate her—for a price. Irene's income is limited to about ten thousand a year, I understand. But there's the matter of two hundred thousand dollars in reward money for anyone who can prove communication with Kalaban's spirit."

"So," Joe concluded for me, "if anybody can scare that secret code message out of Irene, the rest is velvet. With the secret code message, the fake spiritualist can hold a séance, use the code message to prove to the executor of the Kalaban estate that connection with Kalaban's spirit has been established."

"WHAT A nasty deal!" she said.

"Okay," I said. "Now Joe, it's your job to see if you can figure out who is putting the hooks into Irene Kalaban. Remember also that Seer predicted the death of Michael Holland. I've got some dope on Holland and one of you might check on him. It's no job for you, Merry. I'd rather you'd get friendly with Irene Kalaban and help Joe.

"Holland was a sort of crack-brained scientist. He worked all by himself in a crummy little lab on the lower east side. About a month ago he was fooling with some poison gas and the apparatus he was working with seems to have blown up. The cyanogen gas got him like fly-spray gets a fly."

"Quick-like, huh?" Joe Harper mused thoughtfully.

"It seems to me," Tim said, "that after the Homicide Bureau, including Inspector Magnus' number twelve shoes, have tracked all over the place, most of the evidence would be slightly obliterated."

"Maybe," I said. "But where the Homicide squad made its mistake was in deciding that this was accidental. They figured it that way, and of course you can get pretty dead just fooling around with cyanogen. But if Seer predicted Holland's death, I think somebody planned that death."

"So we do what?" Merry asked.

"Tim," I said, "how about you investigating the Holland death on your own?"

I felt certain he would enjoy playing a man's part for once, and would play it well.

Tim stood up, put his hands behind him, tilted his cigar, and paced the floor. The president of a corporation planning a merger couldn't have looked more profound.

"I'll take you up on that, George," the little man said. "I'll ferret out the evidence."

"And remember," I said, "Glenn Saunders is in the death house up at Sing Sing, taking a rap for a murder he didn't commit, because he's supposed to be me, convicted of a murder I didn't commit! Unless we solve this mystery, and solve it fast, I'm going to reverse the substitution, get Glenn out and put myself in! All right, let's get going."

CHAPTER XIII

SPIRIT TEMPLE

EAST 127TH STREET near Lexington Avenue doesn't look like the convening place for the souls of the blessed dead. It is a narrow street with littered gutters and worn block sidewalks. Signs swinging from iron brackets attached to the front of closely crowded buildings advertise cheap lodgings, tailoring, hairdos and what-not. Narrow stone stair treads bound by ornate black iron rails lead up to the main entrances and down to basements. Some of the buildings look wrong-side-around, what with fire escapes zigzagging across their faces.

Such is the street where Dr. Seer, Prophet of Doom, had his "Temple." And it was to this temple that I went the night following the conference with my aides. I wore the disguise that can identify me as the Ghost when I will it to. But when I paid my two dollar fee to the squat, gray-haired woman in black at the door, you can be sure that the Ghost was completely "turned off." So I entered Dr. Seer's domain without attracting as much attention as my money did.

The place was pretty well filled. I could see that there was going to be a shortage of seats and for that reason I simply stood at the back of the large room, not far from the exit. People in the aisle near me were writing questions on billets of paper and these were handed to one of

Dr. Seer's assistants who immediately burned the billets and tossed the glowing ashes into a large brass vase that rested on a wheeled table.

I watched the man doing the message-burning. He was quite an artist at his billet-switching, and needless to say the billets he burned were not the ones with the questions written on them. The question slips, I was certain, were perfectly whole and were preserved in a special compartment in the vase, deposited in that compartment when the assistant put the ashes of the burned billets in the vase.

As soon as I had learned the secret of the billet-switching trick, I turned my attention to the audience itself. Near the front in a sea of unfamiliar faces, I saw the rugged, granite-hard visage of Robert Martin, who had proclaimed Dr. Seer the greatest of all mediums previous to my spirit-show on the night of the murder.

Such a determined believer was Martin that I would have been greatly surprised if I hadn't seen him among those present. Nor was I surprised to see that equally determined non-believer, author Carl Van Borg.

Van Borg was seated half-way toward the stage and well over to one side. His dark, leathery countenance was illuminated by a wide smile. It must have been perfectly clear to everyone around him that he was greatly amused by the credulous people who composed Dr. Seer's clientele.

SEER'S STAGE was a simple black-draped platform, raised a foot and a half above the floor of the room. It was completely draped in black. Shortly after I entered, curtains were drawn back on rods disclosing the lanky, thread-bare prophet seated in an ornate chair which might have been picked up when some lodge had auctioned off its props. There was a small table in front of him and it was covered with black velvet. Resting on the stumpy pyramid in the center of the table was a large glass globe.

Seer's head was bare. Had I been in his place, with that colorless crop of fuzz on my head, I certainly would have hidden it with a turban. Dr. Seer, I learned, knew absolutely nothing about showmanship—the first requisite of a fake spiritualist. At least he didn't use any. The fact troubled me. It hinted that Seer might be sincere, and that didn't fit in with his prophesies of death followed by murder.

Seer's lack of showmanship, it appeared, didn't prevent him from having a large following.

Lights were dimmed, the audience hushed. The door near me was closed. Dr. Seer rose to his feet, gaunt, starved-looking.

His angular body bent over the glass globe. His fingers closed upon the globe, stroked it gently as he spoke.

There were questions to be answered first of all before he attempted any spirit manifestations, his high-pitched, curiously magnetic voice announced.

As he stroked the glass ball, as his lean, ugly face contorted, the crystal began to glow with a purplish light that quickly changed to pale yellow and then green—each of the colors contributing their peculiar effect to the hollow-cheeked face of the mystic who bent over the globe.

It was the same old hooey, the same run of questions. Is my girl two-timing me? Can you tell me where that diamond cuff-link I lost is? When will I be married? And of course Seer gave the questions such complicated answers that the person who had originally written the question could interpret the answer to suit himself.

But the audience was definitely impressed. You see, a mentalist's job is really done for him when he is able to repeat questions that have been "destroyed." When he does this, his answer doesn't matter, because he already has his sucker hooked. I don't suppose any of those who had written down questions ever thought that if the papers on which they had written were really destroyed there would have been no possible reason for them to have been asked to write them in the first place!

Seer hadn't done any of the work himself. If there was any "art" connected with the racket it had been accomplished by that billet-switching genius who had apparently burned the messages in the aisle. And the cheapest assistant to a side-show mentalist could have done what this billet-switching assistant of Dr. Seer had done.

Seer, I was beginning to believe, was simply the ornate fringe of a racket. But if that were so, why hadn't a man with more showmanship been picked?

THE QUESTION and answer part of the show complete, Dr. Seer threw himself back into his chair, seemingly exhausted. But his eyes continued to stare at the glowing globe in front of him. I saw his lank body gradually stiffen, and as though the audience knew what was coming, I noted a certain animal pricking-up of the ears among Seer's "congregation."

And the mystic's crystal ball glowed pink. The pink deepened to rose and then glowed steadily a blood-red. Beneath Seer's platform somebody, presumably friend Satan, beat on a brass gong.

When the reverberations of the gong had died, every member of the audience was on its feet. Dr. Seer also stood up, his reed-like body waving back and forth above the blood-red ball.

"This is my third prediction!" his voice shrilled as he squinted down into the globe. "Three days from today a man shall die. His name is—his name"—he passed a hand over his forehead—"his name I can see clearly now, Dr. Matthew Salvo Livingston. Three days from today, Dr. Matthew Salvo Livingston will die!"

The gong crashed again, masking the excited murmur that ran through the audience. Across the ball, I saw Carl Van Borg get half out of his chair and then sit down again. And I was about as startled by this announcement as he was. For wasn't Dr. Livingston the man who was responsible for sending Eric Emboyd to the leper colony?

With the idea of getting beneath Seer's stage to see the mechanics of his miracles, I turned toward the door. As I did so, I bumped into a man. I steadied him by putting a hand on his shoulder. He blinked up near-sightedly at my face. Though I could not be sure in the gloomy interior of the room, I thought this was the man Irene Kalaban had named as Harold Harkness, executor of the Kalaban estate.

The meeting was breaking up in a lot of noise, so I slipped out of the door, through the hall, and to the front exit. I hurried down the narrow stairs to the sidewalk, rounded the base of the stairs to the basement door which was directly beneath. The door was locked. I was certain that I would be a good deal wiser on the subject of Dr. Seer after I had investigated that basement.

CHAPTER XIV

GUNS OF THE RACKET

I HAVE DUPLICATED Houdini's classic escape from a Chinese water cell, and if you have ever seen that stunt on the stage you can well imagine that I had no great trouble picking the lock of the door that led into Seer's basement.

The door closed behind me, I stood there for a moment, eyes closed so that the pupils of my eyes might open to their fullest. When I opened my eyes I could see fairly well in the faint glow from the street which passed through the dirt-encrusted panes of glass in the basement windows. Dr. Seer's assistant seemed to have departed.

If there were any noises in the basement, I couldn't have heard them because of the rumble made by the shuffling of feet in the chamber above my head. I moved across a furnace room which was directly connected with a coal bin under the sidewalk in front of the building. I knew just about where Dr. Seer's stage was located. At the back of the furnace room was a good sized cubicle cut off from the rest of the basement by walls of unpainted wood.

Feeling my way along the wooden wall, I came to a door that yielded to my touch. If the door creaked when I opened it, I couldn't hear the sound because of the noise upstairs.

Inside, I was in the sort of darkness that clung to the eyeballs. I pulled my tiny pocket flashlight and thrust its needle beam around until I located a light switch on the wall. I turned the switch on and a closely shaded light in one side of the room showed. Above my head I could clearly make out the outline of the base of Dr. Seer's stage. It was a mere shell of construction, which accounted for the closely shaded light—no tell-tale rays would pass up through the stage.

There was a large, old-fashioned roll-top desk in one corner of the room. Two or three good-sized packing boxes might have served as furniture. There was a tiny elevator with a foot-square platform connected with a sliding trap in the stage—

My investigation was cut short. It was cut short by the shadow of a man falling suddenly across the floor. Dr. Seer's assistant was back.

I didn't turn around just then. I simply kicked out with my foot at the lamp which was near the floor, smashed the bulb with the toe of my shoe.

"You're covered," a muffled voice said. "Don't move."

But before the man could spot me with a light, I had slipped my cigarette case from my pocket, clicked it open, and removed the third cigarette from the end of the row. When the flashlight beamed at me, I was simply holding the cigarette case in one hand and the cigarette between my fingers in the other hand.

There were two other men behind the man with the flashlight—Bull and Shark-face. Shark-face had his right arm in a sling, a memento of the set-to at Palmer's. The face of the man with the light was a blank. I mean a white curtain mask covered him from forehead to chin. Maybe his aspect wasn't as threatening as the faces of the two hard-looking eggs near the door, but there was menace enough in the determined jut of his gun.

THERE WAS no way out of the room except the elevator to Seer's stage and the door. I had put my head in a perfect trap and getting out was going to be plenty tough. The door might better have been closed and locked than blocked off by these men. And because of the noise upstairs I couldn't have been warned of their approach.

My lips peeled back from the yellow shell teeth I wore. My eyes stared blankly. All the indications of animation disappeared from my face. In short, I "turned on the Ghost."

The effect on the three men who blocked my entrance was evident at once. The gun in the masked man's hand wavered a little. The two toughs bunched close together.

Those of the criminal element in New York who have never had direct contact with the Ghost nevertheless know of his existence, have heard descriptions of him. These three knew they were having contact with him now, and were speechless.

It must have been something like digging for treasure and then finding that the spade you've been using has been hammering on a dud shell that is apt to go off at any minute.

I dropped the cigarette from my fingers to the floor. It showed up dimly against the dark concrete. I took a side step so that the toe of my shoe touched the cigarette.

"What are you doing down here?" the man in the mask asked unsteadily.

"I'm not here," I said. "I'm elsewhere, see?"

I brought my foot down on the cigarette with a scuffing motion. There was a sharp explosion, a flash of flame, and a column of smoke rolled upward, enveloping me.

The masked man dropped his light, scrambled for it. He cursed and yelled to the toughs to block off the door. He didn't need to bother, I wasn't going anywhere.

The masked man told someone to turn on the light. But by the time the light was on, I wasn't within sight. A pillar of smoke that mushroomed out as it met the ceiling was all that could be seen of the Ghost. For as soon as I had dropped the cigarette and set it off with the toe of my shoe, I had dived for the roll-top desk, shoved the rolling curtain back, curled up on the top, and rolled the curtain down in front of me. I had to move fast, but I'm used to moving fast after spending most of my life in Magic. The small sounds I made were covered by the shuffling of feet overhead.

"Where'd he go?" Shark-face gasped.

"He disappeared—disappeared in a cloud of smoke!"

"Nuts!" said the muffled voice of the man in the mask. "The man's human. He couldn't have got out of here. Look behind those boxes. Get busy. We've got to find him. He's dangerous."

CRAMPED UP inside the desk, I managed to wiggle out my little automatic which I held ready for a surprise just in case the baffled men got realistic and looked in about the only place that I could have hidden.

The trick I had pulled is known as "The Devil's Whisper." Needless to say the cigarette had been carefully prepared. It was simply a cushioning roll of tissue around a mixture of chlorate of potash and red phosphorus, a couple of chemicals which won't stand much jolting around when brought together. Actually I simply use the trick to produce sudden and surprising misdirection which is sufficiently startling to permit me to make a few moves which usually go unnoticed.

"He's not in here," the masked man said. "Search the basement."

"He couldn't have got by the door with me standing here." Bull objected. "It—it just ain't human."

Human or not, the trio went out to hunt for me. I kept to the desk, and a little bit later I heard the audience in the hall upstairs going out. Possibly my basement explosion was the most successful "spirit" manifestation Dr. Seer had ever produced.

Somebody came back into the room beneath the stage and turned out the light. Then the last whisper of footsteps died, and I wedged my fingertips under the edge of the desk curtain and raised it.

I tiptoed to the basement door and found that I was locked in. It was worth a laugh. Undoubtedly the spook racketeers had taken particular pains to lock up thoroughly to keep the Ghost out of their basement.

Back in the under-stage room, I made a pretty thorough investigation. I found the metal vase which had been used to handle the burned messages of the members of the audience. There was, as I had supposed, a separate compartment where the messages themselves were preserved. Ashes of duplicate billets were in the other compartment.

The crystal ball and its secrets, by means of which Seer read the questions, was subtle. A narrow shaft in the ceiling of the under-stage room reached up into the hollow center leg of the table which Seer had on his stage. A piston-like arrangement on a long handle was made to fit exactly into this shaft and on the flat surface of this piston the messages written by the audience could be attached. But covering this piston was a silk curtain on tiny spring rollers. The silk curtain was part of the focal plane shutter of an old camera, I believed.

I puzzled over this for a moment. If Seer *knew* that he was a fake, there was no point in the shutter arrangement on the piston, because the messages thrust up into the shaft which probably ended at the bottom of his crystal ball couldn't be seen by the audience. There could only be one explanation—the shutter arrangement was to fool Dr. Seer himself!

IT WORKED in this way: One of the messages was placed under the shutter curtain and the curtain closed. The piston was thrust up the shaft to the illuminated crystal globe. Because the globe rested on a velvet topped table, Dr. Seer wouldn't know when the message was in place until someone down below pulled the shutter release. Then the message would fade into the globe.

That accounted for the evident sincerity Dr. Seer got into these meetings. He really believed he had supernatural powers.

Even the illumination of the crystal globe was so carefully concealed and operated from the room beneath the stage that I doubted if Dr. Seer understood it. And the trap in the stage which was connected to the elevator in the room below was a masterpiece of careful construction. When Seer materialized spirits by means of this elevator and trap he didn't know what he was doing. What was merely mechanical he thought was spiritual.

There was nothing in the roll-top desk of much interest save a ledger which indicated the profits the spook racketeers had made up to now. During six months of operation they had netted about ten thousand dollars. They had yet to make a really big killing.

A spook crook, you see, waits until some wealthy client in a moment of spirit-inspired confidence, reveals something out of his or her past that isn't savory. Then the spook crook becomes a blackmailer. Any blackmailing that this outfit had done hadn't got into the higher brackets, though it was evident the crooks were eating.

I might easily have taken this ledger to the police and had the whole gang rounded up. But first I had to establish what all this hocus-pokus had to do with murder. As far as I knew, out of two predictions of death, Dr. Seer had been a hundred percent right. First Michael Holland, the poor inventor and scientist, and then the wealthy and distinguished David Palmer.

Tonight he had made a third prediction. Dr. Matthew Salvo Livingston was to die three days from tonight. I had never met Livingston, but I intended to meet him now without delay.

There was a phone in the under-stage room and I consulted the directories and eventually found Dr. Livingston's address on Beaumont Avenue in the Bronx. He didn't have an office phone, so I took it that his doctor's degree was something besides medicine. Possibly, considering his location, he was on the Fordham University staff.

As it turned out, just to show how wrong you can be, Dr. Livingston had a medical degree and also that of doctor of philosophy. He had retired on a small income and spent most of his time as a consultant for the Bronx Park Botanical Gardens.

It was about ten o'clock when I phoned Livingston's house. I asked if I couldn't see him for a few minutes on a matter of extreme urgency. He pumped me a little, trying to find out what it was I wanted.

Finally I said: "It concerns your death, Doctor," and hung up. Even if he didn't want to see me, I was pretty sure he wouldn't be asleep when I got there.

CHAPTER XV

I WARN
THE DOCTOR

B EFORE I lock-picked my way out of Dr. Seer's spirit temple, I took out my compact makeup kit and altered my disguise. I removed the wire ovals from my nostrils and got my nose back into shape again, took out the celluloid shells that covered my teeth, used a cloth to remove the powder and eyeshadow that did much toward making the Ghost.

With "plumpers" in my mouth to fatten my cheeks, a few extra years tacked on me by means of a lining pencil applied to the corners of my eyes and mouth, I no longer looked like the Ghost. I didn't look like George Chance either. In fact when I added dignity to my makeup by dusting my temples with powder and then borrowed some wisdom from a pair of Oxford glasses, I had stepped again into the identity of Dr. Stacey.

As Dr. Stacey I had done a good deal of investigating in the past. It's one of my favorite disguises and one which I thought might make an impression upon Dr. Matthew Livingston. At least Livingston and Stacey had titles in common, though Stacey's title had come out of the Ghost's makeup kit rather than a university.

From the brief chat I had with Livingston over the phone I got the impression he was a garrulous old man. After my taxi had put me down in front of his house in Beaumont Avenue and I actually met the man, I found I was wrong on one count—Livingston was not old.

Livingston had a flat-topped head. The flatness was emphasized by the fact that his oily black hair was combed from a middle part and stood out over his ears like eaves. Oily black eaves overhung his eyes so that it was next to impossible to determine their color. When he opened his mouth his lower teeth stuck out a little like a bulldog's because that was the way his jaw was made.

He was a man who didn't carry much weight around his body but plenty around his head. I don't mean he was a fathead. He was probably bright enough. But he had evidently resolved in his mind to be as unpleasant as possible.

A servant, who looked as if he had long suffered beneath the tongue lashings of his master, let him in. Livingston dismissed him in a way that was pretty definite.

"Get out, Jeffry!" he said.

Livingston and I were in the small central hall of the house. There were two occasional chairs in the hall, but I wasn't asked to sit down. Livingston didn't sit down either. Merry White would have said: "He don't look like he could bend."

"Are you the damned ass who called me on the phone an hour ago?" Livingston demanded. "You are, aren't you? Dr. Stacey, eh? Never heard of you!"

"What a coincidence!" I said pleasantly. "I was on the point of remarking that I had never heard of you either until tonight."

Livingston snorted. "You've heard of me, eh? Heard of me tonight. What did you hear of me?"

"Maybe you'd better sit down," I said. "This might be a bit of a shock."

LIVINGSTON SHOOK his head savagely.

"Nothing shocks me. No news you could have could shock me. My family is all dead except one, and I wouldn't care if he was."

"You care about yourself a little, don't you?" I asked. "This bad news is about you, Dr. Livingston. I heard you were going to die three days from today."

If this made any impression on Livingston, I couldn't detect it.

"Go on," he said. "What else?"

"After you're dead," I said, determined to break through the man's crust if possible, "there isn't any else."

"Bosh!" he said. "What are you talking about? Do you think you're God, telling me I'm to die in three days?"

"I didn't say it. A man named Doctor Seer said it and he's predicted the deaths of two other men with awful accuracy. Dr. Seer is a spiritualist."

"Never heard of Dr. Seer either. Spiritualist! Twiddle-twaddle. You can go back where you came from and tell Dr. Steer or Speer or whatever his name is that if he comes around here with his unadulterated bosh I'll tweak his nose for him."

"Good!" I said. "We've got something in common. We both believe that Dr. Seer is full of—well, you've called it twiddle-twaddle. Just the same, I'd like you to answer a few questions. Dr. Livingston, have you any enemies—people who might want to kill you?"

"Rot!" he said.

"The impression that you've made gave me the idea you might have a lot of enemies," I said, watching the angry doctor carefully.

That did it. Livingston sat down as though he was a deflated balloon. He was breathing rapidly.

"Look here, Stacey," he said, fingering a fraternity key that dangled on his watch chain, "you got me a bit upset with your damned phone call. I have been doing some intensive research for the botanical gardens here and I didn't want to be bothered. But you're so determined—what is it you want, anyway?"

I offered him a cigarette, took one myself when he refused.

"Did you ever hear of Eric Emboyd?" I asked.

"I have indeed. One of my close friends of former years. The poor devil's out in the Philippines in the leper colony. I had him put out there to be cured. My private opinion was that he was too far gone to be cured, but there's nothing like giving a poor devil hope."

"Eric Emboyd is in New York," I said gravely. "Isn't it possible that he might be looking for you with murder in his heart?"

LIVINGSTONE SNORTED again.

"If Emboyd is back in town," he snapped, "he'll avoid doctors, not seek them out. Why, if I saw him, I'd send him packing back where he came from. What's all this got to do with Dr. Seer? Emboyd isn't this crazy mystic, is he?"

I shook my head.

"Then your spirit *fakir* pulled the wrong number out of the hat this time, Stacey. Matthew Salvo Livingston isn't good material for mysteries. Or for murders either. Why, when I die, I'll have just enough money left to bury me."

"Everybody has to die sometime," I said. "The question usually is how and when? It's possible, you will admit, that Emboyd might be out to kill you for sending him to the leper colony."

"I say bosh again," Livingston said with a harsh chuckle. "I'd like to see him try it. I'd like to see anybody try it. Good night, Dr. Stacey. Sorry to rush you off. I have a hard day's work ahead of me and I'd like to get some sleep."

And he opened the door suggestively for me.

I saw that I could get no further with him. If ever a man believed himself perfectly able to take care of himself, it was the crusty Dr. Livingston.

It was midnight by the time I taxied back to the vicinity of the Ghost's haunted rectory. When I slipped through the back door of the squat, dark building, and went down into the basement, I found Joe Harper having a tall drink from my little bar. He was stretched out on the couch as completely as it was possible for him to be and still drink without pouring the stuff all over his face.

I could feel Joe's beetle-black eyes following me as I went to the bar for a bit of a drink myself.

"Where did you get, Ghost?" he asked me.

"Seer is a fake but doesn't know it," I said. "He thinks he's on the receiving end of all the telegraph lines leading from heaven or wherever our ends are rough-hewn for us. Under his crystal, which he alone looks into, there's a sort of camera shutter device that lets messages flash in under the crystal like magic. He wouldn't be trying to fool himself, would he?"

"If he doesn't pull the strings, who does?" Joe asked.

"A gang of crooks."

"I get it. Dr. Seer is the scenery. The crooks fool both him and the public and split the take. Well, that's your story. Merry and I made out all right with Irene Kalaban."

"How?" I asked.

"Well, Merry and I were looking the house over from the outside when a car drove up and out gets Irene Kalaban. Like a flash, Merry pulls a fake twist of her right gam and falls down on the sidewalk.

"Mrs. Kalaban asks what the matter is and Merry goes into her act. She's hurt her ankle. Irene says: 'Aren't you the young woman who assists George Chance?' Merry says she is. Irene takes Merry up into her house for the night."

THE PHONE rang. Joe and I both reached for it, but my reach was the longest. Tiny Tim's voice came shrilly from the receiver:

"I need help and need it quick! I'm locked in. I think he's going to fire the place. I—"

There was a sputtering crackling sound and then the steady line buzz of the phone and nothing more.

I dropped the phone into its cradle, turned, bumped into Joe Harper.

"What's up?" Joe demanded.

"Tim's in trouble. Sounds bad. Somebody cut the line before he could tell me where he was. But I sent him to Holland's so that's where he must be."

"Let's go," Joe said.

"You stay here. Merry may call any moment."

And I ran from the rectory.

CHAPTER XVI

MURDER FLAME

JOE HARPER'S car, or rather one that he had bought and I had paid for, was the one I used in getting to Holland's laboratory on the lower east side. I didn't spare horsepower or rubber getting there.

The laboratory was a disused livery stable on Water Street and as I passed it in the car the place looked dark and quiet enough. I parked the car up the block a little and hurried back. I tried the door of the place and found it locked.

I started around the building looking for a convenient window through which I might enter. A shed-like addition was attached to the rear and piled against the wall of it was a number of packing boxes reaching nearly to the low roof.

This looked like some sort of a stairway which Tiny Tim might have constructed. I climbed up it to the roof of the shed and saw that a hood ventilator pipe about a foot in diameter had been removed from its flange. Here was obviously the means of entrance which Tiny Tim had used, but it wouldn't do a full-sized man any good.

From the roof of the shed, I got to the roof of the main structure. There was a skylight up there and I knew I could pry the thing up and get into the laboratory that way. But as I was going across the roof toward the skylight; I heard the sound of a motor car starting. The sound came from the north side of the building. I ran to the edge of the roof and looked down.

Below me was an old model sedan, standing in the drive, motor warming. It was an eight foot drop from the roof to the top of the car, but as the car started to roll I sprang from the roof, landed flat on the top of the car. Had it been one of these newer models with a steel roof, I'd have had the wind knocked out of me.

Whoever was at the wheel knew well enough I was up above him. His first idea was to shake me off as a bronco tries to shake its rider. As the car hit the street, the driver skidded it around a corner. But I was looking for something like that and the toes of my shoes hooked down over the edge of the car top, keeping me crosswise of the car when centrifugal force would have thrown me off.

I got out my knife. Any more such twisting around and I'd drive the blade into the fabric of the car top and use that for a handle to hang on with.

The car turned at the next corner, headed for the river. The driver spurted for one of the piers and I rolled toward the back of the car. Nothing kept me from flying off except my knife. I drove the blade deep into the fabric. The cloth was more than half rotten. The knife didn't hold until the blade struck a cross member.

My weight sagged the top of the car, weakened now by the long gash my knife had made. I heard threads pop as the car jolted over a bump. A sudden lurch and the top tore all the way across. I hinged in the middle, went all the way through, my back and shoulders meeting the rear cushions, my heels coming down on the shoulders of the driver.

I KNEW I was in the tightest spot of my life. I rolled myself off the cushions to the floor, got my legs down from the back of the front seat. At the same time, I went for my gun. I scrambled around, got onto my knees, thrust upward with my gun to the place where the back of the driver's head should have been.

At that moment, the smell of gasoline fumes came to my nostrils. A match flamed, arced above my head, struck somewhere behind me. The interior of the car was suddenly bright with flame. The car was going mad. I saw its driver standing on the left running board, giving an imitation of steering with one hand through the window. How close the wheels were to the end of the pier I didn't know. I simply pulled my gun around and fired at the man on the running board.

Only, he wasn't on the running board then. At the very moment I applied pressure to the trigger, he must have dropped off. What became of him after that, I had no chance of learning. The back of the rear cushion was a sheet of flame. The car without a driver was rushing toward one side of the pier, throttle wide open. And as I started to roll over into the front seat in a desperate effort to get control of the machine, I saw Tiny Tim Terry huddled in one corner of the rear seat, nicely bound and gagged.

I flopped to the front cushion, glimpsed the side of the pier just ahead of the nose of the car. I got my left hand to the right side of the wheel, yanked the car away from the water's edge. Before getting my feet around to the clutch and brake pedals, I pulled the hand-brake back and jerked the hand throttle to a retarded position. Rubber burned as the car skidded; brake lining was seered. But the car stopped crossways of the pier.

The sudden stop must have rolled Tiny Tim to the floor of the car. Or perhaps he had managed to get there in his frantic wriggling to get away from the flaming rear cushion. Anyway, I got out of the car, got the back door open, dragged him out. The sleeve of his coat was burning, but I smothered it out. Then I put Tim down on the pier and looked around. The man who would have made torch victims of Tim and me was nowhere to be seen.

I cut Tim's bonds, pulled the gag from his mouth, rushed him away from the car that was now a flaming torch. Not so far away a fire alarm sounded. I picked Tim up in my arms in order to make better time. This was no time to stand and argue with firemen about the origin of the fire.

It was not until Tim and I were safely hidden in the shadow of a warehouse that I was able to get his story.

TIM HAD investigated the neighborhood in which Holland had his laboratory by daylight. From a talkative tailor, he had learned that Holland was a victim of hard luck. Holland had produced some sort of a triple-phase radio tube.

"And what do you suppose happened when Mike Holland applied for a patent?" the tailor asked Tim. "Somebody had beat him to the same invention by twenty-four hours! Here he had all that money invested in a machine for blowing glass tubes and extracting the air from them, and his invention was worthless to him."

Tim failed to learn anything further about how Holland had died. Everyone seemed to agree with the police opinion on the matter.

That night Tim had entered the laboratory through the ventilator pipe on the roof. He was giving the place the once over when somebody unlocked the front door and came into the dark interior. Tim ducked through the door of a little office set apart from the main room of the laboratory and from there watched the prowler.

Guided by a flashlight, the man searched a cabinet, found a sheet of paper which he examined closely in the light of his torch. The paper was some sort of a map, Tim was certain of that. In an attempt to get a better look at the piece of paper, Tim stumbled over the leg of a stool.

The man in the dark swung around, spotted Tim with his flashlight. Tim ducked into the office and slammed the door, bolting it on the inside. The man tried to follow him, couldn't get the door open.

Tim crouched inside the little room, holding his breath. He could just see through the key hole. He saw the prowler apply a match to the paper for which he had searched. In the flicker of flame from the burning paper; he could see two things: the man wore a white mask that covered his face completely. And at the man's feet was a red can that might contain gasoline.

It was then that Tim got the idea that the man was going to set the laboratory on fire. Frantically, he looked for a phone in the office, found it, called the unlisted telephone number of the Ghost's rectory.

"But," I said, when Tim had concluded, "the man didn't use the gasoline to fire the laboratory. He simply wanted to destroy this paper you say was a map?"

"That's it," Tim piped. "He used the gasoline to soak the cushions of that old jalopy he was driving. It took him some time to break down the door of the office. Then we had a bit of a fight. I'm kind of hard to catch, you know. But once he had me, the fight was over. He must have intended either running his car into the river with me in it or setting the thing on fire."

"Probably both," I said. "Wanted to make it look like an accident. But tell me this, Tim—in your struggle with the man, did you make out a single identifying mark? Did he say anything so that you might have a chance to recognize his voice if you heard it again?"

TIM SHOOK his head.

"He didn't say a word. And in the darkness I didn't get much of a chance to see any identifying marks. Afraid we didn't net anything at all except the knowledge that the prowler wanted to destroy some sort of a map. And where will that get us?"

At the time, I was inclined to agree with Tim—that we knew nothing more than we had known before. But later the scene that Tim had witnessed through the keyhole turned out to be of the utmost importance.

CHAPTER XVII

SHAKE-DOWN

NOT UNTIL late the following afternoon, as darkness fell, did I hear from Merry White.

"I guess I'm wonderful," she said gayly over the phone. "It's Mrs. Kalaban's maid who has been putting those nasty warning notes around the apartment. She's in the business with a Lexington Avenue photographer. I followed the maid to this man's picture shop. He's a man with one leg that would be shorter than the other if he didn't wear a built-up shoe. You go upstairs to his shop. I would think being lame he would have his place on the ground floor, but—"

"Where are you now?" I asked.

"At Mrs. Kalaban's. The maid is out and so is Mrs. Kalaban. She went out with her boy friend, that nice Robert Martin. I'm all alone now. Mrs. Kalaban would like to adopt me, I think. And I found the picture."

"What picture, Merry?" I demanded. "Stop talking riddles."

"The picture. The one they're using to shake-down Mrs. Kalaban. I don't understand it. It's a photo of a man lying on the street in front of Mrs. Kalaban's car. And it shows Mrs. Kalaban getting in her car. The man on the street looks dead. On the back is penciled: 'We want two hundred thousand dollars or that something just as good.' Do you suppose that refers to the secret code message that could be used to collect the reward money?"

"Yes," I said positively. "Now listen, Merry. I'll drop by and pick up that photograph inside of an hour. And don't let me forget to tell you that you're wonderful."

I hung up and turned to Joe Harper.

"We're going to go after a shake-down artist, Joe. There may be some rough stuff so maybe we'd better look the part. I begin to see a little daylight in this business. Running into those thugs at Palmer's, and then into another pair at Kalaban's, sort of confuses the issue. This affair has more than a single thread, it has at least two, and my hunch now is that even though they've tangled, they're separate in origin and perhaps in motive. Let's go."

When Joe and I left the Ghost's rectory, we were a couple of hard-looking eggs. I had broadened my nose so that it looked like something that had stopped too many fists. And I had built myself a pugnacious chin. We both had on the oldest, sloppiest clothes we could find in the Ghost's wardrobe. Joe even traded his green felt hat for a cap and his piped vest for a turtle-neck sweater. He slid a sap into his pocket.

Merry was out in front of the apartment building where Mrs. Kalaban lived. She gave me a hello kiss, handed me the photograph, and then a good-bye kiss.

The picture was just about what Merry had described. The face of the man on the street was clearly shown, and he did look plenty dead. And Mrs. Kalaban was easily recognized, too.

JOE WAS driving the car, and when I gave him the address of the photo shop which Merry had given me, Joe said he would bet a fish he knew the photographer. His name was Oscar something and Oscar something didn't mind doing anything for money.

On the way to this photographer Joe called Oscar, I stopped at a drugstore and bought a photo-flash bulb and a box of writing paper. I came out of the drugstore, emptied the paper into a street receptacle, but saved the box. I took the photo-flash bulb and shorted it across the two ammeter posts back of the instrument board on Joe's car.

"What do you think you're doing?" Joe wanted to know.

"Getting something to stick our photographer with," I told him. Then I put the burned flash bulb into the paper box and told Joe to get going.

Up Lexington, not far from 128th Street, Joe pointed out a sign that hung over a door and read:

PHOTO FINISHING

"That's Oscar's, I think," Joe said. "Probably he lives there, too."

The building was an ancient red brick tenement. We parked, got out. I carried the box with the bulb under my arm. The doorway under the sign opened on a flight of steps. We went up to the second floor where another sign, identical with the first, was hung on a door. I knocked at the panel.

Pretty soon we could hear footsteps, half of which sounded as if made by a built-up shoe such as a cripple might wear. The door was opened, and Joe asked if this was Oscar. Anybody could see that it was—a largish man, lame, wearing a rubber apron to protect his clothes against photo acids.

"I've got some pictures I'd like to show you," I said. "I'd like some enlargements made."

Oscar took a rank smelling cigar from between snags of yellow teeth. He asked us to come in, not very cordially. Maybe now that he was in the big blackmail racket he didn't care about stooping to pick up an honest penny.

We went into a small photographic shop with a dark room walled off in one corner. A door at the other side of the room opened into what was probably Oscar's living room and bedroom combined.

"What d'ya want?" Oscar asked.

"This," I pulled out the photo print that Merry White had given me. I shoved it under Oscar's nose and kept my eyes on Oscar's face. Beneath the dirt and beard stubble, Oscar's cheeks went pale. He gulped, wet his lips. He was not a good actor.

"You want me to make an enlargement of that? Have you the negative?"

"No," I said, "but you have. You took that picture."

"You're a damned liar!" Oscar said. His right hand went for his hip pocket, but Joe Harper cracked him across the wrist with the sap. Joe's fingers reached into Oscar's pocket and pulled out the automatic.

OSCAR SAT down on a stool. He was trembling a little.

"I didn't take the damned picture!" Oscar declared.

"You did," I said. "I've got proof. When you got through snapping that picture, you took out your flash bulb as you crossed the drive of the filling station near where the accident took place. You dropped the bulb and it landed in the coiled-up air hose of the filling station. The bulb didn't break."

I was just making this up as I went along, but if he was a professional photo-snapper, the chances were he really didn't know what he had done with the flash bulb any more than he would have known what he did with the butt of a cigarette he had smoked some time ago.

I opened the writing paper box under my arm and showed him the flash bulb I had bought in the drugstore.

"This is the bulb," I said. "And if you'll look pretty close you'll see what a nice set of finger prints is on it."

I didn't say whose finger prints were on the bulb, but the implication was all that was necessary.

"Cops?" Oscar looked frantically from me to Joe.

I took the shield that was part of my Detective Hammill disguise and let Oscar get a flash of it. I asked him if he knew what the penalty for blackmail was in this state.

"Listen," he said, "I honest to hell didn't know there was any black-mail connected with this. I was hired to do it, that was all. I just took the picture. You got to believe me."

Somehow I did believe him. His eyes looked earnest and his forehead had broken into an anxious sweat.

"Who hired you, then?" I asked.

"McTeeg," he said. "Augie McTeeg. You know him?"

I knew him. Who didn't? Maybe his name has been forgotten now, but once he had had the questionable honor of being listed on the roster of public enemies.

"Okay," I said to Oscar, "we'll see what McTeeg has to say about that."

Oscar jumped up and grabbed my arm.

"Don't tell McTeeg I said a thing," he pleaded. "McTeeg would kill me."

"Don't worry," I assured him. "If you've played on the level with us, we'll play on the level with you."

Joe and I returned to the car.

"What do we do now?" Joe asked. "This Augie McTeeg is one tough guy, what I mean, even if he is so fat he looks like he'd dent if you shoved a finger into him."

Joe couldn't tell me much about McTeeg I didn't know. During my ghostly escapades I had run into him before.

At the present time he was getting his living from a numbers racket over in Harlem. He always kept a pretty close eye on his source of income so it wasn't peculiar to find him living in an apartment on Lenox Avenue right in the colored district.

JOE AND I drove over to within a block of the building where McTeeg lived, and then got out and walked.

I asked Joe if he felt up to doing a bit of burglarizing. He said he guessed he might as well feel like it. So we got out and walked to the apartment building where McTeeg lived.

McTeeg was on the second floor front. From the street we could see a light burning in the front window. Joe ran across the street to the drugstore and telephoned McTeeg's apartment. I waited for him outside. He returned a moment later to announce that a man had answered the phone and said that McTeeg wasn't in.

"It wasn't McTeeg who said that, was it?" I asked.

"No. I'd know the guy's voice anytime. He squeaks like a juvenile's understudy his first night on stage."

I remembered that thin voice of Augie McTeeg's pretty well myself.

As we went up the steps I gave Joe my plans. Whoever answered the door was to get Joe's sap back of the ear. Then we would go on and go through the place with a comb, try and find the negative of the picture, and then get out as soon as possible.

I knocked at McTeeg's door. A voice on the other side asked who it was.

The vocal cords in my throat tightened. So close an imitation of McTeeg's squeaky voice came from my mouth that Joe Harper gave me a startled look.

"It's Augie," I said. "Open the door."

A key turned in the lock. The door opened. Joe and I jumped the man, had him before he could make a move. Joe's sap went up and came down again and the man melted to the floor, face up. I closed the door of the apartment.

"Well, I'll be damned!" Joe said.

I turned around, looked at the man on the floor.

Maybe if he hadn't been stretched out on the floor just as he had appeared in the picture, we wouldn't have recognized him so readily.

You see, this man Joe had knocked out was the man in the photo— the one who looked as though he had been killed by Mrs. Kalaban's car. He was undoubtedly a professional dummy-chucker who made his living by having accidents and then filing suit for damages.

This time he had simply flopped in front of Irene Kalaban's car. Oscar had been planted where he could snap the photo easily. It was all a put-up job, as I had half expected. And so long as the man Irene thought was dead wasn't dead, McTeeg really didn't have anything he could blackmail her with.

Joe had the same idea that I did about the blackmail stunt. "There's no percentage in us sticking around here now, is there?" he asked.

"We'd better take a look around while we're here," I said.

It was in an unprotected drawer of a dressing table in McTeeg's luxurious living room, that we came across the negative of the shake-down photo. Joe and I were about to leave the bedroom with our prize when I heard McTeeg's shrill voice talking to someone.

"McTeeg's out there," I said to Joe.

"Yeah. We're in a spot."

CHAPTER XVIII

HIDE AND SEEK

HAD I been alone, caught in this manner, it wouldn't have been half as bad as it was now. I could have faced McTeeg, pulled some sort of magic stunt, and depended upon my wits to take me the rest of the way out of the jam.

But if I got out of this jam with magic and McTeeg saw that Joe Harper was with me, he might put two and two together and get the idea that the Ghost was George Chance. Like this: George Chance is a magician. The Ghost is a magician. Now if the Ghost has a friend known as Joe Harper, then the Ghost is George Chance, the magician.

So when Joe said we were in a bad spot, he hadn't exaggerated a little bit. There was no fire escape outside the bedroom window. Outside of breaking our collective necks by jumping out the window, there just wasn't any way out except through the door and into the living room. And I could hear McTeeg coming for the door now.

"Stay where you are," I whispered to Joe. "And if you get a chance to run for it, do it. No heroics. I'll get out."

I turned out the bedroom light, opened the door, walked right out into the living room. McTeeg stopped in the middle of the room and pulled his gun. Behind him and a little to one side was Artie Meyer, McTeeg's strong arm man. Artie had his gun out.

A mirthless grin slit McTeeg's fat face. He was one of the flabbiest men I have ever known. His number three chin spilled down all over his collar. He even had bulges of fat above his eyebrows. He didn't look as though he had been born; he looked like the product of a jelly mold.

"A visitor," he squeaked. "How nice. You didn't knock when you came in, but you knocked *after* you came in." A fat-handed gesture indicated the man Joe had sapped when we had entered the apartment.

Artie Meyer had the features of a cigar store Indian—high cheek bones, a Roman nose, thick kips. Also he was as expressionless as a wooden Indian.

I pointed at the dummy chucker on the floor.

"Irene Kalaban won't pay you much in the way of hush money if it leaks out that guy she thought she killed is alive."

McTeeg looked slightly annoyed. After all, it must have been quite a shock to learn that his blackmail scheme had got out.

"But," he said, "just as long as Mrs. Kalaban doesn't know anything about it, it's no monkey wrench in my machinery, is it? And if we bump you, you won't be in a position to tell her, will you?"

I said I didn't know about that. I thrust my right hand into my coat pocket and snipped the lid off a little box I had there.

"Take your hand out of there!" McTeeg warned.

"I'm just looking for cigarettes," I said. "Maybe you'll lend me one."

I knew McTeeg didn't smoke. Artie Meyer did and he was standing over by the phone which was not far from the door and consequently not far from the light switch.

"Give the 'condemned man' a smoke, Artie," McTeeg said.

ARTIE FUMBLED in his pocket. I brought my own hand out of my coat pocket, but not until I had scooped a good-sized piece of magician's wax onto the back of my thumb nail. I accommodated Artie by crossing the room to get the cigarette. I held the cigarette between first and second fingers and Artie flickered a lighter for me.

"Thanks," I said, and pushed the cigarette into the lighter flame. All the time Artie's gun pushed into my middle.

I took a couple of pulls on the cigarette and then secretly scraped the wax from my nail onto the end of the cigarette. No matter how close Artie was watching me, he didn't see that move. If he had I doubt if he could have guessed its purpose. But he was suspicious of me and had moved back just a little way so he could see all of me at once.

I reached out my hand as though to use an arm to prop myself against the wall. Then I turned out the light switch.

I didn't have to move fast. Put yourself in Artie's place and you'll understand why. Wouldn't you expect me to make a dive for the door? Artie did anyway, and McTeeg expected the same thing.

"Watch the door!" McTeeg squealed.

What I did first was to move to the west side of the room where I stuck the glowing cigarette to the wall by means of the wax. Then I simply walked away from the cigarette, walked to the bedroom door and kicked it open.

Artie fired at where he thought I was but where only my cigarette was. The cigarette didn't move and it sounded to me as though both McTeeg and Artie were closing in on the place where they thought I was.

The bedroom door open, Joe Harper knew the way was clear for him. I felt him brush past me. Whether he could get the door open and get out depended a lot on how much time I could give him. I knew that Artie and McTeeg were just about to converge at the point where they thought I was. I tightened up on my vocal cords and said:

"Look out, Artie! He's right beside you."

The voice that came from my lips was McTeeg's voice. There was a scuffle and it sounded as though Artie had clubbed McTeeg. McTeeg's soft padding of fat was equal to a lot of punches. He shrilled a curse that informed Artie he had made a mistake.

Across the room I heard the door open. That would be Joe Harper going out. I followed at his heels, but at the door I employed ventriloquism again. Using Artie's voice I said:

"I got the guy over here near the bedroom, Augie!"

And that created sufficient confusion so that I could get out of the door. I ran down the steps behind Joe Harper and sprang into the car that waited for us outside.

AFTER WE were traveling, Joe looked at me and asked:

"Now where are we?"

"We've snapped one thread and done Irene Kalaban a favor," I said. "Let's be glad of that."

"It doesn't get Glenn out of the death house," Joe said.

"I know it," I answered grimly. "Incidentally, tomorrow is the day that Dr. Seer predicted Dr. Livingston would die."

"Tomorrow?" Joe grunted. "Say, it's tomorrow now. Look at the clock on the dash."

It was two A.M.

"We're turning back," I said to Joe.

"What do you mean?" Joe asked, giving me a bleak look.

"Livingston's house is near Fordham," I said. "We're going in the wrong direction."

"Livingston will thank you for getting him out of bed at this time of night to ask him if he's dead yet."

"Murdered yet," I corrected. "Seer isn't grabbing these predictions out of thin air. There's a carefully directed murder machine behind all this. I don't know what the reason is, but the murder machine is guided by a reason. Livingston is in danger but too stubborn to believe it."

The doctor's house on Beaumont Avenue was dark, as might be expected at this time of night. Joe rolled the car past slowly.

"Everything is okay in there, George," he said. "It's as quiet as backstage in a deserted theater."

I nipped Joe's arm and ordered him to brake. I was on the side nearest the house and could get a better view of the place than Joe. It seemed to me that the front door was standing open.

"That door's open," I said to Joe. "I'm getting out for a look."

I hurried up the approach-walk to the house. The closer I got, the crazier it looked—the house dark, the hands of the clock nearing three in the morning, and the front door standing wide open.

I stepped to the door and listened. The place was as quiet as a grave. If you can qualify silence, this sort of silence struck me as uncanny. I stepped through the open door, groped along the side of the door for a light switch, found a plate of three switches and turned the first one on.

Nothing happened. I tried the second and third switch, but no light came on. I pulled my flashlight and beamed it around the little reception hall in which I had talked with Livingston nearly three days before. Light globes were in the center lighting fixture.

It was a peculiar situation. What was I to do—try to wake the doctor up, or just look through the house and see that everything was okay, running the risk of getting shot as a prowler?

CHAPTER XIX

TOMORROW'S MURDER

C LOSING THE front door behind me, I decided to search the lower part of the house. To my right was a dining room. I entered it, my light beam pushing ahead of me. I went into the kitchen. A door from the kitchen opened onto a back porch. I just gave the porch a glance, was about to turn away, when I saw the fuse box was open. Perhaps someone had pulled the electrical switch open.

I crossed to the fuse box and looked inside. The switch was closed. But the fuse—there was the trouble with the lights—the mica window in the plug-type fuse was blackened. I opened the switch to avoid getting shocked and unscrewed the fuse. If I placed a nickel behind the fuse the circuit would be completed. Lights once on, I would be more hesitant about looking around the house.

But when I unscrewed the fuse and fingered my nickle into place in the socket, I found that some sort of a coin had already been placed back of the fuse. I picked the metal disk out and looked at it in the light of my torch.

It didn't look like a coin. It was rather more like a washer except that the hole in the center was square instead of round. The disk was made out of some white metal that resembled silver yet felt lighter. Of course, with that hole in the center, the disk hadn't made contact with the tip of the fuse.

I traded the strange metal disk for my nickle, put the fuse in place, closed the switch. I went back into the kitchen where I tested my repair by switching on the kitchen light. I left the kitchen light burning and returned to the central hall. On the side opposite the dining room, there was a living room. I turned on a light there.

Here again, that same silent emptiness.

At one side of the living room was a sturdy-looking panel of oak which possibly opened into a library or downstairs bedroom. I tried the knob of the door, found the door locked. I listened at the keyhole, heard no sound. I tapped at the door.

"Anybody home?" I called.

And there was no answer.

I turned, went back to the central hall, and hurried up the stairs to the second floor. Two bedrooms and a bath in the top floor, all empty, all in perfect order. My scalp prickled. It was getting to be just a little too much—this loneliness and silence, this haunting idea of mine that something was wrong.

Whatever was wrong had to be behind that locked door. I went back to the living room and tried breaking in the door by ramming it with my shoulder. It was a solid piece of woodwork.

I turned to the living room fireplace and got hold of a heavy poker. Back to the locked door, I hacked at a portion of the panel that was nearest the lock. It was a slow job and noisy. When I did get a hole, it wasn't big enough to get my hand in. Finally, I inserted the tip of the poker in the opening I had made and used the poker as a wrecking bar to rip off a section of the wood. I got my hand in and twisted the key in the lock.

I pushed open the door. Before me lay a small square room. Except for a single window, the walls were lined with books. A lamp burned on an end table beside a chair. And in the chair sat Dr. Livingston, mouth and eyes wide open.

Need I add that he was dead?

IT WAS one of those things that you more than half expect. Yet I was not prepared to face an incredible situation like this. This was murder. Regardless of what anyone might have told me to the contrary, I knew it had to be murder. Dr. Seer wasn't endowed with any supernatural powers and he had accurately predicted this man's death. Therefore the death itself had to be premeditated murder.

But what material evidence was there to support my opinion? One thing—a knife sticking out of Livingston's chest on the left side. Yet it required only one look to convince me that the knife hadn't killed him. It had struck no vital spot and Livingston had not bled enough. Livingston, it seemed to me, had been knifed after death.

Here was a room thoroughly and completely locked—window and door both locked, though the door could have been locked from the outside. There was no place the murderer could have hidden. There was no visible murder weapon except the knife, and I was positive it wasn't the murderer's weapon, no poison darts anywhere. I knew all this because I gave the body a pretty thorough going-over before leaving the room. I even noticed that the pupils of the dead man's eyes were constricted.

Had I gone so far as to have ventured a medical opinion, I would have said that Dr. Livingston was strangled. Yet there were no finger marks on the throat, no possible way that fingers could have reached him. Truly, the impossible crime.

I left the doctor's library, closing the mutilated door behind me. I went to the phone which I spotted in the living room, intending to call Ned Standish and inform him that the Prophet of Doom had clicked again.

I had hardly raised the phone when I heard the front door creak. I put down the phone, slipped my little automatic from the gimmick clip that holds it beneath my coat. A white-faced man wearing a chauffeur's cap slipped into the hall and with trembling hands closed the door behind him. It was Dr. Livingston's servant who had admitted me when I had first visited the doctor.

I cleared my throat.

The servant turned, took one look at me, jumped toward the door.

"Don't," I warned. "I'll shoot."

The man's knees were visibly knocking together. He raised his hands above his head. His eyes implored me not to shoot even if his quivering lips were incapable of speaking.

"Come in here," I ordered.

THE MAN obeyed, his hands down now, sensing I meant no harm.

"Look!" I said.

"My God," he cried, seeing Livingston, "what's happened?"

I gave him a flash of the detective badge I was carrying in my pocket.

"Murder," I said.

"Good heavens!" the servant gasped. "The man with the hideous hands—"

"What's that?" I cut in. "Don't mix this up now. What's that about a man with hideous hands?"

Was this killing the work of the leper, Eric Emboyd? Or had Eric Emboyd entered after death, and thinking Livingston alive, knifed him?

"They were more like claws than hands," the servant said. "Horrible! And his face—I-I've never seen anything like it."

"The beginning, please," I said patiently. "What are you doing running around this time of night?"

The servant took a moment to collect his thoughts and get the events of the evening in chronological order.

"Dr. Livingston," he began, "was out to a scientific meeting of some sort until late. He came home about half past eleven. He went to his library as usual to read like always for an hour or so before going to bed."

"Does he always lock himself in?" I asked.

"No sir, though he don't like to be disturbed. He's said to me many a time, sir, that when he's reading, he don't want to be interrupted no matter if the sky falls or the house catches afire."

"How could he read when the fuses were blown out and there were no lights?" I asked.

"I'm coming to that, sir. The lights were all perfect until after midnight—I don't know just how long after. Usually I wait up for Dr. Livingston to get to bed, but tonight he must have had something unusually interesting to read because he didn't make any move toward bed, and I think I should up and assert my rights a bit and go to bed myself.

"I went upstairs to the doctor's room to turn down his bed and open his window, which I did. Back of his bed he's got a bridge lamp because he sometimes wakes up in the middle of the night and goes to reading in bed by that lamp. The lamp is near the door. And tonight, when I shut the door of his room, the lamp cord got caught in the hinged end of the door like it sometimes does, only tonight was the last time for that lamp cord. I mean, it got pinched one too many times and there was a short circuit and the fuse blew.

"I thought how terrible it would be for me, blowing a fuse when Dr. Livingston was reading. It would be an interruption, sort of, and he don't like to be interrupted when he's reading. I was all a fluster, it being my fault for pinching the lamp cord. So I ran out of the house and down to an all night drugstore to get a new fuse."

I BELIEVED he was telling the truth.

"Did you shut the door?" I asked.

"I shut it, but the night latch wasn't on yet. I remembered about the night latch when I was half-way back to the house with the fuse. But when I got all the way back, the door was shut just like I had left it and I felt it was all right.

"When I went into the house, I turned on the flashlight I had been carrying since the fuse blowed out and I was going back toward the kitchen when I heard a noise out there. I said, 'Dr. Livingston, sir?' and there wasn't no answer. And then *he* came out of the dining room door."

"Dr. Livingston?" I asked.

"No. Not Dr. Livingston. If I live to be a hundred and ninety, I won't forget what did come out of that door. He was a thin man with the ugliest, twisted-up, boney face, and his skin was like old paper stretched over bones. And his fingers were crooked like claws. They *were* claws, a lot more like those of a bird than anything that you could call human.

"It was like in them horror pictures of Frankenstein and Dracula and such. I let out a yell you could heard to Hades and turned and ran out of the house. And just now I got nerve enough to come back."

"Okay," I said. "You go up to your bedroom and stay there until you're wanted."

The servant obeyed me.

As soon as he was up the stairs, I took up the phone and called the apartment of Commissioner Standish. Ned had got me out of bed in the wee hours many a time and now I returned the compliment.

"Listen, Ned," I whispered, "Ghost speaking. Dr. Seer called another shot, and hit it on the nose, I think. He may have been a few minutes off, but I don't think so. Dr. Livingston on Beaumont Avenue, this time. And the servant has a story to tell about the man with claws. That's the second time Eric Emboyd has turned up at a murder. That doesn't make him the murderer however. You'll see from the set that Livingston was knifed after death. That was either done by Emboyd or somebody else—somebody else if Emboyd was the murderer. Anyway, Emboyd is no myth!"

I hung up and hastily left the house to rejoin Joe Harper. The sooner Joe's shrewd eyes got back on the trail of the man with claws, the better. When we all knew all there was to know about that hideous individual, we'd be a long way toward solving the mystery.

CHAPTER XX

COIN OF THE DAMNED

WE **HAD** a clue—the round washer with the square hole in the center of it which I had found the night before behind the burned-out fuse at Dr. Livingston's house. It was the only material clue I had been able to pick up so far.

I asked the hardware dealer what sort of machine such a washer came from, and what its particular use was. He examined the thing closely, said it was stamped from steel stock and added that he had never sold anything like it or seen anything like it. If it was a washer, then it must fit on a square-shank bolt, and there wasn't any such thing.

So I put down another zero in my long column of zeros.

Gray templed, unsmiling, my eyes looking a bit severe behind Dr. Stacey's Oxford glasses, Merry White still found me an agreeable companion when we lunched that noon in an obscure corner of a restaurant on Sixth Avenue.

She had taken a look at the morning papers before going into court that morning and was familiar with the details regarding the death of Dr. Livingston. I showed her the impossible steel washer clue and told her where I had found it.

She wrinkled her brow over the thing and bobbed her head knowingly.

"What do you think it is?" I asked.

"Oh, I don't know. But then you don't either. You don't know it's a washer. You just have to have a name for it, so you call it a washer. It's more like a Chinese coin."

"The thing is made of steel," I said. "I never heard of a steel coin before."

"You're right," she said. "But people steal coins, don't they?"

"Don't pun," I said.

Merry put her cool hand on mine.

"Poor boy," she whispered. "I don't like to see you worried. You mustn't worry, because everything will be all right."

Many a time I had played Merry White's hunches and won. So I did not overlook her idea that the disk I called a washer might just as well be a coin. I paid a visit to a coin dealer who sold every sort of coin to collectors.

The coin dealer took one look at the steel disk and shook his head.

My heart sank a bit. I supposed he didn't know what it was either.

"It has no value," he said. "A curiosity, perhaps, but I wouldn't give you anything for it."

"I don't want to sell it," I protested. "I want to know what it is."

"Oh, it's a piece of token money used in leper colonies. When a person is sent to a leper colony out in the Philippine Islands or some place like that, they trade all their money for these disks which are used entirely within the boundary of the colony as a medium of exchange."

I LEFT the coin dealer and hurried over to Police Headquarters Building where I was admitted at once to the presence of Commissioner Standish.

"Emboyd was at Livingston's place last night," I said flatly. I showed him the coin I had found in the fuse box.

Ned Standish sighed.

"We'll pick Emboyd up some way," he said. "But you're solving every murder except that of David Palmer."

"The two are connected," I said.

"How do you figure that?"

"Dr. Seer predicted both deaths. Either he attends to the killings personally or somebody who knows of the killings ahead of time tells Seer about them. Livingston was murdered, wasn't he?"

Standish stroked his square of moustache and nodded.

"He was murdered. Suppose we bring Seer down to Headquarters and give him a going-over?"

"Leave Seer to me," I insisted. "What killed Livingston?"

"Poison gas," Standish said. "You were right about the knife. The gas was cyanogen, or something equally potent. Traces of the gas were detectable in the room where Livingston died. How it was introduced— well, we're stumped there. And we considered every possible way."

"How deadly is the gas?" I asked. "Why wasn't I overcome by it when I broke into the room?"

"Demarest says you can put enough of the gas under pressure in a globe the size of a small orange to kill several men if they get a sniff of the stuff right away. When you broke in, the gas was pretty well mixed with the air in the room and probably floated out the door, especially inasmuch as you had such a time getting that opening in the panel."

"Incidentally," I said, "the homicide boys must have been a little confused because I had smashed that door."

"That's right. Magnus thinks somebody made the hole in the door while Livingston was sitting calmly inside the room, stuck a hose through the opening, pumped the gas in. He says that sounds fishy, but that's the only way it could have been done."

"How about laying a little bet on something?" I asked.

"Speak your piece," Standish urged. "Only I don't bet with the Ghost. If you fumble now it will be the first time."

"It will also be the last, I reminded him. "But here's what I'll bet: Inventor Michael Holland, David Palmer, Dr. Livingston, were all killed by the same man."

I COULD hear Standish's gasp.

"Holland's death was listed as accidental—"

"Holland," I said, "was killed by the same gas that got Livingston."

Standish nodded. "And Palmer was killed with a poison dart."

"Very probably because the killer would have had some difficulty using poison gas to kill one man in a room that was filled with people."

"I hope that's it," Standish said gravely. "If any man ever gambled his life, you're doing it now, my boy."

"Maybe you don't think I realize that."

"Got any ideas as to the motive?"

"I'm just playing a hunch," I said, "but I think the Kalaban reward has something to do with it."

And I wasn't more than about fifty percent wrong.

Still troubled by the Eric Emboyd angle, I tried to get in touch with Randolph Curtis, whom Carl Van Borg had mentioned as being a possible enemy of the exiled leper Eric Emboyd, or rather the other way around, since Curtis had married Emboyd's fiancée.

Curtis was out of town. His charming wife did not expect him in until late that night. I asked her if the name of Eric Emboyd meant anything to her. At the mention of the man's name, her lovely face paled a bit.

"Yes," she admitted, "I knew Mr. Emboyd some years ago."

"Look," I said softly.

"Excuse me," I said, "but I understand that you were engaged to marry him at one time."

"That is true, Dr. Stacey," she said. "Why are you concerned about the matter?"

I explained that I was doing a little unofficial investigation in an effort to assist Police Commissioner Standish.

"Is it true," she asked, "that Eric Emboyd has escaped from the leper island?"

"It is," I said. "How did you know?"

"A friend of mine, Carl Van Borg, warned me. I suppose that word 'warned' sounds a little melodramatic. But then Carl is melodramatic. I hardly think Eric would hold anything against me."

I left the telephone number of the Ghost's rectory with her and requested her to call me as soon as her husband returned.

CHAPTER XXI

THE FOURTH
PREDICTION

M **ERRY WHITE** had reached the rectory ahead of time and
was curled up on the couch, staring at the wall, a pensive and
not particularly happy expression on her face.

"It's such a muddle, darlin'," she said. "Such an awful muddle."

I held her tightly in my arms. Even as I did I fancied that I could
feel the warden of Sing Sing tapping me on the shoulder, telling me
that my time had come to take that last short walk.

"You're not losing your courage, are you?" I asked her. "You mustn't."

"Why can't the police see that the same person who killed David
Palmer is also responsible for these other deaths?"

"They can't see it," I told her, "because outside of the predictions that
Dr. Seer has made, there just isn't anything to connect them."

"But this crazy leper—"

"We can't prove that the crazy leper ever knew David Palmer, let
alone was an enemy of Palmer's," I interrupted.

Merry took a long breath and patted my cheek.

"I'm all right now," she said. "See, I'm smiling—"

I kissed the smiling lips.

Ten-thirty came. No word from Mrs. Curtis. No word from Joe
Harper who was out hunting for Eric Emboyd. No word from Standish
who had all the available police hunting for Emboyd. And then I heard
Tiny Tim's footsteps on the basement stairs of the rectory. Merry and
I got up to greet the little man.

"Little man looks like he's had a busy day," Merry said.

Tim's babyish brow crimped into a tight frown.

"Cut it out, frail!" He tried to reduce his small voice to a grumble.
"What I want to know is where this is going to end?"

"Where what is going to end?" I asked of him.

"These killings. He's done it again."

"Emboyd?" Merry gasped.

"Emboyd? Who's Emboyd?" Tim hadn't been brought up to date on all the developments. "I didn't say anything about anybody named Emboyd, did I? I'm talking about Dr. Seer. He says somebody else is going to die. Tonight."

Tim fumbled in the inside pocket of his perfectly tailored coat and brought out a scrap of paper.

"I wrote it down for you, George. I don't know whether the name means anything to you or not. Randolph Curtis. I stopped to look his address up in the telephone directory."

"Don't bother," I said. "He lives out near Locut Point on Shore Drive. I was out there this afternoon. Did Seer predict Curtis' death?"

"He did. I just came from one of Seer's séances," Tim said. "Curtis is going to die tonight, according to that moth-eaten mystic. Hadn't we better get out there?"

"Not 'we,'" I said. "You and Merry stay right here. I don't know that Curtis is home yet. I hope not. I've got to be there when he arrives."

I WENT into my dressing room and quickly removed what was left of the makeup which identified me as Dr. Stacey. Time was too precious to permit me to make any elaborate changes in my appearance. I simply slipped into the Ghost's black suit, altered the shape of my nose with the wire ovals. In short, I simply became the Ghost again.

I kissed Merry more hastily than she deserved and then hurried out to pick up a taxi at a stand over on Madison Avenue.

Seer was calling his shots more closely this time. The killer was becoming more sure of himself with each murder, it seemed, for if Randolph Curtis was to die tonight the killer only had about an hour and a half to do the trick in. Unless Curtis was already dead. I doubted that, because Seer's prediction wouldn't be a prediction if that was the case. A newspaper man might call it a scoop, but not a prediction.

The Curtis house was a small, newly built place of brick and stone, beautifully situated on spacious grounds that overlooked the sound. My taxi driver let me out at the gate of a concrete drive and I hurried toward the house.

It is true that I had called on Mrs. Curtis that afternoon disguised as Dr. Stacey. She would not recognize me as the man who had spoken to her earlier in the day, for I was now wearing the makeup of the Ghost. But that was the way I wanted it.

My reason for this was simply that if I arrived ahead of the killer I might be blessed with the chance to catch the man red-handed. And if I had been disguised as Dr. Stacey and then employed the methods of the Ghost in the capture of the killer, any chance observer would understand that Dr. Stacey was the Ghost. The alias of Dr. Stacey was too valuable to me to risk anything that would compel me to stop using it.

Lights were burning in the front hall of the house. But as I approached the door that inexplicable sense of uneasiness came over me. The place was too damned quiet.

However, a house that contains a lone wife waiting for the return of her husband may well be perfectly quiet. I sounded the brass knocker of the front door.

There were no answering footsteps. Was this to be a repetition of what I had experienced at Livingston's? I knocked again before trying the knob. The door was locked.

I left the small front porch and hurried around the house, testing the windows as I went until I found that one window at the back, though locked, was readily accessible.

A fortunate thing the Ghost had had chosen to enlist his arts on the side of the law. He would have made a first class burglar. I had the window unlatched inside of ten minutes and then crawled across the sill to find myself in a small, neat kitchen.

I stepped from kitchen into dining room and from there into the lighted hall. The house was perfectly silent. You could almost feel its emptiness.

In front of me and across the hall was a door which I opened on the living room. It was a long room, a fireplace at one end in which a log fire glowed. At the other end of the room, light banked up against the wall from floor to ceiling from a desk lamp which had fallen to the floor.

THE GREEN shade of the desk lamp was broken and the bare globe shed its glaring light on the recumbent form of Mrs. Curtis. One outstretched arm lay across the bronze base of the overturned desk lamp.

I crossed the room, stood there staring down at the woman. Her normally pale skin was a ghastly shade of gray. Her blue eyes were open, her mouth open and jaw set—a mask of tragedy molded in flesh. Flesh without blood.

She was dead, I knew, before I dropped to the floor beside her. Her hands were cold, stony. One shoulder felt warm to the touch, but only because of the proximity of the light bulb.

Without disturbing the body to any great extent, I searched for wounds, found none. The flesh of one arm had been scraped a little by the edge of the lamp base, but there was no other mark.

I stood up and tried to reconstruct the moments of her life which had directly preceded her sudden death. There was no chair in front of the small spinet desk. The lamp had rested on one corner of the desk. Mrs. Curtis had been standing up and over the light, reading a folded newspaper that rested on top of the desk.

I glanced at the newspaper. She had evidently interested herself in a column of beauty hints—something she could have had little use for, I thought.

I looked at my watch. It was within two minutes of midnight. Had Dr. Seer's "spirits" made a slight error when they had predicted the death of Randolph Curtis? Perhaps they had meant his wife—the woman who was to have married Eric Emboyd.

I stood as nearly as possible in the exact spot where Mrs. Curtis must have been standing when she had fallen to the floor. I looked up to the ceiling, at the wall with its two small etchings hung in black frames. I looked to either side. There were no doors or windows in direct line with the place where I stood.

But why doors or windows? Hadn't death been *with* her in the room? The house was locked. Death had been locked into the house, too.

MY PULSE hammered against my temples. Was it possible? What kind of a brain could have conceived murder like this? The undetectable, the all but perfect crime again. She had died as Livingston had died. Perhaps the same subtle weapon had been used—poison gas. How introduced? The central heating plant was not in use. Besides, I notice that the house was heated with hot water radiators so that the heating plant could not have been the means of introducing the gas.

I crossed to one of the bracket lights at the side of the mantel at the other end of the room. I unscrewed the cold bulb from the socket and took it back to where Mrs. Curtis lay. I dropped to my knees again.

Using my handkerchief as a glove against the heat of the bulb in the desk lamp, I unscrewed the bulb and in what little light there was from the fireplace, I screwed the cold globe into the lamp socket. The room was again flooded with light. I wrapped the hot bulb I had taken from the lamp in my handkerchief and put it in my pocket.

I had started for the phone to inform Standish of my discovery of the body, when I heard the click of a key in the lock of the front door. I stopped, stood perfectly still in the center of the room.

CHAPTER XXII

I MEET THE
MURDERER

RANDOLPH CURTIS called out as soon as he had the front door open.

"I'm back, honey! The train was late."

He advanced to the center of the hall, both of his hands occupied with briefcase and Gladstone bag, before he noticed me.

He was a large man with a broad, happy-looking face. He was happy to get home, happy to get back to his wife. That's what got me. That's why I couldn't say anything to him for just a moment.

So we stood there staring at each other, the smile on his face changing to a look of bewilderment into which a little fear might have crept.

"Mr. Curtis," I said finally, taking a few steps toward him.

"Who are you?" he asked. "What are you doing here?"

"It doesn't matter who I am," I said. "I am afraid I have some bad news for you."

"Bad news," he echoed dazedly. "Where's my wife?"

I went up to him and put a hand on his shoulder. His frightened gaze searched my face, a not too pleasant face even though I had "turned off the Ghost."

"This will be a terrible shock for you, Mr. Curtis. Your wife isn't here."

It was hard for me to frame the picture with words. His wife was here. Her body was here.

"Isn't here? Where is she, for heaven's sake?"

"Your wife is—is dead," I finally worked out.

"You're fooling," he said huskily. His voice wasn't the same voice that had called out to his wife when he had entered.

"I wish I was," I said. "She's been murdered. The police have not yet arrived."

He dropped his bags.

"Where is she? I've got to go to her. Let go of me, damn you!"

I let him go into the living room. When he saw the body, he advanced slowly as though he didn't know what his feet were doing. His big body wilted. I saw his shoulders shake with silent sobs as full realization came upon him. Finally he collapsed in a chair and buried his face in his hands.

For fully ten minutes I sat there with him. Then I spoke gently.

"Your wife has been murdered. You must help me find the murderer."

He raised his head. I was afraid that he would get the idea that I might easily have been her slayer. But apparently no such thought crossed his mind.

"Yes," he whispered. "Yes. Anything. I'd kill him with my own hands." He covered his face again.

"Did you ever hear of Eric Emboyd?" I asked him.

HE NODDED his head without taking his hands away from his face.

I shook him. He looked up quickly.

"Emboyd?" he said. "Emboyd? He didn't do this. He's in a leper colony. Livingston and Van Borg sent him to a leper colony."

"He's in New York now," I said. "He had reason to hate you, didn't he?"

"Because of—"

Curtis looked at the body of his wife. His shoulders shook. For a moment he couldn't say anything at all. He just nodded his head and kept looking at his wife.

I went out into the dining room to a cellarette and poured a stiff drink of brandy for Curtis. When he had taken that down he seemed to have a little better control of his emotions.

"Don't leave her there," he begged. "God! It isn't human."

I pulled down one of the drapes and covered the body.

"The police have to get here before we can move the body," I told him. "Now you'll best help by telling me what you know of Emboyd. Do you think he might have killed your wife?"

Curtis stood up. He seemed to get a better hold on himself by pacing back and forth in the room.

"I have to think that now, don't I?" he choked out. "And yet he once loved her. And I—I always loved her, I guess. I tried to steal her from him when she was engaged to Emboyd. If Emboyd was jealous, why didn't he kill me when we were down in the wilds of Mexico together?"

What was this, I wondered. Mexico? Was this a fresh thread?

"You were in Mexico with Emboyd?" I prompted. "What region?"

He stopped his pacing and looked at the desk, at the pitiful, draped mound at the front of the desk.

"There's a map in my desk drawer," he said. "Our expedition is pretty clearly marked. Yes, he could have killed me there. Only perhaps he was afraid of the others. We weren't alone, you see, and he might have been afraid that—"

"Was Michael Holland with you?" I asked.

He stared at me, surprised, and I saw that I had hit something. Here was something that might tie up. Holland had had some sort of a map which Tiny Tim had seen burned by the prowler in Holland's laboratory. And now Curtis has a map.

"Mike Holland," Curtis said, "was with us. And—"

A single pistol shot crashed thunderously in the silence of the night. A bullet snicked through the lead glass of the large window in the living room. Curtis' eyes seemed to bulge and cross a little. A dead blank expression froze on his face. He fell forward stiffly like a statue toppled from its base.

I picked up a chair as I ran toward the window. I flung the chair ahead of me through glass and leading, cleaning out a jagged opening which I got through without opening an artery by some miracle. I landed on hands and knees in the middle of a shrub, scrambled out, got to my feet.

That smooth acting gimmick-clip delivered my little automatic into my right hand. The shadowy figure of a man, dimly discernible in the gloom, raced across the lawn a good two hundred feet ahead of me.

I wished then that I wasn't the mediocre shot that Commissioner Standish says I am. But even if I had been a marksman, I doubt if I could have clipped the murderer, for in another instant he was lost in a forest of small trees and shrubs that artistically landscaped the lawn and made the escape of a murderer comparatively easy.

I put in five minutes of hunting before I drew a bead on a man and told him to stick up his hands. When I got close enough, I saw that my catch was none other than my cab driver who had got out to see what all the shooting was about. He wanted to know if he shouldn't call the police. I told him he shouldn't, I had already done so.

The reason behind that little lie was that I didn't want to be bothered with the police until I had taken a look at the map Curtis had said was in his desk. I hoped it was still there. Because the killer had destroyed the map that Holland had, I hurried to get back to the house. The murderer might have doubled back on his tracks to try and beat me to the map.

I entered the house through the front door which Curtis had not had time to lock. I went into the living room. Curtis was dead. Probably he had never known what had struck him, for he had been shot square-ly in the back of the head. Poor soul. Perhaps he would not have found life worth living anyway, after what had happened.

I went to the desk, stepped over the corpse of Mrs. Curtis, and pulled open the desk drawer. There must have been half a ream of bond paper lying inside the desk drawer, a pile of old letters, some paper clips and rubber bands. At the very bottom of the stack of letters, I found the map.

Rather it was a part of a map of the Coahuila district of Mexico, cut from what must have originally been a very large map of the country. The part of the map concealed in Curtis' desk was about the size of a sheet of letter paper.

I was stooping over, trying to get some of the rays of the upset lamp to fall on the surface of the map, when a whispering voice said:

"I have you covered."

I straightened, dropped the map into the open drawer of the desk. I turned around slowly, my face freezing into that skull-like mask that identifies the Ghost.

From the window which I had broken, a man stepped into the room. His crooked fingers were covered with black gloves. A curtain domino mask covered his face completely. His right hand held a heavy auto-matic.

CHAPTER XXIII

STALEMATE

// **THE GHOST!"** the man whispered.

I think he was just a little afraid. He might have killed with impunity, he might have laid murder plans cleverly, but the legendary reputation of the Ghost carried a little weight even against this master criminal. But his gun did not quiver.

That was the main thing—his gun did not quiver.

I had seen a sample of his marksmanship that night and the position of target was not a comfortable one to be in. I reached down to the desk drawer for the map, picked it up.

The eyes in the mask watched my fingers closely. The man knew the Ghost's reputation for trickery. I knew that he would kill at the first sign of it.

I picked up the map, turned it around so he could see the face of it. "This?" I asked.

The masked man nodded. He took a step toward me. I took a sideways step away from the desk and toward the end of the room where the fireplace was. At the same time, I turned the back of the map toward him. At least, he thought it was the back of the map.

I folded the map once and deliberately tore it in half, or so it must have seemed. The eyes in the slots of the mask watched me closely.

"Give it to me, I said," the masked man repeated. He took another step toward me and I backed toward the fireplace. My eyes were locked on his trigger finger. And at the same time, my own fingers worked rapidly, folding the paper and tearing it until I had a pile of scraps about two inches square.

"You want it, eh?" I laughed. And my laughter was that taunting, gruesome laugh of the Ghost's. And then I flung the scraps of paper into the fireplace where they blazed up.

Yellow flame cast dancing shadows upon the wall of the room.

The masked man chuckled.

"I only wanted the map in order to destroy it, Ghost," he whispered. "You have saved me the trouble. I must warn you not to cross my path too often. I am rather deadly."

"When you know you're good it isn't bragging, is it? Yes, I've seen evidence of your deadliness."

We stood there facing each other like a couple of fighters in an arena, neither caring to make the first blow. My attitude was entirely bluff based on the Ghost's reputation for doing the impossible. He could have shot me easily enough. And I didn't know how far I dared strain his nerves. Something had to break soon. Though I knew that I was taking my life in my hands and juggling it, I made the first move.

My eyes fixed on a point in space some five feet from me, and I reached out toward that spot as though to pick something out of the air. The sudden forward and upward movement of my hand threw my knife out of the loop inside my sleeve and into the palm of my hand.

The masked man saw the glint of the knife blade. He had heard of its deadliness. Fear hastened his shot before it was well aimed. I never knew where that bullet landed, but I heard its whine. It was a clean miss, and I had not yet thrown my knife. I threw it now.

THE MASKED man was in motion. He sprang toward the desk. My knife, intended for his heart, needled through the padded portion of the shoulder of his coat. The weight of the knife hasp carried it clattering to the floor as the masked man swooped down upon the lamp to jerk the cord from the socket.

Because of the glow from the fireplace, the room was not in total darkness. The masked man fired at where I had been, but by that time I was behind a chair, my own gun out. In the matter of misdirection, he was no mean magician himself, for he threw a vase or something toward the broken window and drew my fire. My gun flame pointed out my position. I felt the impact of his heavy slug as it struck the chair in front of me.

The masked man was on the move again, running toward the door. I came from behind the chair, saw the living room door, fired. Before the door slammed, he tried another shot through the crack. It went wild.

Instead of following him through the door and into the lighted hall where I would have been a swell target, I took the same exit I had before—the broken window. I thought I might get around to the front door and head him off. I felt certain his exit would be slower than mine because he would be expecting me to follow through the door.

Around in front of the house, I took up what I supposed was a strategic position behind a tall spike of juniper. But the front door of the house didn't open. Tense seconds ticked off, and still the door didn't open.

I was about to enter the house and face it out with him when the whine of an automobile starter sent me running across the lawn toward the street. It was my own taxi that had got under way. And riding in it, his gun very likely at the head of the driver, was the killer.

I have never been able to watch the front and back door of a house at one and the same time. The killer had simply used the back door while I watched the front.

His victory it was, but not entirely. The map of Mexico—well, *I hadn't burned it.* There was some consolation in knowing that I had pulled a trick right under the man's nose.

Remember, I had dropped the map back into the desk drawer. I had taken care to drop it squarely on the pile of bond paper in the drawer. In picking the map up, I had also picked up a piece of the bond paper. When I had showed the masked man the map, the bond paper had been behind it. When I had turned the map around, it was the bond paper he had seen, not the map.

In folding the map, I had also folded the bond paper. But it was the bond paper which he had watched me tear. With every fold and every tear, I had crimped the map up into a smaller parcel, but always kept it whole behind the pieces of torn paper.

So I had the map safely in my pocket. Perhaps it was the vital clue to the whole mystery.

I was feeling the need for sleep. I decided to get some and did—not much but enough to keep me going. The following day, Standish, who felt the desperation of the situation as keenly as I, did what I had asked him not to do. He had Dr. Seer taken up and brought to Headquarters where the prophet was given a working over that frightened but didn't give the police any information.

Seer took his grilling with the air of a martyr. But he wouldn't budge from his opinion that he got his predictions direct from the spirits.

All that resulted from the commissioner's earnest efforts was that Dr. Seer temporarily locked up his temple.

Joe Harper was still searching vainly for Emboyd. Merry White, Tiny Tim, and I puzzled over the map which I had brought from the Curtis house. On it a route was clearly indicated leading down from the Texas border. Then there was an arrow pointing to a spot on the map marked with the word "ours." This point was enclosed with a penciled circle and inside the circle was the word "He."

We had a nice pair of personal pronouns that meant exactly nothing.

I thought of Glenn Saunders in Sing Sing, and my heart was heavy. How was he standing the confinement? The question troubled me, and I knew I could not proceed with a clear head unless I first paid a visit to Sing Sing. I went as a clergyman.

Glenn was thinner than when he had left my house to fill my shoes in prison. Worry had done that to him. His high cheek bones stood out like doorknobs above hollow cheeks. He was pale. His eyes were red-rimmed with lack of sleep.

I took my place opposite him and my thumb and forefinger formed the letter "G," a sign by which he knew me in spite of my disguise. He repressed an expression of joy. He was full of curiosity. I told him all that I knew. He gripped my hand.

"I'm not worried," he whispered. "I know you're—on the job. I can stand this if you can."

When I left, we both felt better.

That night I telegraphed to the Mexican government for information about the region indicated in Curtis' map.

CHAPTER XXIV

THE FIFTH
PREDICTION

DR. SEER re-opened his temple. I paid him a second visit in the disguise of the Ghost. I waited until the crowds were packed into his building, watching the place from across the street. He was really packing them in. Believers and nonbelievers—all were curious to see the man who predicted death with unfailing accuracy. And the crooks who were backing the prophet boosted their entrance fee to five dollars a head.

I didn't need an entrance fee. When the séance was well started, I crossed the street, unlocked the door of the basement of the temple building by means of a key I had made, and entered the basement.

I was surprised to find that no one was on guard at the door. The under-stage room at one end of the basement had a light in it. As I moved toward it, somebody in the under-stage room beat on a gong. I stopped, listening to what went on in the hall above.

Dr. Seer's strange voice rose, shrilling above the excited murmur of voice in the audience:

"This is my fifth prediction! Five days shall pass and then a woman is to die. Her name—it is somewhat indistinct. Her name is Irene Kalaban!"

My automatic dropped into my right palm as my left hand seized the knob of the door of the under-stage room. There was only one man in the room—one of the toughs I had encountered on my first visit to the temple. He was in the act of putting down his big brass gong when I entered.

He dropped the gong, made a fumbling effort to draw his gun as his staring eyes met the blank, skull-like face of the Ghost.

I took two strides to him and slapped him down with a blow from the barrel of my automatic. He fell without a groan. I sprang to the platform of the tiny elevator which was used for spirit manifestations. On my first visit I had acquainted myself with the mechanism of the elevator. I had only to trip a lever with the toe of my shoe and I shot upward toward the stage with astonishing speed.

The trap above me opened and the platform of the elevator took its place in the floor of the stage. It was an all but instantaneous change. The Ghost must have appeared to materialize out of thin air. I was within two feet of where Dr. Seer stood over his glowing crystal globe.

Gasps, screams from the audience, and even Dr. Seer who admittedly was a friend of the beings from another world, didn't look sure of himself. He shrank back from his spirit table. I reached out my left hand in which I had concealed my small flashlight. I picked up his crystal ball with my fingers, at the same time thumbed on my flashlight. The light beam passed into the crystal ball so that the ball continued to glow even while it was in my hands.

My right hand reached into the hollow beneath the glass and I picked up a small square of white paper. I merely glanced at the paper, saw that it carried Dr. Seer's prediction, neatly typed. The spirits must have encountered a typewriter salesman!

I knew only one way I could get out of the building, and that was down through the audience. The elevator that was responsible for my appearance on stage was operated only from the room below.

HOLDING THE glowing crystal ball at arm's length, I stepped majestically from the platform. The audience melted back before me as though I was Poe's gruesome figure of the Red Death. To put teeth into my bluff, I recalled a portion of a biblical passage:

" 'Nor let there be any among you who seeketh the truth from the dead. For the Lord abhorreth all these things and for these abominations. He will destroy them at their coming.' "

So I passed through the hall and no one so much as touched me. It was too bad I couldn't have walked through the door at the rear without opening it, but that is a little beyond my magic.

Once through the door, I stood at the top of the stone steps leading down into the sidewalk of East 127th Street. Not far away I could see Irene Kalaban, more than half supported by the stocky Robert Martin. Mrs. Kalaban was sobbing. Martin was telling her to be brave.

I vaulted over the iron railing that bound the steps, hid in the shadows below.

"Get control of yourself, my dear," I could hear Martin pleading. "You mustn't take that message as final. There is surely some escape."

A sedan, its back shades pulled, started from the curb a few hundred feet east of Seer's temple. Its right hand tires didn't leave the gutter. The car braked alongside the spot where Martin and Irene Kalaban were standing. Two men got out. I saw the flash of gun steel before Martin did.

One of the men from the car was Artie Meyer, McTeeg's wooden-faced henchman. The other man I didn't recognize. Martin, struggling furiously, was beaten back to the car where hands out of the rear compartment seized him. Irene Kalaban was gun-shoved into the car by Artie Meyer. I think it was Artie who got in under the wheel.

I left my hiding place on the ran, sprang onto the back bumper of the car as it got under way and clung to the spare tire carrier.

It was the wildest ride I ever took. The edge of the bumper seemed to be cutting through the soles of my shoes. My feet were as unfeeling as blocks of concrete by the time the car came to a stop in front of an old loft building.

I stepped off the bumper, but kept hidden behind the car while Artie Meyer and his pals got Martin and Mrs. Kalaban out of the car and hustled them into the building. I got a glimpse of the last man to enter and had no trouble recognizing the flabby figure of Artie's boss, McTeeg.

I had succeeded in putting a crimp in McTeeg's blackmail efforts to extort money from Irene Kalaban. Now he was up to some new scheme but with that same motive in sight, no doubt the two hundred thousand dollar reward money that was to be paid to anyone proving that they had communicated with the dead Kalaban.

AS SOON as McTeeg and his captives were inside the building I came from behind the car and followed. They had gone to an open doorway beyond which were stairs leading up to the quarters above. I was about to go up the steps when the door at the head of the stairs opened. I ducked back, flattened myself against the building, and waited for someone who was coming down.

It was that henchman of McTeeg's I had not recognized. McTeeg had probably sent him down to watch out for cops if what went on upstairs got noisy enough to attract attention.

When the man came out of the door, I flicked my knife from my sleeve and sprang in behind him. I let him taste the steel of the knife between his shoulder blades.

"Try anything funny," I said in the Ghost's flat, chill voice, "and I push it all the way in!"

"What the hell?"

Turning his head, the man looked into the skull-face of the Ghost. I brought the knife out of his back and hammered the hasp of it to his temple. As he went limp, I crouched, catching his body across my shoulder. Then I carried him up the steps to the landing at the top and dropped him in front of the door.

I listened at the door. I could hear McTeeg's voice squeaking.

"Now listen here, Mrs. Kalaban, you're coming across with the secret code that you and your husband arranged before he died. You're coming across right now. I'm not asking. I'm telling."

"I never will," Irene Kalaban said. Her voice quivered. "I know what you want to do. You want to use the code in order to convince those who hold that two hundred thousand dollar reward that communication has been established with my dead husband. You're after that reward, aren't you?"

I heard Artie Meyer laugh.

"How'd you guess it, Mrs. Kalaban?" McTeeg said. "That's just how it is. Of course, if you could hand over the two hundred grand to me yourself, then I wouldn't have to bother with this secret code business."

"Don't tell, Irene," Robert Martin's voice warned.

"Now you listen, hard guy," McTeeg said, evidently to Martin, "the way we're going to persuade Mrs. Kalaban to talk is by pulling out your toe nails with a pair of pliers. If she doesn't seem inclined to talk then, why we'll just start in with *her* toe nails. See how it works?"

"You touch her and I'll break every bone in your fat body, you damned swine!"

I think McTeeg hit Martin in the face.

I did not wait any longer. If McTeeg was getting rough, it was time I stepped in.

I RETURNED my knife to my sleeve, took a gun out of my coat pocket. Then I started to groan as though I were the unconscious man at my feet. I heard the man speak just three words when I had encountered him at the foot of the steps, but I now imitated his voice fairly well, calling out in anguished tone to Artie and McTeeg for help.

I could hear somebody approaching the door from the other side. I stepped to the side of the door, waited for it to open. It was Artie with his wooden-Indian face who came out to see why his pal was lying in front of the door groaning. I reached out and tapped Artie on the back of the head. He toppled down on top of his pal.

I swung around the edge of the door to enter the room and slammed squarely into McTeeg himself. I think I bounced back a little from his rubber belly. McTeeg's right hand went back to his hip pocket where he always carries his gun. I rushed him at the same time and my hand went around to his hip pocket also.

What I did was simply shove the gun I was carrying within easy reach of his grasping fingers. When I shoved him back his draw was so hurried he simply pulled my gun from my fingers instead of his own. Then I rocked his big body back a few steps with a punch to one of his chins.

McTeeg brought around the gun which he thought was his own, pointed it squarely at me and pulled the trigger.

I don't know why it is, but I simply have never been able to break myself of having a little fun at the expense of men like McTeeg. When McTeeg pulled the trigger of that gun I had been so careful to hand him, a banner of green silk about a foot square and bearing the word "Bang" in white letters, was expelled from the barrel of the gun. It's just a comedy stunt I've used a lot on the stage. The gun itself is of the "scare" variety, a perfect duplicate of the real thing in appearance.

To say that McTeeg was amazed is putting it mildly. He took one look at the gun in his hands, at the green streamer that mocked him. He thought that the Ghost was the devil-incarnate, thought, maybe, that the Ghost had actually changed his own gun into this harmless thing he had in his hand.

McTeeg dropped the trick gun, never thought about drawing his own and much more deadly weapon, and rushed at me like a mad bull. His one desire at the moment was to get out of the place.

His fear and rage made him an easy mark. In spite of that padding of flesh, I finished him off with half a dozen blows. The man just didn't have any guard. He was too nervous after the gun trick. So McTeeg fell within a couple of yards of where his henchmen lay.

I had time to look around the room. McTeeg hadn't got far with his torture. Martin's shoes hadn't even been removed. Both Martin and Irene Kalaban were tied in straight chairs. I cut them loose with slashes of my knife.

"Y'know, that's damned decent of you!" Robert Martin sputtered as he got out of his chair. "Thought Mrs. Kalaban was in trouble for a moment."

MRS. KALABAN grasped both my hands in hers. There were tears in her lovely eyes as she thanked me.

"You must tell me who you are," she said. "Are you—are you this poor leper the police are—hunting?"

Maybe I did look like Mrs. Kalaban's conception of a leper. I smiled with my eyes and I think the Ghost's face looked less dead and certainly more happy.

"I'm the Ghost," I said. "You may have heard of me."

"Yes," she said, "but I thought the Ghost was—was a sort of criminal—"

"A detective, my dear," Martin said knowingly. "He's a private detective, or something of the sort. Smart man."

"Whoever you are, I want to thank you sincerely," Mrs. Kalaban said.

Little did she know she was thanking her old friend, George Chance!

"I happened to hear Dr. Seer's prediction tonight, Mrs. Kalaban," I said. "Don't worry too much about it. Take every precaution, of course. You see McTeeg seems to be only one of the persons who has designs on that two hundred thousand dollar reward. Someone else has a similar idea."

"What do you mean?"

I turned to Martin.

"Will you run downstairs and see if you can find a cab in which to take Mrs. Kalaban home?"

Martin hesitated. Perhaps he didn't like to leave Mrs. Kalaban alone with a ghastly-looking stranger. But she urged him to go.

As soon as he was down the stairs, I smiled at Irene Kalaban.

"Someone may be trying to scare you into revealing the secret code which would enable them to claim the reward money," I said. "I believe that in a little while you will receive another message from Dr. Seer. When you do, inform me immediately by putting a potted plant in the front window of your home. I will see it and communicate with you. Do that, please. Will you promise? I am trying to help you and others, too."

"I will promise," she said gravely. Again she took my hand. "Thank you, Mr. Ghost."

Left alone with the three unconscious crooks, I telephoned Standish and told him to send men to pick up McTeeg and his pals. I told him that Mrs. Kalaban would gladly swear out a warrant for their arrest on the charge of extortion.

"Can you pin the Palmer murder on McTeeg?" Standish demanded.

"I can't," I sighed. "I can't pin it on anyone yet."

"We haven't found a trace of this Eric Emboyd," Standish said, and his voice sounded grave. "I have a piece of unpleasant information for you. The Court of Appeals handed down its decision on Glenn's appeal. The sentence stands. George Chance... must die... in the electric chair."

CHAPTER XXV

THE ESSENTIAL CLUE

S LEEP WAS not for me that night. I worked. Scarcely moving in my chair except to light a cigarette or look at the material clues I had picked up during the adventure, I still worked harder than ever before in my life.

Slowly the tangled threads of the mystery unrolled before me. The four material clues I had gathered dropped into their places and fit—first the leper's coin, then the Mexican map with its cryptic pencil notes, then the message I had stolen from beneath Dr. Seer's crystal, and finally the light globe which had come from the murder scene in the Curtis house.

In the morning, my mental notes arranged, I went down to Centre Street in the disguise of Dr. Stacey to pay another visit to the office of Police Commissioner Standish. Standish was at his desk and in the company of Merry White and Robert Demarest. Merry had tears in her eyes. The commissioner was looking grave and worried. Demarest lolled in his chair, his lips looking as though he had a sour taste in his mouth, his heavy eyelids drooping.

"The condemned man looks as though he had eaten a hearty meal," Demarest said as I entered. "A meal consisting principally of the fruits of despair."

"Don't, Dr. Demarest!" Merry pleaded. "This is serious."

"Serious, did you say?" Demarest raised one eyelid a little higher and gave Merry a look. "You don't hear me chortling with glee over anything, do you?"

Standish gripped my hand hard, a glum look on his face.

"Have you got anything?" he asked quietly. There was a hopeful light in his eyes.

"I've got a lot of work laid out for Demarest," I said. "And for you, too. I don't know what strings you have to pull to do it, but I want the body of David Palmer exhumed!"

"An exhumation order takes a while to get," Standish said calmly. "But I'll take a short cut. Why do you want it?"

"Because," I said, "I think Demarest made a mistake in the cause of Palmer's death. A very natural mistake," I added lest Demarest be offended. "The poison thorn was found in the back of Palmer's neck. He had every symptom of curare poisoning. Curare, when it acts fatally, strikes the respiratory system, producing a paralysis of the body's breathing apparatus."

"You've been reading up on the stuff," Demarest said. "Well, maybe you're right about us missing the cause of Palmer's death."

"Isn't it right that you can't tell much how curare is going to act on different individuals?" I asked.

Demarest nodded.

"Personally, I didn't think there was a lethal dose of the stuff on the thorn in Palmer's neck. But as you say, it's a funny poison."

"Couldn't poison gas have killed Palmer?" I asked. "The same gas that killed Livingston and Holland and Curtis' wife?"

DEMAREST NODDED again.

"I suppose so, though naturally we didn't make any tests for poison gas. To poison one man in that room filled with people by means of gas sounds more fantastic than the poison thorn. Besides, we could see the poison thorn and we could detect curare."

"You forget," I said, "that when Palmer died, he wasn't in a room filled with people. He was in a spirit cabinet, smaller than most closets. Gas introduced into that cabinet would have passed upward because of the construction of the cabinet itself. That cabinet would have acted like a chimney, air coming in at the bottom and out at the top, carrying the gas upward where it would have been lost in the upper reaches of the stage itself and carried out by the ventilators."

"I'll be damned!" said Standish. "Had you thought of that, Demarest?"

"It's logical," Demarest said. "But why the poisoned dart?"

"Simply because the murderer brought *two* weapons with him," I said. "He wasn't expecting to have the opportunity of using the poison gas. But he *did* have that opportunity. Then after Palmer was dead, he shoved the poisoned thorn into the back of Palmer's neck to throw us off the track, planted the box of thorns in my pocket to give Magnus somebody to pinch right away."

"Goody!" Merry said, clapping her hands. "Then that proves George Chance couldn't have killed Palmer!"

"Does it?" Standish asked softly. "If the poisoned thorn was to throw the cops off the track, how can we prove that George Chance didn't employ the poison gas, too? I'm not trying to be contrary. I'm showing you how hard this thing is to break down."

"No use borrowing trouble," I said. "We've got to depend on getting further medical evidence. Meanwhile, puzzle over this."

I put the small piece of paper bearing Dr. Seer's fifth prediction down on Standish's desk. My friends crowded around, studying it. It was simply a typewritten note which Standish read aloud:

This is the 5th prediction. Five days from today, Irene Kalaban will die.

"Where did you get this?" Standish asked.

I told him. I pointed a finger at the typed numeral "five" which numbered the prediction. Directly above the figure five were two tiny marks that looked like dots.

"Take a look through a magnifying glass," I suggested. "I think that's our essential clue. Whoever typed that note accidentally touched the shift key of the typewriter just a little as he wrote the figure five, so that the character which is mounted above the five on the same type-bar showed up. A common typist's mistake."

Merry jerked one end of Robert Demarest's watch chain from the doctor's vest pocket. There was a magnifying glass on that end of the chain and she looked at the tell-tale mark through the glass.

"Above the figure five on the standard typewriter keyboard is a percent sign," Standish said. "That doesn't look like a percent sign. Looks like two little dots."

"Not dots," Merry corrected. "Two little *lines*. And they both slant in opposite directions as though they might meet like the peak of a roof. Only these don't meet."

"They would have met," I said, "had the shift key of the typewriter been completely depressed. Since I believe the killer is working entirely alone, we can make a close guess that the person who made that typewritten message is the killer. And those little marks above the five tell the tale."

"I don't get it," Standish said, "but I know better than to ask for the answer at this moment. What do we do next?"

"A lot depends on what Demarest finds out," I said. "There isn't a whole lot of time, but in that time I may hear from Mexico."

"Mexico?" Merry gasped. "What's Mexico got to do with it?"

I remembered that I had not shown them the map I had taken from Curtis' house. I showed it to them now, pointing out the penciled markings—the arrow labeled with the word "ours" and the encircled letters "He."

"More Greek," Merry said.

"Literally Greek," I said with a smile. "I think the 'He' originally came from the Greek word that means 'sun.'

"Now," I went on, "in case nothing turns up before the night of the execution, I want to arrange a little party. Our guests will be Robert Martin, Irene Kalaban, Carl Van Borg, Dr. Seer, Harold Harkness, McTeeg, Artie Meyer, and if Emboyd should show up, he'd better come along too. Maybe I can get the killer to try and make a ghost out of the Ghost.

"This party," I went on, "will take place at the house of George Chance. Not the Ghost's rectory, understand, but the house of George Chance. I have my reasons."

CHAPTER XXVI

THE LEPER

ON THE day following, Joe Harper came into the rectory. He didn't say hello to me, but then he seldom does. He simply walked down the basement steps into my presence, his cigarette dangling from his lips, his face bearing a haggard look, and started to strip off his clothes.

"I want to take a bath," he said. "Flop houses and lepers—the association sort of has me itching."

"Lepers!" I gasped. "Joe, have you found Eric Emboyd?"

"Found him? I slept on a mattress about six feet from the one he slept on," Joe paid. "In the morning I offered to buy him a breakfast and he was half starved. So he followed me to a meal. Who am I to go around setting up bums? Let the city attend to it, I thinks. So I led him into the hands of the cops."

Joe sauntered over to the bar and began looking for a drink.

"I could use some internal antiseptic, too!" he explained, pouring whiskey. "Emboyd looks like one of Demarest's cadavers. I didn't touch him. I let the cops do that. Not only has he got leprosy, but he's nuts, too. He tells everybody that he killed Dr. Livingston and Michael Holland—and Curtis and Van Borg. But Van Borg hasn't been killed and Emboyd doesn't know how he killed any of them. But he may have done it."

"What about Palmer? Did he confess to killing Palmer?"

"No, he didn't," Joe said. "So you're still in a black spot. Emboyd never heard of Palmer."

That was the way it was. That was how it had been all through the case. I seemed able enough to prove nearly everything except that I did not kill David Palmer.

That afternoon, I passed Irene Kalaban's house and saw in her front window the potted plant—the signal that she needed the Ghost. In a hotel washroom, I switched my makeup to the Ghost disguise and went immediately to her house. She had received a communication from Dr. Seer who offered to contact her husband's spirit and get Kalaban's spirit to intercede for her with the fates that had promised her death.

He could do this, Seer claimed, but only if he had that secret code that Mrs. Kalaban and her husband had arranged. He was sure he could contact her husband's spirit and that Kalaban's spirit would be able to persuade the fates to "lay off."

It was as clear a case of extortion as the one McTeeg and Artie Meyer had tried to pull. It was, perhaps, more subtle. I am certain it would have worked had it not been for the Ghost's intervention, because poor Mrs. Kalaban was worked up to such a hysterical pitch by Seer's prediction that she would have parted with anything to appease the demons of doom that threatened her.

I assured Mrs. Kalaban once more that she needn't worry. Then I got in touch with Standish and told him to have the cops pick up Dr. Seer. This only resulted in some collective headaches down at Headquarters, because all that could be got out of Seer was that he had gone to Mrs. Kalaban with that proposition because the spirits had told him to do it and had threatened him with certain death if he didn't.

MR. SEER was easily the most sincere and determined believer in spiritualism I had ever met. And he made a perfect dupe for the unscrupulous murderer I was hoping to catch.

Still no word from Mexico. I visited Robert Demarest in the morgue on the north side of Bellevue Hospital.

Demarest took me into his private room, sat down wearily in a chair, motioned me to do likewise.

"Well, we've done things," he told me. "Exhumed the Palmer cadaver, gone over the whole territory of his anatomy. Cyanogen gas got him, too. But right there I quit. How the devil the gas was administered, I don't know."

I took from my pocket the electric light globe I had taken from the lamp in the Curtis home. I asked Demarest if he remembered the overturned lamp which was almost directly beneath the body of Mrs. Curtis. He nodded.

I took a pin from my pocket, used it to explore the frosted glass of the light globe I had removed from the lamp. At that portion of the globe where the trade mark is usually stamped, I showed Demarest a hole into which I could put the pin.

"And yet in spite of that hole, you can screw the bulb into a socket and it will light up," I said.

"The bulb's double then," Demarest said. "The inner bulb contains the light filament."

"And the outer contained the poison gas under pressure," I said. "This tiny hole here was sealed with some transparent cement which was melted by the heat from the inner globe, allowing the poison gas to escape. You can see some of the melted cement still there."

Demarest showed considerable excitement, which means that he opened his drooping eyelids a bit wider.

"Cyanogen was a perfect choice," he said. "Extremely deadly. A single whiff of it will kill. Yet it dissipates rapidly, leaving but little trace. But if a globe like that was used to kill Palmer, where was it placed?"

"Inside my own spirit cabinet! In that close little booth where David Palmer was tied! The globe was simply screwed into the blue-shaded lamp inside the cabinet. It's there right now and it's just like this globe I brought from the Curtis place."

"Remarkable," rasped Demarest. "Remarkable the lengths you go in order to prove yourself a killer."

"*Anyone* could have had access to the stage to examine my spirit cabinet inside and outside with the curtains closed," I told him. "I invited people up on the stage to look the cabinet over."

"How damned easy," Demarest said. "And just as damned deadly. But where can you get globes like that—double-bulbed, filled with poison gas?"

"THE TRUTH is, Bob, that you can't get them now. They must have been made to order by Michael Holland. Holland had the equipment. He could make the gas, because according to you he died of a dose of the gas while making it in his lab. He had glass-blowing equipment. And anybody who could make a triple-phase radio tube could certainly construct a double light globe."

"And according to you, Holland was murdered?" Demarest murmured. "Ghost, you poke too many holes in the dignity of the office of Chief Medical Examiner Demarest. I said he died an accidental death."

"We won't fight about that," I said. "The only thing there is to indicate murder in that case is the fact that Holland's death was predicted by Seer. Holland and the killer had planned to work the scheme together. After Holland had made up some of the poison gas globes, enough for the killer's purpose, how easy for him to just happen to drop something on the apparatus that was being used to generate the gas. The gas would burst out into the killer's face. The murderer would simply hold his breath and walk out."

"But what's the motive?" Demarest insisted. "The case has as many convolutions as a human brain."

"Wait until tonight," I said. "We'll net killer, motive and all."

"Or," he concluded sourly, "we'll each net a nice little boudoir out there." He gestured toward the next room where the cadavers were kept in their individual coolers.

By eight o'clock that night, I was ready for the little party that had been arranged in the home of George Chance. Inspector Magnus and two of his plainclothesmen were on the reception committee in the hall. It was their duty to search the suspects as they came in.

Van Borg was the first to arrive. While some of my guests would have to be dragged to the house, Van Borg came voluntarily, smiling his charming smile. Through a secret peep hole in the wall, I watched what went on.

"What poor devil, Chance!" he exclaimed to Magnus as he entered. He tapped a rolled up newspaper under his arm. "I've just been reading about his scheduled execution."

"Well, murderers will be murderers," Magnus said. "You don't mind if I search you, do you, Mr. Van Borg?"

"Not at all!" Van Borg put his newspaper into Magnus' hands and raised his arms above his head. The two plainclothesmen went over him very carefully. Then he was led into my little auditorium.

For the entertainment of my friends, my house has a room which is equipped with a small stage on which I sometimes do magical tricks. It was from this stage tonight that I expected to point out the killer.

AS SOON as the guests had been assembled, Police Commissioner Standish stepped out onto the stage. He got quickly to the point.

"I have brought you here at the suggestion of the Ghost, that mysterious individual who has the uncanny knack of getting at the bottom of mysteries in a hurry. The Ghost is of the opinion that George Chance did not kill David Palmer. The Ghost delights in irony, and he thought it would be quite ironical if the real killer was brought to justice in the house of the man he had framed. Before I turn the meeting over to the Ghost, I want to say that I have never once supposed George Chance guilty of that crime for which he is scheduled so soon to pay the penalty of death. I sincerely hope that there may yet be time to save him from the chair."

Standish stepped down, and instantly I made my appearance from behind black curtains. My face was the skull face of the Ghost, my eyes expressionless as I looked out upon the little audience.

McTeeg and Artie Meyer were sitting close together. Police were on either side of them. A single policeman watched where Eric Emboyd sat a little apart from the others. Emboyd, his face made hideous by his disease, his thin hands like claws, was a more frightful-looking person than the Ghost.

Then there was Irene Kalaban, beautiful and serene. At her side was Robert Martin, his craggy face looking like a mask of granite. Van Borg lounged in a club chair behind them, his newspaper lying in his lap. Beside Van Borg was that near-sighted, bald little man Mrs. Kalaban had introduced to me as Mr. Harkness, executor of her late husband's estate and keeper of the coveted two hundred thousand dollar reward for proof of Kalaban's spiritual existence.

Dr. Seer's starved figure was perched uneasily on the edge of a straight chair. His eyes moved furtively from the police to me. Only one door at the back of the room was unguarded. Perhaps he planned to make a break for it if the opportunity arose.

In the flat, emotionless voice of the Ghost, I began to speak:

"In this room is a murderer. And inside of half an hour, the finger will point unerringly to him. There is no escape. Do you understand that thoroughly? *There is no escape.* McTeeg—"

"Who? Me?" McTeeg jerked nervously up in his seat.

"McTeeg," I went on, "you were extremely interested in getting your hands on that two hundred thousand dollar reward which according to the will of the late Kalaban must be paid to anyone receiving from the spirit world a code message. This code message you tried to force Mrs. Kalaban into giving you so that you could hoax the executors of Kalaban's will into giving up the reward.

"You tried first of all to blackmail Mrs. Kalaban on trumped-up evidence. The price she was to pay for your silence was the code message which would enable you to claim the reward. Blackmail failing, you tried brutal extortion with the code message as the price of mercy."

"I didn't kill nobody," McTeeg said.

"I know you didn't," I said. "Because the motive behind the murders was *not* to get the two hundred thousand dollar reward. It was something larger than that. Look to your right and at the wall."

AS I said this, I pressed a button with the toe of my shoe. Lights in the room went out. By means of a projector, a greatly enlarged image of the Mexican map I had found in Curtis' desk was thrown on the wall.

"You see, Mr. Murderer," I said mockingly, "the Ghost's fingers are quicker than your eyes. I didn't destroy the map, did I? You would have destroyed it, because it points clearly to the real motive.

"Before he died, Curtis told me that he was one of several men who formed an expedition into Mexico. The route of this expedition is indicated by the pencil marks on the map as you see.

"You will also note a region which has been encircled and marked with the letters 'He.' Now 'He' is the chemical symbol for the gas helium. In as much as Livingston, Holland and Curtis were scientists, we can assume that they discovered a deposit of helium gas in Mexico. You will also note that an arrow on the map is marked 'ours,' which would indicate, perhaps, 'our property.'

"What happened was that the five men discovered a profitable supply of helium in this region, kept the secret to themselves, bought up the property for a song. The five men held joint ownership of this helium property. The deed to this property can be checked with the Mexican authorities.

"Since the property was owned jointly, a motive for murder is at once apparent. Livingston is dead. Curtis is dead. Holland is dead.

"Since the United States government has a monopoly on helium with the chief deposits in the entire world located in Mexico, the value of this property can scarcely be estimated," I went on. "So we have a motive for murder. Mr. X must destroy all the co-owners of the property except himself in order to become a very wealthy man."

"Helium," a voice croaked out of the darkness. "That was it. It was helium. And we didn't want to develop the property because—"

I stepped on the button that turned on the lights in the room. The croaking voice had come from the leper, Eric Emboyd. All eyes turned on him. Realizing this, he stopped talking.

"You recall something, Emboyd?" I urged.

"I do," he said. He passed a hand over his forehead. "It is so vague. Hate has crowded out so much. But those men I hate were with me in Mexico when we discovered helium there. We bought the land, as you said. Then after we bought it, some of us thought it was wrong to develop it because it would destroy our country's monopoly on the gas. If the gas was sold to foreign countries and used in the foreigner's dirigible balloons, we might be destroying our advantage in case of war. So we never spent a penny to develop the land and sink the gas wells."

My deductions checked with Emboyd's testimony. Considerably more confident that I could force the killer into making a break which would positively identify him, I stepped to my small draped magical table which was sitting on the stage. It held not a single piece of visible apparatus except a lamp without a shade. I lighted the naked globe.

I made no comment. My idea was just to let the killer sit there and watch that light globe and worry about whether or not I knew his murder method.

CHAPTER XXVII

THE FINGER OF LIGHT

STEPPING A little to one side of the table, I continued my little lecture on murder.

"Emboyd has spoken of men he hates. And Emboyd's hatred has made him a perfect fall guy for the murderer! Realizing that Emboyd had escaped from the leper colony determined to be revenged on his enemies who had sent him there, the killer had nothing to do to frame Emboyd except let the police draw their own conclusions. Emboyd was afraid of the police because he didn't want to be sent back to the leper colony, so naturally his movements were furtive. And Emboyd was determined to be revenged on the men who had sent him to the leper island. Emboyd actually *did* stalk some of the men who were murdered with malicious intent. He actually did stick a knife into Livingston in the dark, not knowing him to be dead. But he did not commit murder!"

"Can you prove that?"

It was the bald, near-sighted Mr. Harkness who spoke.

"I can," I said. "First of all, consider the murder of Dr. Livingston. And Livingston's death is the only one in the group in which there is any actual evidence against Emboyd. Emboyd visited Livingston the night of the murder as attested by Livingston's servant.

"The servant had accidentally blown a fuse in the house. He had left the house to go buy a fuse. When he returned, he met Emboyd coming out of the house. A bit later Livingston was found murdered. But Livingston died in the light, not in the dark as he would have done had his death occurred after the fuse had been blown out. The constriction of Livingston's pupils at the time the body was found proves that he died in the light.

"Yet Emboyd did not arrive at Livingston's house until after the fuse burned out, plunging the house in darkness. We know this, because in order to hunt out Livingston, Emboyd's first act was to go to the fuse box and try to repair the lights. He used the usual emergency method of making such a repair—by putting a coin back of the burned out fuse.

"Reaching into his pocket for a coin, Emboyd's diseased fingers could not distinguish between a coin and a leper's token which the police have now on exhibit. He put a leper's token back of the fuse and the lights still did not come on because the hole in the center of the token prevented the proper contact to be made. Emboyd groped in darkness, found what he thought was the living Livingston.

"Then the return of the servant frightened Emboyd away. Now, if Emboyd did not kill Livingston, he did not kill the others. Why? Because it is very unlikely that two criminal minds could have thought up the same clever, subtle murder method that was employed in each murder case except the last.

"For in the last murder, the killer intended to remove Curtis by the same means he had killed the others—by poison gas. But Curtis' train was late and it was Mrs. Curtis who stumbled into the death trap the killer had arranged. Curtis then had to be shot."

"What does all this have to do with the killing of David Palmer by George Chance?" Robert Martin asked. "Y'know, I'd like to see Chance cleared of this crime."

I mentally echoed Martin's wish.

"I'm coming to that," I said. "For Palmer, too, was killed by poison gas, not by a poisoned thorn. Chief Medical Examiner Robert Demares will bear me out in this. To throw the police off the track, the killer put the thorn into Palmer's neck and planted a box of thorns in Chance's pocket. The killer had probably intended to use thorns and a blow gun on Palmer, because he was afraid he might not have the opportunity to use his poison gas.

"But why kill Palmer at all? Was Palmer one of the joint owners of the Mexican helium property? There is no evidence to support an affirmative answer. But Palmer knew about the helium property and who owned it. The killer, in order to try and get money advanced to develop the helium property, broke the secret to Palmer. Palmer was a clever investor and the killer thought Palmer would be willing to back development of the helium land with money.

"Palmer refused, but you can rest assured that he did not refuse without first making a careful investigation which proved to him that the killer was not the sole owner of the Mexican property and therefore had no right to develop the gas wells. Then Holland died a violent death. Put yourself in the killer's shoes. Could the killer start eliminating the co-owners of the property while Palmer lived? Not without arousing Palmer's suspicion. And Palmer's suspicions must have already been aroused by Holland's death—at least so the killer thought. So we have the motive for Palmer's death.

"Of the co-owners of the Mexican property, Holland, Livingston, Curtis were to be murdered. Emboyd was to be framed for the murders and die in the electric chair, leaving the killer the sole owner.

"But now let's consider Dr. Seer for a moment."

When I spoke his name, the gaunt Prophet of Doom got to his feet. A policeman promptly pushed him down again.

"The killer, in order to realize on his murder-investment," I went on, "had to have money to develop the property. He hit upon the same source of money that McTeeg did, namely the two hundred thousand dollar reward money in the Kalaban estate. But the killer's methods of getting at that money were more subtle.

"Since he was going to kill Holland, Palmer, Livingston, and Curtis anyway, the killer decided to predict his victims' deaths ahead of time—predict them in such a manner that Mrs. Kalaban would be sure to hear those predictions. In the company of Robert Martin, Mrs. Kalaban was attending all of Dr. Seer's séances.

"Now Dr. Seer isn't a fraud, not consciously a fraud, anyway. Dr. Seer is simply the ornamental fringe of a gang of spook crooks who have been duping the public for some time. Dr. Seer really believes in spirits.

"The killer simply made a deal with the spook crooks behind Dr. Seer. The killer furnished the crooks with the murder predictions. And the crooks, by mechanical means, made these predictions appear in Dr. Seer's crystal."

I GAVE them a minute to let this sink in, then went on.

"Why these predictions? Simply to build up Mrs. Kalaban's belief that Dr. Seer had supernatural powers and could predict death. If he could do that, the killer was certain that when Mrs. Kalaban's own death was predicted, he would have her sufficiently frightened that she would reveal that secret code message which she and her dead husband arranged. And that code message is the only key to the two hundred thousand dollar reward which the murderer needed to develop his helium property."

A gesture of my hand signaled to Joe Harper in the wings. Except for tiny footlights at the stage edge and the light globe which burned on my magic table, all the lights in the room went out. I stepped to the table.

"A few hours from now, an innocent man will die in the electric chair if the real killer of David Palmer isn't found," I said in a grave voice. "But George Chance was framed for that killing—framed for a definite reason. Perhaps the killer might have easily cast suspicion on Emboyd for the Palmer crime as he did for the others. But George Chance had to be removed from the picture. Why? Because everyone knew that George Chance was out to break the spook crooks—to prove that Dr. Seer was a fraud. If Chance had done that, the killer's chances of getting his hands on the Kalaban reward were slim."

I unscrewed the lamp bulb from its socket, stepped off the stage and into the audience.

"This globe may not be as innocent as it looks," I said. "I want each of you to examine it closely."

"What's the meaning of this tommyrot?" Robert Martin growled.

The meaning was that I was trying to scare the killer into making a break. I didn't tell anybody that, though.

After the globe had passed through the audience, Augie Meyer handed it back to me and I went up on the stage.

Now, because I was going to switch light globes and get hold of a trick one in place of the one I had passed for inspection, I had placed a little mark on the base of the bulb I had handed out. When I took a look at the bulb in my hand, my heart gave a bound. It wasn't the same bulb I had passed out. Clever to the very end, the killer had panned off on me one of his deadly gas-filled globes, hoping that I would screw it into the lamp socket where it would have shortly delivered its deadly contents into the room. But more importantly, directly into the Ghost's face.

Somewhere, out in the darkened end of the room, I detected the opening and closing of a door. The killer! He had slipped out. He didn't care to be around when the room was filled with poison gas. But what he didn't know was that he had sneaked into a dead end. There was no exit that he was apt to find from that room except the door through which he had passed!

THE DEADLY bulb in my hand, I vanished into one of the black art wells of my magic table at the same time that the second well delivered the trick bulb into my hand. My idea originally had been to perform the floating light bulb illusion, cause the globe to float right down to where the killer sat, and at the same time explain how the murders had been accomplished by light globes. If the killer made a break for the next room through the only exit unguarded, my globe would have followed him through the wall.

Now my moves were essentially the same, only I didn't have to explain anything.

The killer in the next room supposed that I was using his deadly light globe in my experiment!

I merely set my trick light globe on top of the lamp socket, though I pretended to screw it into place. The trick globe was powered by flashlight batteries concealed in its shank, and I lighted it by simply screwing the brass base of the globe.

A system of silk threads operated by reels concealed in the front portion of the house had been arranged for the floating illusion. There are a number of other ways of causing the levitation of a light globe, but here I had to have an assistant manage the trick while I pursued the killer. Merry White and Joe Harper were actually responsible for the trick.

While the audience watched, I waved my hands over the globe. The thread they couldn't see tightened and the globe, still lighted, floated up from the socket and out over the heads of the audience. They were so intent on watching the globe, they didn't see the Ghost vanish through the trap in the floor of his stage.

Instantly I was in the basement of my house, running in the direction of the room above my head in which the killer waited. An elevator and trap arrangement very similar to that which had been incorporated in Dr. Seer's stage, gave me instant access to the room where the killer was.

I stepped onto the platform of the elevator and was virtually shot up into the room above. There was no light in the room, but the Ghost would furnish that shortly!

I could hear the killer moving about in the room, trying to find a way out. Once he whispered a curse. It was then that I uttered the rollicking, ghoulish laugh of the Ghost.

"Wh-what was that?" the killer whispered.

I laughed again.

"Don't you know, murderer? Don't you know who it is? There isn't any escape," I said. "We will simply wait here for the light to come."

The killer said nothing. It sounded as though he was moving toward me. I wondered if he had the nerve to come to grips with the Ghost.

He must have been half-way across the room when he stopped. He stopped because light was coming into the room through the wall. It was my trick light passing through an opening which was cleverly concealed by a tightly stretched silk curtain painted to resemble wall paper.

THE BURNING globe apparently passed through the solid wall, floated on its unseen thread across the room. The killer didn't move. Fear must have frozen him.

"The deadly light globe," I whispered. "And you are the only man who had the opportunity in each murder case to plant those deadly globes where your victims were bound to light them.

"But your big mistake, Mr. Murderer, was using your typewriter to write the predictions which appeared in Seer's globe! Because you made an error on your last prediction note—a simple typographical error. You accidentally depressed the shift key a little when you made the figure five. The character on the upper part of the figure five type bar came in contact with the paper and showed us two tiny lines slanting toward each other like the peak of a roof.

"That was how I knew your identity," I whispered. "On an ordinary typewriter, the character above the figure five is a percent sign. But on your typewriter you have a piece of special type, a special character particularly useful to men of your profession!"

The light globe floated nearer and nearer. I could see the killer's face clearly illuminated. He was white as death. His eyes followed the floating globe that for all he knew contained the deadly gas that might be discharged any moment.

"That special character on your typewriter was a caret mark, particularly useful to authors, Mr. Carl Van Borg!"

As I said that, I reached out, tweaked the silk thread that carried the light globe. The light globe fell to the floor, shattered. And Van Borg—well, Van Borg simply fainted. You see, he really didn't know but what I was using the deadly gas-filled globe he had panned off on me!

THERE IS very little more to tell. The party Merry White and the Ghost put on in the Ghost's rectory for Glenn Saunders, on his release from prison, was memorable. Besides Glenn and Merry, Tiny Tim Terry, Joe Harper, Robert Demarest, and Ned Standish were there. We talked about the case of the Prophet of Doom quite a bit, naturally.

Standish's message to the governor saying that he had found Palmer's real murderer, enabled the governor to stay the execution of "George Chance." Van Borg when he came to and found himself hopelessly caught, confessed to all the murders. His confession corresponded quite closely with the evidence we had gathered.

One thing that came up that night of the Ghost's party was the question of how Van Borg had got his gas-filled light globe into the house at all that night I exposed him. Standish claimed that Van Borg had been searched carefully, just as the others had.

"And how did Van Borg know you were going to pull the floating light globe stunt and thus give him a chance to substitute the deadly bulb?" Tiny Tim piped.

"He didn't," I said. "He didn't know I was going to pull the floating light globe stunt. If that hadn't given him the opportunity to use his globe, he would have simply gone to the door, thrown the globe across the room to break against the wall, hoping that by holding his breath he could slip out while the rest of us breathed in the gas."

Merry White sat down on the arm of my chair.

"Suppose you tell us, smart man," she said, "how Van Borg got that gas-filled globe into the house when the policemen so carefully searched him. You're trying to dodge the important question."

"I am not," I said, giving her hand a playful pat. "While Van Borg was being searched, good old Inspector Magnus was holding the deadly light globe. It was rolled up in Van Borg's newspaper. Van Borg smilingly handed his newspaper to Magnus, took it back after the search was over."

I had never heard Robert Demarest utter a hearty laugh until that moment.

"If Magnus knew that," he said, "he'd come into the morgue and curl up on a slab!"

"Here's to the Ghost's next case!" Tiny Tim cried, raising his glass.

"What's your hurry?" Joe Harper asked. "Can't a man get some rest around here?"

But he knew, and I knew, and we all knew, that there would be a next case, and that when it broke, the ghost would walk again.

www.ingramcontent.com/pod-product-compliance
Lightning Source LLC
Chambersburg PA
CBHW022013010726
47494CB00003B/1015